The Magpie's Nest

A Summer School

Rosemary Pavey

The Midnight Oil Artisan Press
2014

Published by The Midnight Oil Artisan Press 2014

Cover illustration and design by Rosemary Pavey

The Midnight Oil Artisan Press
www.paveypenandpaint.com

Printed by CreateSpace

ISBN: 978-0-9927463-1-5

To J

Who Lit the Touch Paper

Acknowledgements

My grateful thanks to all who have patiently helped and encouraged me. Also to the cultures and storytellers whose tales and folk-wisdom have provided inspiration for this novel. Every attempt has been made to acknowledge my sources and trace copyright holders. If any omission has occurred, please contact me. I would like to remedy the oversight.

Quotations
"*Those are pearls...*" William Shakespeare, *The Tempest* 1,ii,397-401
"*Thrice welcome...*" William Wordsworth, *To The Cuckoo* l.13
"*One for sorrow...*" Modern version of a traditional Nursery Rhyme

Fables which are retold in the text
The Tale of the Hodja, adapted from a tale found in *Masnavi I Ma'navi VI,ix* by Jalaluddin Rumi
The Tale of the Tomte, based on 'Moving House' from *Scandinavian Folktales,* trans. and ed. Jacqueline Simpson. Penguin 1988
White Wolf, Black Wolf, from a legend of the Cherokee nation.
The Magpie's Nest, adapted from the folk tale collected by Florence Holbrook in *The Book of Nature Myths,* Houghton Mifflin 1902.

The Author
Rosemary Pavey was born in 1960 and works as a writer and painter in Sussex, dividing her time between her studio in Ditchling and Stoneywish, a local Nature Reserve.

Also by Rosemary Pavey
The Beehive Cluster - *A Novel for All Ages*

Forthcoming Titles
Christmas Ghosties - *Tales for a Winter Night*
Painting and Chaos

To find out more about any of these or exhibitions, talks and other events please visit: ***www.paveypenandpaint.com***

Contents

Chapter 1

A Place to Start

The Sump lay at the bottom of the garden - a derelict patch of woodland which belonged to the Water Board. It had once been part of the Sewage Works and before that, belonged to the Fraisey Manor Estate, but now it was an island of neglect in the busy landscape of Bockhurst. From the road, you would hardly know it was there and it formed no more than a green backdrop to the lives of Beckley Road. But Trudi and Jurgen knew another side of it.

Long ago, in summers they could barely remember, they had fashioned a hole in the fence - hardly more than a scrape beneath the stiff chain-link - and had made forays there with their father. That was before he got so busy. And 'Sump' was the name they had invented then - a sort of mongrel term, somewhere between sewage and dump, which fitted the place exactly. Sven Larsson, in those days, was the perfect leader for an expedition: a kindly Goliath, with burnished skin and a giant's curly, brown hair and beard. They would arm themselves, all three, with biscuits or melting ice lollies and make for a secret camp in the fork of a giant beech. And there the children would listen to stories and examine caterpillars and warm themselves at imaginary camp fires. That was when Trudi loved Sven most, his hair full of twigs and leaves, his huge frame crammed into a child's space and all the world saturated with his irrepressible good-humour. It never occurred to her that he belonged with the grown-ups. He didn't condescend to play with them as grown-ups did, but threw himself into their games as if the adventure was new and he had never been a boy before.

Once or twice they had ventured further into the wood. In the leafy depths they came across a black lagoon, and derelict sheds and hoses: a creepy reminder of times past. And once they had found a heap of moss-covered boulders, which Sven laughingly called the Trollstones, thinking of Swedish tales. Worse still, were some sinister pens, which had owls' eyes painted on them, where little brown birds pecked in the dirt. These things belonged to an alien

1

world and Trudi was glad to return to familiar ground.

Five years on, everything had changed. Trudi was growing up and her father's work absorbed all his time. The children had become too busy for idle games. Nowadays they hardly thought of the Sump, except when a 'stink' blew out of the Sewage, as it did from time to time. So when news came that the land was to be sold, they were not especially concerned. Secretly, Trudi felt glad. It bothered her that there should be dark corners so close to home and secrets lurking, which had no place in her sunny life.

Today, she was sitting on the edge of her bed, taking stock of things, because today was the first day of the Summer Holidays and she had that delicious sense of anticipation you get when you are going to be free. Well, maybe 'free' was not the right word, for she actually had six weeks of carefully planned events and activities to look forward to. But this, surely, was how holidays were meant to be. Her mother saw to all that.

Kirsten Larsson, a genius at organization, saw to everything. And it was she who always ensured that life flowed along in its seamlessly comforting way: piano lessons, swimming lessons, rounders matches, dance, tea, homework, music practice. Under her direction, the holidays became dynamic programmes with skis and canoes and trips to the theatre. Sometimes the family accompanied Trudi's father to the far-off places where he conducted his botanical research. Sometimes they simply followed the sun. This year, Sven was leading a field trip to the Florida Swamps. Kirsten herself would be away at a design conference in Helsinki and the children would attend summer school until they could all go together to paddle and relax in the Seychelles. At least, that was the plan. Summer School would begin in just a few days' time: Drama, this year, for Trudi and a Woodland Crafts camp; for Jurgen, a Junior String Master-class and football. All their friends would be there. And then next term, she would start a new school, with a smart, navy blue uniform and hockey and Latin. No wonder she had butterflies in her stomach.

But today was going to be special in another way too. She swung her legs over the other side of the bed and frowned into her dressing-table mirror. Grandfather Larsson was coming from Sweden today. In the few brief moments before they set off to collect him from the airport she made a mental review of her world, wondering what the old man would think of it and whether he would see it as everyone else did. This was a game she often liked to play.

So, here she was: Trudi Larsson. Ten years old. Tall for her age, with apricot-blonde plaits and a pale, almond-shaped face. Fine eyes of an indeterminate colour. Wilful, curious and rather too clever. She thought he would approve and imagined what fun it would be to surprise him with all the wonderful things she knew. This was how she usually won admirers and she had perfected the technique to the point that visitors who frequented the Larsson house never tired of praising her and telling her how she was just the image of her beautiful mother. And though she modestly shrugged such flattery aside, in her heart she knew it to be true, and it was with quiet satisfaction that she noted her gradual development from little 'Toodi', the toddler, to the pretty and graceful young girl who now faced her in the glass.

Already she could pass her school exams with ease. Her teachers spoke of her as '*exceptionally gifted*' and classmates forgave her, even when she was overbearing, because she was a champion of the sports field. But she had never played teacher's pet. A renegade gift of mimicry and a readiness to perform any dare had always ensured her favour with the more subversive elements, for if ever a volunteer was wanted for acts of danger - trespass, forgery, subversion, a school séance - Trudi could always be counted on to oblige. And since she looked so angelic, she invariably got away with her crimes and no one even thought of calling her a swot. Her only critic or tease was her younger brother, Jurgen, and she had ways of dealing with him. Trudi seemed to have it all. She was a heroine, just waiting for a story and ready to take up the tale herself at the slightest encouragement.

"Let me show you our house," she began, taking her imaginary grandfather by the hand. Everything would be new to him and she would be so proud to open one door after another. This is how it was when you went to tea with new friends. The first visit gave the real flavour, a sense of the spirit of the house, while the people who invited you showed off. Later, when first impressions faded, it was harder to remember what was special. To see your *own* home with fresh eyes was like going under-cover; an interesting challenge. Anyone coming to the Larssons' would first have to pass through the village. Bockhurst and Foxden were twin hamlets, which had grown up, beside the railway as it carved its way through open fields, and now these settlements almost met in the middle. There were still enough trees to remind everyone that they were in the country, and enough shops to keep the streets busy, like a town. The Larssons' house had a foot in either world, with the Sump sequestered behind, and tiled, Victorian steps in front, leading down into the street.

"Our house is not really like other people's houses. It looks boring on the outside - grey, with big sash windows and a fanlight over the front door, but Kirsten…" (Yes, I'm afraid Trudi did sometimes give herself airs.) "…Kirsten Larsson is a designer and loves surprises, so this is a trick to make you think you are nowhere special. Those are her hydrangeas in pots and the crazy paving is retro - all very English - but then, when you open the door... Padaam! Every house, as you know, has a unique flavour - a special smell of its own. It might be furniture polish, or onions frying, or carpet glue. Some houses are damp or smell of smoke - I once knew one that smelt of apples - but if you come to tea with us - you will find that our house smells of wood. Pine. And this is what you see from the doorstep: a long, polished, pine hall with stairs beyond and wood-panelled rooms, so that for a moment you think you have stepped into another country - and so you have! We're Swedish. Kirsten was born in England but her parents were Swedish and Sven grew up in Stockholm and still speaks English with a foreign accent.

"Our house is a kind of laboratory where we make things happen. This is where my mother does her sewing - she designed the furnishings for all the rooms, except my father's study. And this is her piano. And this is the painting of the forest my father gave her. Look! There are wolves' eyes between the trees. She doesn't really like it but she can't say so and hurt his feelings. This is the kitchen where everyone talks. We all take our shoes off in the house." Trudi was warming up. "Upstairs is Jurgen's room. It's full of horrible, plastic warrior-toys and football posters. Forget that room. This is mine, all different shades of green, but I think I'm bored with green now. I don't like lots of pictures. It's not cool. And this is where we do our homework. Mummy and Daddy's room - boring. And Daddy's office. We're not allowed in here but this is where he writes all his papers. He's got hundreds of books and scientific journals -

4

usually all over the floor - and hundreds of plant specimens from his research trips. He spends hours and hours up here and forgets to come down for dinner. Mummy won't tidy it up, so it simply gets worse and worse, but he loves it just the way it is. I can't decide whether I want my room to be like this, busy and clever, or like Mummy's workroom. She calls hers Zen. There's nothing to look at but two pebbles in a bowl. It's supposed to make you calm.

"From here you can see right down the garden, which is a little bit untidy, because that's how Daddy likes it, all the way to the Sump. I can't take you there. We're not really allowed to go and anyhow it's all wild and overgrown. I don't even like thinking about it. At night, sometimes, you hear horrible things - rabbits screaming in the wood. It freezes your blood. And the *kelet* live there, though of course they don't frighten me. Nothing frightens me now I'm grown up.

"Mummy and Daddy have parties in the garden and clever people come and talk and laugh under the lanterns on summer evenings - and Jurgen and I hand round the crisps and wine. And that's our world. Oh, except for the neighbours.

"That's the '*creepy*' house over there. It's all run down and you have to hold your nose when you go by or you will catch germs. A mad, old witch-woman lives there. She talks to the birds. And on this side are the Stringers, who are terrible people. They are rich and look down on us and they have a dreadful dog. Look, there! Can you see that huge, black thing lying under the table in their garden? He's a man-eater. He's bitten Daddy three times but we can't do anything about it because he did it on private land and the owners don't care. When you walk down our garden he comes after you and tries to jump over the fence. The fence is two metres high but he can reach the top and he snarls as if he could eat you. I have bad dreams about that dog. The Stringers' son is the same age as Jurgen, and there's a baby daughter, though we haven't seen her yet. The boy is an albino. His hair is pure white and he has a nanny who is a vampire."

She paused a moment, picturing in her mind the henna-haired, hip-swinging Amber, in her skin-tight clothes and high heels. She never spoke, but you only had to look at her white face and burgundy lips to know she was a vampire. Professor Saxmund laughed about it all. Lovely Professor Saxmund. He was her father's Head of Department, an ethno-botanist, and when he was in the house it seemed that everything would always be all right. He was like a lion, grizzled, wise, watchful, never more alert than when he pretended to be dozing, and just when you thought he might be cross, breaking into peals of laughter. Everyone, her father, especially, adored him. Even though he told the most terrible stories - it was Professor Saxmund who had told them about the *kelet*, for example - and he who had teasingly suggested there might be something strange about Grandfather Larsson - you nevertheless felt safe when he was there. He seemed to know the answer every problem and they all depended on his affectionate goodwill.

Now Grandfather Larsson was coming to stay! Having painted her side of things, she proceeded to call to mind all that she knew of him. She could see him quite clearly, for though she had met him only once before on a visit long ago, her memory was still fresh and vital, as those of tiny children often are. Somewhere in a great forest of pine trees in Sweden, she recalled a wooden hut, and inside the hut a confusion of sights and smells - things she had never encountered before, so that bound into the memory were also the unfamiliar scents of oil and fish and resin which tainted the air.

There, just as she had seen him, was Per himself - a giant in a thick-belted coat, who picked her up and sat her on a table by his side, so that they could study one another's faces - hers, pink and perfect, wide-eyed, and his, deeply-lined, bearded, fringed with grey hair, but remarkable for a pair of penetrating eyes the colour of ice. She could not understand what he said, but she was captivated by the richness of his voice, and by the soft fur seams on his sleeve that her fingers shyly touched. In that moment they had forged a silent bond, and the other fragments of the memory were like things remembered in a dream. Vaguely, in the shadows, she recalled her mother restlessly moving about, smoothing her daughter's hair where Per's big hand had ruffled it. And her father stamping outside and bringing in the wood. Something was not quite right, though at the age of three she could not tell what it was. An awkwardness, a coldness somewhere? Something that made her uneasy...

These memories were buried deep; separated from everyday experiences and stored apart, in the mind's outlands, along with other mysterious and inexplicable things. For, unlike Professor Saxmund, Trudi did not yet understand everything. And however dazzling her performance for the world at large, she was privately troubled by the knowledge of another, less-than-perfect Trudi; one who was fascinated and appalled by things she did not know. This untold self sometimes woke to unspeakable terrors in the night, felt scared of being alone and made superstitious charms to ward off bad luck. She was hidden away so well, hardly anyone suspected her existence. But Trudi had a feeling that Per's searching eyes might find her out. And the possibility raised a shiver.

"Trudi! Come on now, we're leaving!" That was Sven calling.

He still cut the perfect father-figure, forgetful, funny, always ready to play the clown, just as Kirsten was a model mother. Everybody said so. Who else looked so slender and stylish? Who had such pretty, smooth hair and beautifully-tailored clothes? And whatever Kirsten did, whether she was running a cake stall, or giving a lecture, or cycling through the traffic, she did it with a natural flair which made her the envy of all. Was not this, after all, what it meant to be a Larsson?

Perhaps Trudi idealized life too much. But they all subscribed to the myth. Now, seeing things through her grandfather's eyes, she had to admit that they did not always match up. In her heart, she knew that her world was changing and that the celebrated Larssons were sometimes in danger of drifting apart.

Oh, everything looked fine on top. They still had summer parties and spiced biscuits at Christmas, and they all threw themselves into their sports with the same enthusiasm. But increasingly, Sven lived for his work and behaved in his own house like a stranger. And the longer Sven spent away from home, the harder Kirsten had to work to keep the family legend intact. It was her energy and efficiency which warded off for the children any dangerous moments of boredom or doubt. All the same, here was Trudi now, just sitting, thinking, and thinking led to wondering. She knew that they didn't really talk as much, or play together as they used to. Like sea-creatures stranded on a beach, they lay, drying out, waiting for some kindly storm to wash them back to sea. They quarrelled more. They ate alone more. Perhaps, she thought, in a spasm of anxiety, their house was not really so special after all. They had been quarrelling today, but then everyone was a little bit anxious today. Grandfather Larsson was coming and it was to turn their world upside-down.

7

Chapter 2

The Unexpected Guest

Sven and Kirsten bickered all the way to the airport, while, slumped behind them in car, Jurgen fiddled with his mobile phone and Trudi went on thinking.

In part, she understood. Her own excitement at seeing her grandfather was mixed with anxiety that his coming might somehow spoil the summer. Her parents naturally felt the same. Any disruption to their forthcoming schedules would throw out months and months of careful planning and yet, here was the old man, announcing a visit, quite without warning, and just as they were about to leave on their various ventures. News had arrived from Sweden that he was already on his way. He could not have chosen a more inconvenient moment. With anyone else, they might have tactfully explained that they were busy. But Per was not anyone else. He was family. They had not heard from him for years and, in any case, he was not coming on a pleasure trip, which could be cancelled. He was coming because he was ill and had no one to look after him in the forest. And that was all that Sven could tell them.

Nobody knew how sick he might be, but the very thought made Trudi nervous, for nothing like illness - apart from the odd bout of 'flu or Jurgen's chicken pox - had ever featured in her life before. Illness, like old age, was something that happened to other people and Trudi shared with Kirsten an instinctive aversion to both. In an ideal world, they would cure her grandfather very quickly and help him return to his forest. Then they could all carry on with their lives and no real harm would be done. It might even be fun in a curious sort of way. But the grown-ups did not seem to share this view. They only saw that Per was trouble and that the next few days would be a testing time.

The summer holidays were very important and must not be wasted if they were to make a good start next term. Trudi had heard her mother say so a hundred times. And she and Jurgen had set their hearts on meeting all their friends at summer school. For their parents, there was even more at stake. The Helsinki conference meant everything to Kirsten. It would give her new ideas and vital contacts for her business - opportunities which might not come again. And Sven was committed to his students in Florida. None of them could see how Grandfather Larsson fitted in.

They had made up a comfortable sickbed for him in the conservatory, with a lovely view of the garden, and filled the room with books and flowers, and set up a private TV. Jurgen even lent his spare computer games in case the old man got bored and they all promised to pop in and see him whenever they could and be terribly nice. Nevertheless, they knew things might be awkward. It was small wonder if they felt a bit on edge.

Trudi shut out the distraction of her parents' voices. She liked going to the airport. She had been lots of times before on holidays and school skiing trips and, despite the fuss with security, she always thought of it as a happy place; an entertaining no-man's-land, where people drifted between worlds, contenting themselves with simple pleasures.

Here you could glimpse figures rarely seen in other places: dignitaries in African costumes, Buddhists with shaved heads, or home-comers, still tipsy with holiday euphoria, now shivering in shorts and sombreros. But today, waiting at the arrivals barrier seemed an eternity. Was Grandfather Larsson really coming? Had he even survived the journey? It seemed that the dribble of passengers would never end and nowhere could Trudi see the shaggy figure she remembered from long ago. Suddenly, her father stepped forward and embraced a shrunken-looking man in a parka jacket. Trudi spared him scarcely a glance and turned back to watch the queue, but Sven called her over:

"Trudi! Trudi! Come and say hello to…"

Then she saw his face.

The old man dealt her a nod of recognition and his pale, blue eyes drilled into her once more. Yes, that was Per Larsson - the magician, Professor Saxmund said! But he no longer reeked of fish and petrol. His rather trembling embrace filled her nostrils with an antiseptic smell, somewhere between ear-drops and disinfectant soap and she felt sad and disappointed. Though she recognized his voice, the strength of his once legendary bass was reduced to rumblings from a

9

hollow chest. Phrases raked with silence.

He had but one case; a battered holdall, which Sven slung on his back. And Kirsten took one arm and Jurgen wedged himself neatly under the other and they made a halting procession to the car.

By the time they reached home, Grandfather Larsson was too tired to have his guided tour. He dropped into a chair in the kitchen and began to doze, his nose half-buried in his beard, his thin, large-veined hands spread on his knees. The family surveyed him in consternation, as if an injured goose had landed in their midst and they were at a loss to know what to do.

Kirsten roused herself first. "I'll unpack his things," she said and hauled Per's bag to his room.

"Is he going to die?" asked Jurgen, with an eight-year-old's taste for doom.

"Not this time," smiled Sven. "We're going to make him better."

"How?"

"Well," Sven considered it. "We'll make him want to live. That's a start."

Trudi felt cheated. Not once, except for that initial nod, had the old man given her any special recognition. And now she was afraid she had missed her chance to be his special girl and introduce him to the pleasures of her world. She had a horrid feeling that he *had* come to die and bring bad luck into the house.

Disappointed and dejected, she retreated upstairs and threw herself on her bed. Life wasn't going to be an adventure, after all. It looked as if the grown-ups were going to be right. Grandpa's visit would be difficult - uncomfortable, difficult and boring - and she lost herself so far in this dreary thought, she did not at first notice the voices the other side of the wall.

Her parents were arguing again. They had taken to their room, and were talking in hushed tones, but on this occasion, a new note of desperation had crept in. Trudi was an expert eavesdropper and she promptly opened her door a crack in order to hear what they were saying. Hugging the old teddy bear which had been her comforter since babyhood, she lay back, listening, open-eyed.

"What could he have been *thinking* of!" That was Kirsten in suppressed outrage.

Sven tried to smooth things over. He hated a scene. "He has his own reasons, no doubt. We hardly know him. How can we understand…?"

"Understand! Sven I'm telling you he has brought nothing - no pyjamas - no toothbrush - no slippers - no medicine - nothing but a cap and boots, a filthy reindeer coat, *which stinks*, and a belt with a hunting knife!"

There followed a pause in which Trudi accurately pictured her father giving a shrug.

"A *hunting knife*. Do you hear me? Sven, it's twenty centimetres long - on a plane! With all those customs officials. *Why*? What was he thinking of? He could have had us all arrested!"

"They are his things," said Sven simply. "They are his most important things." Another pause. "He *was* a hunter, you know."

"You don't understand. You don't even want to admit how crazy all this is. We live in suburban England. We live…"

"No, *you* live in suburban England," interrupted Sven. "*I* live in many places. My world is not as closed and narrow as yours."

"Someone has to be here now to look after him. He can't go globetrotting with you!"

"Yes, yes, I know."

"So, will *you* stay? You understand him best."

"You know I have to go."

"Oh yes, of course, then *I* must stay. Give up my one chance to do something important, so that you can have an easy mind!" Trudi had never heard her mother so angry. "I say he should go into a nursing home," she continued. "There are the children to consider. It's not good for them to be dragged into it. And for his own sake…" she softened a little. "He would get better care."

"No!" shouted Sven, driven to exasperation. "We can find another way."

"Yes. Like all your other ways. You have the idea and then someone else has to do it."

"Perhaps we can get a nurse to come in…"

Trudi almost wished she had not heard. She thought of the old man asleep downstairs and felt suddenly ashamed that they didn't want him. Curled on her bed, she let the voices drift out of range and seized instead on the cause of their concern. She felt strangely elated to think that her grandfather had brought his traditional costume with

11

him. She could envisage so clearly, the coarse, hide coat, the boots, the curious belt...

Perhaps Grandfather Larsson had not come to die after all. Perhaps he had not come to be boring. Suppose he had not. And suppose he had come, instead, to bring her an adventure - say, the kind of adventure she had been waiting for all along - well then, she might be the one who came to his rescue, looked after him and made him want to live again. Saving her grandfather might turn out to be more interesting even, than going to summer school...

She sat up. The idea sounded mad, but then she liked a challenge. All her life long she had dutifully followed her parents' wishes. It had seemed the obvious thing to do. But now the grown-ups couldn't agree amongst themselves. Perhaps the time had come for her to strike out on her own. Perhaps she, of all people, would find the answer to their problems because the answer was something so simple only a child could see it... Of course, there would be difficulties, and she did not quite know how she would manage, but when she watched Per, later that day, pushing away his food and sitting like a captive, with his eyes downcast, she felt so sorry for him she vowed then and there she would do what she could to help.

First of all, there was the question of the luggage. She knew how strong-willed her mother could be - how she always brought Sven round to her side. If she wanted Per's possessions out of the house, *and she did*, she would throw them out, for Kirsten kept everything spotless and there could be no place in her cupboards for a shaman's ragged coat. Trudi racked her brains, wondering how she could stage a rescue, but she did not have to worry for long. Life with Per, she would learn, was full of surprises, not to say miracles - and the first occurred that night, when Sven picked up his father's belongings and made a stand against his wife.

"You will not lay a finger on these things," he flashed. "You will not meddle with things you do not understand."

And the second was the note from Auntie Barbara.

Chapter 3

Trudi makes a Decision

Auntie Barbara was not like Kirsten's usual friends who drank herbal tea and went to yoga. Auntie Barbara was American and fat and full of fun. She had a broad, mischievous face and dark hair in a top-knot and she wore outlandish flowing clothes which harked back to her days as a student. She had been at college with Kirsten, who for some reason, allowed her liberties no one else would dare to take. Barbara spoke her mind about everything. She always wanted to wash up at the end of a meal, regardless of the fact that there was a dishwasher and she always arrived with a box of animal chocolates for the children. Kirsten could only freeze in disapproval as they all hunkered down on the sofa and indulged in a ritual share-out: "The kittens are mine! You can have the butterflies!"

"Lord save us!" Auntie Barbara would cry whenever Kirsten said something particularly moral and correct. "The boy can practise his cello *any* time. Let him play football first!"

She was a stupendous cook, - hence, perhaps, her impressive size - but she made a mean opponent at badminton, nonetheless, and she knew all the gossip, for she talked to *everyone*. Kirsten had moments of doubt about Auntie Barbara, but after five minutes in her company, her infectious good-will would always win her over. She was one of the last people still to write by hand, for she had an old-fashioned affection for her fountain pen. A lifelong love affair with books had given her a flowing style and her letters, frequently enlivened as they were, with comic cartoons and absurd anecdotes, always left the reader feeling better. Yet it was not a letter, but a text that came the day after Per Larsson's arrival, and it produced an unsettling effect.

Kirsten read it, then put her hand to her mouth and suddenly dashed from the room. Sven followed her, and Trudi, so as to be within earshot, slipped after them.

"What is it? What's happened?" asked Jurgen later, when the two children were alone together. They were crammed, knees up, on the window-seat of the 'homework' room upstairs.

"Tod's died," said Trudi with a certain dramatic relish.

"Tod?"

"Auntie Barbara's partner."

"Yes?"

"Well - that's it! He's just died, like that. In a car crash. And Auntie Barbara is very upset."

"Oh." Jurgen was clearly disappointed. He had hoped for something more.

They were all very fond of Tod. Tod had been there ever since the children could remember; a gangling Yankee who gave them aeroplane rides and did party tricks. He had a teasing, dry sense of humour, so you couldn't tell if he was joking or not. And he would tell extravagant fibs until Trudi and Jurgen almost cried with frustration.

"You don't believe me? It's true! Look. I've got five fingers on this hand and seven on that. Five here and two - oh - yes here they are!" Barbara doted on him utterly.

Jurgen considered all of this and then continued with his interrogation.

"So?"

"So they are going to ask her to come and stay."

"Here?"

"Here."

"But we're all going away."

"Just for a few days, so we can cheer her up. She's going to be all sad and grumpy like Grandfather."

"Like *everyone*."

They fell silent for a moment at the thought.

"She didn't even tell them about the funeral," said Trudi.

Then Jurgen shrugged it off. "I'll thrash you at '*Viking Raiders*' if you like."

"Do the tennis game."

"The tennis game is so boring. Do the motor racing trials."

"No, tennis."

"It's too boring."

"But I like being the star with the big hair."

"Idiot!"

14

"Slug-belly!"

"Ugh! Bat turd!"

"Mould-slime!"

"*Kelet*!" Jurgen knew that this would silence her. Whatever the game, he would thrash her anyway on the computer. Girls were so slow. And he was quite right about Auntie Barbara too.

When she arrived, she looked thinner, paler, and hardly talked at all. Kirsten took her out for walks and showed her all the designs for the conference, in secret, in the piano room. Sven retreated to his study. And Grandfather Larsson slept in his chair. But Barbara was very attentive to Per. In fact nothing seemed to cheer her up so much as cutting up his food, or settling his cushions. Trudi couldn't get near him. When he had finished sleeping, he would sit staring emptily at the floor, but Trudi's attempts to engage him fell quite flat:

"This is my homework project... these are the photos of our holiday... this is my new dance routine..." None of it brought any response beyond a murmured: "Min Trudi," and a restless movement of the hands.

On the third day she got angry and challenged him to his face.

"*Why* are you so sad?"

Per started and his eyes shortened their focus. "I am an old wolf," he said simply.

Trudi persisted. She was not used to being fobbed off. "Don't you *like* us?"

"Min Trudi..."

"*Don't* you like us?"

"Perhaps... I miss my home."

Now she had him! "Tell me - tell me about your home."

Per stumbled in English. He knew the words but they were far away and wouldn't come when he wanted them. Now his hands gripped the arms of his chair, and he scanned the room, looking for an answer that eluded him.

"My home - is - very big."

"Your house?"

"No. House very small."

"I remember your house." Trudi tried to prise open his memory like a thief slipping in a jemmy and levering for all she was worth. "I

15

remember the table and the window and the boxes of things."

Per looked directly at her, but he did not see her with his far-away eyes. He was seeing his own abandoned room, the low sunlight filtering in.

Trudi persevered. "And I remember the forest…"

"The forest is very big."

"*Tell* me about the forest…"

But already she was losing him. He heaved a long, hollow sigh and patted her on the head. "Min Trudi." He was gone.

"I don't give up, you know," Trudi warned his sleeping figure. "I'm more stubborn than you can believe. Even more stubborn than Mummy. You know even *she* has to give in when I really dig in my heels."

Barbara assessed things at the Larsson house very quickly. She saw that Sven was hiding in his office too much and that Kirsten was bossing the children too much. She saw that Per pretended to sleep too much and the children were by turns angry, preoccupied and genuinely apprehensive, and her natural interest in human affairs began to tickle away beneath the numbness of heart she felt over Tod.

"Hell, Kirsten," she said bluntly one day, when Trudi just happened to be in the hall, "You *have* to go to Helsinki. You are a terrible nurse. You just stand and look at your patient in a kind of frozen horror. You are a priceless designer and you've worked so hard for this chance to show what you can do. Sven *must* go to Florida - he's booked. All the students need him. The kids are off to summer school. *I'll* stay and look after old Grandpa."

"You?"

"Sure. I'll be fine. I think he likes me!" She gave a characteristic wink. "And I'm better living in someone else's house. Mine gives me the creeps right now."

"I can't let you…"

"You can't *stop* me." Barbara cut her short.

"Oh Bee -"

"Now don't you dare get emotional, or I *will* go home. You know me. Bury it and button it up tight!" Barbara brushed her sleeves with her hands as if that was settled and then added: "You have to teach me, though, how to use that goddamn cooker of yours," adding, in an

16

exaggerated accent: *"I ain't never done digital cooking."*

Better than that, Kirsten made her a complete wall chart of all the workings of the house, the children's agendas, the internet shopping system, and timetables for public transport. Barbara surveyed the sheet in disbelief, while Kirsten gave her a final briefing:

"So then, the children go off next week. Don't let them watch too much television - fresh air as often as possible - and no more than one piece of chocolate a day. Trudi has five days at the Drama course and then Action Camp. There's a dance workshop in London in the middle of August - and then French exchange week at the school. But by then we're back for our holiday, if we take a holiday. It's looking pretty unlikely now. Anyway, I'll give you all the details. Jurgen has his music for a whole week..."

"Stop there!" Barbara put up her hand like a traffic cop. "You write it down, in triplicate, in purple and orange, and *I'll* figure it out!"

With Barbara in the house some of the tensions eased, but there were still tricky moments.

Sven left on his travels first, with a pile of luggage. "Goodbye my diva!" he said picking Trudi up. "Be a good girl." Trudi offered a cold cheek, offended by such generalities. She was too old to be told to be good and she really didn't want him to go. She suddenly thought of a hundred projects they could embark on, as they had done when she was little, and now, just when they might share some time together, he was off again. How could he go, and look so pleased. She was not yet able to allow that grown-ups hide their feelings and her gesture genuinely hurt him. Unable to catch her eye, he gave a hapless shrug. Per hardly looked up.

Only Barbara sympathized and clapped him on the back. "Don't worry, heart. Everything will be just fine. She's upset to see you go, but it's only four weeks and a lot can happen in four weeks. She'll welcome you back right enough - you'll see."

Kirsten's departure came next and she left for the airport in a taxi, so calm and chic in her travelling clothes, her bags immaculate.

"Don't be difficult with Auntie Barbara," she chided gently, kneeling down to straighten the children's fronts. "And e-mail me - promise? You've got my address. Every day, mind. I'll phone you when I get to Finland." All of them looked for a signal that wasn't

17

there and felt relieved when the parting was over. Trudi dashed upstairs and burst into angry tears. Jurgen wandered aimlessly about.

"Come on guys," said Barbara, at last. "Let's watch a movie. I know where there's a big bar of candy. And Grandpa needs a rest."

That night Trudi sat up at her window, watching the dark shadows of the garden and trees beyond.

Those had been Kirsten's last words to them all: "You know the rules. No going into the Sump at all. Promise me!"

The Sump, so dark and mysterious and full of unknown dangers. Trudi wondered how it would be when it was sold. The grown-ups thought there would be houses there, just like everywhere else, and then the danger and the mystery would be gone. But several parties had shown interest in the sale and nothing was certain yet. Trudi had hardly had time to think about it, but when she did, as she was doing now, a cold thrill ran through her.

Out there lay another world, where drama and French and dancing seemed to have no relevance. The ban which her parents had imposed, cut her off from a lost past as well as an uncertain future. She shuddered at that pool of darkness, conjuring all the terrors that swarmed in the night, but as she sat, other thoughts crept in as well. These were summer memories from long ago, deeper, sweeter, harder to define: the smell of wet earth, and a drift of leaves overhead; moss on tree bark and little banded snails. Her father's work now took him away on greater adventures, leaving such trifles behind, but the Sump remained for Trudi her nearest 'wilderness'. Here nothing was organized and graded. The regulations of school did not apply. There was no fear of being late, or untidy, or stupid. Time hardly existed. There was just life and death; sunlit seasons of an eternal here and now and shadows with their own wolves' eyes.

Grandfather Larsson would understand. He belonged to the wilderness. As Trudi climbed into bed she realized that she too might fall in love with it. Drama and French could wait for another year, but the Sump would soon be gone, and Per might never come again. It would be her boldest undertaking yet to explain to the adults that Summer School was off. But she wasn't afraid of that.

Chapter 4

Rebellion

To be fair, Auntie Barbara didn't fuss. There were long periods when she seemed still sunk in her own thoughts, so perhaps that made a difference. She gave a knowing shrug, when she heard Trudi's news, as if she had half expected as much, and turned to Jurgen.

"What about you?"

Jurgen was not to be left out. "I'm not going either."

"You know what this means?" Barbara continued, providing her own reply: "It means, my dear children, that your mother will go completely crazy. If I listen to you and let you skip your courses, she will never speak to me, or allow me to look after you again."

This much was irrefutable.

"*Daddy* wouldn't mind," said Trudi.

"That only makes it worse." Barbara sighed, anticipating distant storms. Any disagreement now, even one via satellite, would certainly spell disaster.

"It's not that we won't work."

"We'll do the homework," echoed Jurgen. "I can practise all day."

"You'll miss your friends," cautioned Barbara. "And your parents have already paid, and they think it's all for your own good. They won't let you stay home."

"They *will*!" Trudi was putting on her best dramatic performance. "They will when they understand this is more important."

"What are you going to do here?" Barbara did not wait for a reply: "I'll tell you what. You're going to mope around and be bored and get under my feet."

"Auntie Barbara, we *never* have free time at home. It will be a different kind of summer school - and - and I want to talk to Grandfather Larsson. And if I go to Drama, the summer will just disappear - everything is always so busy - and he will go back to Sweden and we will go back to school, and then I will never find out..."

"Find out?"

Trudi had said more than she meant to, but having got this far, she blundered on: "I'll never find out if Professor Saxmund was right when he said Grandfather was a shaman."

Barbara felt like a ship's captain caught napping at the helm. One minute she was sailing smoothly by her charts, everything calm, the rigging safely secured; the next, she had headed into a squall and needed all hands on deck.

Her proper course of action was to do exactly as she had been told: deliver the children as and where directed, and continue with her own rest and recuperation, watering window boxes and not upsetting apple carts. She loved Sven and Kirsten far too dearly even to consider betraying the trust they had put in her.

It would be completely *improper* to lend Trudi a sympathetic ear, no matter how much she felt tempted to do so. Barbara had no children of her own so she was free to hold whatever opinions she chose about the best way to bring them up. But she could not try out those ideas here. That would never do. All the same she could not help believing that her young rebels had a point. She often felt that Trudi and Jurgen were over-burdened with work, and needed more time off. She even suspected that what Trudi said was right. Getting to know Per Larsson might be a very special experience for them - and their companionship could only do him good. How sad for both to have to miss the chance!

The shaman business, of course, was poppycock. Professor Saxmund, in the course of his research, spent so much time investigating ritual practices, he had come to assume there was mystery everywhere. For half the year, he travelled the globe, studying the medicinal value of plants, and listening to the campfire stories of far-flung tribes. Of course, plants and magic went together in the old days, no matter where you lived, and Professor Saxmund had gathered ancient lore from the tropics to the snowy wastes of Siberia. Once home, he was far too happy to relate these tales over supper, while the children hung on his words. But what he understood as metaphor and myth, was living fact for them. Barbara disapproved. She frequently told him so, but he always laughed at her concern. "Nonsense! Children need to know about things - about good and evil in the world. They are perfectly able to handle such stuff. Better than you or I, I promise you."

"What *is* a shaman?" Trudi asked, and Barbara felt herself honour bound to fob her off.

"A shaman is like a tribal medicine man. He cures the sick people in his village. And he looks after the land."

"But he does more."

"Honey, a lot of it is just made up - fantasy - like Father Christmas."

"Tell me."

"Well they talk to the spirits of the ancestors. And they talk to animals. And they do strange dances and go into trances. Most of it is just for the tourists now."

"How do you know if someone can do that?"

"You don't. Unless you are born in a place and you grow up with the people. It doesn't happen here. Hasn't done for hundreds and hundreds of years. You have to go to the rainforest or the Gobi desert. And even then, it's all over and done with now. They do western medicine."

Trudi gave her a penetrating look. "*You* don't believe in it."

Barbara shook her head. "You need to do what your mother says. Work hard. Be a clever girl. There'll be lots of time later to find out about these things."

Trudi held on tight. "What about shape-shifting?"

"It's a story."

"Tell me."

"The shamans in some cultures pretend to turn into animals, just like witches and wizards in children's stories."

"Why?"

"So they can find out what is going to happen in the future, or travel long distances, or escape from danger. In some countries in the old days, pagan beliefs were illegal and people were locked up for them."

"Was Grandfather Larsson locked up?"

"No! Never. You've got to forget all this."

"Why did Professor Saxmund say it then?"

"Say what?"

"That Grandfather was a magician?"

"Because he's a tease. You know. He's always saying something

21

outrageous. He thinks it amuses you."

"No. Mummy and Daddy were cross he said it. But they didn't contradict him, did they?"

"Oh darling, it was late I expect. I can't remember."

Trudi ignored this banality.

"Do they do good magic, or bad magic?"

"Both, I guess." She felt she was being compromised. "The good ones do good and the bad ones take people's money and cheat them."

"I need to know if he's good."

"Of *course* he's good! How can you doubt it?"

Trudi smiled. She had 'got' her, at last.

"*That's* what you really believe!" she said with a flash of triumph. "You *do*, don't you! And you will help me?"

On the day of the Drama course, Trudi came down with a terrible cold and Jurgen immediately followed suit. There was no question of either of them leaving the house.

Barbara set up quarantine right away. The last thing she wanted was to lose the old man with pneumonia. She informed Sven and Kirsten and kept them posted with copious medical reports: temperatures - appetites - medication – sleep.

Hot and miserable, the children thrashed about in their beds and swallowed doses of lemon-and-honey and sat, glassy-eyed and uncomprehending, as she washed their faces and tidied their hair and read them cheerful stories.

Finally Per, who had been watching her in her whirl of activity, suggested: "Let them come down. We can all be together, and your legs will not have to run so far."

Barbara gave him a look.

"It is okay for me. No problem. I don't catch the 'flu. Anyway they are over there. I am over here. It is more friendly, though."

The cosiness of this arrangement seemed to assist recovery. By now, camped top-to-tail on a sofa, it was a pleasure for Trudi and Jurgen to be helpless and have their pillows plumped. Barbara devised invalid lunches with the food arranged like faces on the plates. She dug out simple board games from the toy cupboards, for the children's powers of concentration were low and even 'snakes and ladders' soon sapped their energy. She struggled manfully with a hail of messages from Helsinki and Florida. By the afternoon, they all felt tired. But afternoon brought the highlight of the day; something they all came to look forward to with pleasure. Tea things cleared away, the children half-asleep, Barbara would pull up Per's armchair and he would begin, in his subterranean voice, to tell them stories from his past.

"Begin in Sweden," Trudi would slyly urge. "Begin in the forest…"

It was delicious to lie there, wrapped in her duvet, with the comforting clatter of Barbara doing something in the background - the summer rain outside - and Per's voice gathering the threads of his narrative. He was finding his tongue now. After a week or more in England, his ear was 'in' and he began to remember and distinguish the unfamiliar words so that sometimes he surprised himself with his fluency. Speaking to the children thus was like talking alone and he enjoyed the novelty of trying out their language. Sometimes Trudi drifted off to sleep and woke again to find the tale flowing on: how old Anders capsized the boat - the day the great storm came - Midsummer fires and Swedish waffles.

Sometimes she took up the story in her head and carried it a different way. The images of the forest suffused her mind and emerged in vibrant dreams. Winter, and the creak of branches under their weight of snow, the cabin hearth-smoke floating out under the stars. And drifts of birch leaves in autumn, gold against the forest floor; reddening berry bushes, mushrooms and carpets of yellow moss that warned of treacherous bog beneath. Spring - just a trickle of ice-cold water and a flood of birdsong. And summer, the best time - long, long days without beginning or end. Lake trout and wild fruit and geese on the lakeshore.

Here Per's voice almost broke into song. He was a boy again, cramming wild strawberries into his mouth, blueberries, cloudberries, lying on his back amongst the ferns, forgetting for a moment the harshness of his peasant's life.

"Of course the peasant's life has gone. Everybody in the north has electricity - washing machines - mobile phones - snowmobiles. Something… " He faltered. "The magic is not the same."

Trudi pricked up her ears. But this story was at its end and Per patted the bedclothes and retreated into silence.

23

'The magic is not the same.' Trudi suddenly felt bored with being ill. Her mind was in a ferment. She had seen a glimpse of the real Per and now she knew just what he needed to get well again. The *real* Per had a secret source of energy. You could see it in his face when he spoke about the forest. As soon as someone changed the subject, he fell back into to his invalid state. He existed for the very thing which had always made her afraid - the wide, dark spaces of the wild.

"Jurgen," she whispered, when she was sure there was no one listening.

"What?"

"Jurgen, you've got to get better."

Jurgen gave her a critical look. Now what?

"You've got to get better," she repeated. "We're going to the Sump!"

Chapter 5

Going In

A day or so later, Barbara appeared at breakfast brandishing a fistful of mail.

"Postcards from Florida!" she announced.

One for each of them, written in Sven's close hand. He liked to cram as much as possible onto the card, scribbling up the sides and even round the stamp.

As usual, Barbara ate nothing, but she kept up a busy banter, filling cups and whisking away the plates. She seemed positively driven, as if afraid to stop and think. She read her card mid-flow, with an indulgent smile. But then they all responded differently. Jurgen had a picture of an alligator with which he pretended to attack Trudi's arm. Per, a mangrove sunset. He seemed mildly perplexed. Trudi hardly looked at hers. She was still too angry with her father to want to acknowledge his distant jokes. There was no room even for kisses on this card. It was all news and facts - nothing about her at all - or about how he should have been missing her. She tossed the thing aside. She would break his rules to spite him.

It wouldn't be difficult to arrange. Per always had a long nap in the morning and Barbara busied about early, but then she liked to brew herself a big mug of foamy coffee and sit down for a rest at eleven.

"We're going into the garden," Trudi casually announced.

"Okay, okay. Don't get into mischief. Do you want coats?"

"Auntie Barbara, it's *summer*!"

"Yes, but you've been ill. Take tissues!"

"It's *hot*! And we're fine. We'll only be a few minutes."

They sidled out through the kitchen door, helping themselves to a colander on the way. And Barbara heaved a sigh of relief.

She was finding life with her young charges something of a trial. No sooner were they back on their own feet, than they seemed to be perpetually under hers. And Trudi would insist on helping. Whatever Barbara did attracted a little commentary of '*Mummy does it like this...'* or *'We don't do that...'* or *'I can show you...'* Such helpfulness, after a while, proved positively irksome. If only they would run away and just be kids and leave her to do the worrying!

The garden, like that of most Victorian villas, was long and narrow, bounded on the east side by a wall and rambler-rose trellis, and on the west, by a high, panelled, wooden fence. According to current fashion, the space had been divided into a series of 'mini-gardens', leading one into another, each with a separate style of its own. There was a Japanese gravel garden, (Kirsten's idea) which doubled as a pitch for boules when Sven was home; then a wisteria covered pergola and lawn, perfect for sitting and talking with guests and a shrubbery, where Sven took the children bug-hunting. Beyond that, stood an old Bramley apple tree and a large shed full of all the tackle necessary for the Larsson way of life: tennis racquets, bicycles, snorkel-gear, a hammock, a croquet set, just to begin with.

They had gone about half way when Jurgen stopped and cocked an ear.

"Wait for the beast!" he mouthed. But everything was quiet next door.

"Don't!" said Trudi. "Don't wake him up."

Jurgen pulled a defiant face and tapped on the fence. Instantly there came a throaty gargling, followed by three or four deafening barks and Sammy, the Alsatian, hurled himself at the panelling from the other side. The fence shook as he lunged again, leaping so high, his black ears and nose came momentarily into view and he rolled his eyes at the children cowering below.

"*Don't!*" Trudi pulled Jurgen away.

Sammy followed them, rebounding with greater fury and did not stop until they reached the relative safety of the shrubbery.

"That was so *stupid*!" Trudi protested. "One day you won't be laughing. He'll come right through and something terrible will happen."

Jurgen made another face - his only way to deal with her nagging.

Already, they had reached the chain-link fence which marked the boundary between the garden and the Sump and somewhere here, must be the secret entrance they had once made with their father. Sure enough, beneath a blanket of goose grass and bindweed they found a place where the wire was lifted up.

"Why are we going?" asked Jurgen, before ducking down.

"Strawberries," said Trudi with an air of authority. "Wild strawberries."

"In *there*?"

"Yes, of course '*in there*'. Grandfather said they picked them in the woods in summer. It's to be a surprise for him, to cheer him up."

"That was in Sweden. How do we know this is the right kind of wood?" Jurgen still demurred.

"*I* know. I heard Professor Saxmund talking about it once."

"About strawberries?"

"About Fraisey Manor - you know, the big house which is a hotel at the end. The Sump was once part of a park that belonged to the manor. The rest of the land got sold off over the years, but originally it was called *de* Fraisey. That was the name of the old family who lived there - and it's French - fraises - strawberries! I *know*. I did it on my course last year. It's written on their coat of arms, and the menus in the hotel have pictures of strawberries all round the edges because the lady who owns it now wants to restore it to its former glory. She's one of the people who are trying to buy the Sump. Well, don't you see? That's where the strawberries must have come from - from the woods - probably in Norman times." She had got quite beyond herself and Jurgen's face now wore the look of beleaguered disbelief which was his refuge when Trudi 'took off'.

"Well, let's at least have a *look*," she urged.

"We promised not to."

"You're scared."

"I'm not!"

"Go on then! Go home baby. I'll do it on my own. I'm sure I remember eating berries with Daddy there, when we made our camp."

Once they resorted to dares, there was no holding either of them, for if there is one thing worse than feeling frightened, it is having to admit the fact, and so, with beating hearts, they wriggled under the wire and tried to get their bearings.

Directly ahead of them stood the ancient beech which had witnessed their infant picnics, years before. Now in full leaf, it spread overhead, a dome of dappled green, shading the ground beneath. Elsewhere, a forest of nettles and brambles formed an impenetrable barrier.

"We can't get through, Trudi."

"We can if we stay under the trees, the nettles don't grow there. Look."

"This is our special place, do you remember?" Jurgen ran his fingers over the trunk.

"Yes, of course I do, but we need to be quick."

"There's my swing." Tied to a branch, like a hangman's noose, hung a length of nylon rope. Trudi had lost him.

"Come *on*!" she urged. "I promised we wouldn't be long and you're going to make us late."

But something strange happened to time in the Sump. There were no clocks. No calendars. Minutes and hours lost themselves in a maze of shifting shadows. Narrow paths, like fox-runs, tunnelled into the scrub and then abruptly halted, leading nowhere. Trudi felt herself sinking. The surrounding greenness, the almost palpable scent of hot leaves, the quietness, punctured by distant birdsong, all created a feeling of unreality, as if she had plunged into an underwater world. Yes. *That* was what struck her most. This place did not recognize her - did not need her. Absorbed in its own secret processes, it hardly needed people at all, which came as rather a shock. After all, Trudi was used to a welcome party wherever she went.

Waves of memories came flooding in but she pushed them steadily aside. Sven was off with other people exploring his wilderness. Well now, she would do the same! Her jealous heart wanted to show him, she could be just as clever, just as brave, all by herself. She didn't need anyone to help her any more.

"Jurgen, we'll play later. Let's find the strawberries first. There's a way through here." She struck out to the right where the nettles had been disturbed. The hulk of another beech loomed, further along the path. In between, a tangle of sapling sycamore and willow and fallen tree-trunks, rotting, where they lay.

Could they be ghosts from the Great Storm? Trudi had heard talk of the hurricane of '87 which flattened whole forests like matchsticks. Already, she thought, she was taking notes, like a proper scientist.

But Jurgen, likewise, had succumbed to the spirit of the place.

And it awoke in him a curiosity, and headstrong will that made him more than usually unhelpful. He didn't want to be told what to do. He wanted to scamper off like a puppy and nose about and climb and scramble. Adults were always giving out boring jobs. And Trudi was sometimes worse than an adult. She had good ideas, but she was too bossy.

"Look, Trood - a skull. I'm taking it home." Memories of midnight rabbit screams made her turn away.

"We'll go as far as that tree," she announced, "and if it's no good, then we'll turn back." But Jurgen was miles away.

"Look at me! I'm walking a tightrope."

He had climbed onto one of the fallen trunks, all damp and slippery with moss. Spreading his arms, like an acrobat, he began to strut about.

"There are weird things growing on this. Whoo! Toadstools! Come and see. Look at me, Trood - I'll do it backwards…"

She hardly turned her head. It was completely predictable that he would tumble off and she felt no more than exasperation when a cry and a crash brought him upside down into a pile of nettles.

"Get up!"

"Trudi, help me, I can't. I've hurt my leg. Help me - I'm being stung all over!"

A crisis. They were so engrossed in their predicament, they did not see the stranger approaching, until he was nearly on top of them and his voice took them by surprise: "What the hell's going on here?"

He was the most alarming-looking person, Trudi had ever seen. Not old, but skinny and wiry. He had a narrow, dark, bearded face with a scar on his nose and his hair hung loose beneath a red, knotted headband. He wore two earrings in one ear, like a pirate, and a gold neck chain, which glinted against his skin. He did not seem to bother with proper clothes. Trudi noted a meagre torso with prominent ribs. A green snake tattoo curled up and over one shoulder. His arms, which appeared more muscular, were also covered with tattoos: Celtic braids, a couple of crossed spears and a skull. From the waist down he wore baggy tracksuit trousers, tucked into builder's boots.

Seeing Trudi, frozen like a frightened rabbit, he did not wait for a reply, but plunged straight in amongst the nettles and pulled Jurgen

29

out by the armpits.

"Don't you know this is private land?" he grumbled. "It's not a safe place for kids to play." He was now kneeling down and looking critically from brother to sister, but his tone had softened.

"I've broken my foot!" Jurgen wailed, feeling the full force of his stings and aware of a mounting pain in his ankle.

Trudi looked on helplessly.

Every instinct in her body told her to run away, but that was impossible. She could not leave Jurgen. And in any case, where could she go? She was in deadly trouble, whatever she did. If Jurgen died now, which he probably would, she would almost certainly get the blame. And if he didn't, if he made it home, his injuries would tell against her. Wasn't the whole calamity her fault? Hadn't she broken her solemn promise to her mother and then told fibs on top? And what chance did they have of ever reaching home? It was much more likely that they would be murdered first by this man in the wood.

The pirate propped Jurgen deftly against a tree and began issuing instructions. "Move this knee, can you? And this one?"

"Like that?"

"*They* move. What about your feet? This one? Fine. That one?"

"Aaoow!"

"It still moves. I think you'll survive. That was a pretty dumb thing to do, wasn't it?" He grinned in what was supposed to be a reassuring way, but smiling revealed a mouth full of broken teeth which made him look more alarming than ever.

"So, what were you doing?" He gently undid Jurgen's shoe and peeled back the sock to reveal a spreading bruise.

Trudi bit her lip. She knew she was not supposed to talk to strangers. She knew she would be dead meat when her parents found out, but what else could she do? This dreadful man was all the help they had. And help seemed quite impossible without trust. Quite spontaneously, she thought of Auntie Barbara. What would Auntie Barbara say if she was here? She could almost hear her voice whisper in her ear: "*Go with it, honey. Hell, it will work out all right.*"

"We were getting strawberries," she said.

"Strawberries?" the pirate squinted in disbelief.

30

"I know it sounds stupid," Trudi ploughed on, "but they were for our grandfather. He's Swedish. They were to remind him of the forest back home, and now it's all gone wrong." She knew she was going to cry. So much for her brave expedition. She was going to cry in front of a stranger.

"Well, you've got the wrong month and you're in the wrong place." Blackbeard began scouting around for dock leaves. "Here. Rub these on his stings. They'll take the pain out. He's quite a Spartan, isn't he?"

"What's going to happen to us?" asked Trudi, still trembling, but rubbing nonetheless.

"We get you home. Where do you live?"

"Over there. We crawled under the fence."

"Could he do it in this state?"

Trudi looked at Jurgen, who was beginning to feel sick and shook her head.

"But you could go, and get your mum."

"She's not there," Trudi wobbled again "Only grandfather and Auntie Barbara and she's too fat to get through."

"Right. Here's what we do then. You go home and tell Auntie Barbara we're coming. And I'll bring -" he paused, "him - home another way. Can you find your way back?"

She nodded.

"I'm Scarp, by the way."

"Do you work here?"

"Not exactly. I live on Jackson's farm, on the other side. Now, what are your names?"

Trudi demurred. Oh well, she'd done everything wrong so far. Might as well carry on.

"Trudi and Jurgen."

"And what number is your house?"

Silence.

"Okay, you stand out in the street by your gate, then. When we come down the road, you wave so we can find you. Got it? Now then, ready?" He swung Jurgen onto his shoulders as if he weighed nothing at all, glanced up to make sure that he was all right and strode off into the undergrowth.

Trudi turned and fled the way she had come. She had done a

terrible thing. Now she had lost Jurgen, too. She *knew* the Sump was a bad place. She *knew* bad things happened there. Why did she come? Why? *Why?* Now the tears flowed thick and fast. Every bramble caught at her clothes. The nettles lay in wait for her. She slipped on roots, barged into branches. *Where* was Sven? Why wasn't he here to take care of things - to make it all alright? The sight of the blue rope-swing brought a moment's respite. At least she was not lost. She could slip through the fence and raise the alarm.

Sammy heard her coming and was ready, but for once she yelled angrily back. On she ran, headlong, through the Zen garden, through the open patio doors, and straight into Barbara's astonished arms.

"Whatever happened to *you*?" she cried.

"I'm all right. It's Jurgen! In the Sump!" sobbed Trudi.

"*What*?" Barbara - assuming the worst - visualized a succession of fatal possibilities, beginning with death by drowning.

"He's broken his ankle - and a man is bringing him home - and we've got to go outside and wait for him."

"Oh, Trudi Larsson - what *have* you two been up to?" Barbara's face crinkled up, though her tone actually said: '*Thank the Lord! Is that all?*' And she grabbed Trudi's hand and set off down the hall.

"*What* man?"

They reached the front door and scanned the empty street.

"That man!" said Trudi, pointing. And sure enough, the pirate was already swaggering into view, with Jurgen on his back.

"Holy Mother!" said Barbara. And then, casting a sideways glance, she added: "You're going to need patching up too, you know." She was right. Trudi had some impressive scratches of her own.

Scarp took his time and duly presented himself at the gate.

"Auntie Barbara?"

"Oh, my gosh!"

"It's not as bad as it looks. I think he slipped off a log. Looks like a sprain only... You know, they shouldn't be in there on their own."

"Are you telling *me*? *They* know that! Well, but thank you for bringing him home. He looks a bit green, doesn't he? Come in, come in. I'm sorry. I didn't catch your name."

"Scarp."

To Trudi's surprise she led the way indoors and Scarp tramped

32

after her in his big, shabby boots, leaving a trail of dirt across the floor.

Whatever would Kirsten have said? Trudi did not need to ask.

Kirsten would have congealed in horror, as *she* had done, and got rid of him on the doorstep. For a moment, Trudi glimpsed inside her mother's heart. And what she saw gave her a start. Was it possible? Was it truly possible that she was frightened, just like an ordinary person? She looked so calm, so wonderfully capable, but underneath it all, even when she was most formidable, was she, too, afraid of things?

It took her a while to process this thought and return to the scene in the kitchen: Per, now leaning forward in his chair, taking note; Scarp depositing Jurgen on the edge of the kitchen table and then standing back, surveying his surroundings with a sudden unease and Barbara, engrossed with the foot, making clucking noises.

The old man held out his enormous hand and Scarp shook it and gave a tacit nod of the head. Then both turned back to the patient.

As for Jurgen, he was beginning to enjoy himself. For once, he was the centre of attention. Normally, Trudi's dramas ruled the house, but today he had upstaged her, and he took a positive pleasure in transferring allegiance from her, (since she had proved such a bad commander), to Scarp, (who seemed a rather good one). Trudi could whistle for attention. She didn't have a sprained foot. And she couldn't perform miracles either, like Scarp. That ride home had been quite a thrill. Scarp knew a secret way out of the Sump, and by climbing along a tree and dropping down into the Sewage Works drive, he had reached the road in a matter of minutes. Once he was certain he wasn't being kidnapped, Jurgen had felt proud as punch to be travelling in such style.

But here, in this domestic setting, Scarp was losing his nerve. He shuffled from one foot to the other, scattering more mud, and rubbed his hands over his arms, as if he wished he had a shirt.

"You may want to get him x-rayed," he said. "But he can move all right."

Barbara nodded without listening and addressed herself, instead, to her patient. "Are you okay, honey?" Then she did that awful thing that kindly adults do, and ruffled his hair like a dog.

"Arnica might help," Scarp went on.

33

"Yes, of course. Well, Kirsten will have absolutely everything, neatly stored somewhere." She straightened up and grinned as Jurgen slapped his hair down again.

"Will you have some tea, Mr - ?"

"No - no mister. Just Scarp. And - er- no, thank you. I'd best be going and let you all sort yourselves out."

As soon as the words were out, he knew he'd given the wrong reply. Barbara's face fell - she really did mean her offer - and Jurgen looked quite stricken. But a mounting sense of panic gripped him now.

"Well, thank you, anyway," Barbara rallied. "You've certainly saved the day. The kids' parents are away and I guess I bit off more than I could chew when I said I'd look after them." Her warm, brown eyes looked close to tears. If only Tod were here... Tod would know what to do.

Scarp hesitated. "Do you want me to strap him up? I can. But you really ought to get him to Casualty."

"Oh, sure. Anyone can see that." Barbara waved the tears away. "But how? I don't drive, see? Stupid, I know."

"Fetch the medicine," said Per softly. "We can look after him here. It is not a problem."

Scarp nodded gratefully and backed towards the door. "That's my mobile number." He produced a much-thumbed ticket. "Keep it. If you're worried, ring me and I'll bring the truck, okay?"

Jurgen's eyes grew wider still. Truck, did he say? A ride in a truck? Scarp winked at him. "As for you, mate - here's a memento. Don't go in *there* alone again, okay? There could be anyone lurking about in there - and if you fell in the pond I couldn't get you out. I can't swim!" He pulled an object from his pocket and dropped it into Jurgen's hand.

Then he was gone.

By the time Barbara returned with the contents of the medicine cupboard, Per had straightened up.

"Give to me," he said. "This is something I can do."

Trudi watched as he gradually came to life, opening jars and sniffing tubes to find just what he wanted - no point in struggling with the labels. And Kirsten, it was true, kept every remedy you could think of: tea tree, balsam, witch hazel, arnica, each in its own

34

distinctive bottle. Then there were dressings of all kinds... His hands moved with a newfound certainty. "This is going to be stiff tomorrow. But you will look very smart. You see?"

Per finally chose an embrocation smelling of turps, massaged it in and wrapped a bandage over it. Over and under, he went, over and under, round and round and then, with a rip and a knot he was finished. A real professional job. How many times had he done it before, Trudi wondered? She heard Barbara's voice again: "*A shaman is a tribal medicine man. He cures the sick people in his village.*" Of course!

"Aren't you really going to tell us off?" she asked, while her own injuries were seen to.

"Guess there's no point," said Barbara.

"But Mummy said…"

"I think the best thing is to forget this ever happened. Your mother doesn't have to know where you were. She will only worry."

"Oh Auntie Barbara, *thank* you!"

"Though you owe me a big favour, in return."

"Anything!"

"Like - you make pudding," Barbara teased.

"*Anything!*"

"And you tell me what you're up to."

Trudi looked away and started to breathe like a horse.

"I know," Barbara went on, ironically. "It's a secret. The Larssons and their goddamn secrets!" She shot a meaningful glance at Per. Sven and Kirsten were little better - always mysteries - mysteries. Barbara didn't do mysteries. She liked everything open and honest and friendly. And here she was, getting dragged into intrigue, despite herself.

'*Hi Kirsten,*' ran her next e-mail. '*Everything is just fine here. Grandpa is doing really well and the kids have completely recovered from their 'flu. I've also got the cooker controls finally sorted. Hope you are loving Helsinki and not working too hard. Jurgen had a bit of a slip today and twisted his ankle. I don't think he'll make it to Football Club - and Trudi is in revolt over the Ecology Camp and says if Jurgen's not leaving the house, she's not going either. I don't know if you can get the money back, but she seems pretty determined. She has forged quite a bond with Per so maybe it's for the best. It seems kind of unfair to split them all up now. Please don't be mad. We're keeping busy! Lots of love, Barbara.'*

She winced as she pressed the 'send' button. Like a pilot, releasing a high altitude bomb, she felt a sudden twinge of nausea. Too late to do anything about it now. She could only wait for the tell-tale smoke that meant she'd hit her target. And, if she knew Kirsten Larsson, there would be plenty of smoke and a few more missiles coming back. Not a good way to start her spell in charge!

They fixed Jurgen up with ski-poles for crutches and he soon found that, using these, he could get around faster on one leg, than he had previously done on two. Per smiled approvingly and the day passed without further event.

Yet when Trudi thought about what had happened, she was filled with indignation. She and Jurgen had got out of a terrible scrape, and Barbara had been simply marvellous. That much was certainly true. But her own plans for winning Per's trust had failed completely. Far from proving how perceptive and original she was, she had merely succeeded in extinguishing herself. Thanks to his fall, Jurgen had scooped all the attention. And when Scarp gave Jurgen his farewell gift, a wave of bitter resentment filled her soul. Scarp had hardly bothered to say goodbye to her. And then, Per had spent so much longer tying Jurgen's bandage than dabbing her little scratches... When she asked about Scarp's present, Jurgen didn't even want to show her. It was something private from his new friend.

"What did he give you?"

"I dunno. Just a stone." Perhaps he wouldn't show because he was disappointed. He sounded disappointed.

Per watched them, his chin cupped in his hand. "May I see?" he asked at length.

Jurgen delved into in his pocket. "It's nothing," he said.

Per took the souvenir and weighed it in his hands as if it were a living thing, feeling the edges with his finger and letting it sit in his palm, searching for the most comfortable grip.

"Jurgen, this is a good gift," he murmured. Both children were curious now.

"This is very old. A tool from Stone Times."

"Neolithic!" crowed Trudi. "It's a worked flint. We did all that at school."

36

But Per paid no heed to her. He was too busy looking.

"This is a hunter's tool - a scraper - for cutting meat from skin or bone - very old – maybe a hundred thousand years. And still sharp."

"Do you think he found it in there?" asked Jurgen.

"I think," Per nodded, "there were hunters there, many, many years ago. When bears were here!" His eyes flashed and he made a playful growl. "Must be a special place!"

Trudi now felt utterly eclipsed. She had organized the trip to the Sump, yet she had come back empty-handed. And it was Jurgen, stupid Jurgen, who had to fall off a log and ruin her expedition, who pocketed all the prizes. Grandfather Larsson liked Scarp and he liked the flint much better than anything she could find.

Yet Per had not forgotten her. "Trudi," he said, when she wished him goodnight. "Be patient, Trudi. You have so many battles to fight - but things will come out right. You will see. You have a good heart. Do not be unhappy. Your time will come and then you will do much."

He was right. She did feel embattled.

She felt responsible for everyone round her - for her father and mother - for Per himself - for Jurgen - even Barbara, and now, in a strange way, for the Sump. Per had said it was 'special', hadn't he? Did it matter that they were going to sell it off and build houses over it? Where would the rabbits and foxes go? And the *kelet*? All she knew was that she had started something. Already there were invisible forces at work, changing the world she thought she knew so well, and it was too late now to go back.

Chapter 6

The Kelet

At two o'clock in the morning, the invisible world came knocking.

Trudi sat up with a start, thinking she had heard a noise, or felt something creeping past her bed, but eventually she decided her own mind had woken her to warn her she was not alone. The *kelet* were somewhere nearby and she was about to experience one of her terrifying encounters with them. Fear gripped her soul. Her heart began to batter her ribs and her eyes, dilated to the full, scanned the palpable blackness of the room.

Where were they? Her tormentors? Which corner were they hiding in - or were they in *all* the corners? Wherever the shadows lay thickest? Sure enough, as she waited, she began to hear them; so quietly at first, they were little louder than her own heartbeat. But then, in a gradual crescendo - a throbbing rhythm - their voices gathered strength.

You would think it the easiest thing to flick on a light and dispel such ghosts, or nightmares at a stroke. But Trudi could not move. She waited, transfixed, peering from left to right with her useless eyes, anticipating how the ordeal she knew so well, would gradually unfold. Before long, soft, white forms, like yeast bubbles, began to detach themselves from the dark.

This ordeal - always the same - had haunted her at intervals ever since she could remember. She might throw herself under the bedclothes, put her hands over her ears, close her eyes fast, but she could not shut out either the insidious voices, or the vision of the crowding, white balloons - the faceless creatures that she named '*kelet*', though she did not know for her life what they really were. In time, the murmur would grow to a roar and the shapes press so close, she could feel their bodies bulging against her own.

Hard as she tried, she never could hear what they said, but it made no difference. She knew, by intonation alone that they were threatening, deriding her, and that at a certain point, she would be further terrified by her own screams, and rush from the room to seek for help from her parents.

Kirsten always made her feel better. She would fold her in her arms, wrap her in her cashmere dressing gown and take her down to the kitchen, where, in the pretty light of the halogen lamps, they would find a drink, a book - the comfort of normal things.

"Trudi, Trudi, it's nothing," she would reason in her oh-so-sensible voice. "You got too hot sleeping and you were frightened by your own pulse beating. There's nothing there, my love. It's just a dream."

Trudi would shake her tear-stained face.

"We'll open the window and let the room cool down."

"No! No! More will come in. They'll come in! I can't go back!"

And such was her fear of returning to bed alone, Kirsten would sometimes let her sleep with her till morning.

"She has got an over-active imagination," Kirsten's friends concluded. "She is excitable, suggestible. Many children are."

Hence Barbara's disapproval of Professor Saxmund discussing his myths and cults in front of the youngsters. The name *kelet*, after all, came from his arsenal of legends. *Kelet* were Siberian fairy-folk with long, hairy arms and legs, who could change their size at will; one minute small as mosquitoes, the next, towering, tall as cliffs. They would catch at night-travellers with their skinny, black fingers. They knew everything - their very name meant 'clever ones'. Before Professor Saxmund could be silenced, Trudi had recognized the *kelet* as cousins of her own nocturnal demons and instantly appropriated their name. Naming gave a face of sorts to the faceless ones, though it did not confer power over them. And Trudi still felt unable either to predict or understand them. If only she knew where they came from... Did they spawn spontaneously in the shadows indoors? Or live in the Sump and creep in through cracks and crevices at night? The Larsson house, after all, was more Swedish than English and the windows were always open. Trudi, alone, insisted that hers be shut - but it made no difference. The *kelet* found her anyway.

On this particular night, however, when the air fermented thick with them, she had no recourse for help. Kirsten was in Helsinki. Jurgen would not understand. Barbara would think her a cry-baby and, after the disasters of the day, she didn't dare lose face again.

39

Only Per, perhaps...

With a supreme effort of will she swung out of bed and stumbled towards the door. "Grandfather - grandfather -" she whispered, repeating the name, like a mantra, to block out the taunts in her ears.

Her arms itched and, she swept her skin with her hands as if the *kelet* were ants which could be brushed away. Now she pattered, barefoot, along the landing. The wood felt smooth beneath her feet. Here were the stairs - three first, then a landing and a turn - then six, then another turn and five to the bottom.

"Grandfather - grandfather..."

The door to the conservatory stood ajar and, by the light of the lamp outside, she could see the white of the turned back covers.

Per's bed was empty.

Trudi tried to reason to herself: Grandfather had gone to the bathroom - he was in the kitchen... All the rooms downstairs lay dark and quiet. From the garden, the scent of summer jasmine drifted through the open window. She could see the white flowers nodding, just beyond the pane.

"Grandfather, where are you?" Why was it that people were never there when you needed them? Trudi flung herself down, weeping, beside the bed and buried her face in the sheets. The place where Per had slept felt warm, and a sense of utter abandonment overwhelmed her.

In a curious way, the sound of her sobbing brought relief. Any human voice was better than none and the *kelet* seemed to draw back when they heard it. Reaching for solace, she hugged the pillow and pulled it towards her and as she did so, she came across something hidden beneath. This something was small and smooth; a carving no longer than her little finger and threaded on a leather thong. It felt cool to the touch. Wood, was it? Or ivory? Bone? Her hands explored the shape as they would do if they had found it in a Christmas stocking. Jurgen always wanted to put on the light, but that spoilt everything, for the whole fun of Christmas morning was guessing in the dark. Sometimes the guessing was better than the gift.

This, she decided, was a pendant of some sort. She passed it from hand to hand, as she had seen Per do with the flint. It was crescent shaped - a bow, she thought - like a miniature hunting bow. Perhaps

Per had used the full-sized weapon when he was a hunter years ago. Perhaps it was for good luck. Professor Saxmund knew about such things. Amulets which were well-thumbed became polished smooth. At any rate, rubbing this one produced a magical effect. In the brief time since she found it, the *kelet* had fallen silent and disappeared from sight. The string was long enough to go around her neck. With one hand cupped over the figure, she straightened Per's pillow and did something she had never managed before - she returned to her room and her own bed alone.

"Don't be angry, grandfather," she whispered. "I'll bring your bow back in the morning."

How quiet her room seemed - and stuffy too.

She loosened the window latch a notch and curled up to sleep, the charm pressed close to her heart. Now she could feel that heart beating slower and steadier and a glow of astonishment crept over her to think that she had withstood an attack and survived.

As she drifted back to sleep she heard again the sound that had first awakened her, a haunting cry, somewhere out over the Sump. She would ask Per in the morning. He would know what it was …

Chapter 7

Deep Water

"Well, you two are grounded for today," said Barbara at breakfast. "I think *you* will practise your cello," (pointing at Jurgen) "and *you* will do some of that history project you have to write, so that I can give your mother good news!"

The day was grey, in any case, and Trudi and Jurgen seemed to accept this pronouncement without demur. In fact, Trudi appeared particularly eager to please and kept an anxious eye on Per, who affected not to notice and for once tucked into his food with good humour.

Barbara had got them all sitting up to table, with piles of fruit and nuts and yoghurt, by express order from Finland. This, though not a traditional Swedish breakfast, accorded with Kirsten's rules on health. And Barbara meant to take no more chances. She would manage the next three weeks strictly day-by-day - no grand ambitions - just see if they could keep body and soul together until Sven and Kirsten returned.

She felt ashamed of herself for showing weakness yesterday. Whatever must that gypsy man have thought? She should have presented a stronger front, if only for Tod's sake. After all, she had dozens of good friends to call on. It was simply a matter of picking up the phone. But somehow she didn't want to revive any part of her old life now. Memories were still too raw. People would insist on being sympathetic and any gesture of kindness simply reduced her to tears again. No. She might be a victim of fate but she was going to do it her own way. She was better here, with a job, however crazy, to do. She enjoyed the anonymity of staying in Bockhurst. Here she could cruise along in a little after-life of her own, imagining that, with her previous existence behind her, she, like Tod, had upped sticks and gone away for good. The little dramas in the household here were absorbing and challenging and she was pleased to notice gradual improvements taking place.

Old Per had certainly become livelier than before. A positive transformation was taking place. And the children - well, they seemed more like children. They had stopped laying down the law quite so much and they were *doing* things, rather than fiddling incessantly with their computers or their mobile phones. In fact, when she suggested that Trudi might like to call up her friends and see how they were doing at Drama, Trudi had shrugged a bit and said it didn't matter. Not that she was depressed. She was simply absorbed in private preoccupations of her own, which Barbara optimistically took as a good sign. Any interest must surely be better than none. And the child would no doubt share her reasons when she was ready.

Overnight, Trudi had changed from being someone who thought she knew everything, to someone who *wanted* to know everything - a more congenial compulsion!

They were just tucking into a second bowl of muesli, when there came a knock at the front door.

"*I* go!" said Barbara, pointing an admonitory finger at the table. "Stay just where you are and finish your helping."

"Oh, it's *you*!" they heard from the hall. "Oh how kind. You really shouldn't have bothered." Ears strained to catch an indecipherable reply. Barbara again. "He's *fine*. We're having breakfast. Come and see. You can join us?" She had that east coast way of turning a statement into a question, with a flick of intonation.

The front door closed and two sets of footsteps approached along the hall.

"Hey, guys," said Barbara, as if it was the most natural thing in the world. "Scarp dropped by again, to see how you were. Isn't that nice?"

Scarp had dressed for the occasion and now sported a navy blue vest and jeans. He had taken the hint, seeing the heap of shoes in the porch, and removed his boots. A vibrant pair of odd socks completed his attire. In one hand he carried a small pot plant which he set down on the table in front of Trudi.

"*That's* a wild strawberry," he said. "But they don't grow in the wood. That one came from Old Jackson's orchard."

Trudi bit her lip and glanced shyly from gift to giver.

"Thank you," she said. It wasn't the plant, but the fact that she had been remembered that mattered, and she was delighted. "*Did*

43

they?" she asked. "Grow there years ago?"

"Don't think so," said Scarp, scratching his beard. "Hard to tell what might have grown there once."

"Coffee? Toast?" Barbara interjected.

"Yeah - great - thanks."

"Sit down, Scarp, please - and welcome," said Per, always formal, holding out his hand.

"Forgive me asking," Barbara spoke for them all, "but what is your connection with the wood?"

Scarp closed his eyes and when he opened them he was smiling. "I'm a trespasser, aren't I? Just like you lot." He crossed one foot over his knee and plucked at his sock. "I live on Jackson's land next door - I'm old Jackson's odd job man, if you like. I'm good with mechanical things, so I fix his tractors and other bits when they go wrong - and I have a kind of workshop on the farm where I can do up old cars, private like. In return, I get to camp free of charge and I raise some pheasants for the son, when he's home from college. He's a bit of a squire you know - hunting, fishing - all that! The wood makes good cover for the young birds and I've set up a couple of rearing pens there. Strictly illegal, but nobody's complained yet. Of course, when it's sold, I'll have to clear out. But I still think of it as my place. No one interferes there, so it's good for nature. A bit of wildwood. I suppose I'm wild too - a squatter. I just slip in and out. No tax - no VAT - no official residence. I'm an endangered species really. Know what I mean?" He stopped to accept Barbara's mug of coffee and gave her a wink. He seemed to have surprised himself with that long speech, and signed off with a toast. "Cheers! - er - any...?" he cringed in a shamefaced way. "Any sugar?"

"And you are archaeologist?" prompted Per, enunciating the word with care.

"The flint?" Scarp had now crammed too much toast in his mouth and had to chew before he could reply. "There are hundreds over there. I pick them up all the time. Cores, flakes... There's a seam of sandstone that runs through the site. That's where you find them. The badgers dig them up. You only have to clear a few feet of ground, especially after rain, and there they are. Don't know why they occur on sandy ground. The flint is originally from the downs, of course. People must have brought it here to make their tools and

44

hunt. Word has it there was once a spring - something called a chalybeate. I've heard Jackson talk about it. Perhaps the hunters were drawn to the water."

"Who taught you to see?" asked Per.

"Old bloke - same bloke who taught me to fish when I was a boy. I've had professional archaeologists turn their noses up at what I find - but I know when it's genuine. It sits in your hand, like. Really comfortable. You can tell just how they held it. The stuff you find here is early. Some looks rough - only worked on one side, but it's genuine all right." He had got back in his stride "The whole place is full of history. An old drove road that was once a Roman road cuts across it. That's why the woman at Fraisey Manor is after it - wants to do something big with the museum at Tilchester - buy it up and make a sort of theme park thing." Scarp snorted indelicately. "Oh, thanks." He allowed Barbara to pile more toast on his plate.

"You had a good teacher," said Per and then, following his own thoughts "I expect you are right about the stream. Good place to wash things - good place to wait for game too."

"Would you show us?" asked Jurgen.

Scarp hesitated. It was all very irregular. He should not get involved. But he felt somehow drawn to this odd little household. They were exotics, misfits, like himself, incongruously tucked behind their suburban façade like peacock chicks under a hen. Nice people too - trusting... Having stumbled across them, he found himself resisting his natural instinct to run away. With educated people he could always feel the waves of disdain or condescension. His accent, his appearance, were enough to keep such folk at arm's length, and sometimes that was literally as far as his fist could reach. But this family had accepted him just as he was. They might have been companions, dreamt up by his boyhood self to fend off loneliness, while his father was drinking and his mother suffering one of her migraines. That old man, for instance... Scarp was something of a 'divvy'. He had hardly attended school but he was quick to learn from life and he had a knack of 'knowing' when something was real. Like the flints... The old man, now, *he* was genuine and there seemed to Scarp's canny eye, fathomless, interesting depths in him.

All the same, he knew the rules. Children should not go off with strangers, especially when their parents were away.

As he stalled, Barbara came to the rescue. "When your leg's better, Jurgen - huh? And perhaps I can come too. I'm kind of interested myself, though how I climb up a log I have no idea!"

"That's no problem," said Scarp. "There are several ways in. Some easier than others."

"Sure. Well, meantime, you guys can catch up on some work."

Per had transferred his attention to Trudi: "Tell me. Why a strawberry?"

"Oh, I..." she fidgeted under his scrutiny. She must give a plausible answer before Jurgen blurted something out. "After your stories about the berries in Sweden, I just wanted to see if we had any here." She almost convinced herself.

Per smiled long and slow. "A humble plant." He hardly seemed to hear her. "Yet once a year it is the queen of the forest. The air even smells sweet when these berries ripen. And their taste is the taste of heaven. A valuable healing plant too... Why should they not grow in the wood?"

He beckoned across the table and then reaching out, pulled the pot towards him, cupping his hands, as though the leaves warmed them. "Your Sump has many secrets."

"*Sump*?" queried Scarp. The only 'sump' he knew was the pan which held the oil for an engine.

"It's our name for the wood," said Trudi.

"Lovely name!" Sump oil was synonymous with sludge.

"Good place," Per concurred, missing the joke. "But the water is very deep."

"Somebody drowned there once," said Scarp, picking up the cue.

"Wicked!" cried Jurgen. "*Who* drowned?"

Though Barbara frowned a warning, the story was out.

"Some old gardener from the Manor."

"No! *When*?"

"Oh, ages - about a hundred years ago. Poor bloke got into trouble with the owners. The original de Fraisey family had it then. They owned all this land. There was a scandal about some missing jewels. First it was pearls and then a gold brooch, a Saxon thing that one of the ancestors dug up before the Civil War. Worth a fortune, so they said. Well, no one had broken into the house, so they suspected the gardener, who was a touchy old devil. He got so pestered about it they reckon he drowned himself. They found him two days later in the pond. Lord de Fraisey went berserk and had the whole thing dredged - they think that's probably when the spring packed up - but they never found nothing. He was in a right state anyway. His son had just left to fight in the war - 1914 - and the boy got himself killed in France the first week he was there. The family went to pieces after that and the place was all sold up. It turned out they had already mortgaged most of what they owned and there were rumours about the theft being a scam. But if it was, it backfired or someone lost their nerve and gave up on it."

"What's a scam?" asked Trudi.

"Well it's a way of getting money. If you insure something for a lot of money and then you lose it, the insurance company have to cough up the value of the thing you lost…"

"Oh."

"…only see, if you're lying and you haven't really lost whatever it is, or you didn't actually have it to lose in the first place - well, that's getting money under false pretences. That's a scam. You can go to prison for that."

"And you think there wasn't a brooch?"

"I dunno. I think there was something fishy." Scarp leant back in his chair and rubbed the back of his head. "Some people at the time said the son robbed his parents. Some people said the son never really died. Some people said the whole thing was made up. I've never found anything Saxon in there - it's all early stuff - but there *is* the old drove road, so I suppose anything is possible. The sad thing is, if the history people get their way, they want to excavate, dig it all up and cut down half the trees to make way for a *Heritage Centre,* whatever that is." Scarp set down his mug. "It's not my idea of history."

Per nodded thoughtfully. "Just listen, eh?"

"That's it. Just listen to the voices."

"I've seen a picture of that brooch in the Museum," said Trudi. She and Jurgen had been lots of times. There was a Saxon skeleton too.

But Scarp seemed to be saying something else besides - something more intriguing. He had heard voices in the Sump. And if

47

that was so, would they be the same voices that she could hear?

Was it possible that her voices were not *kelet* after all but ghosts from a violent past, including the corpse of a drowned man? Things were suddenly looking worse than before.

"Fiddle-de-dee!" said Barbara, noisily gathering the dishes from the table. "You'll give us all the creeps! I say that's all just local gossip."

"It will be the local economy if the Museum lot win. 'Major tourist attraction' according to them."

"Very likely."

"*I* think it will be a giant car park." Scarp realized, belatedly, that he had said more than he ought and made his farewells. "I'd better be going. Thanks for breakfast - and I'm glad you're going on all right with your foot."

To Trudi who was quiet, he added. "Plant that somewhere under a tree. It won't be hard to grow - a bit of shade - a bit of sun. It looks scruffy now, 'cos it's tired. The fruit comes in June. Next year it'll be fine."

Trudi put on a brave face. "Oh yes. Fine. Thank you."

She had wondered about planting it just beyond the fence, hardly in the Sump at all, but outside the garden, where it wouldn't be disturbed. But now she wasn't sure. She didn't know if she would be brave enough to return to the Sump. One minute she felt she could take on any danger. The next, she was just a child afraid of the dark. But the Sump had got into her soul and kept calling her. Perhaps, when no one was looking, she would plant her strawberry there, near the old camp and make a secret garden. Perhaps the ghosts would even like that - and maybe, then, they would leave her alone.

Barbara saw Scarp out rather sharply, and he fumbled with his boots at the door.

"Sorry. I've put my foot in it haven't I? I talk too much here. What did I say?"

She gave him a lemon-pip smile. "Don't take it to heart. You aren't to know. Come and see us again if you want. I think the kids would really like to go flinting."

Scarp nodded and hobbled away, his laces still undone.

Chapter 8

Pandowdy and Apple Slump

Later that morning, with the soulful scrapings of Jurgen's cello resounding from the homework room, Barbara set about her latest report to Kirsten:

'*Hi, K darling, everything is just fine.*' She was putting a creative gloss on things. '*The kids are working hard and I've managed to book them on a local archaeology course for a day, when Jurgen's foot is properly healed. Per is feeling much better and starting to eat. He even shuffled out into the garden today. Don't worry about a thing. Lots of love, Barbara.*'

Send. No, Delete. Send. No, Delete... As she vacillated, the phone in the hall went off, followed seconds later by her mobile and she winced and closed her eyes. Multiple phone calls could mean only one thing. War was breaking out.

Sure enough, she had Sven *and* Kirsten on the line, both offering contradictory advice. Trudi was to go straight back to her Summer School. Jurgen was to see a physiotherapist. The Football Camp would still be able to take him, even if he was in a wheelchair. Trudi would be lost without her friends. Both children must have fresh air every day. Perhaps it was best to keep them together. Barbara must not wear herself out. Were they eating enough vegetables? Barbara wriggled and squirmed between the two.

Per watched this performance until he could stand it no longer and then weighed in himself.

"Give me my son," he said, beckoning for the phone and launched into Swedish, in a determined voice.

Trudi, listening discreetly at the door, thrilled at this development and wondered what calamity would now follow. But the adults were giving nothing away today and the question of going or staying was not raised again.

After an excursion into the garden and some poking about in the bushes, which drove Sammy into a frenzy next door, Per found himself a lump of dead rosewood, about the size of a fist, which he

49

brought indoors. He then spent the next hour or two in his room moving boxes and padding about until Barbara's patience wore out.

"What is he doing in there?" she complained. "What *is* he doing?" Perhaps it was better when the old man stayed asleep.

"Barbara..." began Trudi, in a wheedling voice.

Barbara braced herself.

"Barbara, do you believe in ghosts?"

"I knew it! *Thank* you, Scarp. Thanks a whole lot!"

"*Do* you?"

"Honey," Barbara was all ready with her reply. "*There's no such thing in the whole world.*" But somehow the words would not come out. She fervently believed that this was what Trudi needed to hear, but had she not caught herself repeatedly, in the last few days, talking to poor, dead Tod, as if he was right there beside her, and feeling quite sure of his answers too? Her behaviour was crazy - she knew that - but the warm memory of Tod provided such pleasant company, she felt happier when she was crazy. The case of the old gardener, however, was another matter, entirely. No one needed *him* around. If *he* was the ghost in question, he could stay at the bottom of his pond.

"Dead people are always with us, you know," she reasoned, treading a fine line between honesty and diplomacy, "in a *good* way. But they're not spooks - not Halloween ghosts."

"I've heard them," said Trudi simply.

"No, no, honey."

"And one sounds like a goose - over there," she pointed to the Sump.

"Well that would *be* a goose. There's water there, isn't there?"

Trudi looked unconvinced.

"Ja!" Per appeared silently in the new slippers they had bought him. "Goose, not ghost!" He seemed very pleased with the joke - his first in English. Language, like slippers got more comfortable with time, and he was wearing both in nicely. He drifted out again.

"No ghosts!" Barbara waved an admonishing finger in front of Trudi's face. "I'm going to get tea and you're going to find something *positive* to do."

"Auntie Barbara, what *is* for tea?"

"Well, you're having meatballs and potato dumplings because

that's kind of Swedish and Grandpa might eat that - and then some fruit maybe?"

"And you?"

"I'll... have something later."

"Why don't you eat with *us*? You don't eat *anything* any more."

"Well I'm not very hungry right now."

"But you should eat something" (Heavens! How she sounded like her mother!) "You would worry about us if *we* didn't eat."

Barbara pondered this and then had a moment's inspiration.

"Okay, Miss Trudi. I will do a deal with you. I will eat with you. I will eat meatballs and potato dumplings. I will eat the most enormous goddamn pudding you can imagine - and you will tell me what all this stuff is about strawberries and ghosts and the Sump."

Now it was Trudi's turn to think. On the one hand, she would quite like to confide in somebody - and on the other, she was afraid that an adult would laugh at her. She did actually need Barbara's help, especially in warding off the good intentions of her parents - and she did actually prefer the old, fat, jolly Auntie who had always defied convention when Tod was alive and never seemed to worry about a thing... Was it possible that a pudding could achieve all this?

"I promised to help you," she said, "so, all right. It's a deal. You teach me to make a pudding and eat it with us, and I will tell you about my idea to make a forest garden."

"*Hallelujah!*" cried Barbara with gospel fervour. "Now we're getting somewhere. You want an English pudding, a Swedish pudding, or a Yankee pudding?" Her arsenal of recipes was legendary for Tod had been a gourmet of the highest order - and together they had toured the culinary delights of the world.

"What's *your* favourite?" said the wily Trudi.

"Yankee! *Of course!*"

"Then Yankee. What's a Yankee pudding?"

"Oh my girl - there's no end to the varieties of the Yankee pudding - and they are all to die for! There's bread pudding, there's flummery, there's buckles and there's slump - not to be confused with a grunt, or a cobbler, or a betty... least of all a fool..."

"I've never heard of any of them."

"You can make them with apples, or blueberries, or raspberries... or raisons, or lemon... and then sweet butter, molasses (that's like

51

treacle), fine flour, cream, nutmeg... Even as she spoke her mouth began to water.

"Are they good for you?" asked Trudi, betraying her upbringing. Yes, thought Barbara ironically, there *were* ghosts and the spectre of Kirsten was right here!

"What is *'good for you'*?" she asked in return. "You mean do they make you *fat*?" She clapped her hands on her stomach. "Can't deny it, can I? But you don't have to eat them *all* the time - and you can always burn off flab with hard work, like they did in the old days. Do they make you feel warm, and contented, and cosy? Yes, they do. And are they good to share with friends? They are the mortar that cements good fellowship. They are the ultimate celebration of the great feast of life, to which we are all invited as guests. And they must be made and given with love. Amen!" They were both transported by her passion. She would make a preacher yet, with sermons like that. "So is that good for you, or not?" she concluded. It was a clever ploy to close with a question.

"It's good," said Trudi.

"Fine! Let's have apple." Barbara ran her tongue around her lips. "You put the things on the table as I pass them to you. No, wait - apron first - and wash those grubby fingers. And we will make the finest of them all. Pandowdy. Can't you just hear the music in that name? Pan-dow-dee! It's like a pie with apple and lemon and spices, all chopped up and cooked again - and served with real ice cream! And we'll have it..." Barbara, now fully animated, was waving a lemon in the air, "as it deserves - by candlelight - as it's such a dull and dreary day."

Trudi marvelled at this glimpse of chaos at work. A few moments ago the day had been doomed to boredom and one chance question had changed it all. Her so ordered, so predictable life, was taking off again, like a runaway cart, and there was no telling where it might take her. Half afraid of her own audacity, half excited by the prospect of stirring things up, she saw the summer itself as a kind of alchemical pudding, whose ingredients might combine to magic effect. There was that word again. *"The magic is not the same..."* She remembered Per's feeble, weary voice. And then she thought of him as he had sounded today on the phone. Now he was, up and about, still rummaging in his room. Whatever *was* he doing?

52

"Right!" Barbara called for attention. "Two cups of flour. *What*? What's a cup? Oh hell, of course you don't do cups here, do you? Okay, let's think… 300 grams of flour, in that scale."

They began to make a mess: loose flour, sticky butter, apple peelings everywhere. Such a thing had never been seen before on Kirsten's gleaming chrome and marble.

"Don't worry. Keep going. We're doing fine." Barbara let Trudi do the work; watched her struggle with the ingredients till disaster seemed all but inevitable and then stepped in at the last minute to right things with a timely stroke or two.

"Look at you!" she said, viewing Trudi's bespattered state, with pride. "Now you're a *real* cook!" Only when the pie was safely in its tin, and the tin in the oven, did she cut to business. "So what is it all about - you and the Sump? You know, you are getting me into frightful trouble."

Trudi gave a fudge of an answer and Barbara filed a mental note: *for Larssons, read crackpots! The whole lot of them! Forest gardens, shamans, talking ghosts…* but she wouldn't give up on them now. She was set on her own intriguing journey and she would see it all through to the end. Her candlelit supper proved a success - a festive party atmosphere, with the pandowdy pudding as its climax.

"Now medicine," Barbara wagged a finger at Per, but he pushed Kirsten's pills away.

"No - no more. This medicine is not good for me. I can do other medicine." And that was final.

Chapter 9

Hobgoblins

The next morning brought two developments. First, a barrage of messages from Sven and Kirsten. No surprises there. But second, and more promising, a smart, blue and yellow football, which had materialised on the lawn overnight, and sat there like an improbable mushroom, fresh with dew.

Barbara took it up and clasped it to her bosom. "Must be from next door. I have an idea how to deal with this."

Today, the hastily tidied kitchen was flooded with sunshine. The scent of hot rolls with marmalade filled the air.

"I ordered you smoked fish. Is that right? Is that what you *really* have for breakfast?"

Per gave a slow, appreciative nod. "One day, Barbara, you can become ..." He hunted for the word. "Yes - honorary Swedish woman!"

"Great!" said Barbara doubtfully, and then put on her brightest smile. "Cheer up kiddies! You're not going back to school today - not yet anyway. And I've made you an appointment with someone special, a real gardener who knows all about plants. He's an old customer of mine..." The children looked unimpressed and when the breakfast things were cleared, Jurgen hobbled back to his computer.

Barbara sat down to write a further report. She felt weary with the seemingly endless tussle over the children. Kirsten was now threatening to come home early and take charge of things herself. Her summer programme must go on. Since speaking with his father, Sven had taken the opposite view and now wanted his family to stay at home. Both sounded miserable and estranged from one another. Barbara, caught in the cross-fire, played Piggy-in-the-middle, but Piggy-in-the middle was a mug's game and Barbara had never submitted to being a mug before.

"Hell, I'm supposed to be resting and recuperating!" she muttered and turned to where Tod should have been, at her side. "And *you're* no help either. I'm probably going mad, too. Here I am talking to myself! I should get out and leave them to it. But... but I can't just run out on old Grandpa. Can't even think about going back to my old life yet. Need to see things through here first." She took a deep breath. "Swedish pastries, I think, with coffee this afternoon. Oh yes - and then deal with the football - and organize outdoor play!" In her own way, she noted wryly, she was simply re-writing Kirsten's schedule, though hers was more flexible - a foraging expedition rather than a route march. She would never have believed that childcare could be such hard work!

"Hi Kirsten," she began. 'Don't you even dream of coming home. We're having a perfect time. I'm arranging for the children to play with a new friend and, oh yes, they have got quite keen on gardening, which seems good and healthy. We're all learning lots and if you could see the kids, you wouldn't worry at all. They're absolutely fine!"

Trudi's face told another tale.

"I don't *want* to meet a gardener!" she objected, slamming the door of the fridge. "I *hate* plants anyway."

"Hate?" said Per. He had unearthed a pair of brown-rimmed spectacles, behind which his eyes seemed to swim without focus. "'Hate' is a big word." He had begun to whittle his lump of wood and the carving was slowly taking shape.

Today everything was contemptible to Trudi.

"Plants are always getting in the way." she said, with venom. "They take up so much time, and then there's no time for anything else."

"Plants do?"

"Yes. They take people away. And make them forget everything that's important." She was thinking, of course, of her father and his folders of crumpled specimens. Sven and his papers and his students. And his endless foreign trips. Today she didn't want to be staying at home.

"Ah," Per began to see her drift. "Trudi is angry."

There was a pause during which her thoughts ran on, so that when she spoke again she had covered some distance.

"You know they are going to get divorced - mummy and daddy."

But Per had gone on further and was waiting for her.

"No, no Trudi."

"They are. Everybody's parents get divorced. It happens all the time." She plucked fretfully at her tee shirt. "They only ever argue now. They don't listen to each other any more."

Per pushed the glasses down his nose so that he could see over the top, with eyes as keen and fierce as ever.

"Trudi, listen. To argue is not a problem."

"They don't have fun any more. *We* don't have fun any more. Just work, work - WORK." Her face crumpled. "I hate work!"

Per saw, for a moment, a vision of another face: fair hair, sun-browned skin, hazel eyes so like Trudi's own... Actually things could break down. Yes, he knew. He had never seen this face that he loved so much, grow old. His wife had fled long ago and taken their only child with her. People *could* drift apart - but he was older and wiser now. It must not happen again."

"You know, sometimes things are not quite as they seem," he said.

Trudi glowered back, her anger directed, not at him, but past him, to the 'authorities', heavenly or earthly, who set courses, ordered terms, decreed that life had to be labelled and classified like a sample in a jar. She didn't want to be in a stuck in a jar. She wanted to be free.

Per could not reach her with reason, so he tried a story: "Did they tell you about the Turkish Hodja?"

"I don't even know what a Hodja is," she objected with a pout.

"They didn't." Encouraged, Per edged onto surer footing and slackened his pace, as storytellers do. "The Turkish Hodja, Mehmet, was a man who always wanted to be one step ahead. He had been to Mecca on pilgrimage, and he had had many adventures. But he always felt that he was too poor to be happy. One night he had a dream. He dreamt there was a hoard of gold, buried beneath the bridge at Isfahan. When he woke up, he was excited as a child." The tale flowed on, with its own persuasive rhythm and Trudi had no choice but to listen.

"He packed his things," continued Per, "said goodbye to his children, and set off for Persia, the land of dreams. It was a long and difficult journey, but all the time Mehmet kept thinking of the gold in his dream and the promise of finding it lightened his step. Imagine all the people back home who would make him guest of honour if he was rich. Think of all those banquets. Think of the power... Now at last, his wife would stop scolding him. When he arrived at the bridge, he waited until nightfall. Then he began to dig. He dug and he dug."

"And found the treasure," said Trudi, losing patience. Nothing seemed amusing today. And why was Per telling a story about Persia, in any case? She did not care about Persia. She hardly listened to his reply.

"No. He found nothing, however hard he searched."

"There wasn't any treasure, then." Her tone said '*I knew it all along*'.

"Oh yes, there was treasure - a great deal," replied Per. "But not under the bridge at Isfahan. Just when he was about to give up he met a man who asked what he was doing. He explained that he had been led a long dance by a dream. 'Oh' replied the stranger. 'Dreams! Who can be bothered with them? I have a dream about treasure myself – and my dream tells me there is treasure in Turkey. Yes! Can you believe it? Under an old man's bed in Istanbul! What kind of a fool would look for treasure there?' And he went on to describe the very house where Mehmet Hodja lived. The old pilgrim hurried home as fast as his donkey would go and sure enough, when he lifted the floorboards, he found that the treasure had been under his bed all the time."

"Well, why didn't he find it before?"

"He didn't think to look."

It seemed an unsatisfactory story to Trudi. "Well there isn't any treasure under *my* bed. I'm not allowed to keep things under the bed."

"Nor I," said Per with a gleam of humour. "This house is too tidy for surprises and my own bed is far away. Not even a hobgoblin could live under a bed here. I know a story about a hobgoblin too."

"There's no such thing as hobgoblins!" snapped Trudi, in her superior '*I know because my father is a lecturer*' voice. "Professor Saxmund says hobgoblins are just manifestations of the subconscious ..."

"Ah yes - quite so," nodded the old man, without understanding. But she had the feeling that he was laughing behind his bushy eyebrows. Now, if there was one thing Trudi found hard to bear, it was ridicule of any kind. Such an insult, even from Jurgen, would put her in an unspeakable rage, but Per's amusement had a sadness at its core that touched her. Perhaps it really was hard for him, missing his own bed, and feeling alone in the spare modernity of a foreign house. His cabin had been crammed with things. Even now, he was sitting, surrounded by a litter of wood-chips that would have her horrified mother.

"Listen, Trudi," he went on. "Some things in the world are bad - some even are *very* bad. We cannot stop all of them, but we must live, just the same. One way to live is to run away - but that is not a good way. Better to stand and fight." His sadness changed to seriousness and when he spoke again his voice had a quiet urgency:

"In days long ago, every house in Sweden had a goblin called a Tomte. You could always know a Tomte because he was small and wore a red cap. He might live anywhere; in a stable, perhaps, or in a corner of the kitchen. The 'old folk', the trolls, liked cobwebs and dirt, and people were very wary of them. But Tomtes like everything neat and clean. Can be useful in the house. Can be trouble too... If you upset a Tomte, say country people, well then beware. You will have nothing but bad luck! Once, a farmer fell out with his Tomte and the creature made his life a misery. This little spirit - how to say - yes, he curdled the milk, he clattered the pans, he spilt the ashes from the fire all over the floor. He tormented the poor fellow until finally he could bear it no more. He decided to pack up and start a new life far away. He collected all his things and placed them in his cart - his pots - his blankets - his furniture - even the goat from the yard. And he said goodbye to his old place with a sigh of relief. Thank heavens! He would be free from trouble at last. As he left the village, a neighbour stopped him. "Anders, where are you off to?" "I'm leaving." he replied. "I can't live in that house a moment longer." But as his cart pulled away, the Tomte poked his head out from under a blanket and gave a mischievous grin. "It's true," he said, "We're leaving home. The two of us, together!"

"But it's not about *stories*," said Trudi. Her anger seemed to have receded. "It's about *us*."

Per paused. "These two characters, Mehmet and Anders, are inside all of us. Treasure is not always gold and trouble does not always wear a red hat. The *real* riches are buried in our lives here

58

and now. We just have to look. The world is full of cares, and sometimes people run away, just to forget them. It is not the plants which keep your father busy. Don't blame the plants. He is busy because then he can forget his worries."

"He wants to get away from *us*!" said Trudi in a spasm of regret.

"No, no. Not you. Me, perhaps? Maybe I am the trouble?"

"He's been busy for *years*. Long before you came."

"Then maybe the trouble is something he does not know himself. Perhaps he does not even feel better when he is away."

Trudi looked up.

"One day he will realize that home is good - is safe. Look, no goblins!"

He lifted his legs and waved them in the air, then peered, beneath his chair, like a clown. At that instant, he himself felt a surge of compassion for the son who had become a stranger, and the cold, incomprehensible woman that son had taken for a wife. Trudi's parents seemed little more than children themselves and just as vulnerable, for all their worldly wisdom.

Trudi threw herself into his arms and sobbed till she felt better. The carving and the knife slipped, forgotten, to the floor.

"So," said Per at length, as much to himself as to his grand-daughter. "We make a good welcome when they come home - and we work a good magic, ja? They will find that the treasure is here, after all!" He smoothed her hair with his hand.

"Yes."

"And you will look after your little plant and find it a good home, over there, in your special place. Not too far away. Clear some ground, maybe, near the fence. This plant wants sunshine too – just like Trudi!"

"Yes."

"And you stay this side of the water, unless you go with Scarp to the far side, where the old sheds are. You can do that? Promise?"

Trudi nodded.

"And I will talk to your mother and tell her some things…" his arctic eyes scrutinized her as if he saw into her soul. At last he nodded and, seeming satisfied, let her go.

And it was not until later, when she turned the scene over in her mind, that she recalled no one had ever told him about the sheds.

Chapter 10

White Wolf, Black Wolf

Barbara had the interview all mapped out in her head. As she stood on the doorstep of the house next door, the football clasped before her, she even rehearsed a few gestures, and mimed a phrase or two in preparation. The scene would start something like this:

"Oh, Mrs. Stringer. I'm so glad I've caught you. You know, the ball came over into our garden. I'm Barbara, by the way - just looking after the children at No. 57 while their parents are away. It must belong to your little boy? Simon? I wanted to bring it back because it seems such a shame for our kids and yours to be playing on their own this summer, when they could have so much more fun together. I wanted to invite Simon over - he could come and play boules in the garden - and we've got cinnamon buns for tea today. What do you say?"

She had seen Simon once or twice - an extraordinary-looking boy, about eight years of age - a pure albino, with white hair, a pointed, porcelain face and colourless eyes; a tiny, spindly chap who looked so much as if he needed to be out in the sun, though of course that was just what was bad for his delicate skin.

"There's a lot of shade in our garden," she added as a mental afterthought.

If one thing seemed ridiculous to Barbara, in her mission to improve the world, it was this feud which existed between the Larssons and the Stringers. Just because of a silly dog! That was no reason for the children not to be friends. Barbara felt that the least she could do was to build some bridges - sign a truce, so to speak - before Sven and Kirsten returned. As she practised her opening lines, her finger on the doorbell, the Alsatian in question hurled himself down the hallway and pitched against the door, barking like a fiend.

For all her brave talk, Barbara recoiled, fearing the glass would break. But somebody on the other side put an end to Sammy's antics. He dropped down as if he had been stunned and Barbara watched him slink away, his sinuous body weaving side to side. The figure who next appeared was not Mrs. Stringer. Barbara knew *her* by sight - large and blowsy-looking, with a baby at her breast - brown, flyaway hair. This person teetered along on high heels and when the door finally opened, after some fiddling with the lock, Barbara realized she was looking at the nanny, who 'lived in'.

Amber was young and beautiful, and there was no room in her world for fat people. Her heart-shaped face boasted a blemish-free, pearly complexion, straight from a cosmetic pack - cheeks, pale, against a luxurious mane of burgundy hair. She wore a crisp, white shirt with a high collar and plunging neckline and a large red, shiny belt, clasping a waist so small, Barbara wondered where in the world she put her vital organs. Black, skin-tight trousers and high boots, though it was the height of summer, added a finishing touch.

She said nothing, but set her chin in an insolently provocative manner and pursed a pair of vermilion lips. A body can speak volumes: "*Well?*" it said. Barbara's opening lines promptly deserted her:

"The - erm - football landed - erm - in our garden? Is Mrs. Stringer there?" Her smile met a rebuff.

"She's busy right now." Amber had a low, melting voice. "Thank you. *I'll* take it." She held out her hand as Barbara floundered on:

"Look, why - why don't you ask Simon if he'd like to come round and play? We'd love to have him. The kids could all have tea together and it would be so good for them to get to know one another. Seems silly..."

"I think we know what's good for Simon," Amber interrupted, rolling the ball on her hip. "He's not advised to play with other children. He's very delicate." She began to close the door.

"If I could just speak to Mrs. Stringer - I'm sure we could work something out..."

But the door had the last word.

"Gees! Did you ever...?" Barbara blinked. "What a witch!"

"What a *witch*!" she fulminated again, from the safety of the kitchen. "I'll swear she has a pentangle tattooed right on her bosom! That poor kid. He's a prisoner."

She was strutting about like an indignant hen, feathers ruffled out. "And that dog! And - and *another* thing..." she paused, unsure whether she had put three or four spoonfuls of coffee into her jug, for

61

she preferred the old percolator to the espresso machine with sachets. "Someone was crying. I could hear someone - a woman - sobbing somewhere in the house. God, what a place!" She recklessly chucked in another spoon. Perhaps the caffeine would calm her nerves. "Well, one thing's for sure, I'll never try and be friendly to *them* again."

"They're just not normal people," said Trudi. "I could have told you."

"Well, *we'll* play boules, anyway. Outdoor play, your mother said - and *you* are going to play *outdoors*. And that dog can bust a gut if he pleases!"

The children raided the garden shed, found the pétanque set and embarked straightaway on the arguments and taunts that always made competitive games such fun:

"You cheated!"

"You just can't play."

"You moved the ball."

"You can't see straight!"

"You're an earwig!"

"Toadstool!"

"One-legged stick-insect!"

Trudi squinted into the sun, adjusting her hat as she considered her next shot. There, at his bedroom window, sat Simon Stringer, watching, his face like a plaster cast.

But the storm over Summer School seemed to have abated. Kirsten swallowed her indignation and decided to stay on for the tour of Finnish design studios. Scarp arrived in time to sample the cinnamon buns and Per finished his carving and pocketed it without a word. The next day they would go flinting if the weather was fine, and in the meantime the children had their dreaded work to do.

"I don't even like the cello."

"But honey, you're so good. You make a lovely sound," Barbara cooed.

"It's too big. And it's not cool! Trudi's all right. She plays the piano. You don't have to carry that anywhere."

"But you could play together," suggested Barbara. "I would have loved that when I was your age."

"Not doing exams," said Trudi.

"Well, forget the exams."

62

"How?"

"Play something else. Play something you've never seen before. There's music by the stack in there."

Trudi heaved a sigh. "Okay. Only for you. Half an hour!"

"And then we'll have some scrambled eggs!" Barbara shook her head once they had gone: "Thank heavens I didn't have children!"

Per peered enquiringly over the rim of his glasses.

"I mean," she continued. "Can you imagine what sort of delinquents I would have raised? I could never have made them knuckle down to anything!"

"Barbara, something I want to ask," said Per, pursuing a separate line of thought. "Can you find me a string, or a ribbon, maybe? Kirsten has many such things in the house I think and I need just a small piece - perhaps so long? Ja?" He held up his hands as if he was playing cat's cradle.

After the eggs and washing up Trudi asked for another story.

"A story - so."

"Tell us about when you were young again. Tell us about the forest."

Per leant back in his chair and rubbed his hand across his face as if rubbing away the years. Then he grew still and began in his deep, down-in-his-boots voice:

"One winter, long ago, when I was still a young man, I went out hunting in the forest, but there came a bad snow storm. One minute, I stopped to fasten my mittens; the next, I had lost sight of my companions.

"Snow was everywhere, thick in the air and so confusing I could not tell which way I had come. The wind drove the flakes like needles into my mouth, into my eyes, blinding me. The trees were swaying, bending as if they would break. It was bitter cold, and I was thirsty, but I had to get out of the wind. At last I found an upturned tree and dug myself a cave beneath the roots - a good shelter to hide in. When the snow closed over me, so, I made an air-hole, a chimney, with my rifle and rolled myself up like a wood mouse. A warm sleep came creeping over me but I knew must not go to sleep - so I made lists of everything I knew - the names of all the people I could remember and the places I had seen. When the blizzard stopped, I crawled out of my cave. It was some time after midnight.

63

Bright stars shining and a moon peeping between the tree-tops overhead. Everything gleaming white. Every branch loaded. And so silent. I kept thinking I must get back before more snow comes. I had lost my compass but I could make out some of the stars, so I knew which way to go. I had travelled by the stars before. That part was not difficult, but the walking - so heavy. My boots sank deep in the drifts - and I could not feel my feet - frost bite, you see. After a couple of hours I hit the road again. Now I was safe. Now I knew my way, even though everything looked new and strange. And I began to think of my little fire and the coffee I would make as soon as I got home. At last I could see my roof. A big fir tree had come down in the wind and smashed into the door, but the rest of the cabin was sound and I felt a great joy. Safe at last! I dropped my bag and my gun and crawled through the fir branches, over the soft pine needles till I reached the room inside - the room *you* saw, Trudi, when you came to visit me. Then I stood up, shaking the snow from my sleeves.

"Can you imagine my surprise?

"There in the moonlight, in my own little hut, was something which made me gasp. A white wolf - a big male - had taken shelter there, crept through the broken door, and was standing right before me, ears back, lips curled in a snarl, ready to spring. A magnificent, big wolf. What could I do? I could not go in. He could not come out. I wanted my gun, but it was behind me and I knew I could not turn my back on this wolf. His yellow eyes were watching me. If I turned, he would certainly kill me. It seemed that one of us must die

"I thought many bad things - many fearful things - old legends about man-eaters. And even I pictured myself round a camp fire with my friends, drinking and boasting how I killed a wolf with my bare hands - and me sitting on that lovely white skin, for a blanket! We waited, and waited - for eternity, it seemed. And then I made a mistake. I moved first and the wolf leapt at me, his great fangs so close to my face. I must have yelled and then I fainted - and when I woke up, I was in the hospital. Frostbite, you see. I was delirious for many days - a big fever - and they thought that I would die.

"Over and over in my mind I saw that wolf again, but when I told the doctors about it, they did not believe me. If the friends who found me had not seen the paw prints in the snow - they would have locked me up for a madman!" Per laughed.

"The wolf didn't hurt you?" asked Trudi.

"The wolf saw the sky behind me when I moved. He saw the sky and the stars - freedom! And he leapt past me, back to his forest. Lucky for him, I did not have my gun. Lucky for me too," Per added solemnly. "He was sheltering in my house and, who knows, maybe I had sheltered in his! Brothers in the storm."

"Why didn't he eat you?"

"Because just then his freedom was more important. For a wolf, a man means death. They are afraid of the smell of us. They will attack if they have no choice, but this wolf saw his forest through my door and when I shouted, he chose freedom rather than death."

"Is Sammy a wolf?" asked Jurgen

"Let's not call him Sammy - that is a poor name for him. He is a big beast. He needs a big name. Let's call him Beor - a strong name."

"Is he a wolf?"

"A very sad, angry wolf. He has no freedom."

"He hates us."

"I don't think so. He just hates. Imagine. He has such powerful legs and he cannot run. Always he is in that narrow garden. He smells all the scents of the world, but he cannot follow them. He sees the birds fly overhead. He hears you walk past. You are in the free world where he longs to be - but he cannot go there. He hates his life."

"But when they call him, he wags his tail. Why doesn't he hate the Stringers?"

"He is their slave. They give him his meat. When he displeases them they punish him. They are his evil gods and he has lost his soul."

In spite of her fear, Trudi felt a shiver of pity. "Poor Beor."

Per looked grim.

"But you got better," said Trudi, returning to the story.

"Yes."

"Did you see the white wolf again?"

"No."

"And your big coat? That is not made of wolf-skin?" As soon as she had said the words she wanted to call them back, but it was too late. Per's eyes changed to stone and he turned on her a blank face that made her wince. "What are you saying? My coat is not a hunter's coat. You saw it when I arrived. Anorak, no?"

Trudi mumbled an apology. "Sorry, grandfather - I -"

"Better not to have a long nose," said Per. Then he relented. "Trudi is young and has many questions. Too many. But Grandfather Per cannot give her the answers. The answers to these questions cannot be borrowed or bought. They have to be found in the heart. Every person must look for himself. Keep your ears and eyes open, Trudi, and wait for things to come to you. Maybe then you will find the answers you are seeking."

Trudi felt bewildered. She had been rebuked and then forgiven, even encouraged, all in the space of a few moments. Just as Per had given freedom to the wolf, he now handed her a glimpse of wisdom beyond her understanding. But the fact that he had confided in her at all filled her with a trembling hope.

She put her hands on his cold hands. "You've still got frostbite," she said.

That broke the spell. Per smiled and the warmth flooded back into his face. "Yes, frostbite in summer. That is what the doctor's medicine does to me! That is also what is called 'old age'."

Trudi had a moment's insight.

"Grandfather, are *you* angry? You said you were an old wolf. Are you like Beor?" She was asking questions again, but this time Per did not take offence. In fact he seemed well pleased with his pupil, since this was the role she had chosen for herself. She had crossed instinctively from fable to fact and back again, like a young animal on pack-ice - unsteady, uncertain, but happy to feel the strangeness of moving two ways at once. Stepping here - drifting there. Where would she end up?

Yes, he had said he was a wolf. He had been many things. But just now he didn't feel like any of them; simply old, robbed of his freedom by age and illness and this chilly way of life the English liked, which had no magic in it. Perhaps it would be better to call it *cold* age. Being cut off from everything vibrant and alive. But angry?

"Are you angry with *us*?" she persisted.

Perhaps he *had* been; angry with Sven for not understanding and frustrated with his own weak hands which had once been so strong.

But not like Beor. Not in a jealous way. This child, with her fresh, open mind, teasing him every day with her hungry curiosity, and Barbara, spilling fountains of love, these blew a warmth on his frozen spirit that felt exquisitely painful. Thawing out was always the worst part, as he knew from many winters - much worse than freezing numb. But now, after resisting for so long, a thaw was what he chose.

"Not with you, little one. Not angry. Maybe old, sad."

"You mustn't be sad," said Trudi, "*ever* again. I won't let you. You'll go out again, like the white wolf. You'll see!"

Per kissed the children goodnight, but at the last moment he called Trudi back and slipped the carving he had made, now complete with its plaited thread, into her hand. "To keep you safe," he murmured. It was a miniature hunting-bow, just like the one she had borrowed. But before she could speak he put his finger to his lips. "Not a word, now. Off you go."

Chapter 11

Setting a Trap

"Oh my gosh!" cried Barbara, as a rotten branch snapped beneath her feet. "What *am* I doing here?"

They were back in the Sump, but this time they had taken a lift in Scarp's truck, parked by the Sewage Works, scrambled along a hedge, crossed a ditch and slipped through an old iron gate, whose padlock had been conveniently 'fixed'.

"When you said the 'easy' route, just what exactly did you mean?"

In the heat of the summer morning, the woods provided welcome shade, but Barbara, unused to exercise of any kind, had turned bright, lobster pink and was perspiring freely.

"You've done the hard bit now," said Scarp, trimming the truth, like a politician. He was not sure how he had coaxed Barbara this far and he had grave doubts about getting her back her again, but his manner today was easy and relaxed. He had reverted to informal dress: long, baggy shorts and a vest with such large armholes, his ribs enjoyed an airing on either side. Bare shins and cavernous boots. His headband, worn Navajo style, was for practical use rather than ornament, keeping the hair out of his eyes.

Trudi and Jurgen grinned mischievously at one another. It was not often that they had the advantage of Barbara, but even with his weak ankle, Jurgen could easily overtake her.

"Now then," Scarp rallied his little team and took his bearings.

The pheasant pens lay over to the left and from here down to the lagoon, the land, untouched by any hand, had followed its own wild inclinations. Straight-poled sycamores and ash grew thick together, with gaps, where single trees had toppled and a riotous under-storey scrambled for the light. The shapes of veteran beeches - some whole, some ravaged by time - towered in the distance.

"The badgers like the sandy soil," Scarp said, moving forward. "Easier to dig, I suppose. *They're* down here." The land suddenly fell away. "Mind your step now."

Where the sunlight dappled through, fat syrphid flies hung motionless on the air, darting aside as they approached and then returning. Speckled brown butterflies spiralled up and down, chasing one another and the blue flash of a damsel-fly signalled water nearby. There were insects everywhere: shiny beetles, sunning themselves on the burdock leaves; dark beetles and centipedes down on the woodland floor; tiny spiders that had winged in on gossamers from the field next door.

"How many of these critters bite, do you suppose?" asked Barbara, warily.

"Oh - all of them!" Scarp was in his element. He had forgotten his awkwardness and assumed a confident tone. "Look - see the earth here? Freshly turned. This is where they've been. This must be a new entrance to the sett." He dropped down on his haunches and started sifting the soil through his fingers. The mound before them rose, almost blocking the wide mouth of a burrow. "If this was a fox hole," Scarp addressed himself to the children, "it would be littered with old bones and rubbish. But this is clean, see? Definitely badgers. But no flints."

Other entrances also showed signs of recent workings.

"What about this?" Jurgen recovered a stone. Scarp took it from him and turned it over.

"'Fraid not," he said.

"How do you know?"

"I'll show you." He squatted again and this time pulled from his pocket two lumps of flint, one like a bitten apple, shiny and black - the other round and pitted, grey, like a beach pebble.

"Where are the Trollstones?" asked Jurgen, his mind already wandering.

"The *what*?"

"The boulders all covered in moss. We found a whole heap of them once," said Trudi, interpreting for him.

"Oh the *greywethers*," Scarp looked up. "Well, my granny used to call them greywethers. The old Sarsen stones? They're over by the sheds."

Jurgen nodded. "And are they trolls?"

"Course not! They're stones. Better than trolls! We'll go and take a look at them another day."

69

"Let's just do these stones for now, huh?" urged Barbara, itching to be done and heading for home. Scarp grinned at her and returned to his lesson.

"This is a hammer stone." The pebble in his right hand. "This is a core." The apple in his left. "To make a tool I knock a piece off the side of this core. You have to hit it hard and straight. There!" With one blow he struck off a flake which bounced onto the sand. "This is what the experts call a micro-lith."

"That means 'little stone'," interrupted Trudi, unable to help herself.

Scarp pulled a face. "Yep. Well, the edges are sharp. You could cut string with that. Who needs a pen knife? You could turn this into a barb for an arrow. Bigger flakes would make arrowheads, spearheads, scrapers. The really old arrow heads are back to front. The pointy bit is tied to the shaft and the blunt end hits the animal and stuns it. Now, look. On the back is a bulge - looks like a shell doesn't it? Those ripple patterns you see there are the shock waves that went right through the flint when it was struck. If you can't find that pattern, it wasn't done by a human."

"You could be an archaeologist," said Trudi, with flattering condescension.

"No thanks," replied Scarp. "Don't get me wrong. Archaeologists are okay. Clever. But they do everything with their heads. If you want to get inside the skin of a Neolithic man, you have got to feel it here. Just think..." he fixed them with his eager brown eyes and punched his heart. "You're sitting here, half naked..." (his vest had become a bear-skin) "...ten thousand years ago. These trees are giant ferns - and there's all sorts of beasts out there: mammoths, giant deer, sabre-toothed tigers... You're just working on this flint..." his voice tailed off into a whisper, "...and you hear something, far off in the forest - the crack of a branch underfoot... Something big and dangerous, and it's coming this way..." With their ears primed, straining into the distance, they were startled to hear a loud rustling close at hand.

Scarp's body froze and he sniffed the air like a primal hunter. Then a triumphant gleam entered his eye.

"Yes!" He whispered, silently clenching his fist. "Listen! Listen. Stay dead quiet, all of you. Don't move. Don't breathe Don't say a

70

single word… *They're* coming and this time I'm going to get them!"

"Scarp?"

"No, no, no. I'll explain later. Back up all of you. Really quiet now. We'll cut them off at the pens."

"Have you gone quite off your head?" Barbara toppled indignantly into a bramble.

"No. I've been waiting for this moment for months. I'll explain later…"

Stealthy as a guerrilla commander he waved them on, closing on his unsuspecting victim.

"Scarp, this is ludicrous! What *is* it?"

"Trespassers."

"We're *all* trespassers. Or had you forgotten that?"

"No - a *real* trespasser. You'll see."

Crouching in the tickliest corner of the undergrowth, with insects now feasting on their tender flesh, they paused within sight of the pheasant runs.

"I don't like them," murmured Trudi. "They're creepy!" Old plastic feed bags dangled up in the trees, just as she had seen them long ago. Someone had drawn eyes on them with a felt tip pen. In the absence of a breeze, they swayed lightly as if by some agency of their own. Gibbets, thought Trudi with a shudder, but Scarp dismissed her objection.

"That's only to keep hawks out. *This* is the real danger. Just watch and wait."

A few moments later the bushes parted and a figure blundered through. Trudi, expecting a mammoth at the very least, was disappointed to see an old woman; her head wrapped in a floral scarf, the rest of her person bundled up in a motley assortment of clothes: rag-bag jumpers and cardigans, and an apron and skirt of different lengths. She must have been impervious to heat, for she also wore grey woollen socks and lace-up boots, and she walked, or rather stumped, doubled over, like a peasant in a fairy tale. Unaware that she was being watched, she beetled straight for the enclosure, dug into her apron pocket and pulled out a hefty pair of wire-cutters.

"Got her!" breathed Scarp, with conviction. "I've *got* her!"

"What's she doing?"

"What's she doing? She's doing criminal damage. That's what

71

she's doing!"

Sure enough, she began to worry at the fence, making hasty stabs and loosening the wire. That was enough.

Scarp straightened up, puffed out his chest and strode down the bank towards her.

"Just what the hell are you up to?" he yelled, waving his arms.

"That's what he said when he found *us*." Trudi nudged Jurgen.

The old woman spun round, her hands - with the incriminating clippers - held aloft, but she had no intention of apologising. Instead, she launched into the attack.

"So *you* are the villain responsible for these *monstrosities!*" She spoke in a theatrical voice, spitting out her syllables with measured emphasis and rolling her 'r's.

"These are my pens," admitted Scarp, momentarily taken aback.

"They are an *affront* - an affront to Nature. What have you got to say?"

"They are here to protect my birds."

"Your *birds*? You call those *birds*?" She did not wait for a reply. "Poor, silly defenceless creatures. Good for nothing but to provide a shooting spree - sport for barbarians. Innocents bred for slaughter!" Had she ever been on the stage? Her manner and diction suggested it. She might have been declaiming Shakespeare, every consonant ringing clear. And it certainly had a disconcerting effect.

Trudi spotted all this from the cover of the bushes, but she noticed more, besides. To her astonishment, the branches of the nearby trees began to fill with tiny birds. Where they came from it was impossible to tell. They arrived in ones and twos, fussing as though disputing seats in a theatre, or filling up the pews in a church. Before long, an entire flock had assembled, fluffing out their feathers and jostling for space. Had they come to watch? Once settled, they grew still and blended into the backdrop of leaves.

A pause gave Scarp time to recover.

"Well?" His adversary was waiting.

"Well, this is my work," he retorted hotly. "And when you cut my wire you destroy all my work, which has taken me months to do. Not to mention the money it costs me. You're taking away my livelihood, 'cos my boss doesn't pay if there are no birds to shoot in the winter. And all you do is let in the foxes, so they can kill everything anyway. What good is that? It pleases the foxes. They have a nice old dinner."

"The pheasants should not be here at all," wailed the old lady. "They are not native birds. They are not part of the natural symphony. They cannot survive as wild creatures, so you keep them as prisoners, but I think one day of freedom is better than a lifetime in captivity. Sooner feed a fox than fatten a good-for-nothing farmer!"

"One all, I think" whispered Barbara, keeping score.

"One what?" asked Jurgen.

"One dumb fight." Barbara replied. "Hold onto your hats - I'm going in!"

She heaved herself up and swung into view.

"Excuse me," she said, emerging centre stage. The whole situation felt absurd, as though they were amateurs, hamming a play. And not Shakespeare either - more like a pantomime farce, with forest scenery. They certainly had the right ingredients: an outlaw, a crone and babes in hiding... As for herself, she must be the dummy, the unlucky fool, who got dragged through bush and briar... No. Somebody had to take control: "Excuse me," she raised her voice, "but I think we need to chill out a little here?"

The two disputants turned round in annoyance.

"And who might *you* be?"

"I'm Barbara. And I'm very pleased to meet you." Ignoring Scarp's look of outrage, she extended her plump hand. "Now, more to the point, who are *you*? We can't possibly have a civilized conversation until we know who we are talking to."

She eyed Scarp in rebuke, but it was the old lady who took her reproof to heart.

"Why yes, of course. How very rude of me. Marjorie Vincent. Miss. How do you do?"

"Miss Vincent, this is Scarp. Scarp, Miss Vincent."

They gave one another a belated nod.

"Now, Miss Vincent," began Barbara, all reason. "You say you are freeing the birds to prevent them being shot? Even though you know they will die anyway?" '*Should have been a barrister!*' she smiled, listening to herself.

"But it's ..."

73

"A–a!" she silenced Scarp with her finger. "Let Miss Vincent speak first."

"Yes. To prevent them from providing profit for people who *call* themselves countrymen, when they know nothing about the country but killing!"

'*Thirty-fifteen,*' noted Barbara. This was better. A verbal game of tennis, with herself as umpire. "Scarp?"

"I look after my birds," retorted Scarp. "Love them, if you like. They have the best of everything. Fresh air, fresh water, proper corn, dust baths, safety from predators. They're not like battery birds. Look at them. Some of them get shot, but every bird dies of something. In the wild, in their native country, most of these would die when they were just chicks. I give them a good and happy life. And if the farmer eats some at the end - even if *I* eat some at the end, how is that different from a cat eating a sparrow?"

'*Thirty all. Well played*'.

"Can't we call a truce?" asked Barbara. Even tennis had its limitations "You are both bird lovers. Anyone can see that, though perhaps you love your birds in different ways. I'll bet you have more in common than you think. We could resolve this better over a cup of something, couldn't we? And I'm being eaten alive here. I can't stick it a moment longer. How far have you come, Miss Vincent - couldn't you join us for tea?"

Scarp put his head in his hands. Women! Women! Every time you are getting into a good fight, along comes a woman and ruins it!

"I live just over there," the old lady pointed towards Beckley Road, then sighed: "Perhaps you should come to me."

"These two as well?" Barbara, beckoned to the children.

"Oh, why not?" Miss Vincent threw up her hands. "Invite the world! But..." And here she waved a warning finger. "I'll ask you to come quietly and make no sudden movements." ('*Even though she has just been roaring her head off!*' thought Barbara.) "As you will observe, I have company."

"*Told you!*" hissed Trudi and poked Jurgen again. Sure enough, as they headed towards home, the little birds took wing and escorted them, flitting from tree to tree.

Scarp stayed behind long enough to secure his damaged fence. Always the man for repairs, was Scarp. That was the advantage of

74

living on a farm and having your pockets full baling twine. He had not, however, simmered down.

'*Why am I doing this?*' he muttered. Of course the act could not close without a soliloquy: '*I'm Scarp – aren't I? A free man - I do just as I please. No obligations, no ties, no trouble. And here I am, suddenly trotting along like a puppy dog... Let's go flinting. Let's drink tea with a mad old coot... I must be going soft in the head!*' Get these kids home safe again - that's what he had to do - and that crazy nut, Barbara. She was a liability, that's what she was. But perhaps *she* could persuade the old woman to leave his pens alone.

Shaking his head, he brought up the rear, his flints all but forgotten.

Chapter 12

Salmonella!

If Barbara had been wondering how she would get back out of the wood, her mind was soon set at rest. Just short of the Larsson picnic camp, Miss Vincent called a halt and began to fumble with some ivy.

Trudi and Jurgen hung back, whispering in the ranks: "I know who she is!"

"So do *I*!"

"She's the woman from the creepy house next door."

"The one who told us off for making a noise in the garden…"

A moment later she had vanished behind the leaves and, following her, they found that an entire section of the fence had been cut away. Easy as pie, they emerged into sunlight on the other side. So those trusty wire-clippers had been put to use here, as well! Miss Vincent had contrived a private entrance for herself - she must have been a woman of some strength to do it - and her curtain of ivy acted as a screen.

Did everyone who lived here take advantage in this way? Barbara could not help noticing that the neighbours next in line were using the land behind them as a dump and had thrown over huge mounds of garden cuttings, together with some sheets of tin and what looked like an old lawn-mower.

"This, here, is holy ground - so please, no noise." Miss Vincent chopped the air with her hand, and hobbled on towards the house. *'Bad hip'*, thought Barbara. *'She can't manage, poor soul. This is even more overgrown than the Sump.'* Struggling amidst a tide of elder and bramble, was evidence of a former garden, now submerged. Lanky roses careered crazily skywards. Baby hollyhocks had seeded themselves in cracks on the terrace. Tiger lilies and mint sprawled for light. On the right, stretched the flint wall and rambler rose, which bounded the Larssons' property. A pair of French windows, yawned agape, and they paused as Miss Vincent took a breath, hauled herself up the step and plunged inside.

Barbara turned to the children with a moment's misgiving and mouthed: "Are you okay?" And they nodded cheerfully back.

The room beyond was dark and it took Barbara's eyes some time to pierce the gloom. When they did so, she gave an involuntary gasp: "*Oh my Lord, Kirsten!*" This was the last place she should have brought the kids. It came straight from the pages of some gothic novel; a mausoleum of forgotten time and she felt that the secrets buried here were just waiting to lay a fateful claim upon them. She might have been an explorer stumbling into Pharaoh's tomb.

Every wall was lined from floor to ceiling with double rows of books. Books lay in piles on the carpet. They filled the chairs, cluttered the desk and, open or shut, filled just about every available space. Yet this was no ordinary library and the contents were not just 'books'. One glance told her that these leather-covered tomes were first editions - fine bindings, as they were called in the trade. And shouldn't she know? Hadn't she and Tod, for the last ten years, run their own inimitable antiquarian bookshop - a bookshop which, incidentally, stood closed until further notice - or until Barbara could begin to put her old life back together?

A large, leather-topped desk commanded a view of the terrace with its numerous bird-feeders. Pots of food littered the paving and tell-tale signs of tiny visitors were only too evident indoors as well. (The room had its own distinctive smell, Trudi noted, she being a specialist in this field: must and damp and leather and something like wet dog-biscuits.) Her eyes were drawn to a large, standard typewriter which dominated the desk. Scattered typescripts suggested that this anachronism was still in use. Against the wall, above the fireplace, hung a pewter-coloured mirror where the room swam in reverse. She could just see herself and the faces of the others, drowning in the depths. What else? A chaise-longue. A tarnished chandelier. Everything, from the corniced ceiling to the hearthrug, spoke of former days, happier days, no doubt, before this dereliction and decay. Here were ancient Christmas cards and Palm Sunday crosses, stuffed among the ornaments, a sepia youth in uniform, smiling from his frame, a signed postcard of the sculptor Gaudier Brzeska...

They all gawped in astonishment - even Scarp - and he had cleared a few houses in his time, but Miss Vincent seemed oblivious to their dismay and stumped through into the hall. Tiptoeing after her, they passed the doorways of two rooms entirely filled with clutter and came to the kitchen; a kind of back scullery, with yellowing tiles and a stove on legs - a butler sink of the type that had recently come into fashion. There were the remnants of a dinner - who knew how old *that* was?

Barbara's heart sank. "*Here we go,*" cried an inner voice. "*Salmonella! That's it. We are all going to die!*"

"You can sit yourselves down," Miss Vincent waved towards a table as she fiddled with her kettle. "Move the things! Make yourselves at home. Now, Darjeeling? Lapsang? Formosa Oolong? Or do you prefer thick, brown, working class tea?"

"That will do just fine, thank you," said Barbara hastily. "He's working class," indicating Scarp, "and I'm thick and brown."

The old lady considered this culturally alien joke and moved on without comment.

"What about the small people?"

"Oh, tap water - definitely!" Barbara insisted.

"Cake?"

Heaven help us! Barbara spotted a half-eaten Battenberg, open on the side, replete with toxic-looking, pink-and-yellow sponge and plastic marzipan. The children would probably love it. She tried not to think of bird poo.

"Well!" Miss Vincent turned to survey her guests, teapot clasped in hand. "You are the first people to come into my house for longer than I can remember."

"It's a lovely place," nodded Barbara, grateful to be able to say this with conviction. In truth, the building *was* a gem - every authentic detail still in place - even the lamps, the window-latches. It had never been re-wired. "Have you lived here always?"

"Pretty much." She did not seem to want to visit the past.

"And your *books*! They are to *die* for. Did *you* buy them all?"

"The library belonged to my uncle, though I've added a title or two. They help with my work."

It required some effort to imagine what this might mean.

"Your work?"

"My research. I write and paint. Mostly the birds. But other things too."

"Oh, I would *love* to see your paintings," Barbara's curiosity was now thoroughly aroused. She seemed to have forgotten the purpose of the visit.

"No, no." Miss Vincent had not. "You came to settle this matter."

But Scarp had also been distracted. His eyes wandered to the window sill where a chaffinch, jauntily perched, was pecking at a crust of bread. Beside it, in an orderly row, lay a collection of hand-worked flints.

"Did you find them?" he asked in a new tone of respect.

"Those things? They are over there by the thousand." Her reply sounded matter-of-fact. "I only bother with the interesting ones." Digging into her cardigan pocket, she brought out two that she had found that day. "It's like looking for mushrooms," she turned to the children. "Once you start, you see them everywhere. You develop an 'eye'."

"These are all right." High praise from Scarp.

"My uncle began it all and I suppose I caught the habit from him. They clutter the place up, but then, I'm a collector - a magpie – can't resist anything interesting…"

Scarp placed his hammer stone and core on the table. "We were flinting just before you came along. I was showing the children."

Miss Vincent actually smiled. "I hope you visited the badger sett - *that's* the place, you know."

"Got my best hand axe there."

"And I got... this…"

She lurched out, leaving them gesticulating across the table.

"What about the pens?" Barbara asked on her return. But neither Scarp nor his companion still seemed interested in the pens. Trudi and Jurgen turned, intrigued, from one to the other. They were thawing out in the glow of their shared enthusiasm and when Miss Vincent's voice rang out next, she sounded almost jolly:

"Come through. Come through! I can't keep on staggering in and out!" And they trooped back to the study together.

In their absence the room had filled with the little birds which had followed them home and now fluttered casually from shelf to shelf, or trotted about on the step.

"You know they are destroying your books!" cried Barbara in dismay. She couldn't help herself. It appalled her to see the damage they were doing.

"*That is* my research," came the reply. "The blue tits are the worst. They really do enjoy ripping a book to bits - and for no apparent reason. Wanton destruction. Look at Doctor Johnson there. You wouldn't think a tiny bird could do that, would you?"

The volume by the great lexicographer lay virtually in shreds.

"But this - this is *terrible*, Miss Vincent. This is a priceless book!"

"Priceless? To me? What value can you put on life, fellowship, knowledge? Dr. Johnson was a man of feeling with a powerful curiosity. I am sure he would have been as interested as myself in the conduct of these creatures."

Well, he liked his cat, thought Barbara, *and the cat would have liked the birds!* "Don't you care at *all*?"

"I care passionately, with my whole being. Why else would I risk life and limb to cross a ruffian such as this," she jerked a thumb towards Scarp. "My research is *everything*. But you asked to see my pictures - well - here they are."

She moved her typewriter and pulled a portfolio from under the desk. This she laid open, spreading the contents on top of other papers and sending a flurry of sparrows in all directions.

Barbara came in for a closer look. The drawings had been done in an H6 pencil, some so faint they seemed little more than a crumple in the paper, but as her eyes settled, she made out a welter of intricate lines.

"These are *extraordinary*," she gasped. "Miss Vincent I was at Art School, but I never saw anything like this in my *life*."

Jurgen leant across the desk and pulled a face, trying to make out something he could recognize. He gave it up. The marks were descriptive not of a form, but of an event. Like a puzzle, they were two things at once - abstract, yet narrative - fleeting, yet drawn with steely certainty.

"Look Jurgen," said Barbara, catching him as he turned away. "This is like a time-exposure photo, but so much better. Here's a wing. See how it moves? This flutter is a little claw of a foot. There's the ghost of a bird in here, just clamouring to get off the paper, but she's caught him. There's the arch of a scapula. Can you see it?"

Jurgen looked at the lines again. He couldn't see a bird, but a pattern - something that made him feel twitchy and itchy. He liked patterns -

80

When Barbara straightened up, she found Miss Vincent studying her with her sharp eyes.

"They're *exquisite*," she gushed.

"Not easy," the older woman replied, "but every time a new challenge. I am not often successful."

"These might outlive Doctor Johnson," Barbara rejoined. "How did you learn?"

"I had my teachers."

Barbara turned involuntarily to the mantelpiece.

"No, no," smiled Miss Vincent. "Not *him*. He was dead long before I learnt to draw. He was a friend of my God-mother's. My uncle knew him. Nothing more."

Nothing more. As if *everyone* had a god-mother with such connections!

"Do you exhibit?" asked Barbara, as the portfolio was folded away.

"My work, my life, are private. I've been a recluse for years."

Trudi, who had devoured every word, now called to mind the front of the house, as she knew it: the rampant shrubs, the gate with its metal post-box and warning signs which had always filled her with dread: "*No hawkers. No circulars. No free newspapers. No milk bottles beyond this point.*" Now all seemed perfectly reasonable. She rather liked the little birds.

For her part, Miss Vincent was at a loss to know how she had let these people in. She certainly felt no need of human company, though once she started, she could certainly talk. Her life with her birds had always felt complete. She preferred her inner world, but recently she had realized that all that was about to change. Letters, snippets on the radio, rumoured that the old Sewage Works, which she regarded as her private territory, was about to be sold. There had been a notice about it from the council and an enquiry from the Museum at Tilchester, who were interested and wanted information from older residents. Somebody else proposed building houses there and had applied in advance for planning permission. "Luxury Eco-Homesteads" they called them. Miss Vincent snorted in disgust.

She tried not to imagine her beloved trees coming down, and her patch of night sky being flooded with solar lighting. The issue of the pheasant pens paled to insignificance by comparison. No, her very existence was on the brink. She and her kind were in retreat, like rainforest lemurs, moving up the mountain. Life, for the moment, went on the same. But as the smoke and the sound of chainsaws approached, she knew she would one day reach the tree line. Where then? Extinction? Her birds twittered on, happily unaware of any threat, but the end was coming, and it made a difference.

"No exhibitions, no." She was now hustling them out. She felt suddenly upset and wanted to be alone. She remembered why she avoided people.

"If it's all the same to you," murmured Scarp. "I'll go out the back. I live the other side of the wood - it's quicker for me to cut through that way..." He nodded all round and slipped into the garden. Miss Vincent watched him go and herded the others into the hall.

"Well, thank you so much..." began Barbara, but the old lady cut her short.

"It's of no consequence. No consequence. Not your fault."

At the door, however, she changed her tune and seizing Jurgen by the hands, forced his fingers open. "You didn't pick up anything?" she demanded.

Jurgen shook his head in alarm.

"Pockets?" she persisted.

"Haven't got any."

"Humph! You?" She turned to Trudi.

"I've got this," said Trudi, prompted by an irrational urge to win her over, and she shyly showed the carving Per had made.

Miss Vincent took it in her hand and peered minutely at it. In an altered voice, she then demanded: "Where did you get this?"

"My grandfather made it for me." Trudi simply couldn't help bragging a little. She scented a conquest: "It's a Sami amulet. For good luck. He's a shaman, you know."

Miss Vincent handed the carving back. "I'd like to meet your grandfather," she said.

Barbara, ever the diplomat, butted in. "I'm sure you *will*. We'd *all* love to see you again." *Why ever* did she say that? Was she *mad*? She thought again of the Battenberg cake, the old, stained cups, the litter of birds' droppings... Better not to think!

But already the front door had closed, reducing the old lady to a blur behind the glass. She wavered a moment, then was gone and

Barbara hurried the children home.

What could one take for the ills they had been exposed to? Barbara made a mental list: Bird 'flu, salmonella, campylobacter, dust mites, fungal spores, just for starters! How did one set up a home-made stomach pump? More to the point, how did one explain to the Larssons that their children had contracted parrot fever? Impossible. Only one course seemed remotely practical - and that was to whistle and pray!

Her e-mail to Kirsten was written in this spirit:

"Hi K, We've had a wonderful, stimulating day today. We did the archaeology course in the morning and then took tea with a local artist who showed us her work. Exquisite! She's an ornithologist, by the way, and the children were able to observe some of the birds she studies at first hand. Everything is just fine. I've contacted someone who may be able to give Jurgen some coaching with his music. Love Barbara."

So far so good. But Trudi was flying too high.

She had come home, as always, fired up and ready to trump everything she had seen. In her over-excited mind, her woodland garden had already grown into a sanctuary where Miss Vincent's companions chirruped from morning till night. Trudi herself, meanwhile, - ever the heroine of her own fantasies - was drawing breathtaking pictures which became the wonder of the world. For a moment she overreached herself so far as to imagine that, with the fortune she raised from her art, she outbid all the contestants for the Sump. She alone would become the proud owner of the woods, the antiquities, even the dreaded lagoon, and install Grandfather Larsson in a secret cabin, where she could keep an eye on him.

She spent the evening working on her first masterpiece: a sketch of the energy spirals in a snail. She thought she had better begin with something slow and there were such beautiful humbug snails on the hogweed leaves that poked through from the Sump. You weren't supposed to touch the leaves because they raised a nasty rash. But she was canny enough to be careful and found a brown, button snail with a primrose-coloured spiral.

The drawing proved more difficult than expected. Her spirals went round and round like hosepipes; her pencil was too dark, her paper too thin. She wisely hid her efforts from Jurgen's mocking eyes, but Barbara also missed the point. Her: "*Oh yes, honey. Very nice,*" might just as well have been: "*Oops! Well, never mind.*" Which baffled Trudi, because it went without saying that she must have more talent than the old woman next door and Barbara had raved about the drawings there. Even allowing that Miss Vincent was an interesting and, possibly, an inspiring person, Trudi still knew, as everybody did, that she was mad. And being mad and old could be no contest for youth and cleverness, could it? And Trudi was special. By simple logic, her drawing must be special, too.

She shyly carried the page to Per and laid it, for approval, on his knees. Per looked attentively and nodded without comment.

"*You* understand, *don't* you?" She suffered a moment's doubt. She could just hear Jurgen now: "*It looks as if a baby did it!*"

Per nodded again. "Of course." But he didn't venture any praise and in a frenzy of self-justification, Trudi now took off at a gallop:

"It's a soul drawing. See? Snails. The old lady does soul drawings next door, but she draws birds. She's mad about birds. They're everywhere in her house. She's like a little old witch, with whiskers on her chin. And I showed her the bow you made me..." galloping so fast, she could not stop, even though a warning note sounded too late in her head. "And I told her about you. About you being a shaman and everything. And she wants... to… meet…" Her voice pattered on for a few more paces, and then, seeing Per's face, faltered and stopped.

Per's blue eyes, the colour of a crevasse, turned on her with a fearsome intensity and a frown gathered between his bushy brows.

"What are you talking of?" he growled.

Trudi swallowed hard, wondering what she had done.

"I wanted her to know how clever you are," she stammered.

"You must never, *never* talk so, Trudi!"

"Wh-why?"

"You must never say such things. You can only do harm. The talisman I gave you was a secret gift for you alone - not for others to see. You have a great deal to learn."

"I'm sorry!" Trudi exclaimed, shocked and stung by the rebuke. "I'm sorry! I didn't know."

"Listen to me." Per took her shoulders in his hands and held her in an iron grip. "You think you can pry and know everything.

84

Everything about me. About everyone. One day that curiosity will be the end of you. Be careful, Trudi! You may stir up things you will regret!"

He released her and, lurching out of his chair, blundered out into the garden, where he stood staring up at the trees. Beor, hearing the sound of his step, raced the length of the fence, furiously snarling. As for Trudi, she dashed from the kitchen, blinded by tears.

In the sanctuary of her pretty, green room she sobbed on the head of Sticky Bear until his fur stood up in spikes.

How could Grandfather be so terrible?

How could she know what to say and what not to say? Life was too unfair! She wished she was a hundred miles away. She wished Grandfather Larsson had never come. She wished Kirsten was home to make everything right again. How could she ever go down and face Per again? He would think her stupid now, forever. And she *was* stupid. Barbara had warned her never to talk about the shaman thing. If only she had listened...

She hated Miss Vincent. She hated the Sump and all the horrid things lurking in it...

By the time Barbara found her, she had exhausted herself and simply felt sick.

"Tea, honey?" She coaxed from the door.

Trudi shook her head.

"I've put your picture on the wall."

"I hate my picture!"

"Your snail ate a little bit of the paper, which I think is just perfect! Come on, mischief! Your Grandpa's not really cross. Just worried about you getting into trouble. Come and have some apple cake. You have to make allowances - he's old and not very well."

Sticky Bear spent the evening on his own, legs up in the air, head stuffed between the pillows where Trudi had abandoned him.

The apple cake was new, and smelt too good to refuse.

Chapter 13

The Magic Flute

The Farmer's Market at Newbridge was held in a parking lot by the river and because it was hidden away from the main thoroughfares, it advertised itself with banners and posters throughout the town. It also generated a substantial din, what with the cries of the stallholders and the sounds of assorted street entertainers, all trying to draw young families in. Local shopkeepers took a dim view of such unregulated trading, but made an extra effort to hold on to their customers, by offering market-day delicacies and bargains - *'two for the price of one'* - on the second Saturday of every month. This entrepreneurial spirit brought benefits to everyone and was typical of Newbridge, for the atmosphere there had always been bustling. Political issues were hotly debated and the locals were forever mounting protests, signing petitions, and calling meetings at which they could enjoy a good piece of gossip. The arrival of city chain stores had only just begun to break up the character of the town, and specialist shops still survived and thrived in its fabled lanes and alleys.

Trees lined the main street. As for the 'new' bridge, which had given the town its name, though it was now a rather old bridge, (a stone plaque nearby gave the date as 1740), it still commanded the same picturesque bend in the river, slap in the heart of the town and children still threw bread to the ducks from its lovely stone parapet, as they had done since time immemorial, while the heavy traffic took a crossing further upstream.

Trudi and Jurgen did not often come to Newbridge. Tilchester was a bigger town with easier parking and Kirsten usually did her shopping there. But Newbridge was where Barbara lived and where she and Tod had set up their bookshop. After Tod's so sudden departure, she had felt queasy about coming back. She knew that there would be piles of bills on the doormat - an answer-phone full of messages - a computer crammed with unanswered e-mails. She had run out on it all, run out in a funk and shut the door and she had no intention of dealing with any of it yet. But there was somebody in the town she hoped to see. And since Scarp had announced he must pick up some tractor parts, and since Jurgen was desperate for another ride in the truck, here they all were on this breathless, hot Saturday, jammed, sweltering in the cab, as they crawled past the summer road-works. Up here, even at the back where the children sat, you had a splendid view, for Scarp's 'truck' was a proper working pick-up with a winch for towing and passenger seats all full of junk. Perched atop a heap of tools and oily rags, Jurgen felt himself king of the world.

Per had waved them off contentedly enough. He had been much occupied with his own thoughts since the previous night, and though he and Trudi had hugged and forgiven one another, they knew that they had crossed a line. Trudi could no longer consider him as a pet to be cosseted and he could no longer view her as a passive infant.

Both had grown in one another's eyes but there was caution now mixed with their affection - shadows, where their mutual knowledge faded out. Trudi's first wish had been to run away and forget all about the intriguing 'otherworld' that belonged to Per. She would have no more to do with Hodja's gold or subversive mysteries, however tempting they might seem. She would be boring and sensible and stop worrying about such things. That was what everybody wanted, after all. But further reflection made her change her mind. The *kelet* and Beor, they were worries too, ugly ones which could not be wished away. Only Per, perhaps, had the power to deal with them and if that was so, she would need more than ever to share his secrets.

Today she seemed unusually subdued. They had come to Newbridge, Barbara explained, to see a man about the forest garden. Trudi did not know if it was any longer right, or wise to plan a forest garden - or if there was even any point, when the holidays were spinning by so fast and the sale of the Sump loomed ever closer. Her efforts in that direction had so far had proved disastrous. Today, she resolved, though it did not come naturally to her, to leave the decision-making to others.

"*Who* are you going to see, exactly?" asked Scarp, steering casually with his left hand while his right hung out of the driver's window, tapping a tune on the door. Barbara, remembering Tod's recent collision, tried to avert her eyes. Yet, if the children had survived Miss Vincent's cake, perhaps they'd be proof against dodgy driving too...

"He's called Tristram Farthing," she called, above the noise of the engine.

Scarp snorted. "Only you could have a friend called *Tristram*."

"He's not a friend, exactly. He's an old customer of mine. Anyhow," she added "he's not what you think. You should meet him. You'd like him."

Scarp screwed his baseball cap down on his head and returned a look which said '*no thanks*!' "I'll drop you by the river and come back in half an hour." He wasn't falling for any more invitations.

"Can you do one thing first?"

"Huh?"

"Can you make a detour down Lion Street? I don't want to stop. I just want to see the shop - make sure it's still standing and check no one has broken the windows."

Scarp swerved obediently to the right and down a narrow turning, where the gabled buildings leaned towards one another. A high wall here, a sundial there - tourist heaven!

"That's it!" cried Barbara and they all craned to see the bow-fronted façade slip by.

"'*Prospero Books*'," Trudi announced.

"It's very small," said Jurgen.

"Bigger inside," replied Barbara, satisfied. "Thank you, Scarp". Everything seemed to be in order.

"What's '*Prospero*'?" asked Trudi.

"Oh, a kind of wizard in Shakespeare. He had a magic island and his own personal spirits to do his jobs for him. We figured that books were rather like that - full of knowledge and able to make things happen through subtle influence."

Trudi liked the idea. If one book could cast a spell over someone and change the way they thought, imagine what a whole library could do? "Can we see inside?" She had been before but it seemed a long time ago.

"Not today. We're going to the market, remember?"

"This is your stop," said Scarp, pulling up. "Meet me here at one o'clock? Don't be late."

They scrambled out and Barbara gave him a sympathetic wink. "What do they say over here? *You're a brick*! Thank you. I'll buy you an ice cream!"

Newbridge Market. Suddenly they were in the thick of it: people pushing - people shouting - a children's roundabout with seats in revolving teacups - a toffee-apple stall, - somebody in a straw boater, selling pies - someone hawking hand-made soap - another cooking cheese on a grill. The cheese smelt like bacon. The soap smelt of seaweed. From the nearby tower of the parish church a clock tolled the half hour. So much to take in...

"There he is!" cried Barbara, and grabbing the children by either hand, sallied forward.

It was the music which reached them first, for they were all too short to see far ahead. From somewhere behind the crowd came the sound of a band, a rhythmic hullabaloo. There must have been several players. They detected the boom-boom! of a bass drum, then an accordionist, a harmonica-player, someone with cymbals and bells... They could have sworn they caught the strains of a flute. But when they finally reached the spot, they found themselves in front of just one man, a character in a stovepipe hat, an undertaker's frockcoat and patched denim jeans. Fancy dress aside, he still cut a curious figure.

For one thing, he was tall and stood lopsided, with one shoulder very much higher than the other. His hair, grey beneath his hat, had been gathered into a pony-tail, and his face, though not that of an old man, was tanned and deeply lined. Grey eyes, sunken cheeks. He gave a nod of recognition when he spotted Barbara, but continued to play, stamping time to the music so that the bells on his legs rang out. And now they could see how he made the rest of his din.

The big bass drum was strapped to his back and operated by a lever at his elbow. He had cymbals at his knees, tambourines on his arms and a harmonica ingeniously attached to his neck. Wrist-bands held his accordion in place and he had stuffed a tin whistle behind one ear. As if this was not enough, he added intermittent blasts from a pneumatic hooter (under-arm action) and something which mooed like a cow. A saxophone and a snare-drum, bearing the legend: *"Corky's One Man Band"* lay at his feet. The playing of these instruments involved much jigging and jerking, but in the noonday sun he showed no sign of fatigue.

People stopped in front of him long enough to gawp and giggle, then shuffled off. Sometimes they threw coins into his open saxophone case. Invariably they found their toes tapping. The music got into their heads and some of them burst into song. At last, with a storm of percussion, Corky bowed low and brought his performance to a close.

"Baarbaaara!" he cried by way of welcome. "How good to see you!" His face suddenly twisted, but before he could find the words she cut him short.

Please, her eyes seemed to beg, *please don't mention Tod or I shall cry. Let's just pretend nothing happened!*

"We've come on a mission," she announced instead.

"A mission from Barbara is serious business," he said, swiftly interpreting her message and divesting himself of his accordion. Now he could pay proper attention. He was gazing enquiringly at the children.

"Oh yes." Barbara remembered her manners. "This is Trudi - this is Jurgen. I'm looking after them for a month while their parents are abroad." Was she? Well, when all was said and done, she supposed she *was*, though she had never thought of herself as being remotely fitted for the task. She didn't know whether to feel shocked or tickled by the thought. "Let's say, we're kind of looking after each other. And we're doing okay, so far. We want some advice about *plants*."

"Oh, that is a *real* mission. Could mean shutting up shop. Well, I'm practically done for the day. I'm all ears. You know, normally it's the other way around," he confided to the children. "*I'm* the one in need of information and Barbara is the genius who finds it for me, tucked away in some corner of her bookshop... Corky, by the way." He held leaned forward and shook them by the hand.

"Is this your job, then?" asked Jurgen, full of wonder.

"One of them." He had watched the boy eyeing the coins in his case. "Not a brilliant day today. A one-man-band won't make you rich, but it does cheer people up. At least I hope it does. Anyway I don't need much money. You can hire me for a party for just fifty pounds - that will keep me for a week."

"Looks more fun than the cello, anyway."

90

"Well," Corky put his head on one side, "a cello *could* be added. There was a man called Virtuoso Violinsky, back in the old days, who played with a bow strapped to his knee - but that would be for piano accompaniment. He used his left hand for fingering, right hand for the keyboard. Difficult to do in the open air, though. I like to be able to shuffle about."

"Can we get you a bun, or something?" Barbara interrupted. "They're selling hot pies over there - and home-made muffins."

"A pie sounds just the ticket. Take the money out of there."

"Like hell we will! You sit tight and we'll be back in a jiffy - and meanwhile, you put your gardening hat on!"

The pie stall smelt divine and they were hard put to choose from the dazzling range of fillings: asparagus and goat's cheese; roasted tomato and mozzarella; spicy chicken; gammon and spinach …They settled for one of each, plus a traditional Cornish pasty for Scarp. When they got back to Corky's corner, he had packed his instruments away and they used the cases now as seats. A proper picnic, with Barbara on the big drum!

"We don't have long," Barbara explained, cramming her mouth and waving her hands till she was ready to speak again. "A friend is picking us up. I'm sorry, I didn't mean you to stop playing."

"Quite glad to stop, today. This is much nicer." Corky had a soft voice, old-fashioned courtesy - not at all what you'd expect from his weathered appearance.

"Well," Barbara was still waving her pie. "We need advice - and possibly plants - to make a forest garden. Pronto!"

Now Corky narrowed his eyes. Politeness gave way to genuine interest.

"Where?" he demanded.

"Foxden, well Bockhurst really. There's an old sewage works at the bottom of the children's garden. It was once beech wood and now it's a bit of a mix - scrub - with a lagoon in the middle. Lots of nettles and brambles - I can testify - I have the scars!"

"And *you* are making a garden?"

"Mm-mm," she had taken another bite and shook her head till she could get the next words out. "Not me. This little one, here." She pointed her pie at Trudi. "We have a house-guest, right now, an old grandfather from Sweden who lived in a proper forest before his heart gave out. He was very sad and sorry for himself when he arrived here - kind of lost, you know. Well, Trudi took it into her head to make a little garden for him to make him feel at home. As a surprise. But the nettles and brambles are too strong. We want to plant some native Swedish things - berries maybe? What would grow in a forest?"

Corky listened carefully, his eyes shining, and I am afraid Jurgen and Trudi both stared at Corky. Stripped of his instruments, he had also removed his hat and they could see more clearly now his beribboned rat's-tail and shoulder hump. This last turned out to be a genuine deformity. They had never seen a hunchback before.

He stroked his chin and smiled back. He was used to staring.

"I need to know a few things first: type of soil, type of terrain - I mean, is it hilly or flat - open and sunny, or in a valley? Then, what else is growing there - apart from the nettles - and how big are the trees?"

"Is that *all*?" quipped Barbara.

"No, no," he replied in good faith. "That's just the beginning. We'll need to know a lot more, but that would be a start. For instance," he turned to the children, "my garden is on chalk, so only chalk-loving plants can thrive there. Plants that need acid soil will die."

"Tristram has a nursery by the old cement works. You know, along the river? By all accounts it's quite something."

"Well you must come and see it!" he spread his arms in welcome. "And pick out some plants for yourselves."

Away, under the churchyard trees someone sounded a horn; a couple of short toots to begin with - then a long, unceremonious blast.

"Oh," Barbara brushed off her crumbs. "That'll be for us. I said we would be back by one. Soon as I can arrange a lift, we'll come! It's a deal. *Thank* you, Corky. I knew you'd help."

"Come whenever you like." Corky rose. "I'm always there, unless I'm here."

Trudi put out her hand like a grown up. "Thank you, Mr. Corky."

"No, no. Just Corky. The 'Mr.' goes with that other name - Farthing. But I never use that. Very pleased to meet you." He clicked his heels and gave a mock salute. "I'm sure we can do something special for your grandfather - there's nothing like plant magic for making people feel better."

He sounded just like Per: "*We work a good magic, ja?*" Did that mean Corky was a shaman too? Did he also know about Miss Vincent's energy patterns? And was *his* magic under the skin of things, like the life-sap in a tree? This time, she had learnt her lesson. She kept her thoughts to herself.

Jurgen, who did not bother with politeness, came next: "What happened to your shoulder?"

"Oh," Corky shrugged it off. He rather liked the young boy's candour and paid him back in kind: "I fell off a horse when I was younger. Silly thing to do. I'd gone to look for plants in the high Andes. South America. I was taking time out, you know, as people do when they get stuck with their studies, and half way up a mountain in the middle of nowhere, my horse stumbled and threw me off. Well, they don't have doctors high in the mountains there, so it was a while before they could set my broken bones. I came out a bit crooked, that's all!" His smile broadened into a grin and he turned his hands over, like a conjuror. Look, no secrets - pockets clean. Trudi didn't quite believe him.

The horn sounded again, this time urgent, insistent and Barbara hustled the children away. At the last moment Corky touched her arm. "We miss you, you know."

"Oh, don't you worry," she rejoined. "I'll be back!"

"I've got a long list of books…"

"I'll be back before you know it. You won't get rid of me that easily!" It was the first time she had talked of the future and the words popped out all by themselves. Did she mean it? Well, the summer was racing on. Sven and Kirsten would soon be home and then there could be no more hiding away. But she had things to do first. Not least, to placate Scarp who had worked himself up into a fine temper in the truck.

"We brought you a pie!" She pushed the children in first and then tried to clamber up herself. But the step was just too high. Once… twice… she couldn't find a footing…

"You'll get me nicked. I shouldn't be parked here!" He was still scowling, but the sight of her face, bobbing frantically up and down, brought on a reluctant smirk.

"Oh, give me a hand, you goddamn, no-good, stinker and stop laughing. It's not funny!" She thrust out an arm and Scarp took hold of her fingers and counted to three. "GO!" With a yank, she was up and they all broke into helpless giggles.

"We got you a pie!" But in the scramble Barbara seemed to have sat on it. Scarp didn't care and shoved the remains in his mouth before driving off. The traffic was slow.

"Get your plants?" He quizzed.

Barbara was lost in thought. "Mmm?"

"I said did you get your plants?"

Still busy, she ignored him and started a new tack: "Scarp, what kind of a cake would it take to persuade you to come out here again?"

"A bloody great big one!" he grinned, with a wink to the children. "Pardon my French." He was now in a good humour.

"Big as you like," Barbara agreed.

"With toffee topping!" The children began to laugh.

"Yep!"

"Okay."

"We need to go to Tristram's nursery to pick up some plants..."

"That'll be chocolate bits as well!"

"You'll like it there - really."

"... and icing in the middle."

"Done."

"Done!"

Tristram, packing his instruments into his little sidecar-trailer, zipped on a set of biker's leathers, stuck a crash helmet on his head, and wheeled his old Harley Davidson out onto the road.

"Look!" cried Jurgen, pointing past the receding motor-bike.

"Yea, *that's* Corky!" said Barbara. "He can make a quicker getaway than us."

"No, *there!*" insisted Jurgen. "*Over there*! Look, it's Amber."

So it was. No doubt about it. There was Amber, swinging her hips and sauntering up to a sports car, parked beneath the trees - Amber, in a translucent, muslin dress which glowed white against her skin, her beautifully-toned legs exposed to the thigh, her stiletto-heeled sandals, designer sunglasses, all screaming '*Look at me*!' The man with his arm around her waist knew it and tossed his head, enjoying

94

the envy of passers-by. Young, tall, easy, with powerful shoulders accentuated by the cut of his suit, his stride also shouted to the world, but his message said: *Look at my money*!

He dropped his hand as they reached the car and, opening the passenger door, indulged in a public and protracted kiss.

"My God, *You're right*!" said Barbara, as they overtook them. "And *that's* Nigel Stringer." He now strode round the car and, throwing a glance of defiance at the world, got into the driver's seat. "It's him with Amber. The rotten, two-timing son of a… Well, I'm shocked." Her tone intimated that she wasn't shocked at all. That this was just what she would have expected of the Stringers and of the world at large. She thought of poor pudding-faced Felicity, in her blowsy maternity wear and remembered the crying she had heard before. Now it all made sense. Poor woman! How awful for her, to be living every day with Amber and knowing she was carrying on so… or *did* she know?

Scarp gave a dismissive grunt: "Him? You don't want to get mixed up with *him*."

"He lives next door," said Trudi, straining to hear. This was grown-up gossip so the adults might hope it would go over her head. All the more important, therefore, not to miss a thing!

"Well he's the Chief Planning Officer round here," Scarp went on. "He's done a lot of damage to people I know, getting them turned off their land, blocking ordinary businesses, helping the wrong sort. Know what I mean?"

Trudi didn't, but she made a mental note to try.

"I *thought* there was something wrong…" Barbara suddenly looked pensive. "Do you suppose he saw us?"

"Oh yes," Jurgen was not going to be left out. "He *saw* us."

"Then we're for it!" Barbara shrugged off her solemnity with a laugh. "That little hussy will be putting the hex on all of us!"

Chapter 14

The Wild Chase

Back in the Sump. Trudi and Miss Vincent were sitting together on the very same log where Jurgen had slipped two weeks before. They had come out to draw at Miss Vincent's suggestion. And Barbara, envisaging a quiet hour for herself, had jumped at the idea, packed them a picnic and waved them off with almost unseemly enthusiasm.

It was another hot day, but under the trees the air felt cool. The light picked up a greenish tinge as it filtered through the leaves. Down here were damp mosses and ferns, where bevies of tiny insects scurried and foraged, exploring the peaty crevices and rotten cavities in the wood.

"You don't mind insects?" Miss Vincent croaked, plumping herself down on a rug.

Trudi did, but she shook her head. She would do as she had done with the *kelet* - look away and say something to distract herself. But where to sit without squashing something? She gingerly poked about and the old lady watched her without comment for a while. Finally, she burst out:

"If you don't like something, draw it!" She lugged her drawing board onto her knees. "The more you look, the more you will be captivated by the wonders you see. When you made your drawing the other day, you chose a snail which you liked already." She wagged her charcoal as a stick to scold with. "Too easy to cling to what you know. Anyone can do that. Better to tackle something new - something you've never studied before, even if it frightens you. Get to know that. Ten to one, you'll find it doesn't frighten you by the end - nor will it ever do so again!"

Trudi listened dutifully. Miss Vincent was the only person she had met who really spoke to her as an equal. Everyone else, even Per and Barbara, had a special way of talking to the young, but old Marjorie made no concessions. You had to follow her meaning, keep up or fall behind.

"Perhaps I should draw a daddy-long-legs, then. They really frighten me."

"Perhaps you should."

"What about you?" The words were out before she had time to consider them and sounded impertinent, but Miss Vincent did not seem to mind. She cocked her head and deliberated for a moment.

"I can't see the things that frighten me," she replied.

"You mean they are ghosts?" asked Trudi.

"Oh no. Ghosts are nothing to be frightened of." She was thinking of her fears for the future - of losing just this independence, this ability to come and go as she pleased and find fulfilment, sitting on a log.

Barbara had packed them some flapjack - she was most insistent about that - and a flask of homemade lemonade and fussed and fretted as if they were leaving for foreign parts. Well, in a sense they were. Talking to a child was certainly unfamiliar territory for Miss Vincent. If she had ever known how to do it, she had quite forgotten the art. Perhaps they should have the picnic first. That would leave their hands free.

Trudi, however, was not ready to eat just yet. : "But do you *believe* in ghosts?" she quizzed. Getting no response, she went on regardless: "I think there are ghosts here in the Sump. I mean *real* ghosts, not just the old cave men. Do you know what I mean?"

She felt certain that Miss Vincent *did,* even if she would not admit it. And it mattered. Marjorie Vincent was 'strange' because she knew important secrets, had insight into things that Trudi needed to know. Knowledge that they taught at school, you could learn that anywhere - you could find it on the internet. But how to understand Life? The answer to that question seemed to be locked up in unlikely or out-of-the-way places and Trudi had begun to look at such places with new interest. People had neglected corners inside themselves, lost spaces, disused dumps, just like the Sump. Most people's corners were not very different or profound. But others were definitely haunted. Who knew what lurked in the wastelands of Miss Vincent?

Trudi tried to picture her as she must have been long ago; first as a girl, then as a young woman, with lipstick perhaps, and wavy hair. She would have been old enough to remember the War. Perhaps she had been a spy or a code-breaker - the typewriter on her desk must date from that time... But the old lady brushed her off. She was not ready to let anyone see such things. Not ready to face them herself. Instead she gave Trudi a straight look.

"Real ghosts are not anything supernatural," she said. "Simply little bits of life that didn't get finished off."

Trudi pictured to herself the photograph of the young soldier next door. A brother? A lover? How would it have been if he had lived to marry? Had raised a family? But the boy in uniform had died, she was sure of it, and Miss Vincent had consoled herself ever afterwards with her birds.

"Have you ever met one?" she persisted.

"Heavens above, girl, can't you *see*?" the old lady expostulated. "I *am* one!" That closed the subject for a while.

Trudi wriggled till she was comfortable, took the paper and charcoal which were unceremoniously handed to her and then looked about for inspiration. Where to begin? At school they were always given instructions: '*draw a tree in the manner of Cézanne*', or '*be a Surrealist. Paint a dream with an egg-whisk and a cactus*'. The teachers said just what they wanted. But Miss Vincent said nothing at all. Trudi longed to do something clever, but couldn't for the life of her think *how* and the fear of repeating her fiasco with the snail ate up all her courage. The paper was so alarmingly white, her mind so blank... Already, her companion had sketched in a mass of confident lines. For a moment she felt tempted to copy her, but she knew from school that only dummies copied. No, she would have to work out something herself, but what? Everything round her seemed too big, or too far away... Leaves began to emerge on Miss Vincent's paper, like tessellated tiles.

Trudi crumbled her charcoal till her fingers were black, then noticed that she had spoiled her paper with dirty marks.

There were those little birds, for instance, which had followed them from the house. They were gathered now, chattering in the high trees overhead, or darting down for crumbs of flapjack. Once or twice they made to settle on the old lady's shoulders, but taking fright at Trudi's presence, veered away. They were too quick to draw. The wood was too complicated. Trudi's eyes roamed unhappily from subject to subject. Time was slipping by and still she could not start.

Finally Miss Vincent, aware of her distress, remarked without looking up: "It's not an exam, you know. The picture hardly matters. It's the looking which counts. And only you will know about that. I *never* like my pictures. I destroy most of them. Look!" She took her paper in both hands and crumpled it up. "Now it's more interesting!" Straightaway she busied herself anew and Trudi felt alone once more. She looked at her page, with its dirty smuts, and her thoughts turned to darker things. To begin with there were those creepy-crawlies, scurrying about beneath her legs - and then the shadows where they lived, so small by day, but at night, vast enough to fill the entire wood.

She thought of the depths of the forbidden lagoon with its drowned man and suddenly she knew that the conversation about ghosts was not closed at all, and all her fears began to limp out into the light. The *kelet*... "*If you don't like something, draw it.*"

There were no crane flies here, but the *kelet* were always hiding nearby, mocking, leering. Professor Saxmund said that when you named something, that gave you power over it. If you named a shaman while he was shape-shifting, the power would kill him. But the *kelet* were still strong.

She forgot about the birds and the Sump and the forest garden. She forgot even Miss Vincent in her thick woolly stockings and shawl. She forgot Per and her father and Beor.

Across the page she began to see the shadowy forms of things moving behind the charcoal. Grey smudges, sidling along. At first, just one or two. Then a long-legs stalking them. Behind him, more creatures, like the boulder-trolls her father used to joke about. As she watched, their pace and number increased until the paper was covered and the scene resembled a migration or wild chase which had no beginning or end. Yes, they were rushing headlong. But what were they? Hunters, or hunted ones? Some looked over their shoulders, their spider legs reaching out in front. Some rolled along like balls of moss. After them all, came the deadly shadow of Beor, his red tongue flashing as he slipped between the trees. A terrible chill ran through her. Then, in an instant, they were gone and she awoke to bird chatter and the dappled light of day.

One sunbeam caught a tuft of lichen on an overhanging branch, picking out its delicate, antlered form, As if guided by an invisible

99

hand, Trudi's fingers now began to trace the pattern she could see and as she drew, her mind let go and gradually filled with light. She was cutting back into the shadows with her little ball of rubber, tracing again and following the labyrinth of lines. She lost Trudi. She lost all the anxieties and ambitions of her driven young life. She was floating on a tiny atom of light - free - completely free!

How long this lasted she could not say. Perhaps only minutes, for the sunbeam moved on and the radiant lichen went out. But the atom of light continued to bob about inside her, filling her with an unfamiliar feeling. And it made a difference.

"I've finished," she said.

Miss Vincent looked with some surprise at her paper.

"Yes. I think I you have. Me too. This log is too damp to sit on long."

She stuffed her drawing and the lemonade cups into her bag and brushed the charcoal from her lap. Then, looking up into the treetops, confided: "What shall we do when we lose all this?" They sat a moment, like comrades-in-arms.

"We shan't lose it," declared Trudi, at last. "We *can't* lose it. I don't give in, you know."

Miss Vincent grimaced. She had little optimism to share "I wish you were right."

But the moment, so swiftly gone, had changed everything. Was this what Per meant by treasure under the bed? Trudi realized with a start that she did not want to lose the Sump. She had only just begun to discover it and what she had found was already too important to lose.

"I'm *always* right," she said, using her old bravura trick. It worked with her teachers at school and sometimes she convinced herself, but would Miss Vincent bite?

The old lady ignored it and picked up an earlier thread instead. "You know, you shouldn't worry yourself about things like ghosts. The real world is so much more miraculous than any fantasies we can invent."

"That's what my father says," agreed Trudi. This time she managed not to spoil it by saying how clever he was.

Miss Vincent inhaled and held her breath while she struggled off the log. Then she breathed out long and slow. "You should show that drawing to your father when he gets home. I think he will like it."

The thought of Sven's return brought an unexpected rush of joy. Suddenly, Trudi had so much to share with him. And of course they would save the Sump together! Her father would know what to do. He always did. She pictured him the way she loved him best, sunburnt and burly, legs astride, hands on hips, his stocky frame convulsed with laughter. That was everybody's picture of Sven. When he laughed, they would all laugh too, even if they hadn't heard the joke, just because he was so funny and his laughter was infectious. They couldn't help themselves. Happiness simply bubbled up when he was there. For the rest of the day Trudi kept hearing echoes of Sven's laughter and, for the first time this summer, she found herself worrying whether he was all right. She had been so mean to him when he left. Was he homesick? Did he miss her in his way?

A tug at her arm brought her back to the present. "Hold still Trudi! We've got company."

Miss Vincent was pointing into the wood and now made a dive for cover. Trudi could hear the voices. Not ghosts, but men, several of them, conferring in easy, confident tones. They must be somewhere by the lagoon and a general rustling and snapping of twigs suggested they were getting nearer.

"Hurry! In here!" Trudi's companion grabbed her arm and pulled her into the bushes.

From their hiding-place they kept a breathless watch. Before long, three men appeared and paused in the clearing before them. They were dressed in business suits, with polished shoes, hardly fit for country walking. Trudi recognized the tall one. He was Nigel Stringer. He held a black clipboard in the crook of his arm and stood, listening to the others with a preoccupied air. Next came a shrivelled, bald-headed man who was wearing tinted glasses. The third, pink, plump and sweaty, kept dabbing his face with a handkerchief. He was ginger, like a Tamworth pig.

"So," the man in glasses waved his arms, "the lagoon will be left as an environmental feature. Have to make it safe of course. We'll fill in part, but the rest will remain at the heart of the scheme. The big trees stay pro tem, oh, and the badger sett, of course - that's a selling point."

Ginger whiskers took notes.

"How many houses altogether?" asked Stringer.

"Twenty-five four- to five-bedroom executive homes. All individual, innovative designs, aesthetically laid-out and fitted with the latest eco-technology." He had practised all his answers. He had virtually written the brochure.

"Solar panels?"

"Underfloor heating. We can use the lagoon for that."

"Wind turbines?"

"Naturally." A pause.

"Now access..."

"From the de Fraisey end. An important part of the scheme will be a network of internal roads which will be useful later. Access is vital, so we need to maintain a very good working relationship with *you*." He turned to the Water Board agent, who was scribbling furiously now.

"Gardens?"

"Minimal. Busy people haven't time for gardening. The public areas will be maintained as gardens until phase two comes in. All this scrub goes."

"The development is quite intensive."

"Squashed up, you mean? That's how we do it these days. Minimum impact on the land and so on. It sounds more green. Then there are the other features: grass roofs, underground parking – cutting-edge design, you know."

"Doesn't quite match the neighbourhood..."

"It's not meant to *blend in*, Mr. Stringer. This is a statement for changing times, an icon, a model for the future. It comes with wireless technology throughout and we're working on the old farmer at the back to get a site for a satellite booster. There's a patch of land behind one of the fields over there which would be ideal. Has a squatter chap on it at the moment but we've spoken to the farmer's wife. We think we can solve that problem. So, first rate reception for everyone."

Stringer tucked his file under his arm and pushed his hands into his trouser pockets. "You know the sale will be by sealed bids. There are several candidates."

"We just need assurances about the planning. We've got the

money. I'm not worried about competition. Our scheme is simply better - for *everyone*. I'm sure we understand one another about that." The director of Eco-Homesteads gave a laugh and polished his scalp with his hand. But Nigel Stringer let the innuendo ride.

He gazed into the distance, and answered with care as if he were in court and his words might be weighed against him. "Well, I think that gives us a good picture. We'll - er - look forward to receiving the plans. You know I shan't be able to handle the case myself. Not at present. As a neighbour, I will naturally have to declare an interest. But one of my colleagues will look after you. Yes, I think I know someone in particular, who will be able to help." He turned to the sandy-haired man. "Mr. Malting, thank you for showing us around. It's a great advantage to have someone sympathetic on hand. Invaluable."

"To be honest with you," confessed the Tamworth, "it will be a relief for us to be rid of the place. We're an unmanned station and no one knows quite what goes on in here. We get trespassers all the time. It's a security nightmare."

"Quite. Quite." Then, an after-thought. "What about smells, contamination and so on."

"Oh we can give full assurances about that," Malting replied. "Mr - er - Beamish - Arnold - I should say, is having full tests done and there will be no problems of that sort on days when clients are viewing."

"Excellent. We don't want any bad publicity at this stage."

"Anything further?"

"Nothing I can think of. Of course we will be able to take care of the waste water here! Very convenient."

"These will be valuable houses," Stringer mused.

"*Very.*" Beamish nodded. "Phase two - when we come to that - will be to reclaim the rest of the lagoon and conservation areas, which will provide land for another 120 houses. These beech trees are old and some are quite diseased. I don't foresee any problem there. Health and Safety will want them down. However, that part of the scheme will be handled by a sister company - 'Comfort Living'. They are specialists in low cost housing, you know: 'Cram them in. Sting them up!'" he allowed himself a giggle, then recovered his gravity. "Also *very* topical, very much needed, in these difficult times. We don't want the Eco-Homesteads' project associated with any of that, however, so we are only seeking outline planning. A promise will be enough to fetch us a return on the land. The rest will follow later."

Stringer nodded. "I may be able to help you more by then."

They began to retrace their steps and soon their voices died away.

"Well!"

Miss Vincent turned to Trudi with a savage gleam in her eye.

"Save the Sump, did you say? You're going to need a miracle, my girl!"

Chapter 15

Thor

By the time Trudi returned, the weather was on the change. The clear sunshine of the morning had congealed into a sticky dampness. Leaves hung limp. Inside the house, normally so cool and spacious, the oppressive atmosphere seemed to have soured tempers.

Jurgen had taken to his room to practise his cello. Since his encounter with Corky he had decided to become a one-man-band and this necessitated a radical change of technique. Holding the bow with his foot left his bowing hand free for percussion. But the result, a drawn-out cacophony, had driven Per out into the garden and was wearing Barbara down. She made a face as she answered the door and jerked a thumb upstairs: "*That* unholy row is my fault! Never, never put dumb ideas into the heads of impressionable children!" She marched back to the kitchen, shaking her head.

"He'll soon get bored," said Trudi, feeling deflated. She had this momentous news to tell about the Sump, but Barbara was in no mood to listen.

"To cap it all," she was scowling at the world at large, "I've had another encounter with *them* next door."

"Oh?"

"You know the foxes had pulled the rubbish out in the night - ripped it all right open and dragged it down the street? Well, after you left I went out to clear up the mess, and just as I was doing it, who should drive up in her great, black car, but the wife? What's her name? Felicity? Out she gets with her shopping and me, being a perfect fool and feeling sorry for the woman, after what we saw the other day, I put out the proverbial olive branch – you know, just a smile and a how-do-you-do? She doesn't even acknowledge I exist. Before I can get one more word out, (and, yes, I know I probably look a sight, bent double, picking up the trash) she sails past and then turns back from the door, positively spitting venom: "Stay away from my son!" she says, as if I was some kind of prowler. "He's quite happy as he is and doesn't need any interference from you.""

And in she goes and slams the door. Did you ever hear of anything so rude? *Weird*! That's what they are!" She had worked up a fine head of steam and Trudi felt it blowing all over her. She didn't want Barbara's frustration.

Ever since they had come back from Newbridge, a gloom had descended over the household. The sight of the bookshop had stirred up painful memories and Barbara, despite repeated attempts to be cheerful, relapsed into bouts of brooding. When this happened, Per closed up his shutters.

Clutching her things, Trudi wandered out into the garden. Other people's sadnesses - they seemed to be all around her and they weighed her down.

She found Per, seated on a bench, with a cloth spread over his knees. He had gathered up all the boots in the house and was busy with a polishing brush.

"What are you doing?" She sat herself down beside him.

Per looked up and then turned back to his work. The boots were lined up in neat rows at his feet, laces turned in. Kirsten's boot box, with polish and creams, waxes, dusters, and brushes, all immaculately arranged, lay open by their side.

"Cleaning boots." The fact was self-evident.

"But *why*, Grandfather? They're clean already?"

Per paused and looked up again. "Because I must do something. All my life I have been a busy man and now I have nothing to do. I feel bored. I need some work."

They sat still for a while, the air of the garden growing heavier round them. Dozy flies settled on the achillea heads in the borders or buzzed across the lawn. The grass had grown in the last two weeks and needed mowing.

Trudi so wanted to tell Per about the men in the Sump, about Miss Vincent, even about the wild hunt, but now did not seem the right moment. She wanted to say she understood, but could not find the words. Instead, she pulled out her drawing and laid it on her grandfather's lap. At first he could not make it out, but then he found his glasses and a slow smile crossed his face.

"This," he traced the lichen filaments with his long, tapering finger: "*This* is my homeland!"

Trudi looked up.

"This *takes* me home!"

She was holding her breath, waiting for more.

"In my forest there are great lichens, long, like a goat's beard. All the trees are full of them."

"Is it dark?"

"Yes, in places. But there are clearings. So many, and all alike. Easy to lose your way. Lichens grow on the boulders, too, the great heaps of rocks you find everywhere." '*Trollstones*' thought Trudi, '*greywethers*', but she didn't say it. She willed him to go on.

"Even in summer is it dark?"

"In summer, yes, in the forest. But though the days are long in summer - there is almost no night then - summer lasts a few weeks only: everything in a great hurry to live before the sun grows weak again. Then in autumn - the beautiful mushrooms - the smell of damp wood - birch leaves." He had taken off his glasses and his eyes sought some impossible point, far away.

Trudi led him gently back. "And in winter?"

"In winter, starlight - and the lakes freeze over. It is very cold. In the far north the forest is thin. Only a scattering of spruce and some dwarf birch trees before the real tundra begins, but there you can see something special - the Northern Lights."

"I know what that is," said Trudi, remembering her lessons. "It's where particles from space hit the earth's magnetic field. The energy produces light."

Per nodded. "Maybe so."

"Have you seen the Lights?"

"Many times."

"And are they really magical?"

"There are many legends about them. Some claim they are a bridge to the world of the spirits. Others, that they are sparks from the tail of a giant fox. The whole sky can come alive with cloudy shapes, moving and swirling like coloured ribbons, bright as daylight, Trudi. They say that in the old days, the ancestors could call the Aurora down to Earth, that it made a special noise and if you listened hard enough you could hear it. That has all gone now."

"I wish *I* could see it."

"When your father comes home, you must tell him. Maybe he will take you."

"Can you see the Aurora from your cabin?"

"From my house? Not often. My house is too far south. You must be in the arctic, where the trees grow small. That is the place."

"How did *you* see them, then?"

Per took a long, deliberate breath. "Tell me, does your father talk about his life in Sweden, before he came to England?"

"He tells us about Christmas there, and..." Trudi thought hard, "...going skating, and the little cakes you have." But no, now she thought of it, he didn't ever talk about his childhood, or his home, or parents... And he had never gone back, except for that one trip, long ago, when his mother died and they visited Per in the forest.

Trudi felt she had ventured into unknown country, a country full of hidden pitfalls, but this time Per was there to guide her. An eddy of wind stirred the garden leaves. Jurgen's cello whined inside the house. Per lowered his eyes.

"This, that I am going to tell you, Trudi, is a secret, for now. Nobody knows it. I do not suppose even your father knows. But you are different. Perhaps I can tell it to you. In life, things are not always what they seem. Maybe *I* am not what I seem."

I know. I know! thought Trudi, but she bit her tongue.

"Maybe I am not even Swedish. I was not born in Sweden. My first memories are of Finland. My father was a Finn, a doctor, who travelled amongst the country people of the far north. Finland is an ancient land with an ancient and beautiful language not like other languages - it lies at a crossroads of great cultures: the Viking world of Sweden and Norway just to the west and Slavic Russia to the east. Very beautiful, this country, with many lakes and forests and further north, near Petsamo, just white snow. Up there is Sami country. Maybe you know it as Lapland, but Samiland is the name the reindeer-herders use and their race have been there for thousands of years. My father fell in love with a Sami girl and married her and took her back to his village and they began to raise a family. It was not easy in those days to marry a 'foreigner' but my father was well-loved and I remember a happy home. Then one day came the war. The Russians invaded our country.

"My father, like all the men in our village, put on his skis and went to fight. We little children were sent to Sweden, to stay with Swedish families where we could be safe. I was just 7 years old, younger than Jurgen.

"They meant it for the best, but for us it was a terrible time. I missed my family and my home. Even though Sweden was a good country and the people were kind, it was all strange to me. I did not know the Swedish language or customs. I could not understand why I had been sent away. I never heard from my parents again. When the war in Europe finally stopped, I was sixteen, a young man. I left my new family and took a job in the forest, where I felt more at home. I buried the anger and the hurt I felt and I thought I would stay - become a proper Swede. I took a Swedish name. Per Larsson. So. Now, nobody could know my past, or complain that I was foreign. For in those days, some people did not want to know a Finn! I forgot my childhood and my homeland. All that seemed dead and gone. I had new friends - new life. I thought my sufferings were over. Even after the adventure with the wolf, even after I travelled to the land of the dead and back, I believed I could be a simple, ordinary man." Per stopped, as if resting a heavy burden before picking up and carrying on again.

"That was when I met Agneta, your beautiful Grandmother." His eyes rested on Trudi. Frozen eyes. Frost crystals. "You will be just like her in a few years…" (Trudi knew this was wrong - she was like *Kirsten*; everybody said so - but she kept it to herself.)

"In 1965, Agneta was a young student. Much younger than me. She and her friends came to study in the forest and, well, we met and fell in love! When she went home, I had no choice but to follow her. I could not let her out of my sight. She was so bright, so enchanting. Slim waist, golden hair - everybody's picture of a true, Swedish girl! So, we got married. But I made a fatal mistake. I did not tell her about myself - about the evacuation - or my father, who was a Finn, or my poor Sami mother. I hid these things as if I was ashamed. That past had rejected me and so I denied it now. I hid my old papers and the hunting bow charm that my mother had given me when I was born. But you know, life in the city did not suit me. I felt I could not breathe there. I was homesick for my cabin and the sounds of the forest. By then we had a little son, Sven - your father, Trudi - and Agneta agreed, for my sake, to return to the country. Here I could find work. Life felt like a holiday, but holidays do not last. All the things which made me happy seemed boring and strange to Agneta.

She was a clever woman, educated, ja. She wanted to go to the theatre and wear nice clothes from fashionable shops. She wanted books and friends and restaurants and music and I was just a rough forester. Then, to make everything worse, one day she found my papers and my Sami amulet. I had to confess about my past. I hoped she would understand. But she was shocked - maybe angry too. She said I had lied. She said I had tricked her. Maybe she was afraid. Maybe she had heard bad stories about the Finns and the Lapps. She thought that my bear-bone bow was a piece of witch-craft, but I could not give it up. It was all I had to remind me of my mother."

Another long pause. This part seemed particularly hard.

"Agneta was so young and had never known hardship before. When Sven was five, she took him back to the city. I never heard from her again. And I did not see Sven until she died, seven years ago."

Trudi felt as if she was falling out of the sky. "But that's terrible. How could you let her go? Why didn't you go after her?"

"Because I could not change her mind. And I was too old to learn new ways. In any case, she had stopped loving me. And, remember, it had happened to me before - losing everything. I suppose I believed it was my fate. That there was nothing I could do. All the same, I had had enough of Sweden. I closed my cabin door and took to the road. I travelled back to Finland. Perhaps in Finland I could a find a place that felt like home. There I learnt that my father had died in the War. My mother, they said, had returned to her people in the north. So I set off in her footsteps and lived for while with the Sami. I did not find my mother, and eventually I stopped looking, but I still had so many questions. Who was I? What was I? Not Sami. Not Finn. Not Swede. Just a stranger. But I found I was not alone. There are other strangers in the world. People who see what others cannot see. People who travel where others do not dare to go. Some I met on my journey and everywhere I went I talked, asked questions." he nodded at Trudi. "*Just like you*! And I was lucky. I learnt many things. The arctic is so beautiful - cruel - wild - free - good country. I saw the great flocks of flying swans, and I saw the Northern Lights."

"You didn't stay."

"No. I understood, at last, that I did not really belong *anywhere*. But I made my peace with life. I returned to my old home in the

110

forest. Well, perhaps I hoped that if Agneta ever came back, she would look for me there. Do you know what people say about the Lapps?"

Trudi shook her head.

"They say they are magicians, because they still believe in some of the old Nature Gods. Here is one now." He smiled as a few fat drops of rain fell on his hand. "You will hear him banging his big drum soon. Ukko! Perhaps you know him as Thor, the thunder god. When he has spoken, the storm will pass and we shall all feel better."

"Don't lose *us*!" pleaded Trudi. She had been so eager to prize Per's secrets from him, but never had she imagined they would touch her so. She felt suddenly dazed and lost. Past, present, future, her very self, in doubt. At last she began to understand her father's awkwardness, her mother's apprehension. How vulnerable they all were! "You can belong here," she promised. "We *need* you."

"Don't worry." Per handed her drawing gently back and touched her cheek with his hand. "I told you, I learnt many things. I will not let you out of my sight till I know you are all safe. And now," he added with a grin, "these old bones must run, or we shall get wet! Take some boots, Trudi!"

Raindrops were pattering round them. Barbara appeared at the door: "Are you guys *mad*? Get yourselves indoors!"

The sky above bulged with a sulphurous light and the trees shivered - but still the storm held off.

All at once, Beor was barking at the fence; Trudy dropped and tripped over a shoe; Per threw a duster over his head and lurched off the seat. They were all shouting now, laughing, as the first clap of thunder split the sky.

Something momentous had happened. Trudi stood on the same, familiar ground but everything looked utterly different. How could they have lived all this time without knowing where they came from? She felt a deep, yearning pity for Per and for her father. A kind of vertigo. It was not treasure which they had under the bed, but a yawning hole.

Thunder again, bringing a double flash of lightning over the Sump.

Professor Saxmund knew about Thor. He knew all the Scandinavian myths. In the old folk tales, he said, lightning pursued

111

the devil's folk. That was how the trolls came to be turned to stone. And there were certain flowers, called thunder flowers. If you picked them, a storm would follow... None of it was true, of course. They were just pretty stories, but the power behind them, that was real. You could *feel* it now, brewing up in the sky.

You could feel how everything down here was silently *willing* the storm to happen: the trees thirsting for rain; the birds, hushed and expectant. When the heavens shook with another drum roll and the rain pelted down, Trudi thought her own heart would burst. Where were her fine plans now? Where was the girl who knew everything? All her pent-up feelings, wishes, desires flooded helplessly away and she went spinning with them.

Above the roar, she heard a small, insistent voice. If only she could stop trying so hard, if only she could float along on this tide, wherever it took her, and forget to worry, to hang on, to be afraid... What would happen then? But trying hard was exactly what she had been trained to do all her life - at school - at home, whether it was swimming, or maths, or playing the piano...

"*Trudi works hard*" was written in all her reports.

She tried to imagine letting go of the Trudi who played safe and won all the prizes. She did not need to go looking for adventure. Right here, beneath her feet were unknown worlds, with values she hardly understood and all around her, ordinary people with extraordinary lives. Their secrets might be closed to the greedy and curious. But they could open up at a touch of love in an almost unbearable way.

Was that why Scarp was against the Museum plans for the Sump? Because they wanted secrets for money?

All day long these ideas chased through her mind, mirroring the clouds that chased across the sky. There were long bouts of rain and sudden gusts that turned the tree leaves inside out. Indoors felt dark and safe and warm - the air had cleared. Barbara sat with the light on to write her e-mail but her spirits had lifted:

'*Hi Kirsten, How's it going? We've had another great day here. You'll be glad to hear Jurgen has been practising his cello for hours! His foot is now much better and he is doing special exercises to get it strong. Trudi had another drawing lesson and Per is now making himself useful round the house. We had a cracking storm, but no harm done. We'll be off to the country for a picnic as soon as the sun returns...'*

At that moment Jurgen appeared in the kitchen. "I'm quitting the cello," he announced.

Chapter 16

The Dream of the Corn

The following day dawned bonny and bright. The down-beaten roses, still heavy with last night's rain, glistened in the sun. All the scents of late summer - blackberries and wet earth and the haunting bitterness of the first dead leaves filled the air.

"That's it," thought Barbara. "Seize the day! No more moping about indoors."

Today would be perfect for that trip to Corky's and with any luck Scarp would arrive, demanding his cake and take them all out to the chalk-pit. She felt disappointed and then angry with herself for caring that he had sent no word. He was just that kind of guy she argued: *here today - gone tomorrow - no explanations*. But then he could surely answer a text! How difficult was it to phone? She tried to think of reasonable explanations: *he was busy; he was away; he'd been arrested* - all were possible. By the end of breakfast, still hearing nothing, she rolled up her sleeves.

"Well kids, we don't need him. We don't need anyone. We'll be thoroughly decadent, dammit and take a taxi! Life's too short to waste time, hanging about."

This, at least, should placate Jurgen. A taxi might not have the glamour of Scarp's truck, but it was something novel, and the one which answered their call turned out to be a traditional black cab, cavernous and smelling of polish, where you sat face to face, as though you were in a train.

"It's called the 'Old Ferry Reach'," Barbara shouted to the driver as she settled the children inside. She then lugged her picnic-basket on board and finished her directions: "You go through Newbridge and follow the river out on the Tilchester Road. Yeah - yeah - the Cement Works. It's right there, on the bend."

Per, declining the picnic, had been left with a Swedish lunch. Today he had recovered his spirits and, equipped with his hunting knife and some branches from the garden, had embarked on a fresh project. Leaves and woodchips lay at his feet and his breath came slow, wheezing, as he bent to his task.

Barbara patted his arm: "You'll be all right, Grandpa? Don't forget to eat. You've got herrings in mustard sauce. That's right, isn't it? And mixed berries for afters."

"Ja - ja," he replied without looking up, his long fingers stroking the cut he had made. "Hup!" He drew breath again and nodded in approval, but not to her. "Good! Ja!"

"What is it? What are you making, Grandfather?" Jurgen had crept up beneath his elbow and his eyes followed the glittering knife.

"Well, you asked me, now it is some days since, '*What is a rune?*'"

"They use them in the Viking computer game. I don't know what they mean. I just thought the Vikings came from Sweden, so perhaps you would know."

Per nodded gravely, but his eyes were laughing. "So, I make you some rune sticks - to show you."

"Rune sticks?" His eyes bulged. "Can't I stay and help?"

"Ney, ney. You are going with Barbara to the nursery. You can see them when you come back."

"Won't you show *me* how to make them?" Jurgen pulled a stricken face. Who wanted to look at plants when they could be making magic sticks?

Per smiled at him. "But of course. One day!"

Barbara fidgeted. "C'mon, Jurgen. Taxi's waiting."

But Jurgen lingered on, watching the blade turn this way and that. He seemed drawn to the knife, with its polished edge and reindeer-antler haft. Like all hand-crafted tools, it had a beauty which cried out to be touched.

Why, oh why, Barbara lamented, were children attracted to everything that was dangerous and unsuitable? Here she was, doing her best to keep them safe and every day they developed new fatal fascinations. She just wanted to preserve them long enough to hand them back in one piece. Was that too much to ask?

"Jurgen - taxi!"

He grudgingly tore himself away, but for the rest of the journey she could see he had left his thoughts behind. Trudi had brought a plastic daisy ring from her weekly magazine and sat fiddling with it, modelling it on different fingers, and admiring her hands in a range of poses. She had a little pink matching handbag and for the moment she seemed to have forgotten about her special destiny and looked just like any other girl of her age. Barbara seized the moment to think.

What strange, funny creatures these children were, to be sure. One minute so canny and sophisticated, the next, just babies, really. And there was no way of knowing what was really in their heads. Were they bored, or did they relish their moments of idleness? Un-time. They were too polite to say. Compliant - that was how they had been brought up. But as time went on, Barbara found herself worrying about it. She had a presentiment that this compliance might not last. She must keep them busy and occupied at all costs.

As the road swung out of Newbridge, it joined the river Teal and snaked along by its side. On the left, rose a flank of downland, scarred by old quarries. The hill, with its smooth greensward and stark, white core, looked like a pudding which had been quartered with a knife. Next came the Cement Works - a long, ugly, prefab on stilts, culminating in two industrial chimneys. Behind - a dirty expanse of worked out chalk, dotted with standing pools and heaps of spoil. High netting, surmounted with barbed wire, fenced the site. At the main gates stood two terraces of workmen's cottages, their doors and windows painted blue.

"It's a turning here - just here somewhere."

The driver pulled into a large lay-by and stopped. Fly-tippers had been busy there before them. A chalky dust coated every leaf and twig. Dust lay on the black bin liners, heaped by the hedge and it had got into the river, too. The water looked a sluggish, milky-green.

"Yep, see? The old ferry landing is down there. 'Lime Pit Hole' is this way." A spur of wood, with home-made lettering, announced an entrance on the left.

"I ain't driving up there," snorted the cabby. "Not wrecking my tyres on those ruts."

"No probs," Barbara leant forward, all smiles. "Can you collect us at three?" She was struggling with the door handle, hustling the children out, fumbling in her purse. Perhaps her tip would coax a friendlier response. But the cabby merely grunted and pocketed his change and her smile continued through gritted teeth.

"Thank you so much! And you have a nice day, too!" She

watched him go. "Hope you get indigestion!"

Now, where the hell were they?

"Oh, Lordy! Who said this was a good idea? Let's hope - let's *hope* it's not a three mile hike! Grab a bag, kids. Got your ring? Got your handbag? Okay."

They struck off along the track, hemmed in on either side by shrubs and bushes. These were hawthorns, but those, with the reddening berries, what were they? And those little flowers, all powdered like moths? On uphill. The picnic basket cut into Barbara's hand. Whatever had made her pack so much? And why had she put on these ridiculous shoes? Trudi and Jurgen, with practical common sense, had dressed themselves for the country, but Barbara was a town girl, and knew nothing about hiking. She had naïvely imagined that Corky's nursery would be at the roadside, with a civilized, stone path. Hey ho! She began to blow like a whale.

"Blackberries!" shouted Trudi.

"Not now, honey! Can't stop. Never get going again."

She toiled on, head down, muttering beneath her breath: "Might have told us! Might have told us it was up a steaming great mountain!" But they had not much further to go. Another sign directed them round to the right and suddenly they were on open ground - a chalk pit hollow in front, with the hill rising behind.

'L.P.H. Research Station' said the sign. Another, salvaged from a building site read: 'Report to Manager's Office'. For a research station it all looked a bit ramshackle. There was a long, dilapidated portakabin, tucked against the hedge. Beside that, a vegetable garden: orderly rows of beans and onions, a poly-tunnel, green with algae and then a hotch-potch of recycled oil-drums, wooden pallets, old windscreens, lengths of hose, boxes and boxes of young plants, swathes of netting, a weather station, wheelbarrows and a couple of reeking muck-heaps. Corky's bike was parked beneath a tree.

Way over, the chimneys of the Cement Works peeped above the skyline, belching into the blue.

"Is this *it*?" asked Trudi. It wasn't her idea of a scenic spot.

"This is it, honey. Now, let's find the man."

They rang a bell, attached by a string to the 'Office' door and this brought a shout from the poly-tunnel: "Halloo there! Come on over. I'm dirty!" And they found him, down on his knees, sifting heaps of

117

compost.

Bent beneath his hump, he looked like a dwarf with a bundle on his back. As they approached, he dropped his sieve:

"Welcome, friends! Welcome!"

"We brought you lunch."

"*Thrice* welcome, then! Shan't be a jiffy. I'm nearly done. There!" He scrambled to his feet and towered over them once more. "You found the place all right?"

"Our friend didn't turn up, so we came by taxi. Terribly extravagant, but we just couldn't wait about any longer. We'll eat Scarp's cake for him and that will teach him to neglect us!"

Corky beamed at his visitors. He was dressed in dungarees, worn plimsolls and a check shirt with the sleeves rolled up. Without his busker's top and tails he looked thinner, older, but his eyes shone with the same boyish enthusiasm.

"Which first - a tour - a cup of tea? Lunch?"

"Where's the toilet?" asked Trudi. It was always her first concern.

"Wherever you like," Corky joked. "Actually, there is a compost loo." He pointed to a hut across the way.

"A *what*?"

"An earth closet."

"Thanks," smiled Barbara. "I'll hold!"

Trudi decided she would 'hold' too. She was quite particular about toilets.

"Lunch then."

"Can I bring anything? I have lettuce, cucumbers, tomatoes..."

"No need. I brought it all - and I mean *all*!" Barbara tapped her bulging basket.

"This way, then." He rubbed his hands on his trousers and led them out on the far side, where the garden gave way to scrub. Wild roses uncoiled like springs from the turf. Here and there were stands of downland 'weeds' - elder, and ash and the pretty wayfaring tree - then denser thickets of bramble and traveller's joy. Trudi counted off the species Sven had taught her. Late knapweed flowered at the edges. A little further on, they reached the heart of the quarry itself and the atmosphere changed again. Here time slowed down. An indefinable energy filled the air. If they listened, they could hear that same hum which existed in the Sump, the vital signature of a place that belonged to itself and lived by its own laws. Here the steep quarry cliffs cut out the factory chimneys and though lorries and dumpers could be heard working close by, they seemed a world away.

"What an extraordinary place," said Barbara, squinting up. The sky was so intense, it hurt her eyes.

"It's a corner that got forgotten," Corky explained. "This is the original pit. The lime was used for farming years ago and all dug out by hand. When Tilway Cement came along, they bought themselves a brand new section of hill. They didn't want this part so it became a dump for the local farmer and a part-time gypsy camp. I've still got some decaying tractors over there, amongst the nettles."

"Did you clear it?"

"I got a lease for twenty years. Land was cheap in those days, but fifteen of my years are up already."

"So what happens then?"

"Ah, that's a problem." Corky stopped at a grassy platform, studded with pin-cushion anthills. "Will here do?" It looked perfect.

"I'm not supposed to live here," he went on, "I can run the nursery, but my lease is quite clear - no occupation."

"But you *do* live here," said Trudi.

"Yes, I do. In secret. I don't exactly have anywhere else to live. But if the authorities knew, I would be turned off. I suppose I'm a squatter. Whether I shall get away with it in future is probably doubtful." He gave a grin.

"Well you're not doing any harm, are you?" Barbara began to unpack lunch and then broke off. "Oh damn and blast!"

The others looked up in surprise.

"We haven't done this properly, have we? I mean, washed our hands and all that." How hard it was to remember.

"Oh, all *that*." Corky grinned. "Well, here's what we do. We wipe our hands on the grass."

"It's covered in poo!" objected Barbara.

"Rabbit droppings? Compost, you mean - the stuff of life."

"Whatever. It's poo. It's got bugs in it, hasn't it? What do you do for water, anyway? No, don't answer. It's best if I don't know." She could just imagine Kirsten tutting in consternation and made an inward plea for clemency:

119

"Look, I'm doing my best, okay? I may not get things right, but I'm trusting, please God, that the kids will be fine and not die of e.coli today. Amen." That should do it.

In point of fact, the children were well-adapted to life outdoors. Sven had furnished them with survival skills and they were far too hungry to care about anything just now, beyond getting their hands on a sandwich.

When hunger was satisfied, Jurgen started to fidget. "Can we light a fire?" His picnic would not be complete without one.

"Well, of course. There is wood over there and you can run around and collect some dead twigs for kindling. Mind the quarry edge. Don't climb up the side where it's crumbly, or you'll start a landslide."

Trudi wriggled down on her front and stuck her nose into the turf. A heady aroma of warm earth and sap, and nectar from the dozen or more miniature flowers embedded there filled her nostrils summing up everything she liked best about the summer. You had to lie flat to inhale this particular scent - so the whole experience was infused with sunlight and the feel of cool grass and filtered itself into a general decoction of lazy memories.

"This is perfect," she said. "When I die, I want it to be just like this!"

"Do you mind not talking like that!"

"I'm not being gloomy. I'd really like it."

"Well, try and 'like it' being alive - just for now. Okay?" said Barbara.

"I mean it feels safe here." Trudi rolled onto her back and gazed up at the sky; then closed her eyes, and let the sun warm her eyelids. That evocative sound of flies buzzing overhead, the contentment of feeling well-fed, little snatches of birdsong in the bushes - all seemed a hundred miles away from the dangers and worries of home. Yes, she could stay here very happily.

Barbara took off her shoes, donned a pair of sunglasses and propped herself against a grassy ledge. After a while, she grew reflective and then stopped talking altogether and there was no way of telling whether she was still thinking or had simply nodded off to sleep. She felt rather bad about carving up the cake she had baked for Scarp - but there could be no help for it. Such things had to be eaten fresh! Her sense of guilt, however, persisted and then it bothered her that she was bothered. Gypsy no-good! She found herself wondering what had become of him. It was too bad that he had missed his toffee topping. She hoped he hadn't really gone off and abandoned them. She hoped he wasn't in trouble... Then she pulled herself together. Whatever was she worrying for? Why should it matter? Scarp had trouble written all over him. One look was enough to tell you that. And, in any case, she had no business to be fretting about another man when she was in mourning for Tod.

Over on the far side of the chalk-pit, she could see Tod, large as life. He was sitting with his back towards her, reading a book. One hand raked his hair in concentration. The sunlight gleamed on his signet ring. *He* would know where that quotation came from: '*Thrice welcome...*' Ever since Corky said the words, it had been annoying her that she couldn't place them. She wanted to get up and go across, put her hands on Tod's shoulders and give him a kiss, but her legs would not move and she realized, belatedly, that she was dreaming. Oh hell, why worry about anything? She stopped struggling and decided to enjoy her dream.

Corky was left to entertain Trudi on his own. "It has taken me nearly twenty years to restore this place. When I arrived everything was very wild and overgrown. On traditional downland, the farmers graze sheep and the sheep eat off young trees and keep the turf short. I can cut down trees, but I don't have enough land here to keep sheep. I have to rely on rabbits to eat my grass, but they want to eat my vegetables too!"

"Do you sell what you grow?" asked Trudi. She was good at this - grown-up conversation.

"No, no. I eat my produce, but the garden is really a kind of living laboratory. I'm writing a book - well several books, though I don't know whether any of them will ever be finished. The trouble is, the more I learn, the more I realize I hardly understand a thing."

"My father writes books," said Trudi without enthusiasm. "He disappears in his study for hours and hours and when he comes down he's not really with us. His mind is still busy writing."

"I'm lucky here." smiled Corky, "I'm on my own, so there's no one to complain if I talk to myself, or forget to eat my dinner."

"I've always hated his books," Trudi went on, following her own thread, "and his plants too, because they took him away from us. He's very clever, you know and we're all terribly proud of him. He's an ecologist, a botanist," she turned to Corky: "Are *you* a botanist?"

"Nothing so grand," he replied. "I'm an amateur, if you like. I just love what I do. And I like doing it in my own funny way. I suppose you could call me a gardening one-man-band! Your father would know a great deal more than me."

"My father's plants are all in exotic places. We go with him sometimes to see them, but when he comes home he's not interested in us. He's too busy thinking about his jungles and swamps. I don't think he can actually see us any more. You're different. This place is your home but it feels loved. You *do* love it, don't you?"

"It is my whole life," said Corky. "I'm trying to see how many plants and creatures can exist together on one patch of land. So you could say this is my library and I am the librarian, cataloguing what I find. The place is too confined to be a proper sanctuary, but my small fry are doing well. I've got over fifty kinds of beetle just in this little patch. The more species there are, the stronger the connection between them. Each plant feeds a different bug, which feeds a different bird. Wild things can be very choosy about what they eat. In a successful environment there is a bit of something for everyone. But I don't need to tell you this. You know it all already. Over there, by the poly-tunnel, are the vegetable beds where my real work goes on. The food I grow there is part of a grand experiment: how to get the largest possible crop from the smallest parcel of land. Suppose a man could double his harvest simply by understanding his soil a little better. That might make the difference between supper and starvation for a subsistence farmer. Perhaps one day I can share what I've learnt."

"But how do you *live*? You can't eat just cabbage!" Trudi ignored the lecture, but she was curious. She forgot about being polite.

"I swap things and use second-hand things that no one else wants. It's surprising what you can do without money. I give the market butcher some carrots and he gives me some bacon. And I am lucky with my heating. A tree surgeon offloads his surplus wood here and that fuels my stove. And then I fish."

"In *that* river?" Trudi remembered the silty soup by the road.

"Upstream it's not so bad. My motor-bike is my biggest expense.

I need some kind of transport to get me to Newbridge and the one-man-band pays for petrol!"

"So you are free."

"Ah! If only..."

"I mean, you do as you like all day."

"I'm very lucky. But when it's raining and cold and I don't catch any fish and the rabbits break into the garden, well, then I grumble and feel sorry for myself like anyone else!"

Trudi took off on her own.

"I'd love to live in a magic place that was free. Everywhere I know already belongs to somebody else. Only the Sump is different, but that's full of nettles and brambles, and anyway, it's too dangerous in there. Jurgen nearly broke his leg. And Miss Vincent says the lagoon is a death-trap. And then there are the old sewer pipes and... and what's the point of worrying when it's all going to be destroyed quite soon?"

"Well," Corky took a different view. "We can never really see into the future. That's a good thing. If you looked at the world right now you might say '*it's all going to be destroyed quite soon*', and maybe that's right, and maybe it isn't. The only thing we can be sure of is Here and Now. And the Here and Now can only be good if someone believes in it and tries to make it better. My little quarry has only a few years left before the lease runs out. Who knows if I can stay? Perhaps it will be developed and spoilt. But today it's a good, happy place to be. The old quarrymen who worked so hard to hew this out must have thought that it would always be a place of toil. They would be surprised to find us sitting here at our leisure. But the land belongs to all of us, past and future. Who knows what the future of your Sump might be? It depends on the strength of your dream."

"My dream?"

"When I was in South America I came across many people in the tribes and villages where I travelled. One day I met a medicine man, a puny, skinny, half-dressed elder, who was doctor, priest and scholar to his people. He told me something that changed my understanding of the world forever."

Jurgen arrived with his arms full of sticks, dropped his load and set off again, like a terrier after a scent. Trudi waited expectantly for the message. She wondered whether Professor Saxmund had met this shaman on his journeys and whether he had talked about him in his lectures. And Corky stretched out his long legs and shifted, as though to ease a pain in his back.

"This man called himself a dreamer. I, being a Westerner, thought dreams were flimsy, romantic things. No, he replied. In order to achieve anything you must dream it first, otherwise nothing can happen. Dreams are the seeds of life. So, according to him, the Great Spirit one day dreamt our earth into existence and the tiny seed of corn that will one day feed a man, dreams of becoming a loaf of bread. The dream of the oak tree is buried in the acorn." The subject fired him up: "Seeds are sacred, for a seed holds a pattern of what is to come - the very future of the earth. And the dreams that are in us weave our own destiny. So here I am, dreaming a paradise garden, and playing music to the plants, like the old pueblo god Kokopelli because they drink in more than just water and sunlight. You put your finger on it when you said this place is loved. Where there is love, magic can follow."

"What if you have a *bad* dream?"

"Bad dreams come, not from love, but from fear. Fear makes people destructive and selfish."

"But how can you love bad things? The world is full of bad things - like the Sump is full of nettles. Can you dream them away?"

"No. You can only dream other things to replace them. I can't make my back straight again. But I can try to make it useful."

"But *stinging nettles*?"

"Half these things are not really so bad." He laughed. "You know, some of our most hated weeds are actually precious plants. Take nettles, since you mentioned them. Butterflies need them. Their caterpillars and myriads of other insects feed on them and you can cook them to make delicious soup. Nettle tea is a herbal tonic, full of vitamins and the fibres in the stems can be woven like flax. There's no end to the uses of nettles. Cultivated flowers are pretty, but the nettle, which we despise and ignore, is a whole medicine chest by itself. And it's free!"

He raised echoes of Miss Vincent: '*If you don't like something, draw it*'.

"Stinging nettles condition the soil they grow in so that other plants can come after them. In nature, the landscape is always

124

changing. Life is change. This here was once woodland, then downland, then scrub - now a bit of everything. When I am gone, it will be different again. Left to itself, Nature would restore great forests here, but that won't happen in my lifetime. Just now I love this phase. I'm one among many guests and there is room for all of us. Shade-dwellers over there. Sun-lovers here. In summer, there is plenty of food; the place is full. In winter, the guests disperse. But they'll be back. Perhaps your wood has room, amongst the nettles, for gentler plants too. We could create a corner where they felt welcome."

Trudi sat lost in thought. At last she asked: "Corky, are you ever afraid here on your own?"

"Everyone is afraid sometimes."

"I am afraid something bad is going to happen."

"Because of the wood?"

"Sometimes I think when you try to do good, the opposite happens. Professor Saxmund says '*the devil is jealous*'. Do you believe in evil?"

"Oh yes," said Corky, without hesitation.

"I have a bad dream that haunts me over and over again." She had never confided this to anyone, but Corky's honesty gave her courage and she went gravely on: "At home we have a terrible dog next door, so wild and angry. He hates us and he has bitten my father several times. In my dream he is chasing me. I can hear him getting closer, and closer, but my legs are heavy and I can't run away."

"Oh, that is nothing," Corky breezed. "Everyone has those dreams. I am carrying Pedro over a mountain and the soil starts sliding, slipping away beneath my feet. Real dreaming, for life, you do that when you are awake! Look, I'll show you something." He pulled a battered wallet from his pocket and plucked out a photograph.

"This garden exists half-way up a precipice. It is a miniature forest. Tall shrubs shelter shorter plants below. Creepers climb through it all like green ladders. At the bottom are crops with edible roots. *Everything* here can be eaten. It is a giant salad bowl! The birds come and go. There are flowers for the bees. Children feast on the berries. This is the garden of my dreams."

Trudi turned the photo over. Beneath it was another of a dark-

125

haired boy, roughly her own age.

"And this?"

"That is Pedro - my Peruvian '*chico*'."

"You have a son?"

"A godson. After my accident, I stayed in a remote village where the people cared for me. This little lad was a baby then, but he was sick. He had been born prematurely and he was blind. Nobody wanted him. It is considered bad luck to have a child who is disabled there. His own family rejected him. So when we travelled on, we took Pedro with us and found him a home in an orphanage."

"You didn't bring him to England?" asked Trudi, in dismay.

"He could not come here. He belonged in his own culture. And I had no home to offer him. But he is loved and cared for where he is. I write and they send me news."

"He's very good-looking." High praise from one who was so fastidious. Pedro had dark hair and strange, silver-patinated eyes, with long lashes.

"Clever too. He wants to be a lawyer."

"Then he can *study* here." Trudi announced, as if that was that. The whisper from Peru had restored her spirits. "And you can look after each other. I'll marry him when he comes!"

She handed the photos back and Corky put them away.

Fanciful child's talk...

Jurgen arrived with more wood and a fossil he had found in the chalk: a prehistoric fern. Yes, it was true. Landscapes were always changing!

Barbara woke up and conversation turned to everyday business: lighting the fire - pouring tea. After that they took a tour of the nursery: the chicken run, herb garden and portakabin. Here were the plants Corky had put by for Trudi. And this was a little reed flute Jurgen might like to borrow. Easier to carry than the cello - easy to play, too, with a sweet, husky tone.

Goodness! It was five to three, already. Courgettes for Barbara and armfuls of dill and fennel. A dash back for the taxi. Profuse goodbyes.

"Come and see us!"

"Come and see the Sump!"

"I'll bring my fishing rod," he called. "We'll find out what's lurking in that lagoon."

Trudi's face disappeared as the taxi sped away and Corky shook his head. She had stirred up long-buried memories with her questions. What did she say? Bring Pedro here and they could look after each other - a likely story!

But then the seed of the idea had been planted, and like the seed of the corn, might dream itself into fruition.

Chapter 17

Passing Time

Three days passed and still there was no news from Scarp, so the children occupied themselves as best they could.

Trudi borrowed gloves and made a start on her garden, clearing a patch of soil for the wood sorrel, wood sage and foxglove that Corky had given her. It didn't look much like a garden yet, but at least the plants would be happy with their roots in the soil. Jurgen offered to play to them on his reed pipe. According to Professor Saxmund, the Hopi Indians played to their crops and Corky thought his tomatoes liked hearing '*Lily Bolero*', but Trudi, unwilling to share her project, rejected the offer, and sent Jurgen away to tootle by himself.

This rebuff was soon followed by another. Jurgen had expected that his rune sticks would be fantastical wands which he could flourish like a sword. All he got were twigs with scratches on them. Furthermore, Grandfather looked disapproving when he tried fencing with them and told him gravely that they were not weapons, they were messages from the olden days - a kind of wooden e-mail - to pray for good health or protection from wolves. Jurgen tried to listen, but the explanations were long and this seemed such a slow, dull kind of magic. He felt sure that Viking Raiders would have insisted on something more exciting - proper spells and curses. Per stopped explaining any more at that point. He said that these sticks were not magic anyway; they were just toys. It would take a real magician to bring one to life and all the real magicians had died out, like the trolls and tomtes. As for curses, they were black magic and never to be touched. He looked troubled, and Jurgen, unable to understand why, took the sticks glumly away and threw them into Trudi's garden.

Meanwhile, Barbara continued to organize... One day the children ate popcorn at the movies. Another, they went swimming. They even played tennis in the park. More postcards arrived from Sven and were given pride of place above the cooker. He promised alligator flip-flops to follow.

128

At last, running out of ideas, Barbara arranged a trip to the Museum at Tilchester. They would travel by train. Trudi and Jurgen had seen the Museum many times before, yet, since their visits there were generally followed by a treat at a smoothie-bar, they raised no objection.

Tilchester Museum was housed on the edge of the town, in a gracious, Georgian manor house with a walled garden full of flowers. The creamy, summer façade gave onto a terrace with a sundial and a flight of fan-shaped steps. Here, from the balustrade, stretched a vista in the Italian style: an avenue of yew trees, cut to look like cypresses and cleverly diminishing in size to create an illusion of space. Trudi had learnt all about that on a school trip: the trees were called topiary and the illusion was called perspective and it was 'Art'. Inside the building, reflections of long sash windows pooled on the dark floorboards. A grandfather clock ticked in one corner. The whole place slumbered gently, just like the nodding steward at his desk.

For as long as she could remember, Trudi had enjoyed coming here. They would call by when Kirsten went to the library or when there was a project to do for school and on each visit she would indulge in the same pattern of childish games which she had begun when she was very small; rituals unique to this place Though she was really too big for such trifles now, she still felt tempted to go through them, for old time's sake: touching the rough stone belly of each pillar as she jumped up the entrance steps and squeaking her shoes on the parquet till the turtle-faced steward frowned; fiddling with the door-knobs; swinging the red ropes in the foyer; running off to look at the stuffed animals... She knew the whole collection off by heart. Most fascinating and horrible, were the albino squirrel, whose desiccated form was displayed under a glassy dome and the Saxon warrior's skeleton, deep, in his narrow grave, his spear and drinking vessel by his side. It was essential to visit these, but there were other things. too, which she could list to herself when she lay awake at night: vases, rings, flints, pottery, all familiar, room by room. At the end of the house came the old nursery, with its hideous, cracked-faced dolls and threadbare quilts and bonnets. Kirsten always shooed her out of here.

They would have arrived, no doubt, with a serious purpose: to find out about the Romans, or to look at the harpsichords. But as a treat, they would invariably hurry back to the hall to watch the big clock strike the hour. This was the highlight of every visit.

Trudi loved that clock. Other things in the museum had suffered from the ravages of time, but the clock seemed to go on just the same forever. The sound of the pendulum, long and slow and the glazed, yellow dial had measured whole centuries go by. And it was unthinkable that they would ever stop. *Whatever happens*, said the comforting tick-tock, *I go on*. Trudi knew. She had seen it. And on the hour, every hour, a painted blue bird, would fly from one bunch of flowers to the other. He never missed and he never came back the other way. Trudi used to wonder if he was the same bird every time, or if there were many, and if so, where had they all gone to? They brought renewal, like a librarian, renewing books, promising more time...

On this latest visit, however, it was clear from the start that something was wrong. Large, metal screens obscured the door and filled the entrance hall, creating a maze of panels covered with architect's drawings and plans. The clock had vanished. In place of the leather-topped desk where the turtle once dozed, stood a functional counter, painted battleship grey. Everything looked drab and Trudi felt affronted, as if her home had been stripped bare.

"Where has it gone?" she asked the angular woman at the counter.

"The clock? It's being restored." She seemed hostile at first, but then her manner softened. "Perhaps you'd like to fill out a questionnaire for us. It's such an exciting time for the Museum. We're re-developing. We have tremendous plans for the place, as our exhibition here explains." This was a well-rehearsed speech and she addressed it now to Barbara. "At last we've got a chance to transform the Museum into a vital community space. Clear out some of the old clutter and modernize. An archaeological site has come up for sale nearby. Very special for us if we can acquire it. It will give us a whole new working dimension - everything we need for expansion."

Trudi took an instant dislike to the woman who had stolen her clock and, while Barbara made polite noises, she wandered away. The flints and spears were still in their places, but the next room had a temporary feel. Two cases - Saxon combs and weaving weights -

130

stood empty and the skeleton warrior lay covered with a blue tarpaulin. She wandered back.

"They're going to make it more user-friendly," whispered Barbara.

"It was friendly anyway," snapped Trudi.

"We're particularly keen to get young people involved," said the curator, bustling over with a fistful of papers. "Perhaps you would like to help us design the new annexe?" *She's got a wart*, thought Trudi. *How horrible! And I hate her glasses.* Kirsten had a pair the same, with ugly, heavy frames and when she wore them Trudi refused to look at her.

"New annexe?" Barbara looked up.

"We've got planning, in principle. Now it's just a question of finding the funds. Five million. A lot to raise - but with that we can transform the rose garden into a new educational complex and restaurant. It will really put us on the map. We've been stuck in a backwater here for so long, but this will change everything. The new Anglo-Saxon project is the most exciting way to launch it all."

Jurgen, bored, wondered what had happened to the ice cream kiosk. Trudi gave the woman a venomous look and took the proffered papers. The headings said it all:

Draw your own plan for the Museum here!
Let's redesign the entrance ...
Which item do you like best in the collection?
Enter our competition and write a poem ...

"Pens and pencils are over there in the 'design station'," said the wart.

With a face like stomach ache, Trudi selected some felt tip pens.

Then she drew. In a fury, she drew the rose bushes she remembered so well - startling viridian, with cherry red blossoms - and filled the remaining space with little birds. They were blue: all the birds that had told the time on the grandfather clock.

Underneath she wrote in capitals:

DON'T DO IT. "There!"

"You can't hand *that* in, honey," whispered Barbara, in alarm.

"They want young people's opinions," replied Trudi. "Well I'm a young person. Jurgen can draw them a building."

Jurgen pulled a face and said he wasn't drawing anything. He wasn't a baby. And was it nearly time to go yet? Trying to stem this rebellion, Barbara led them back to the screens.

"Jurgen, we've only just arrived! Did you see this?"

"No - it's boring."

"No, look. This photo here with the trees. *Look* at it. I think it's your Sump."

Sure enough, you could see the black rectangular outline of the lagoon and the drainage beds of the Sewage Works in the adjoining field.

"That's our road," said Jurgen, pointing out a strip with long, green plots alongside.

"That's our *house*," said Trudi, now taking an interest. "That's our shed and look! And that's the Stringers'." A brown stain showed the path Beor had worn as he patrolled his boundary. "Why is it here?"

"Well, because the wood *there* is coming up for sale and, Scarp was right, they want to buy it up and excavate it. The plan is to develop it as a Saxon Resource Centre and part of the de Fraisey Project, whatever that is. They reckon there is more gold in there, like the brooch Scarp told us about."

"They can't have it!" objected Trudi.

"Well they're gonna try."

"They can't have it. They don't know anything about it."

"Look, it says it all here. They've got a document from the last of the de Fraisey's stating where some old boy called Wulfstan died. That's the geezer in there, isn't it?" Barbara tossed her head towards the skeleton within. "So - da-di-da-di-daa -" she was skimming the text: "Yep. English Heritage is interested and the British Museum have said the letter is genuine and the National Trust might come in on it with Fraisey Manor. No, hold on. Fraisey Manor want to buy it themselves. Seems a bit rash, buying it before they've done the dig, but then, time is running out. At any rate, they say the wood is a unique relic of 18th century landscaping. Is it, indeed?" This was Barbara at her most sardonic. '...*the Wolf Stone, part of a collection of ancient Sarsen Stones ... the rest of Wulfstan's hoard ... the tragic death of the young heir...*' Well, there you have it. They have a dream of reconstructing the whole thing. with computer simulations. Sounds like Viking Raiders all over again to me!"

132

Trudi started at the word 'dream'. What would happen if two people had different dreams at the same time? Or three people, or four... Whose dream would win? Corky didn't explain that. She remembered Scarp's scornful prediction that the Museum would turn the Sump into a Car Park. Could that really count as a dream? What would Corky say? And what about the wood itself? Did it have a dream of its own? Did it really *want* to be a car park? And what would then become of Scarp and Miss Vincent? Like the blue birds...

"Let's get out," she said.

"Honey, we haven't gone in yet."

"Can't we have a drink? It's so stuffy in here."

Barbara cast an apologetic glance at the counter. "Kids, eh? What can you do?" But the curator, who had overheard every word, glared after them long after she had put their questionnaires in the bin.

* * * * *

Life at the Larsson house had by now settled into a regular rhythm, largely dictated by meals. Barbara's cooking gave shape and purpose to the day and the tempting aroma of fresh bread and pastries constantly filled the kitchen. Indeed, Barbara found baking so therapeutic, the family could not keep up and she was forced to look further afield for mouths to feed. She had failed with Scarp, but perhaps there were others...

As the summer slipped by, the Sump breathed on, dense and green, serenely unaware of the threats that hung over it, but every so often there were hints of trouble ahead: a letter from the council; another troop of visitors in white, construction hats. Per observed these things without comment, but his own days seemed enlivened by a new sense of purpose. Having completed his rune sticks, he now embarked on a larger project and instead of watching Barbara vacantly from his chair, he began pottering about, collecting things from the garden, or drawing pencil patterns in a shaky hand. Faced with the children's inquisitive attentions he remained politely inscrutable. Barbara, herself bemused, attempted an explanation:

"Look, kids, he's old and there's no way of knowing what goes on in an old person's head. Perhaps he thinks he's back in Sweden.

133

Perhaps he's lost himself in past memories and dreams. It's one way of coping if you feel fed up. So long as he's happy, just let him be, huh?" '*Live and let live*' - that was her motto, though the advice was easier to give than follow! Per started to request the strangest things: beads from Kirsten's sewing box, a hacksaw, a baked bean tin. And he was making a mess!

One day, to her horror, Barbara discovered him mashing up bark in Kirsten's pestle and mortar. A blood-red dye, (it was alder bark), had stained the beautiful stoneware and left an indelible trail across the draining board. However were they going to explain that away? She scolded Per and he looked duly repentant, but he carried on just the same. He had no idea of place!

In any normal house, someone would have taken charge and banned further experiments, but Barbara could not help noticing how the muddle seemed to do Per good. Once surrounded by a comfortable litter of moss and twigs, he began to relish life once more. She caught glimpses of the man he must once have been - keen, determined, full of vigour - and watching the transformation, she had not the heart to stop him. She guessed she had money - all that money from Tod that the solicitors were sorting out. Hell, she could buy a new pestle and mortar - a new kitchen if need be!

On the day that Corky came fishing, she had made an old-fashioned seed cake with a sugar crust on top. She set it on a doily and laid a clean tea towel over the top.

"Here. Take this round to Miss Vincent, Trudi. She must be just about sick of Battenberg, by now. Tell her I'll have the plate back when she's finished."

Trudi was happy to go. Another glimpse of the catacomb would be interesting and since their last visit to the woods, she felt that she and Miss Vincent were now confederates. The old lady answered the door, brandishing a letter.

"I thought it might be you," she said, dispensing with pleasantries. "Will you just look at this - the *affront* of it!" She led the way inside and cleared a space between the marmalade jars and fish wrappers on the kitchen table. "What is that, child? Oh, cake! Good show. Now, the thing is... Where did I put my glasses? Yes. The wood - the 'Sump', as you call it... I've had a letter from the Water Company, or rather, from their agent. Quite a nasty, threatening sort of letter about trespassing. Now who could have told them that I went in there? Did they see us the other day? Or is someone spying? I don't like it."

"Perhaps they followed the path to your fence."

"Perhaps. But it feels all wrong. I believe they're working up to something."

Trudi told her about the exhibition at the Museum and the Saxon Centre plans.

Miss Vincent snorted. "Buried treasure! Fools! I could tell them a thing or two about that."

"You know about it?"

"Not now. Another day. The question *is* - what do we do about *this*?" She tapped an arthritic finger on the letter.

"We need to talk to Scarp," said Trudi, playing conspirator and loving every moment. "He will know."

"Scarp, yes. That young man." Miss Vincent brooded a while, then straightened up. "Well, you must get back. Thank dear Barbara for me. She is very kind." She nodded, her eyes shining. "Good people. Hard to come by."

Trudi slipped out of the door and down the steps and stopped, seeing Amber in the street ahead. Amber had parked Felicity's big car outside the Stringers' house and was loading baby Belinda into the back. Today she wore green - a smock-type chemise in floaty chiffon and pale, cropped trousers with sling-backs. The shoes were red, to match her handbag. She was too busy to notice Trudi, but Beor caught sight of her through the hatchback window, and worked himself up into a frenzy, baring his teeth and barking, his black tail lashing about. Even though she knew he could not reach her, Trudi felt too frightened to pass and when Amber finally looked up, she spotted her, cowering against the wall. With a gesture of impatience, she did something to silence the dog and he dropped down, rolling his eyes. What was it Per called him? An unhappy slave?

Trudi made a dash for safety and bumped slap into Simon Stringer at the gate. For a moment they stood, confronting one another face to face and Trudi, who had never stood so close to him before, was struck by the hostile pallor of his face. He put her in mind of the white squirrel at the Museum. His bones sharp beneath the skin. He only needed a glass dome to set him off...

Looking straight into her startled eyes, he screwed up his nose and

135

muttered: "You watch it, you. We're going to *get* you!"

And Trudi winced as if she had been struck. She had heard such threats in the playground a hundred times and always laughed them off. But this was somehow different. Here the words sounded grimly prophetic. Perhaps she half-believed them already. It bothered her that she did not know who 'we' were. Simon and Amber? Beor? Nigel and his associates? Or all of them together? And why were they against her? She hurried indoors without reply and when Barbara asked her what was wrong, gabbled something of no consequence.

"*We're going to get you.*"

Wasn't that what the *kelet* had been saying all along in their mealy, mumbling voices?

She went upstairs and sobbed to Sticky Bear.

Chapter 18

Secrets of the Deep

She had just about put her face right when Corky arrived with all his fishing tackle. He was in high spirits, eager to get his first sight of the Sump and once again he showered Barbara with gifts from his garden.

Per took an immediate liking to Corky and after the formal handshakes, broke into smiles and animated chatter. This public unbuttoning in someone naturally so solemn, astonished everyone and by a sympathetic process they began to chuckle too. Fishing! Per and Corky shared a passion for it and it forged an instant bond between them. Soon they were inspecting rods, comparing tales, sharing casting tips... Corky had brought his flute and drum and it seemed as though the day would end in festive mood.

Only Barbara felt uneasy. After all, the Sump was still forbidden territory. Kirsten had spelt it out before she left: "*Don't go near the Sump,*" she said and they had all duly promised... Yet somehow, from that moment on, the place had drawn them in. It was a magnet, and it had spelt disaster for others before them.

"Are you sure it's okay to go to this lagoon?" she ventured. "You know, there are so many bad stories…"

Per waved her objection aside. "Nonsense Barbara. This will be good for the children. A taste of real summer. Bring us some fish for supper, Corky, and we can have proper Swedish party. You know, August is the month for summer feasts in Sweden!"

Trudi had heard her parents talk of their own student parties; revels which lasted into the early hours through dreamlike August nights. They were still fond of outdoor feasts, come rain or shine, with lots of 'Skål', the old Viking custom of drinking toasts, which left a haze of happy memories behind.

"I don't know about fish to *eat*," laughed Corky. "We'll have to see what the water is like first."

Barbara's heart sank lower. She could just envisage her next progress report: '*Darling K, Both your children are at the bottom of a pond and Per and I are just dying of cadmium poisoning.'*

"Don't worry!" said Per slapping her affectionately as she stood by his chair. "The water will be good. Bring us a catch to remember: a pike, or some crayfish!" He was now remembering sorties of his own. He winked. An unthinkable thing for Grandfather Larsson to do!

"Well, *I* shan't be coming on this one." Barbara recalled all too vividly the bites and stings of last time. "I'll put on a kettle for you here, and you be home by three o'clock sharp, or I'm calling the police, I swear!"

"We shall defy the monsters and return unscathed," boasted Corky waving his arms.

Trudi noticed that Corky put on his showman's cap whenever he had something difficult or doubtful to do. Perhaps it gave him courage. Or perhaps he was merely excited. They set out with their buckets and nets and Barbara waved them off from the step.

"I still don't like it." she muttered "Something is going to happen. I can feel it in my bones." Per ignored her, but a little while later he called for her again:

"Barbara, where would they keep things like lanterns for the garden? We should do this well, you know. Those who live with the brief summers of the north know that light is a precious memory for times when days grow dark. So - every lamp can be a tiny sun – ja? - for winter-wanderers."

Busy with her own thoughts, and secretly planning how to exchange Sump fish for something from the freezer, Barbara gave a vague reply.

"Lanterns? Oh, they have them. Sure, I've seen them in the past, though Lord knows where. Listen, we can have pancakes and blueberries - that's Swedish *and* American. And Per..." this in exasperation, "what in the name of heaven, are all these leaves doing in the sink?"

"Hawthorn leaves for me. Old man's medicine. I need them. Truly, I need them. Trust me, Barbara!"

Trust! What was that supposed to mean? How can you trust anything at all, when the earth has just opened up and swallowed your nearest and dearest? She hated to let the children out of her sight. She still worried, though she knew she shouldn't, about Scarp -

about that daft old dame next door - even the Sump itself and the house... And what was the point? You couldn't take care of everything. And you went plain crazy if you tried. The task of keeping things ship-shape here was certainly imposing a strain. She loved a tidy room, but faced with a choice between housework or half an hour in the garden - well, she reasoned, the cobwebs could wait. And if she had let her domestic duties slip, surely that was only because there were other, more pressing things to do!

Her natural love-affair with life - her pleasure in books, letters, *biscuits* and other such delights, which had been snuffed out when Tod died – *belief in a future,* all were beginning to revive. She could see the tentative tendrils poking through the dust... For now she would ignore them. She was too busy. Too preoccupied. But she supposed she *trusted* they would grow. One day soon, she might attend to them again and then there was no telling what she would do!

Corky scrambled under the fence while Jurgen held up the wire and Trudi passed the picnic hamper through.

"This is where I started the garden." Trudi showed the heap of nettle stumps where she had scratched the soil.

"Next year!" Corky promised, "There will be something new here and all along these grassy fringes we can introduce more flowers - stitchworts and campions and lords and ladies. There may be lots of seeds already in the soil, just waiting for the chance to grow."

Next year! Trudi nodded without conviction. The day was sunny again. A magpie chattered in a tree above them. Evil birds, Miss Vincent called them and she chased them out of her garden. Trudi would wake to hear the young ones squeaking and scolding outside her window, balancing clumsily in the trees with their long tails. She had always liked them before and kept an iridescent tail-feather in her room. But they were birds of omen. One alone was said to be unlucky. And she superstitiously looked around for another. After all, they were heading for the lagoon and the lagoon was out of bounds.

Jurgen marched ahead, carrying Corky's buckets with an air of self-importance - he had conveniently disowned the boy who slipped off a log - and Corky followed, taking mental notes and gallantly holding back branches for Trudi, as she brought up the rear. He was reading the wood, just as Scarp did. But whereas Scarp kept his eyes on the ground, Corky glanced around in all directions. He pointed things out from time to time, and Trudi nodded, though she walked in a world of her own. She was thinking about her father and wishing he could be with them now. He was the natural leader for any expedition. To have conquered this last part of the Sump and braved the mysteries of the deep together, that would have been a splendid thing. But fate had arranged things differently. This adventure would be like facing the *kelet*. She would have to manage alone.

After a few minutes they came to a halt. Miss Vincent's path steered left, towards the badger sett and pheasant pens, but the lagoon lay straight ahead and the vegetation here grew lush and undisturbed, towering high above Trudi's head.

"We'll have to cut a path," said Corky and he unpacked from his kit a long beater with a metal edge. "This should do it. I'll go first and clear the way and you follow carefully and mind your legs. We could eat over there where the trees are thinner." He strode on, slashing the nettles on either side with sweeping strokes. Before long, they reached a forest of willow-herbs, lanky giants with vibrant, pink blossoms.

"They're beautiful!" said Trudi. Hidden away behind the scrub, you would never have guessed they were here.

"Another weed," called Corky over his shoulder. "Good one to find here. This is the great, hairy variety. Loves wet ground. Pinch the baby leaves and sniff your fingers - it smells fruity. In the old days this plant was called 'Codlings and Cream' or 'Apple Pie'!"

"We should take some for Barbara!"

"Alas, you can't eat it. But there is a sister plant with larger flowers, which tribesmen in Siberia used to make beer. They sprinkled in a little poison mushroom and Poof! One sip would blow your head off!"

"We could make that," said Jurgen.

"Better not!" Corky was firm on that, but Trudi wondered whether Per had tasted any on his travels.

They came upon a clearing, with a grassy platform close to the water's edge.

"What about here for lunch?"

140

Jurgen demurred: "I wanted to sit on a stone."

The Sarsen stones lay further on, near the derelict sheds, but as Trudi was reluctant go that far, they settled down where they were. "Food first, then fishing," said Corky, distributing bread and tomatoes. Barbara had packed enough for a platoon: plates, napkins, little paper screws of salt and pepper - a rug, and books in case they got bored! How would there be time for fishing? Corky poured out tumblers of juice.

"So, tell me about this lagoon."

"It's a fathomless pit with a dead body at the bottom," announced Jurgen, narrowing his eyes. His appetite for melodrama was fresh as ever.

"It's part of the old Sewage Works," Trudi continued primly. She picked the cucumber out of her sandwich and ate it separately, seeds first, then flesh, then skin. After that, she felt more expansive. "There *are* stories about it, though. Miss Vincent says it's older than it looks and there was a spring in it, years ago. The whole of the Sump was part of the Fraisey Manor grounds. We did that all at school. One of the de Fraisey ancestors made a Druid Circle out of the stones, just for fun. You can't see the circle now, because the Water Company cleared them away and piled the stones up in a heap, but on moonlit nights, it's said, they put themselves back in a ring and Sir Vivian's ghost walks round them." She was frightening herself with such talk but having started, she could not stop. "And a hundred years ago, Perkins, the old gardener at the Manor, was accused of stealing a brooch and drowned himself in there."

Corky laughed. "What gruesome stories!" he said.

Trudi had surprised herself. Normally, others told the tales and she rather wished they hadn't. Today though, sitting beneath the rustling leaves and pulling the crusts off her bread, she felt close to the past and happy to be so. She could imagine the workers who had dug out the lagoon, stopping for a break just where she was sitting now, and the crinolined ladies of the Manor, a century earlier, strolling beneath the beeches. It would have been parkland then. *There* was old Vivian de Fraisey, the antiquarian, with his silver-topped cane and buckle shoes, stepping round his boulders and tapping them with a proprietary air, and the Saxon women of Wulfstan's camp, combing their hair. Last of all, Scarp's

Neanderthals, knapping flints by day and fending off the wild beasts with their cooking fires at night. Perhaps they *ought* to go and look at the stones... Perhaps it was silly to be afraid. These ghosts seemed friendly today and didn't bother her.

"They dredged the pond," she heard herself saying, "But they couldn't find the brooch." They all peered down into the depths. "The people at the Museum think that the brooch was part of Wulfstan's burial hoard. That's why they're bidding against Fraisey Manor to buy the land and do a proper survey..."

"If it's true," said Corky, "surely they'll do the survey anyway."

"...but Scarp says it's rubbish. There *are* flints here, but they are Neolithic. And the biggest Sarsen stone has got markings on it. Legend says it was an old 'sanctuary' stone, called the Wolf Stone. Everybody wants to make their own story for this place. Most of the stories are creepy!"

"Muffin?" offered Corky.

"Professor Saxmund says there are spirits that live in lakes and rivers. They're called Näcks and they tempt people into the water and drown them. Perhaps the old gardener met a Näck."

"There might be a huge fish that swallows people whole." said Jurgen.

"I think there is *something* in there," added Trudi. It was pleasant to sit here in the sunshine contemplating doom.

"I think that's all nonsense," Corky laughed. "I'll tell you what. We'll bait a hook and prove it. Ten to one there's nothing there at all and we shall all be going home empty-handed. It looks a bit murky to me."

They studied the lagoon again. The banks shelved steeply at their feet and the surface shone, flat as glass, giving no hint as to what might lie beneath. Columns of midges spiralled in a far shaft of sun.

Corky felt that when honour was satisfied, perhaps he would be glad to get out of this place. An echo or a presentiment bothered him. He couldn't quite put his finger on it, but he knew it made him shiver. Without exactly hurrying, he began to assemble his line. "Pass me that bucket, Jurgen, and the tub with the bait. We'll put some water in there in case we are lucky. Then we can examine what we've caught." He took a deep breath and called for quiet as he prepared his first cast. "No sudden movements now," he warned.

They watched the line fly out over the water and the sparkling ripples widen round the bait. When the ripples settled they could see Corky's feathered float, quietly bobbing on the surface. Gingerly, he held out his rod. "Here Jurgen, take it in this hand. That hand goes there. Fingers on there. If you see that crow's quill move, we've got a bite. Nudge me and we'll reel it in." Jurgen had fished before, but he felt honoured, all the same.

"When you are tired of holding it, we'll set it in this rest here and you can relax." Trudi lay back gazing up into the trees and finished her muffin slowly, crumb by crumb. How lovely it was, doing nothing! Why ever had they made such a fuss about the lagoon? She wasn't really interested in fishing, though. She might slip off and look for those Trollstones... She scrambled to her feet and wandered away, leaving the others behind. "Don't go far!" murmured Corky. "Stay where I can see you."

She picked her way along the edge of the water, where the plants were shorter. Already she could see the old pump-huts, their doors hanging open to reveal a mess of wires and broken dials and meters. Birds had nested in them. A little further on, lay a patch of darker green. This must be the place! The stones were jumbled together any old how, in a pile about two metres high. They were huge and smooth, some pitted with curious pockets, holding dregs of rainwater, some shaggy with dusty moss. Which would be the Wolf Stone? She worked her way round, feeling with her hands. The stone was like a living thing, cool in the shade, warm on top where the sun's rays rested. A sudden rustle beneath her fingers made her jump. An adder slipped into a crack and disappeared...

Corky looked around in consternation. Trudi had ignored him and vanished and he could not call her back without spoiling Jurgen's chance of a catch. But he should not go after her and leave Jurgen alone by the water... Where had that girl run off to? Softly, he stood up and edged away, peering through the pools of light. "Don't move." He whispered. "I'll be back in a jiffy." Jurgen sat tight, frowning with concentration.

Corky crept along like a crab, looking out both ways and teasing the foliage apart. "Trudi!" he whistled, but the wood was quiet. A few paces more, then another, and another...

Suddenly there was a shout: "I've got something! I've caught

143

something!" Jurgen had jumped up and was furiously winding his reel, but this 'something' was big. Corky saw the rod bend in an arc. The more the boy pulled with his little hands, the more the line strained and the soft earth began to slip beneath his feet.

"Hold on, Jurgen, I'm coming!"

Trudi, alerted by the voices, was just in time to see her brother toppling towards the water. For a ghastly moment she envisaged the splash, the gurgle, the bubbles, which would mean he had gone... Perhaps he was right after all about the man-eating fish? But Corky was quicker. Just as Jurgen lost his balance Corky reached him, threw his arms round his waist and tossed him up onto the bank.

The reel flew out of his hand and he landed face down in the picnic. When he next looked up, his face was covered in jam and his tee shirt had a liberal splattering of yoghurt and cranberry juice!

Corky, however, had landed in the water.

By the time Trudi reached him, he was submerged up to the knees and sinking fast in a silt of rotting leaves.

"Throw me my stick, can you?" he called. His boots had filled with sludge and he could not lift his feet.

"Stupid. Look what you've done!" Trudi threw Jurgen a reproachful look and passed the handle of the beater.

"No, no," insisted Corky. "Not his fault. Mine, for not watching properly!"

If only he could catch hold of that overhanging branch, he could haul himself to safety... Whatever was Barbara going to say? And what about his beautiful rod? The fish must have got away for the rod lay floating, just out of reach. His best hope now was to find some firmer ground... He prodded the lagoon bed with his stick. Ah! Something solid there. A sewer pipe, perhaps, that he could balance on? But no, this something was quite small. He probed some more... flat and square, it was. Loose too. No help at all. By a desperate effort, he reached the branch and steadied himself with his good arm. His feet made ghastly squelchings in the mud.

"Jurgen! Are you all right?"

"Yes!"

"Can you throw me a net, the one with the long handle?"

Something might be salvaged here. The children watched in awe, as he began to drag the margin, hanging over the water at a perilous angle. There! Got it! At least he had caught something! The mystery object tumbled into his net. Probably a brick, though it felt metallic. Now for the painful business of lugging himself ashore. He had given his shoulder a nasty wrench, but he kept up a cheerful banter, laughing at his muddy legs and landing his catch, this time away from the picnic!

"Oh dear!" he lamented as he sat on the grass. "What a shambles! We shan't be trusted to go out together again! And look at you! I'm so sorry. I forgot the picnic was there. Are you sure you're not hurt?"

"Jurgen always manages to fall in something, observed Trudi archly. "It's quite normal for him."

Nonetheless, she could not help thinking that Corky's inexperience showed. Kirsten would never have left the jam and yoghurt lying about. She always packed a meal away as soon as it was finished. But then Kirsten would have lost her cool and told them off and Corky was so kind, he never had a cross word. He had nearly come to grief himself, and had messed up all his fishing things, yet he didn't seem to mind at all. It had been quite a scare, watching him thrash and struggle and not knowing if he would ever get out again. In that moment, Trudi felt certain that his jesting hid a fragile soul.

Corky *emanated* goodness. She knew that his deformity didn't matter, but it made him seem lonely. She suspected that he was secretly in love with Barbara, though he would never tell. And she also sensed, with a child's precocity, that Barbara did not return his feelings. She was too fiery, too mischievous for his gentle nature, though of course she cared for him. Anyone could see that. No, Barbara preferred arguing with Scarp. It was all rather sad.

Jurgen, not being troubled by deep reflections, rubbed himself down with a napkin and licked the jam off his face, like a cat.

They began to pack away the cups and, with the help of some rope and a stick, retrieved the fishing rod.

"I *would* have caught that fish!" said Jurgen. "I'd nearly got it. It was a man-eater!" He was already composing a better version of events.

"I expect it was a tiddler, about as a big as a finger," said Trudi.

"Well?" came Jurgen's retort. "Where's *your* fabulous secret, then?"

They all turned their eyes upon the net. Oozing slime, Corky's catch lay on the grass beside them. Old and smelly, it looked like an antique cash-box, or corroded biscuit tin. Perhaps one of those old sewage workers had kept his lunch in it. She could just picture him, in his flat cap, his handkerchief, tucked, like a napkin, under his chin. He would have had bread and jam and cold tea... But this box had a lock which would not give way to the jigglings of a pocket knife. When they shook it they heard the thud of something heavy inside.

"Perhaps it is Wulfstan's brooch," suggested Jurgen.

Impossible. The lagoon had been dredged and in any case this had been in the water no more than a few weeks, or there would have been more sediment on top.

"We'll take it home," said Corky, thinking they had had enough adventures for one day and feeling the mud, cold, and sticky between his toes. "We'll go home early and give Auntie Barbara a surprise."

So they all trooped back and lined up, meekly at the door. As surprises went, this proved a good one. Indeed, the sight of Jurgen's crimson shirt made Barbara shriek.

"Saints alive, what have you done to him!"

"Oh that," Corky smiled. "He was attacked by a giant crayfish, but he manfully fought it off."

"Don't give me that!" Barbara scolded before hustling Jurgen off to the bathroom. "And look at the state of *you*. You're worse than the children! You're not fit to come into the house!"

"I know. Truly sorry," he mumbled to the closing door. He left a reeking trail wherever he went.

Per looked up expectantly. "Fish?"

"Not today, I'm afraid. We hooked a monster but he escaped. No matter. One day, I'll bring you a feast. I promise. We caught something else, though - a bit of jetsom, submerged by the bank. Needs a wash."

Per shook his head. "No fish - no supper."

"No fish? Oh darn, that is *too bad*," grinned Barbara, on her return. "Well, we'll just have to have prawns instead - they're fishy, aren't they? Look, *'from the pristine waters of the Arctic'*. Says so on the packet. Not quite Sump water, but heck, who cares?" She felt a surge of relief.

"We'll eat in the garden anyway, if that dog will let us. And we'll light the candles again, since I can't find those goddamn lanterns. And we'll all drink 'Skål' with elderflower-water, and pretend it's something stronger. You, Corky, must get those wet things off. Trudi can find you some pants, or whatever it is you call them. There must be lots of Sven's clothes upstairs... And *slippers!*" she called, as Trudi disappeared. "*Trousers*, that's the word. I guess they'll be a bit short, but you won't mind, will you? And once you're decent, we'll go outside and relax. You kids can find a game to play and you two can talk about fishing and I'll - I might even go back to my book."

Her book, Corky noticed, was her beloved Shakespeare - a battered copy of *The Tempest*, whose sorcerer, Prospero, had given his name to the bookshop. Trudi picked up the volume, later in the day and read a few lines:

> "*Full fathom five thy father lies,*
> *Those are pearls that were his eyes.*
> *Of his bones are coral made*
> *Nothing of him that doth fade*
> *But doth suffer a sea change*
> *Into something rich and strange...*"

Her thoughts naturally returned to the Sump. The struggle in the lagoon that afternoon had shown how easy it was to drown there. That must have been what happened to poor Perkins all those years ago. Doubtless, he slipped in, just like Corky, but there was no one nearby to throw him a line before he was sucked down to his death. Horrible to think of. But who could have guessed, just from looking, that it was really such a swamp?

Life was full of lagoons - all smooth and tranquil on top and full of hidden perils. Here in Bockhurst, life flowed calmly from day to day, giving little hint of what was really brewing underneath. Appearances. Perhaps nothing was really what it seemed.

Each time she set foot in the Sump she felt she had entered a different world. Today, a dump, tomorrow a corner of Eden; a place of death - a place of miracles... The lagoon wasn't exactly evil, merely a trap for the unwary.

Complex, beautiful and terrible. That was how life looked when you approached it through the Sump. Every visit made things stranger.

And that was even before they opened the box.

Chapter 19

A Night Visitor

Later, in the dark, Trudi took stock of the day. The warm air was full of scents: wasp-eaten apples from Miss Vincent's garden, and the bittersweet smell of dahlias and nasturtiums from Kirsten's borders. Throwing open her window, she gazed once more towards the Sump. From far off, she could hear the throb of a combine harvester working on Jackson's farm. A crescent moon was lifting behind the trees. Next month the full moon would be a Harvest moon, fat and golden like the paper lanterns her mother used for parties...

She tried to picture life on the other side of the Sump, where Scarp lived. They had crossed one of the fields there the day they went flinting, but she found it hard to place this land anywhere on her mental map of home. 'Over there' existed as a floating, imaginary world and she was not even sure which road you would take to get there, but during supper, news of this vague 'somewhere' burst unexpectedly into their lives.

While Barbara cooked supper, Per and the children attempted once more to open the box. They tried levering it and oiling it and poking it with a screwdriver. They even tried sliding bits of cardboard under the catch, but nothing worked. By now, the pond-water had drained out and the contents made a rattling sound when shaken. Trudi, deciding that they were probably bones, felt secretly glad that they could not be extricated. At any rate, the lock held fast and, rather than force it, Corky suggested that they should leave it until they thought of a better way and clean up the outside, instead. Accordingly, they got a rag and scraped away the grime, and almost immediately they uncovered an inscription on the lid. Ornate it was, with letters like the scratches engraved on Per's rune sticks, but when Grandpa put on his glasses to have a look, he shook his head. These were not runes. Then Barbara tried and declared that she thought the writing was Old English, but her memory was so rusty and the words were so badly corroded, she could not make them out.

149

Stumped again, they deposited the box on a pile of newspaper, sat it on the microwave and turned to other things.

Supper first. They ate in the garden, as planned, but just as they were about to start pudding, they were interrupted by a loud knock at the door. Barbara 'went', and shortly afterwards they heard her inimitable squeal:

"Oh my God! That's *terrible!*"

Ears pricked up. Smitten with curiosity, the children crept closer to hear. Barbara was still exclaiming while an unknown voice made reassuring noises. After a pause, they heard front door close and footsteps returned along the hall.

"Guys, this is Hubert Jackson!" Barbara ushered a stranger into the kitchen and Trudi, Jurgen and Corky, agog at the back door, nodded in welcome. Only Per sat on, alone with his thoughts, outside. "Hubert is from the farm where Scarp lives," said Barbara; then turned around.

"Oh heck, don't worry about your shoes. Nobody else does. In any case, we're sitting in the garden. You're just fine as you are. Come on through. We're eating a bite of supper. Won't you join us? Or at least come and have something to drink."

Hubert was straight-backed and wholesome-looking; clean-shaven, blue-eyed. He wore the type of clothing that you saw in country magazines at the dentist's: moleskin trousers and a farmer's cap, even though the night was so mild.

"Very kind of you." Taking off his cap, he pushed his fingers into his hair. He was blond, and muscular and affable. "I feel rather bad, busting in on your party…"

And Barbara took measure of him in a trice. This one was just a wee bit laddie, for all he looked so grand. Probably still at college. She could handle *him*. She put up one plump hand and pointed towards the door.

"What will you have? Tea? Coffee? Or something stronger? Beer?"

"Oh gosh, really!" he gave a little guffaw. "Well, a beer - just a mouthful. I don't want to be a nuisance."

"Out!" Barbara ordered, with a grin. "Look here, meet Corky, a dear friend who has just fallen in a pond. Excuse his trousers! And the children, Trudi and Jurgen, who are the only ones who really *live*

150

here. Their Mommy and Daddy are away. Out there, you will find Per, the Swedish grandfather. I'm coming right away."

She dived to the fridge for a bottle, grabbed an extra plate and trundled outside, where Per was completing his formal introductions.

"Sit! Sit Hubert! Jurgen, you can move over and make room. Now, will you have a pancake? No? They're really good. Okay. Okay. Let's have the full story then."

Confronted with five earnest faces, now a-glow in the candle-light, Hubert began his tale. His bashfulness fell away and he slipped into the rhythm of a practised speaker. Once, Trudi glanced up at the Stringers' house. The dog must have been locked away, for he was quiet. A light in a top floor shone steadily and, with a shiver, she noted Simon Stringer's face, pressed against the window. When she looked again, both light and face were gone.

The news was to do with Scarp. Hubert had just returned from a fishing trip in Scotland. Delightful place on the Strathspey - salmon - a rather good year. (Corky bit his tongue for this was not the moment to digress with fisherman's tales and Hubert returned to his theme.) He had been called home to help with the harvest for the week or two before college term began. He was a final year student at the agricultural place at Bedham, just west of Tilchester. Anyhow, as soon as he arrived, he called by to see Scarp, as he always did when he'd been away, and found the poor chap in a devil of a state. Scarp didn't exactly hit it off with Hubert's mother, so neither of his parents knew anything was wrong. But Hubert had always had a soft spot for Scarp... He drifted off, then pulled himself together. Well, to cut a long story short, Scarp had asked him to come round here and explain why he had been missing for so long. "He seems to have taken a real shine to you," Hubert said. "And he's worried. He thinks he might have caused offence, especially to *you*," he turned to Barbara. "He'd promised to take you somewhere?"

"Never mind all that."

"What *happened*?"

"Is he okay?" The voices chipped in one after another.

Barbara was shaking her head. Trouble! Didn't she just know it!

"He's fine now," Hubert assured them. "But he looks a bit of a mess. It seems that you had a big storm the other night?"

They nodded.

"Well a gust of wind turned his caravan over. He had had a couple of beers and gone to sleep and knew nothing about it till he woke up with a larder shelf on his head. Two black eyes and a nasty cut on his cheek."

"Why didn't he come for help? Someone could have patched him up."

"I think he passed out for a while and simply stayed put, nursing his wounds until the storm passed over. There was nothing he could do about the caravan on his own."

"Well where were his friends? Doesn't he have friends? Why didn't he phone them?"

"Perhaps you don't know Scarp. He's a funny chap. Very secretive. I only know him so well because he let me watch him work when I was a boy. I used to sit up in the big barn when he was mending the tractors, and he'd tell me stories. He's had a few enemies in his time! He's quieter now, but he was a regular handful, years ago. Always up to his neck in something. The friends he had were mostly bad news."

"So what now? What about the caravan? Where is he staying?"

"He's sort of camping out," said Hubert. "It'll take several strong men to get the caravan up again. I can help organize that."

"And Scarp?"

"He's fine, really. Almost his old self. I think he was a bit sorry for himself at first." Hubert pulled a crumpled package from his pocket. "He sent this, as a kind of peace offering. I think he'd like to come and see you."

Barbara inspected the package and shook her head. Chocolates from last Christmas. She might have expected as much. Then she burst out, momentarily forgetting that she was also, in a manner of speaking, 'camping out': "Saints alive! What can you *do* with the man! He must come and stay here. He can't live in the woods!"

"I would be happy for him to move in with *us*, but, as I said, there are difficulties. I don't think he would consider it. Do you really think you might take him in?"

"It's not an invitation, it's an *order*," said Barbara, now feeling truly terrible about the cake she had eaten last week. She peered across at Per to see whether he would object, but he was already nodding his head. "That's settled then. Tell him we're expecting him and we don't care what he looks like."

"You're a true friend. Scarp doesn't really take orders. But I'll tell him what you've said. There's just a chance he might just listen to you. I must say I was worried when I saw him today... Thank you." Hubert rose to go, but Trudi had a question and it simply would not wait any longer:

"If you've known him a long time," she said, very sweetly, "Do you know? Can you tell us? What does 'Scarp' mean? Why is he called that?"

Hubert laughed aloud. "You should ask him," he replied. "He tells it best!"

With that he was gone and the scent of his fine aftershave went with him. Sitting at her window, Trudi found it hard to imagine that the same man was driving the combine she could hear. Of course, farm machines were all clean and air-conditioned now. Scarp had said so before. The Jacksons had all the latest equipment. Really, you needed a computer, not a mechanic, to mend them now. And Scarp - where was he? Sitting under a tarpaulin somewhere, with earwigs in his blankets. She was glad he was coming to stay. It felt safer, somehow.

Barbara struggled so much with her report to Kirsten, she actually shirked most of it. After all, she reasoned, this latest complication was a temporary hitch. No reason why others should worry about it. With luck, the whole affair would be over and done with before anything leaked out. There was an entire week still to go before Kirsten's return and if the children played along, well, perhaps she need never know.

'*Darling K,*' she said, lying by omission '*We're all fine. Nothing much happened today. The children played boules. Hope you are well and enjoying your tour. Lots of love, Bee.*"

Chapter 20

Life and Death

That night, heavy rain came in and though the next morning dawned fine, there was a nip in the air. The sun rose red and dull, through early fog.

Before breakfast, an urgent thumping at the door brought Trudi flying down in her pyjamas, thinking Sven's parcel had come. On the doorstep stood Scarp, looking leaner and more dishevelled than ever, with two black bundles in his arms. His beard had grown, and the bruises under his eyes had faded to lurid green. An unhealed cut on his cheek gave him a desperate look.

"Is Barbara about?" he asked, ignoring Trudi's stare.

Trudi turned and called out Barbara's name.

"We need the oven on, very low, or an electric fire, maybe. Got any old towels?" Without bothering about his boots, he marched straight to the kitchen, where Per was setting the table. The two men nodded to one another.

"Morning," said Scarp, "Sorry. Can't shake hands."

"What is it? What have you got?" Trudi was now hopping up and down, and he gave her a teasing wink before dropping onto his knees. Jurgen burst in, followed by Barbara.

"It's *lambs*!" cried Trudi. "Two baby lambs!"

"They're an accident," said Scarp, now smiling all round. "They shouldn't be here at all. It's the wrong time of year for lambs and these are the wrong colour. The woman at Fraisey Manor keeps Hebridean sheep, for show like, to look pretty in her meadow. Hebrideans are black, with fancy horns and she likes all that. Anyway, one day, in the spring, her ram got in amongst some yearlings Jackson had bought. We caught him up pretty smart and put him back over the fence, thinking no harm was done, but here we are, six months later - two black lambs in August. The problem is, the mother has died and these little things, just born this morning, are orphans. I spotted them out in the field. But the Jacksons don't want them - they're busy with their harvest. Anyhow they are furious

154

about losing a sheep. Two black lambs are no use to them.

"I thought perhaps you could get them going - you know, have them as pets for a bit. Then perhaps we can persuade the Fraisey Manor lot to give them a home."

"They need food," said Per coming over and casting a knowledgeable eye.

"Warm up first. They're cold and wet." Scarp set them gently down and they collapsed on the floor. "I'll go and see if I can get some milk. You wrap them up and put them in a warm place. With any luck, they'll come round."

Trudi leapt in. "I'll hold one. I'm warm!"

She touched the tightly curled fleece with her finger. The lamb made no response.

"This one's the weakest. He might not make it," warned Scarp.

Thanks, Lord! thought Barbara. *Just what we need now - a death in the family*!

Out loud she was her usual, stoical self. "We'll cope. You go. Are you okay to go?" she looked him in the eye. "Yeah, well, we'll sort you out, too, when you get back."

They wrapped the smaller lamb in a towel and popped him in the bottom of the oven. The other was bundled up and placed in Trudi's lap, while Jurgen hovered nearby, offering help and advice and itching to push Trudi out of the way and take on the job himself.

"No shoving!" admonished Barbara. "You'll get a turn. There'll be plenty of time to hold him when he's recovered."

The lamb had shiny black hooves, like old-fashioned buttoned boots, cold as marble, and large, soft ears; a neat, finely-chiselled nose and black lips. Eyes closed, head down, he lay quite motionless.

"Trudi, see if he sucks. Put your finger in his mouth."

Timidly, Trudi did as Per told her. She could feel the fish-bone pattern on his upper palette, the tiny tongue, but the lamb was cold inside as well as out. His mouth felt icy.

"Then give him time." Per seemed so calm, so sure. Trudi wondered if he had revived baby reindeer when he was in Samiland. She couldn't ask him now. That would be to betray his secret.

How slow Scarp was! He must have been gone more than an hour and they all began to wonder if he was coming back at all. When he appeared at last, he looked unhopeful.

155

"No good," he announced. "The animal feed places don't sell supplies for lambs at this time of year. They'll order some in for me but it'll take time. I bought some goat's milk at the supermarket. That's the best I could manage. And I got this baby bottle but it's the wrong shape."

"Rubber gloves!" said Barbara in a flash of inspiration. She might not know about bottle-feeding, but she knew how to improvise. She set a kettle to boil and pulled out the contents of the cupboard beneath the sink. Sure enough, there were rubber gloves, neatly packed, in a choice of sizes.

"Pink or yellow? Guess they can have one of each. Now, bottles... of course *they've* all been recycled."

"I do have *this*," Scarp pulled a half-bottle of whisky from his pocket.

"Excellent!" Barbara pounced on it and poured the contents into a jug. "Save that for later. Well, they say spirits are warming! Now, give the bottle here." A severed glove finger fitted perfectly over the neck.

"*Small* hole," advised Per, watching closely. "They will not swallow much at first." A tiny prick sufficed. They scoured the larder for a second bottle, rinsed them both and warmed some milk over hot water. Per tested the temperature on his hand.

"This is good!"

The preparations proved so absorbing, no one noticed Trudi's lamb lift up his head. He gave a powerful bleat, and then sank back, exhausted.

"Even better!" said Per. "Try him first."

This lamb was not all black. He had a tiny top-knot of white wool, a gift from his white mother. He dribbled and sneezed and his eyes opened in alarm as the milk seeped into his mouth.

"Not too fast," urged Per. "Let him breathe."

"Oh, *let* me try!" pleaded Jurgen almost bursting frustration.

"Okay, honey. You've been good. Let Trudi try the little lamb and you take this one."

Scarp quietly guided his hand. The lamb gulped and gargled and took some gasps of air.

"Hold him tight - he's sliding away." They tucked his long legs under his body and tried again. This time, miraculously, he began to

156

suck. He swallowed four or five good slugs of the milk. "Enough! Enough, for now!" The lamb kicked out with his legs and made a feeble attempt to stand.

"This one is good!" cried Per.

Now the other. This one, coal black, was smaller and weaker, but he opened his eyes as Trudi gently prised his lips apart. She could feel his heart beating beneath his wool. Like his brother, he choked and sneezed.

"Gently. Let him clear his throat." His black eyes shone and his ribs shook. When all was calm, they tried again. But this lamb hadn't the strength to swallow. He choked again, his eyes half closed and his breath came in uneven bursts. Trudi hugged him close, willing him to revive, but his body suddenly slackened and he laid his head upon his shoulder.

"What's happened?" cried Trudi, noticing the change.

"Nothing," said Per, his voice now quiet, resigned. "He has gone home."

"He's *died*?" she gasped. "You mean I *killed* him?" A wave of grief engulfed her and her eyes instantly filled with tears. For once, she didn't care if she looked a baby or a fool. She didn't care about herself at all. Barbara froze in horror. Scarp swore an oath and shook his head.

"Trudi, Trudi," Per went on as she tried to lift the lifeless head. "Don't be sad, Trudi. It was too hard for this one to come back. But he is safe. Look, he's sleeping. He's not cold now."

"He was my lamb," sobbed Trudi.

"Then you will look after him," said Per. "You can give him back to the earth - where he will feel at home. You will look after him till then. We all come - we all go. These creatures do not *belong* to us. They are just companions for a while."

Trudi looked into Per's strange, fathomless eyes.

"We should have *saved* him!"

"We shall save the other. He has life in him - he is happy to stay."

"But *Jurgen's* got *him*," Trudi's tears had turned to self-pity too.

"We will find a good place for this one - and then we will *all* look after the other."

Trudi was astonished that Per's words sounded so natural. Her lifelong horror of death and dead things had meant that she could not even pick up a fly-corpse without a shudder of revulsion. She and Jurgen would dare one another to do such things, but the primitive fear never left her. She had never witnessed a death like this before. But Per talked as if it was something quite ordinary and she turned to him, as though she were stuck on the a perilous cliff-ledge and he alone could guide her down: "Put this foot here - now move your hand - slowly... hold here - don't look down - next foot... nearly there."

Barbara woke up from her stupor.

"Darling we'll bury him somewhere beautiful - somewhere close by, so you know where he is. Somewhere *you* choose... *Won't* we?" She looked around for support.

Scarp pulled a face. Of course it was strictly illegal to bury a farm animal at home. They had to be officially incinerated. But these people knew nothing about that and to mention it right now would be pointlessly cruel. Nothing suspicious had happened, after all. The lamb had simply died of exposure. What harm could it do, staying here? Besides, Scarp was not *in principle* averse to breaking the law. He decided to keep quiet.

"Sure," he nodded. "Sure. I'll go round the health food shops. Someone must sell sheep's milk and we'll keep this one going on that till I get the right stuff from Weatherby's."

Trudi remained thoughtful for a while.

"The dead one has got to have a name. We'll call him Pumpkin. And we'll put him in the Sump. Then Mummy won't mind."

"Oh, honey, you know the Sump is going to be sold," protested Barbara. But Per cut in.

"Not a problem. Stay close to the big trees. The builders should not dig up that ground." Scarp reflected wryly that '*that ground*' was going to be practically impossible to dig at all, what with the dryness and the roots and all. But having started this whole business, he had brought the trouble on himself. He did really feel for Trudi, so he swallowed all objections.

While the other lamb slept, they found a spade. Scarp took Pumpkin and led the children in a solemn little procession, down to the camp and Jurgen brought up the rear, glad to be under his captain's command again.

Barbara started to clear up.

"Poor little kid," she murmured.

"She will survive," said Per. "She is a strong girl. Lot of spirit." Then he added: "This lamb needs a box to sleep in, and perhaps I should feed him again before they return. Might be better if I care for him until he is really strong."

"*Did* she choke the other one?" asked Barbara.

"Who knows?" Per shrugged. "Maybe. But that lamb had already gone too far. He was in the land of the spirits when Scarp brought him in and it is a dangerous journey between that world and this." He spoke with a quiet authority.

"I'll get a box," said Barbara. In her head she could still hear Trudi's words: '*Otherwise I'll never know if Professor Saxmund was right when he said that Grandfather Larsson was a shaman.*' Had Per himself made that perilous journey to talk to the spirits in their other world? And did he really know more about life and death than ordinary, simple people? She thought of Tod making that journey all alone and wished that Per could have been there to give him some advice.

After his next drink, the surviving lamb took his first steps, his hooves skidded on the kitchen tiles. He staggered, slipped and let out a louder bleat. And you could not help but feel a surge of joy, seeing this tenuous life flicker into existence. When the funeral party came back, he was curled up snugly on a towel in the recycling box. Only then was it possible to consider other things.

Chapter 21

Owning Up

They showed Scarp to the homework room, where he would camp for the next few says.

"Is this all you brought with you?" asked Barbara, frowning at the carrier bag he had left in the hall.

"I put my tools in the truck," He seemed offended that anyone should inspect his personal arrangements. "They're safer locked up."

Barbara nodded. Yes, better not fill the house with wrenches and pressure pumps. A lamb was clutter enough!

"Sure. You know best. I'll leave you to it," she said. "I'm making coffee downstairs. Come and join us when you are ready."

They talked about Scarp's caravan, which was now uninhabitable, and about Jurgen's attempts to play the flute; the trip to Corky's nursery, the visit to the Museum, the forest garden, oh, and the fishing adventure. Scarp had little to say about his own affairs, but he did ask after Miss Vincent. Was she all right?

"Trudi's in charge of Miss Vincent," said Barbara. "I gather she's as cranky as ever, right?"

"Right," nodded Trudi. She had still not confided to anyone the things they had overheard in the Sump. Hugging this information gave her a feeling of independence. In some way she could not explain, she shared the old lady's relish for secrecy.

"But what about the *box*? What about the *box*?" insisted Jurgen. How much more time would they waste on nitter-natter when the really important questions remained unanswered?

"Oh yes, why yes, the *box*." Barbara bustled off to fetch it. "We tried but we couldn't get it open. We rubbed it down and look, there's an inscription on the lid. Don't suppose you are any good at picking locks?"

The aside was meant as a joke, but Scarp cocked an eyebrow and grinned.

"Am I good at picking locks? Are ducks good at swimming?" He gave the box a professional once over and then stood up. "Got my tools in the truck, haven't I?" With that he sidled out.

Barbara put her head in her hands. Idiot that she was! Of *course* Scarp would know how to pick locks - just as he could probably empty gas meters, and fix car alarms! Jurgen swelled with pride. A real, proper burglar. Scarp was a genius! He came back with a length of wire, which he poked into the keyhole, teasing, testing, listening and swearing softly in encouragement. After a while, there was a satisfying click and the catch slid back.

"Right, are you ready for this now, whatever it is?" He was enjoying the attention.

"Dead cat!" murmured Trudi.

"*Smells* like a dead cat!"

"No, the pearls," said Barbara.

Scarp lifted the lid to reveal a good deal of putrid silt and some well-rotted rag. It looked like a mummy. Underneath the rag, another bundle. The first fell apart to reveal a piece of cheap-looking metal, brassy, shiny, with dull red and green stones stuck in it.

"That's gold," said Scarp, wiping the mud off with his thumb. "That's Wulfstan's bloody brooch!"

But it didn't look like the drawing in the Museum. And in any case, how would it come to be here? This was shaped like a buckle, with a serpent's body wound in a ring. Scarp continued to peel away the cloth and out fell a quantity of coins and some red and blue beads; a gold mount from a shield; two stone weights with holes in the middle and the rim of a drinking horn, embossed with running hounds.

"Well, bugger me!" Scarp was speechless. To find an ancient hoard like this was a chance in a million. But none of the evidence added up. The box itself could be no more than a hundred years old and it had been in the water barely a month. Had Perkins, the gardener, stolen these things too? But then why drown himself? Why not make off with the loot? And why was this cache never reported missing? The de Fraiseys only complained of losing their pearls and brooch. More to the point, what should be done with the treasure *now*? Did it belong to the Water Company, or to the Crown, or to Corky who found them, or to the lost heirs of Sir Vivian?

"That would be the Jacksons," said Scarp, rubbing his beard. "They're related in a roundabout way. When the boy, Edward, got

161

killed in the war, his parents gave up hope. The mother died soon after and the father took to drink. He copped it one day, driving in the Park. Death duties swallowed most of the estate. The big house and the lands were sold and the home farm went to a spinster cousin who lived in London and rented her land to a tenant. When the old girl died, the property passed to a niece, and she turned up here in 1940 looking for an escape from the Blitz and offering to help with the War Effort. To cut a long story short, she moved in and kept house for the farmer, which caused a bit of local scandal. That was Bert Jackson - never had a girlfriend before – he was something or other in the Home Guard. Eventually they married, which is how the Jacksons came to own Manor Farm. Walter Jackson, my boss, is their son." He stopped and whistled between his teeth. "Looks as if the old cat might get her way after all!"

"What old cat? What way?" said Barbara, struggling to keep up.

"Well Hubert's mother, of course."

"The one you don't like?"

Scarp shifted in his chair and ignored the question. "She's put in a bid for the Sump, you know. She's..." he pursed his lips. "She's a bit above herself, you could say. She went to private school. Got ideas of being a grand lady - mixing with the nobs round here. It's why she doesn't want me around the place. She thinks I'm a bad influence on Hubert. She's trying to get me out, so she can play lady of the manor and show off to all her friends how she's married into the aristocracy. It's all b..." He caught Barbara's eye. "All rubbish, of course."

"What would *she* do with the Sump?"

"Oh, build a horse school and invite her horsey friends." He dropped his sardonic tone. "Truth is they're already flat broke. The farming subsidies have run out and all the new barns and new machines over there are bought on credit. She'll bankrupt them."

"Why doesn't old Jackson stop her?"

"She's quite a force to reckon with," Scarp tilted his head. "And Jackson likes a quiet life. *He's* all right. He's a decent bloke. He's stuck up for me over the years. He just wants to dig his garden, have a pint at The Wheatsheaf and keep himself out of trouble. He's always let her have her head."

"So what now?" asked Barbara. "Where do we go with the

treasure? To the Museum? The Police? Who's the authority on these things?"

"Miss Vincent," said Trudi quietly.

Everyone stared.

"Miss Vincent said when it came to buried treasure, she could tell people a thing or two. I think she will know." She stretched out a finger and touched the coloured beads. There were more ghosts here, lots of them, but they felt homely and rather sad.

"Well, we'll bother her later." Barbara felt quietly relieved. If they had to make public confession that they had been trespassing, well, there would be no way on earth that she could hide the fact from Trudi's parents. And she was still clinging to the hope that she could present a clean front when Sven and Kirsten returned.

She felt like Pandora, trying to cram the lid on a whole world of prpblems. The faster she popped them into their box, the faster they wriggled out again. The concept brought a smile. After all, wasn't that just what had happened with Wulfstan's brooch? The thing wasn't meant to come to light, was it? It was hidden evidence. She could see that now. Someone had got themselves into more trouble than they could handle with this little hoard, so they wrapped it up and ditched it. But who had done it? And why? Her thoughts were interrupted by Jurgen:

"The lamb's awake!"

Oh heavens! What a day! With much knocking and thumping the lamb had scrambled to his feet and was staring at them over the rim of his box.

"Quick, more milk."

Trudi lifted him out and set him on his legs and he stumbled across the floor. He wanted to be somewhere dark. He was looking for the shelter of the mother he had lost. Anything with four legs would do. A kitchen chair looked promising, but the cross bars tripped him up and he landed in a heap. No sooner was he rescued, than he made for cover again This time he slithered under the long bench by the window, and when Jurgen fetched him out, he was festooned in cobwebs.

"Oh Lord! That's my cleaning for you!" shrieked Barbara. "Poor little mite!"

"That's his name," said Trudi.

"*What* is?"

"Cobweb. He looks as if he's got a cobweb on his head anyway. Let's call him Cobweb."

Since no one came up with anything better, that was agreed. And a new routine of life-with-baby began to take shape. Milk - run - sleep - run - milk - run - sleep... There was quite a lot of mopping-up to do and the routine, in time, became: milk - quick! - run in the garden! - sleep - run in the garden - milk - and it all worked out pretty well. Scarp brought in sweet hay for Cobweb to sleep on.

The treasure lay quiet for the moment, though Per, like Trudi, returned often to look at the beads and sometimes rolled them between his fingers.

Scarp took himself off to work, returned late, scoffed his supper and made his excuses. He liked an early night. But if he thought he could slip away without explanation, he was mistaken.

Barbara, seizing a private moment, caught up with him in the hall.

"Well?" she said, blocking his way.

Now I'm for it, he thought, backing against the banisters. How he hated confessions.

"Scarp, it's not true, is it?" She was trying to engage his eye, but he would not look at her. His business was private. He stared steadfastly at the floor.

"...about the storm?" she persisted.

No reply.

"Scarp?"

"What?" He could play deaf *and* dumb. Anything to hold her off... Once Barbara made up her mind, though, she didn't let go.

"It's not *true, is* it?"

"Nope," he replied, at last.

"What happened?"

"Nothing."

"*Scarp!*"

"Okay. Okay, okay."

"It *couldn't* have been the storm. The storm happened at four o'clock in the afternoon. You would have been working and if you had come back in daylight and found the caravan wrecked, you would have gone for help. But you were injured. If, as you say, it was later - and I know the wind kept up all evening - then your lantern would have been alight. You don't have electricity, do you? I've heard you say so - So the lantern would have started a fire. If you were knocked out, you would have gone up too."

"Clever, aren't you?" said Scarp.

"So - what happened?"

He grudgingly gave in: "There were three of them. Big blokes. Bigger than me, at any rate. I'd gone to check the pheasants, in case the storm had damaged the pens, and they closed in on me there - like they'd been tipped off. The pens were open and I was mad. They threatened me. Told me to clear out and never come back. Well, you know me. They don't call me Scarp for nothing. If there's trouble, I'm the first one off out of it! Scarper! I'm good at running. But I was going to give them a mouthful, first." He paused. "I didn't really get the chance."

"They made a mess of you," Barbara clucked.

"Yeah. They were like - like professionals - you know, posh-talking. I dunno what their game was - but they meant business. When I came round and crawled back to the caravan, they'd done it over - tipped it right up."

"Why didn't you get help?"

"I wouldn't go to *her* at the house. I just thought I'd lie low for a few days - try and find out what was going on."

"You could have come here."

"Oh, yeah. You need people like that over here, don't you!"

"Could you describe them?"

"What is this, the police?" He wasn't joking any more. "Like I said, they were big. Can I go now?"

"Sorry. But it doesn't make sense. Do you think it's got something to do with the box Corky found?"

"Nah!" Scarp shook his head. "How could it? He didn't dig that up till days after this happened. This is something else. Something bigger."

"Are you okay?" She hadn't finished with him yet.

"I'm fine. Just forget it."

"What about the caravan?"

"I'll fix it."

"We'll *all* fix it."

Scarp looked aghast. He hugged himself and rubbed his arms.

165

"No thanks! I don't do charity." Then, seeing the hurt in her eyes, he relented. "Don't get me wrong. I don't mean to be rude. It's just that I look after myself. Always have done. It's how I am." He did not want her kindness. Such kindness only made him feel weak - brought home the fact that he didn't have friends of his own he could trust - proper friends who might help... In his world it had always been every man for himself.

Yet the day had been a good day: rescuing the lamb, joking with the kids and opening their box... He actually cared about this odd little family. All the same, he knew he was bad news. Wherever he went, trouble was sure to follow. No one would ever change that and he didn't want to bring his problems here.

Barbara backed off. Perhaps she had misjudged him. Perhaps he was right. Mixed up in things she shouldn't know.

"We'll see," he said, wriggling past her. "I appreciate you caring. I'm just no good with words."

"No matter," said Barbara. "Good night, Scarp."

"It'll all come out okay. You'll see."

"Good night."

Scarp escaped and Trudi, who just happened to be listening at the top of the stairs, heard him coming and fled back to her room. Intrigue upon intrigue! This news added another dimension to the puzzle. But gradually she was fitting the pieces together.

Otherworlds were not only outposts of mystery and magic, they were also *under*worlds, lying right here, like Sump mud, under the surface of every day. This innocent-seeming neighbourhood, so ordinary, so safe, was really seething with treachery. There was the man next door, cheating on his wife; the developers and their duplicitous schemes; now actual thugs beating people up. Suppose those men had been lying in wait for them when Corky took them fishing yesterday?

Beside their murky intentions, the darkness of the Sump seemed harmless, friendly even - like the shadow of Pumpkin, sleeping beneath the moon.

Chapter 22

Evidence

Cobweb needed no coaxing to drink the following morning. He wobbled giddily round the kitchen and collapsed, when he was tired, in the darkest corners he could find. He tried out the broom cupboard, the gap beside the pedal bin and the corner behind the kitchen door. Soon he protested about returning to his box. The box was confined and he wanted freedom. As he explored, his senses awoke to a world of discovery. Everything tasted interesting and he nibbled the knobs on the kitchen cupboards and sampled and spat out all the debris Per had scattered beneath his chair. His nose twitched at a bewilderment of smells. But of all the things he sniffed and tasted, milk was by far best. And when he drank his milk, the delight got into his tail and made it wriggle like an eel

Scarp tucked into toast and marmalade at breakfast and shot off early to do some work on Jackson's trailer. Per laid a hand on his arm as he was leaving and his long fingers closed like a vice. "My friend," he murmured, low. "I am making a gift for Jurgen, but some things I need and I cannot find them here. You go out in the world and maybe you can help."

Scarp nodded. "Just tell me what you want."

Barbara found herself tuning in as she cleared the table.

"The present I am making is a drum. Jurgen has this idea to become one-man-band, like Corky, the friend of Barbara. I, myself, once played the drum. So I would make him one. I have the frame already - ja – this is good. But now I need some animal skin – mm – to stretch over, to give this drum a voice."

"What kind of skin?"

Per broke into a smile - then a laugh. "Reindeer, of course!"

"Oh, is *that* all," said Scarp.

"Can you help?" He was earnest once more. "There is not much time now. I really must have it!" His eyes ignited with a pale fire and the grip on Scarp's arm tightened.

"I'll see what I can do," he promised and all the time he could hear another voice in his head: '*Brilliant! Well done Scarp! Now you've just got yourself into another fix. Where are you going to find a thing like that? Young Hubert goes deer-stalking with his posh friends up north, but not till October. And you don't just walk into a reindeer in Tilchester High Street. Or do you think you can buy one on the internet? Even if you could, you don't do computers, remember? Computers mean reading and you don't do reading. And you don't even have anywhere to plug a computer in. So, now what are you going to do?*' His brown eyes shone back. '*Think of something*'.

"No problem - I'll sort it!"

Per nodded and smiled. His hand relaxed.

"Shake on it."

"Slap hands - that's the gypsy way."

He prized Per's palm open and brought his own down, wallop, to close the deal.

"Nice boy," reflected Per after he had gone.

Barbara heaved a sigh: "Mmm. Slippery fish, though."

"Slippery fish stays out of the net," said Per in approval.

Like the serpent in the lagoon, thought Barbara. Hey ho!

* * * * *

A grand meeting was arranged for after lunch. Barbara phoned Corky - he must be present, since he had discovered the box in the first place - and Scarp said he would put in an appearance, and Trudi was dispatched next door to tell Miss Vincent.

"You go, honey, you're her friend. She trusts you. Ask her if it's okay for us to come over."

Trudi felt excited. A shiny ball was bouncing up and down inside her. She could feel it tickling her tummy. Everything was going well today. The sun was shining; the lamb was looking stronger, and she had managed to water her garden without disturbing Beor. Today was bin day. People who left for work early put their rubbish out the night before. As she stepped out of the gate, she noted that the foxes had been busy again, ripping open the bags up and down the street .

Next door, was particularly bad: chicken bones and chocolate wrappers - lots of shredded paper - strewn right across the pavement.

Trudi picked her way through the worst of it, but one particular item caught her eye.

This was a smart-looking envelope, lying face-up by the kerb. Cream vellum - laid. It had 'Strictly Confidential' stamped across the top in red and the label, printed bold, was addressed to one 'Mr. Beamish, Eco-Homesteads Ltd.'

Mr. Beamish, she remembered, was the man with glasses who had met Nigel Stringer in the Sump. She prodded the envelope with her toe and then bent down and picked it up. There was no postage mark. The flap was stuck down fast. The letter must have been written, stamped and sealed and then lost or thrown away before it could be posted. She wondered whether that was by accident or design. And if it was by accident, was somebody looking for it? And ought she to do something about it... ?

She agonised for a moment. Auntie Barbara would say *'leave it - serves them right'*. Per would say *'other people's business is other people's business'*. But the letter might be important and the bin men would be here any minute. She could not post an envelope all covered in goo. She could not take it back to the Stringers. If she kept it herself, that would be stealing, but then if she didn't keep it, someone else might find it, and then she would never know what it contained...

Eco-Homesteads, after all, were the developers who wanted to buy the Sump; who were planning to push Scarp off his land. And perhaps this letter held vital information about the sale. With a beating heart, she tucked the letter under her arm and continued on her way. She hurried into Miss Vincent's hall like a fugitive on the run.

The old lady immediately pounced on the letter and, with Trudi in tow, lumbered off to the kitchen where her arrival caused the usual flutter of feathers. All the little birds, which had made themselves at home, suddenly bolted for the garden. One robin, alone, remained behind; a scruff who was bolder than the rest, and who, determined not to leave his sausage roll, stayed on window-sill, pecking crumbs and fixing them with his eye.

"Let's see - let's see - you clever girl!"

Miss Vincent, having none of Trudi's scruples, slit the letter open without delay and spread it on the table:

"Dear Arnold," she read aloud *"This seems the safest way to communicate at present. Do not trust anything to e-mail or mobiles, and shred this as soon as you read it. Just to let you know that the deal is on. My colleague from the Planning Department will contact you shortly. Terms as we agreed. Blythe will take care of the sale. Tell your surveyors to proceed as necessary. Contact me only in an emergency through Phillimore at the office. My advance fee should be paid to a separate account: Miss Amber Beldam, South Downs Amicable Building Society A/c No: 2903346857. In anticipation of a successful outcome, Yours sincerely, Nigel Stringer."*

"Sounds nervy, doesn't he?" Miss Vincent grinned.

"What does it mean?" asked Trudi.

"It means skulduggery and dirty deeds in the forest!" She patted Trudi's hand and squeezed it. She sounded almost gleeful.

"In the Sump?"

"Where else? But maybe now, through your cleverness and curiosity," her eyes positively twinkled, "maybe we shall *catch* them. It's not quite the miracle you need to save your woodland garden, but it's a start."

Her hand, leathery, like bird's, let go.

"Will you tell the police?"

"We don't have proof of anything *yet*," replied the old lady. "We need to be patient a little longer. Crimes, like novels, take time to mature."

"Actually, that's not the reason why I came." Trudi remembered her mission and nervously tugged her fingers through her hair.

"Oh?"

"Lots of things have happened." She launched into the tale Scarp's 'accident' and the fishing party and the buried box of treasure. "We wondered if you could help. You said that you knew about it."

Miss Vincent scowled in concentration. "I thought I told you not to go to the lagoon."

"The thing is," Trudi went on, regardless, "that Scarp's accident was not really an accident. I'm not supposed to know," she added hastily, "only I overheard him say. He was beaten up by three men in the wood. It's a secret. Nobody knows but Barbara."

"And you," added Miss Vincent. "And now me - and doubtless

170

your Grandfather. Knowledge has a way of slipping out round here!"

Trudi looked alarmed.

"Don't worry, I shan't let on," she promised. "We're allies, aren't we?" Then she fell silent, wrestling with some private question which she did not share. Perhaps she found the answer, for at length she roused herself and continued talking aloud: "As I said, crimes take time to mature. You had better come, yes, all of you, and bring this 'treasure', and I will tell you what I know. As for *this*," she touched the letter and then tapped her nose. "We will keep it to ourselves for the moment."

Trudi smiled and hurried back to the house. Corky's motor-bike stood parked in the street outside. The rubbish had been cleared away. What if one of the Stringers had seen her steal that letter? She glanced up, half-expecting to see Simon's face at the window, but he was not there today.

In the Larsson's kitchen, Barbara had brewed coffee. Corky, Per and Jurgen sat expectantly at the kitchen table. Cobweb lay fast asleep. There was, as yet, no sign of Scarp.

"She'll see us," Trudi announced. "She's in a good mood today."

This would be the first time Per had ventured out of the house. He put on his shoes with slow care, smoothed his beard and worked up some deep, body-shaking sighs over the absent Scarp. "It is very bad to be late..." he fretted.

"Perhaps he's..." Trudi bit back her words. Surely he couldn't be in trouble again!

"He doesn't own a watch," explained Barbara, "and his mobile is never on. It's a miracle he can find his way about at all."

For Jurgen, who could never understand why adults took so long, the waiting was a torment: "Can't I carry the box? *Can't* I? Let me just hold it. *Please!*"

Barbara thought not. "You could take your flute and show her that. She'd like that."

Jurgen scowled. He did not want to be humoured. He wanted to hold the treasure. Corky only made it worse by backing her up:

"You know a flute is more magical than gold. A flute breathes like a living thing. It can call to the spirits of plants and encourage them to grow. It can call birds out of the sky. In America the Indian hunters made special pipes, called yelpers, out of wing-bones. If they wanted to catch a turkey, they only had to make a wing-bone call and the bird would answer."

Now Per chimed in: "Yes, a flute is very useful. In the old days my people would play the flute and drum, to bring their hunters luck."

"But I'm not a hunter. What can *I* hunt?" asked Jurgen, still unconvinced.

"You can hunt for truth. Truth is the most difficult thing to track down. Takes real courage."

"That's just silly," Jurgen objected.

"No." said Korky. "It is what all true hunters seek, from stone-age flint-makers, to modern detectives. Today we are detectives, following this treasure trail. Another day, if you like, we'll make a 'yelper' and summon some birds."

Jurgen knew he was out-gunned. Adults always had an answer - knew best - saw more, because they were taller. His own longing to be the leader, the one who decided things, ended up crushed time after time and he would resort to playing the clown, just like his father, to hide his disappointment. But one day, one day he would show them all. He would discover something by himself which no one else knew - and he wouldn't share it with anyone, especially not with Trudi, who always got in first and claimed his conquests for her own. Then he would no longer be the clown, covered in mud and jam, but a proper man!

"Jurgen will come with me," said Per, guessing something of his frustration. "I need someone to steady me and Jurgen is strong - can hold my arm."

That put an end to the matter. He had a proper job.

At last, Scarp's truck came rumbling down the street. He swung out of the cab and jumped down. "Ready, are we?"

"What about your keys?" said Barbara "You're not leaving them in the ignition, are you?"

"If someone wants to steal that old heap, they're welcome, the exhaust is going."

"But all your tools! You don't want to lose them, surely!"

"Nag! Nag! Nag! Who'd live with a woman?" Scarp winked and retrieved his keys. "Happy now?"

They all proceeded next door, where the big study had been

172

prepared to receive them. Miss Vincent had driven out the birds and cleared the desk.

"Where *were* you?" Barbara hissed as they shuffled along the hall.

"Looking for something, wasn't I." If his mood was anything to go by, he had not found it.

"Can I help?"

Scarp huffed and puffed. "Maybe."

He kept his eyes down and stayed away from Corky whom he viewed with a sullen mistrust. Educated. Posh bloke. Corky, for his part, said nothing, but his eyes shone at the sight of the study. He was enjoying himself.

Miss Vincent and Per greeted one another with old-fashioned courtesy and she seated him, as guest of honour, on her buttoned, leather chair.

"Well, what have you got?"

She shot a searching look at Scarp's mutilated face. How difficult it was, having all these people together. You could sense their passions and fears sparking up against one another, like ruffled cat's fur. It made for a very prickly atmosphere. She remembered why she preferred the company of birds.

Corky set his box on the table and slowly emptied the contents. Miss Vincent seemed unsurprised to see them and counted the items off as they appeared.

"Well?"

"They are all there," she affirmed. "Beautiful, aren't they?"

"*And?*"

She paused to look round the expectant faces and gave a sigh of resignation.

"Tell us - *please*! The suspense is killing us!"

"These are *not* real Saxon jewels. Oh, they are real gold, right enough. But they are all fakes." She waited for this to sink in.

"How do you know?" asked Jurgen.

"Oh I know... because I know who made them... *and* who put them where you found them."

"Was it *you*, Miss Vincent?" asked Trudi, eyes round as saucers.

"I have the designs for them, but I did not *make* them," the old lady went on. "This is a long story, so perhaps we should sit down

173

and make ourselves more comfortable."

She crossed to the French windows, threw them open and dragged back the heavy curtains to let in more light. "Bring those chairs here. A story should be told in a circle." Per nodded approval. "And preferably on a winter's evening, but this will be a summer tale, with birdsong… Where should I begin?"

She sat with her elbows on the arms of her chair, hands clasped before her, turning the rings on her misshapen fingers, considering her best course. Should she start with the letter from the Museum? Or perhaps further back, way back in history, when this place and the whole of the county were under Saxon rule? Yes, that was as good a place as any. She would make her beginning there.

Chapter 23

What the Raven Knew

"According to legend, a man called Wulfstan was ruler here. Brave in battle and generous in peace, he was a wise judge, and a mighty hunter, unrivalled in his time. Who had not heard of Wulfstan? Of the mead-cups, the honey-wine that poured from his stores and the great tales which were told round his fires, while the deerhounds lay sleeping and the villagers rested from their daily tasks? Wulfstan's people had all they wanted: bacon in winter, herbs in spring, homespun cloth and wood for the fire. Warm thatch kept out the frost. And many were the treasures won and traded from hand to hand across the kingdom. Wulfstan brought prosperity. Why else did folk call him their loaf-keeper? After a day in the forest, he loved nothing better than to stretch out his legs and listen, while his companions boasted and taunted one another over the feats of the day. Then with a belly full of hog's flesh, and the mead flowing warm in his veins, he would set them games and contests:

"Tonight some riddles!" he would announce. "Whoever can solve a riddle will receive a ring." And there would be a roar of approval, for if the Saxons were good at anything, it was telling riddles."

"It is so with my people too," said Per, quietly nodding. Miss Vincent paused to throw him a glance, then carried on.

"On the night of my story, Aldfrith told one about the sun, and Godweord told one about a spear. And Eadric sat in his corner, racking his brains but unable to seize the answers. Eadric was Wulfstan's age, and the two men had grown up together, even resembled one another, so some folk said. Like brothers, they fought and hunted together, feasted and snored in one another's company. And Eadric was valiant, too, a marksman without match. But he had a jealous soul. The freer Wulfstan became with his wealth, the more Eadric guarded his little purse. He hungered for gold, as a hawk hungers for meat, and his heart ached every time the feast-prize went to another.

At last an old greybeard stood up.

175

"I have a teaser," he said:

"*My belly is empty*
Whatever I eat.
My hands chase my eyes;
Ruin follows my feet."

A silence descended on the company.

"Famine," called a voice, but greybeard shook his head.

"A wolf!" called another, but this was also wrong.

Wulfstan rose to his feet, well-pleased. And maybe it was the wine talking by now, for he said: "I'll raise the prize. Whoever can answer this riddle, wins my cloak-pin. Think well, my friends!"

With that he retired to bed.

Now Eadric had always admired that pin, with its bright dragon-face and red, garnet eyes. He longed, with a terrible longing, to win the jewel. But Eadric had a dark side to his soul. And since he could not solve the puzzle by honest means, he went that night to the Raven, who had magical powers. "Teach me the answer," he begged, "and I will do whatever you command."

'Raa - Raa!' said the raven. 'You must do my bidding first. Then, I promise, you will know.'

Eadric nodded eagerly.

'Go into the forest tomorrow and shoot the first creature that you see. Then you will have your wish.' And away flapped the Raven.

Eadric hugged himself with joy. This would be an easy task. He rose at dawn and entered the forest alone. The sun was just rising and the light dazzled low through the leaves. There he sat, still as a stone, till something stirred nearby. A boar, could it be? A deer? He set an arrow in his bow. Now he let the arrow fly. His arrows never missed. The invisible quarry fell. But Eadric had done a terrible thing. When he reached the place, he found it was not a deer that he had killed, but Wulfstan, his own brother in the hunt, who had come early to the woods and now lay with an iron barb through his heart.

"At that moment Eadric understood the answer to the riddle. It was GREED. Greed, which could never be satisfied, which guided men's hands towards whatever they could see, and which brought destruction in its wake. Too late now, he felt remorse for his treachery.

'Raa, Raa!' laughed the Raven from a nearby tree. 'Now you

176

know! Now you know!'

Wulfstan was buried with great honour, his spear, his shield and his drinking horn at his side. But Eadric met a dark and ignominious end. He was thrown into the black mire of the weald wood. As for that ill-fated brooch, it was lost till Sir Vivian found it, centuries later.

So much for Wulfstan. None of this would have been known but for a Saxon Christian scribe, who jotted the legend on the fly-leaf of his psalter. And there it lay, unnoticed for centuries, in the library at Tilchester cathedral. This sets the scene for our own tale of intrigue and death."

Miss Vincent looked around. "Perhaps we should have a drink of something?"

Reluctant to miss a word, Barbara slipped out, plugged in the kettle and then hovered by the door.

"Yes. Now, these baubles, here." She clasped her hands over the 'treasure' and worked her thumbs together.

"I think I mentioned before that I was taught to draw by an uncle, who lived in this house before I was born. His was a family with theatrical connections. The Bohemian fringe, I would call it. Sculptors, writers, poets came here in my grandfather's day. (Hence the photographs of the famous which I keep on my mantel-piece and which you have observed before.)

"My uncle was born deaf, but his parents lavished every attention on him, and though he never learned to speak, he developed a remarkable gift for communicating through pictures. Young Roger soon became the darling of the household with his clever ways. He possessed an unfailing memory. He could mimic any pattern on paper and his talent was not confined to drawing alone. It seemed he could he could turn his hand to any skill. Acquaintances who demonstrated crafts to amuse him were astonished to see him take up their tools and copy what they did with ease. And all his life long he remained hungry for knowledge. He it was who built up the library that you see before you. Even as a boy, he devoured books, and filled whole volumes of his own with notes and sketches. He did not waste his time on other children. They, in any case, could not understand him. Instead he lived in a world of his own imagining.

"Of course he did not go to school. The state made no provision for deaf children in those days, so the family hired private tutors and before long, Roger had mastered pretty much all they had to teach him. He would wander off on his own researches - natural history, archaeology, geology - rambling all day with his collecting jars and a simple satchel of food.

"The railway came to Tilchester in 1847 and established a tiny halt at Bockhurst Gate, but at the time that my uncle was catching his butterflies, (some time after 1900) this was still a feudal hamlet, in thrall to the local manor and surrounded by open fields. In fact, our road, Beckley Road, contained some of the first independent houses to be built here, for, although it was not then common knowledge, the local gentry were already strapped for cash and had begun to sell off parcels of their estate in a bid to pay their debts. This house and your house too, sprang up on such land. Not that that alone could halt the rot. Vain, weak and prone to panic, the de Fraiseys had chosen a course which could only lead from loss to loss. Yet I cannot help thinking they were victims of fate aswell. Many landed families were to suffer financial hardship at that time, but for the de Fraiseys, life had worse in store.

"They had pinned all their hopes on their son and heir, a boy just a few years older than my uncle. If only he could make a good match, they thought, find himself an heiress to marry, perhaps new money would save the day. They sent him to Eton and to Oxford, but alas! Edward was not interested in learning, though he was clever. He was interested in girls and parties and horses and cars. He gambled money faster than he could borrow it. And when the girls threw him over and he could no longer borrow money, I'm afraid he turned to crime."

"The pearls," said Barbara, prophetically.

"Precisely. He staged a robbery against his own mother. The family pearls were smuggled to London where a crooked jeweller broke them up."

"You've known this all along?" asked Barbara. "And never told a soul?"

"Some things are best left buried." Miss Vincent pointed a finger at the box.

"Edward crossed my uncle one day, as he wandered on de Fraisey ground and held him at gunpoint, whereupon, my uncle, unable to defend himself in words, showed him the sketches he had made. Amidst drawings of moths and seed-heads, were copies of his lapidary work, his scripts and archaeological finds. Edward gasped in astonishment. At once he recognized my uncle's talents and his mind began to devise a use for them. He had always harboured fond regrets about the Manor. He, too, dreamt of restoring the former glory... Only imagine the parties he could throw - the power he would enjoy - if he could lay his hands on some new source wealth. Perhaps this inarticulate youth could help...

"He did not shoot my Uncle Roger. Instead, he befriended him and it was not long before he visited him here in this house and witnessed the full extent of his artistic activities: paintings, etchings, woodcarving, metal-work. My uncle could do it all and showed off his work with bashful pride.

"Now Edward began to elaborate the audacious scheme which would prove his ruin.

"Amongst other heirlooms which might have gone to auction, the de Fraiseys owned an ancient brooch, which Sir Vivian had found several hundred years before. It was made of solid gold and worth a king's ransom. Yet this item could not be sold, on account of one of those good old English curses (so convenient for guide books and writers of romantic novels) which linked the brooch with the de Fraisey fortunes. If the brooch left the Manor - according to legend – the family would suffer a similar fate. Therefore this gem was housed in a special safe in the study. Whenever Edward felt tempted to sell it, as he had done with his mother's pearls, the memory of the curse would stay his hand.

"Well, the discovery of my talented Uncle Roger changed all that. Suppose, reasoned Edward, that my uncle could make a replica, exact in every detail, then that allowed for a very different plan of action. They could hide the original somewhere in the Manor - thus protecting the future of the line - announce its theft and pass off the fake on some unscrupulous collector. The Black Market lived and thrived on such transactions. Not only that. They would cash in on the attendant publicity by raising the ghost of Sir Vivian and re-creating the rest of Wulfstan's hoard.

"Roger, like the poet Chatterton, could pen an antique hand with a quill. He and Edward would fashion false documents to authenticate

179

their fakes. There would be new legends, new discoveries, new provenances to rouse a storm of interest. Item after item would be knocked down to the highest bidder and money would flow in as sure taking eggs to market.

"For all his cleverness, my uncle had no knowledge of worldly affairs. Perhaps he was gullible. More likely, he was flattered, imagining his work in great museums, and himself the darling of the society. Besides which, these forgeries would be a challenge, a positive pleasure to make. My guess is that Edward concealed the criminal nature of his plan. The scheme would be an elaborate hoax, he said, a secret game of their own. And there would be handsome rewards when the game was over. At any rate, my uncle took the bait and embarked on his research.

"They made palimpsests, rubbing down old vellum documents from the family archives and writing new letters on them using ink which my uncle prepared. In these documents, my uncle described the items which he was about to make, and he signed them in Sir Vivian's hand. The 'treasure' would be planted by the Druid Circle, just as the documents predicted. This done, they set to work on the 'finds' themselves.

"My grandparents, used to Roger's eccentric ways, certainly suspected nothing. Edward visited when they were seeing friends and the coast at home was clear.

"What I cannot verify is whether Lord and Lady de Fraisey had any knowledge of the scheme. They certainly accepted the insurance payment for the pearls. Within a few weeks, a gold snuff box, some garnet earrings, a pair of candlesticks and Wulfstan's brooch had also disappeared. Staff searched in vain for the missing pieces. Meanwhile, my uncle received the loot: most of it to be rendered down and re-fashioned; the brooch itself to be preserved and copied. And he duly began his work. He also fashioned everyday Saxon objects, beads and loom-weights, to be mixed in with the hoard, for authenticity. Just as you see them, before you.

"By this time though, the plan had run into trouble. For one thing, war had broken out. After a flurry of threats and promises the powers of Europe leapt at one another's throats, and the economies of the world spun into turmoil. As a result, the insurers stalled on issuing further payments, until a thief was apprehended. A dark cloud descended over the Manor and all who lived there, for suspicion destroys all fellowship. Everyone in the house knew something to incriminate somebody else.

"Perkins, the gardener, would have been in the best position to observe Edward's comings and goings and I think, perhaps, he saw him making his clandestine journeys here. I'm sure he knew that something odd was afoot.

"Edward volunteered early for the army and was sent up-country with his regiment. And my uncle, who could not be considered for active service, and who felt Edward's departure keenly, worked on alone, fashioning Wulfstan's grave goods with a dogged determination. He became reclusive, difficult, like an alchemist, working through the night. His family, barred from his studio, and knowing nothing of his motives, feared for his health. And all the while, events were hurtling on.

"When he returned on leave, Edward was sullen and jumpy. Perhaps the prospect of leaving for France had made him thoughtful. More likely, Perkins had spoken to him. Either way he seemed to have lost interest in the Wulfstan scheme.

"Instead of praising my uncle's progress, he ordered him, in no uncertain terms, to destroy the work he had done. Quite threatening he was, too. Well, with his creditors and the police and now a possible blackmailer on his tail, I suppose one could not blame him. He wished to distance himself as quickly as possible from the entire undertaking. The gold was to be sent to a London address. And Roger was to cease all contact until such time as it was considered safe to resume their friendship. As for Perkins, my guess is that Edward denounced him, to get him out of the way.

"At this point, my Uncle Roger began to see young de Fraisey as the parasite he was. The disappointment must have hurt, for Edward was a man of great charm and my uncle had no other friends. He certainly felt badly used.

"The night after Edward left for France, my uncle packed up all his work and buried it here in the garden. He, too, had received a visit from Perkins and he was now afraid. But the following morning, Perkins was found dead in the pool and the rest of the story you know.

"Edward lasted barely a week in the trenches and the news of his death left his parents utterly bereft. His mother turned to God, but died of the Spanish 'flu and her husband, who consoled himself with drink, ran himself and his Bentley, shortly afterwards, into a tree. Death duties wiped out what was left of the estate. The coroner pronounced a verdict of suicide on poor Perkins.

"The Manor and all its lands were sold and a distant cousin from London inherited the farm. The Sump, as you like to call it, was purchased by the Water Company, and a sewage works established on the site. Though the big trees remained, much of the land was cleared when they enlarged the main lagoon. Then forty years ago, they modernized; abandoned half the site and concentrated all their energies on the automatic plant, which is functioning still. Our end, as you know, re-wilded itself.

"As for my uncle, he was never the same again. When his parents died he lived on here alone, but all the sociable times were over for this house. Although we visited, and he was very kind to me, he locked his studio door and except for giving me lessons in drawing, never used his artistic skills again. You are wondering whether he had anything to do with Perkins' death? I have to say I do not know. It is possible that Perkins tried to blackmail him as well. It is possible that, in an attempt to throw him off, he told him the treasure was in the pool. It *is* a treacherous place..."

Corky nodded with feeling.

"But the uncle that I knew was a gentle, shining soul. He had not a grain of malice or self-interest in his being. He it was who taught me to call the birds and he who took me on expeditions to find butterflies and flints and grasses when I was young. I suppose I was a loner too and I had a knack of understanding him. My parents lived in London and when war broke out again I was sent down here for safety. A refugee. Just fourteen. Our house in Bloomsbury was bombed in the Blitz. Somehow I never went back."

Per looked up and scanned her face. The sun had swung round and lit the lines and furrows time had written there.

"I really cannot tell you very much more. The one thing I know is that my uncle did not keep the brooch. That was already hidden at the Hall. As for Perkins, perhaps poor Uncle Roger *was* involved. Perhaps the old boy really did kill himself... Perhaps the rumours are true and Edward murdered him before rejoining his regiment... Some even say that Edward did not die at all, but absconded and began a new life somewhere else. It is all sad. All past. Better left forgotten."

"So how did those fakes up in the pond?" asked Barbara, setting down the tea.

"Oh, I'm afraid that that was me." Miss Vincent stirred her cup. "Just before my uncle died, he thought better of his silence, unlocked the studio and showed me all his work. I then learnt the tale I have just told to you. But a few months ago I received a letter from the Museum at Tilchester. Some old papers relating to the de Fraiseys had come into their possession. The Museum are very keen on anything like that.

"Well, this collection contained letters by the last Lady de Fraisey, some vellum documents and a journal belonging to young Edward. The journal, in particular, caught their interest. There is mention of my uncle and hints about a venture he and Edward were pursuing together. There is also talk of the treasure. Apparently, one of the documents is a manuscript in Sir Vivian's hand, dated 1665, recounting the legend of the Wolf Stone. I have no doubt my uncle forged it.

"The Museum wanted to know about my brother and his friendship with the de Fraiseys. They wanted to see his drawings.

"I panicked, I suppose. I'm not afraid of the police, you understand, but of the *publicity*. People coming here, asking questions, frightening the birds... I have lived quietly for so many years. I dug up the box my uncle had buried, opened it with the key from his desk and checked off the contents. Then I dropped the whole thing into the lagoon. That seemed the safest place - a fitting end for it. I thought it had gone right down. I did not then know that they were planning to sell the land, or that you were going fishing!"

"But you kept the papers," said Barbara.

"I have touched nothing else. My uncle's work may have been illegal, but it is still exquisite. I thought I could destroy other evidence later if necessary."

"So your uncle made the box that he buried the treasure in, too?"

"Of course. The inscription is his - a bit of playfulness, I think - another Saxon riddle."

"And the answer?"

"Ah, that you must work out for yourselves."

"It's quite difficult to read," Barbara objected.

"Well, I think *I* could still decipher it. Old English was not my uncle's strongest point. I could hazard a rough translation."

"Oh, please!" cried Trudi.

"Let me see," she squinted askance. "'*Ic hæbbe dīegol...*' The original is in verse, which I cannot convey, so bear in mind this is something of a fudge: 'I hold a secret which no man can tell. It is more valuable than treasure. You cannot lock up this secret. And those who pursue it will lose it.'"

It sounded unsatisfactory, and though Trudi had a vague feeling that she had come across it somewhere before, she could not remember where and gave the matter up.

Barbara returned to her original question. What, exactly, should they do now? To whom did these things belong? It seemed as though any number of people might stake a claim. Corky and the children had found them. Did that give them a right? Then there was Miss Vincent. Her brother had created them. Then the Water Company owned the land where they were found. The Jacksons? Their ancestors had once possessed the gold. The Museum? That was the natural home for items of historical interest. Or the Crown? According to the law, such findings were treasure trove and belonged to the Queen. It was all so complicated.

"Should we go to the police?"

Barbara said it with a heavy heart. One look at Scarp's horrified face confirmed that his sentiments matched her own and Corky had no desire to be noticed by the authorities.

Only that morning Barbara had received troubling news that the Larssons might be back sooner than expected. They were both feeling homesick, said Kirsten, and missing the children. They thought they would sneak home a little early.

Time was running out.

"I know what *I* think," said Miss Vincent decisively. "I think we should let sleeping dogs lie. Wulfstan's burial gifts should go back where they were originally intended - underground!"

This met with silent dismay.

The old lady went on: "Whatever happens to the poor old Sump, *someone* will excavate the site before they build. The Museum will insist on that. So, *they* will find the treasure and *they* will have to

184

deal with that problem, not us."

Trudi felt a wave of disappointment. How sad to lose sight of these things again.

"But they are so beautiful!" she sighed, puckering her brow.

"Beautiful and bad!"

"Hup!" Per agreed. "Troll's gold. Never brings good luck. All the same," he reached out and touched the beads again. "I could use some of these."

"Oh those," replied Miss Vincent. "I have drawers full of those in my uncle's studio."

They followed her upstairs to a large, high-ceilinged room with an iron balcony, smothered in jasmine and Russian vine. A cool light filtered through the window. Tendrils had worked their way under the lintel and dangled irresolutely in the air.

"This is where he worked," she said, stumbling through the boxes that littered the floor.

In the muddle, they saw half-buried evidence of a kiln, a jeweller's bench, a lathe. Tools lay to hand as though ready for use: stonemason's chisels, pens for calligraphy...

"Here we are, look. He made so many trinkets when he was practising - just tin and clay. They are of no value now."

Opening a drawer, she grasped a handful and came back beaming. "A gift!"

She poured them into Per's cardigan pocket.

"Miss Vincent, we have to go home now and feed the lamb - but how can we thank you?" Barbara took the story-teller's hands in her own.

"A lamb?"

"Well, yes. We have a lamb. Well, come and see him! Let's all go back together and celebrate our criminal collusion!"

Miss Vincent didn't refuse, but she continued to reminisce as they descended the stairs.

"Of course, Edward would not have ended there. He had other plans for inscribing the Sarsen stones - that cock and bull story about the Wolf Stone. My uncle didn't approve of that. At heart, he really cared about history and art. Stones have their own souls, you know. You can't just write on them. That would be a violation."

Barbara continued her own train of thought.

185

"We've got chocolate brownies and blueberry juice. Coffee for grown-ups."

"We can do better than that, I think," old Marjorie replied. "This calls for a proper toast. Chateau Pavie '61? My uncle was a wine connoisseur, but I have never touched the stuff. There is a cellar full of bottles, down below."

Corky laughed. "Who needs gold when they have Saint Emilion?"

"Do you like it? Then you can help me bring some."

Chapter 24

Yoik!

Simon Stringer saw them trooping back, quite merry, as if they had already drunk the wine. Even Scarp and Corky had exchanged a nod or two and now seemed to accept one another. Scarp made an appreciative inspection of Corky's bike as they filed past and Trudi clung to Per's arm, though it was hard to tell whether she was propping him up, or sheltering behind him, till they were safely back indoors.

Cobweb had knocked over his box and scattered a trail of hay in all directions. His legs were now taking on a new life of their own and every so often would twitch with irrepressible convulsions. Down would go his head and up would come his rump, lifting him quite off the ground. Then he would look round in surprise before startling himself with another hop and a skip.

"Feed this baby!" demanded Miss Vincent.

"Yeah! Yeah! Scarp, you find the milk - fridge door, left-hand side. Corky, wineglasses are up there on the top shelf. There's a corkscrew in that drawer. Trudi, darling, you get the plates, and Jurgen - where is Jurgen?"

"Gone to get his flute. He wants to play it, now."

"Okay. *I* get the brownies. Per, are you all right with that lamb? Oh, I say, just look at the decades of dust on those bottles! Makes me feel a whole lot better about my housework. That's it. Kettle's on there - just push the switch. Oh no, - not for the children. Not wine..."

Trudi swung round with an indignant face: "But we helped to find the treasure. If Jurgen hadn't lost his balance, Corky wouldn't have gone in the water..."

"Oh I know, I know, honey, but this is all getting out of hand. Well, make these glasses *small* - or water them right down!"

Per hooked the lamb under one arm and gave him his milk.

"Outside!" yelled Trudi, as soon as the bottle was empty and chased Cobweb into the garden.

Barbara now had charge of the wine: "Pass this along to Miss Vincent. Corky, you've got no cake."

Jurgen reappeared with his pipe and all at once Per clapped his hands.

"A party!" he chuckled. "Jurgen, give us a tune."

"Don't know one."

"Don't need to - just play!"

He shuffled over and picked up a wooden tray. "Give me something - that thing - that porridge stirrer thing over there."

Corky's eyes lit up. Music! He quietly helped himself to couple of spoons.

"I give you a toast!" shouted Barbara, pausing to let Trudi return for her glass. "Here's to us all - and to life and friendship!"

"Cheers!"

"Skål!"

"Clonk!" Jurgen crashed his glass against Scarp's.

"Now, a tune. Let's have a proper yoik."

Softly, Per started to beat on his improvised drum. The sound came, insistent, steady, spell-binding - a murmur from the edge of the world. Then Corky's spoons began to dance in his hands - a jingle - now quiet, now sharper, now interspersed with a bell-like note or a thud as he tapped his glass - the table - his knee. Per called softly and the rhythm changed.

Trudi slipped into the rhythm. She was no longer here in Bockhurst. She was whirling along to a new beat, the drumming of hooves, the jingle of harness, the hiss of runners over gleaming ice and all around her, an infinite frozen space, a star-crowded sky. She was nowhere at all, with Grandfather Larsson driving his reindeer.

His voice broke out of his chest, deep and rich, a haunting stream of song that flowed seamlessly on, like a river, like a journey and lost itself out across the plain. So this was yoik, the Sami song that the reindeer herders of the north sang on their long migrations. This was the secret language that Professor Saxmund spoke of, which only the spirits could understand and which had been forbidden by the Scandinavian Christians, years ago. You could die for singing it in the old days. But here it was, marvellous and free!

"Jurgen, play!" commanded Per and Jurgen put his reed pipe in his mouth and blew out long notes and Per's voice wound over and

188

around them, improvising, gathering strength. Suddenly, Trudi wanted to dance. That same spark which made Cobweb twitch for joy, had touched her too and she grabbed Barbara by the hands.

"Come on!" she cried.

Barbara stumbled to her feet, and Miss Vincent caught the madness and took hold of Scarp and Scarp momentarily forgot that he was an outsider who couldn't let go. He was a little boy again, back in his grandmother's house, with his gipsy kinsfolk round him and somebody playing on the squeeze-box.

Barbara, soon puffing, out of breath, broke away and started to clap instead. So she was the first to notice Kirsten in her crisp, cool linen coat, standing silently at the door.

The kitchen lay in utter disarray. And Trudi's so-sensible mother was gazing in horror at the scene before her. It looked like a bacchanal, an orgy of excess, with characters whom she had never seen before, feasting, dancing and making free with her children, as if they had lived there all their lives. There were open wine bottles on the table, and a coal-faced lamb treading unmentionable things across the floor.

Barbara knew at a glance that nothing would save her now. She was doomed. She was finished. And the whole spirit of kinship too... She breathed an inward valediction: '*Here we go - Geronimo!*' and headed into the abyss.

"Kirsten!" Her voice rose above the din. "How marvellous!"

Trudi heard her and turned, all smiles. "Mummy, *mummy*! Come and join in." She flung herself into her mother's arms and Jurgen piled in after her.

Per stopped his yoik and put his hand across his mouth. The others stood with blank faces, rooted, speechless.

"Everyone," said Barbara, bravely forging on. "Everyone, this is Kirsten, Trudi and Jurgen's mom. Kirsten, it's so *wonderful* that you're back early. You didn't say! These are the friends we've made while you've been away. Really good friends. Erm - This is Miss Vincent, you know, from next door. And ah, - Corky, an old customer of mine from the bookshop. And - Scarp - he's..." As she floundered, Per stepped in:

"Welcome home, dear Kirsten!" He spread out his arms and Kirsten, with her glacial good manners, sailed forward, and took his hands in hers.

"Father, I'm so pleased to see you better." She smiled a smile that cut like a knife. "Well," she looked round at the assembled faces. "I'm sorry. I seem to be spoiling the party. Please don't stop for my sake. I'll - erm - take my things upstairs and then we can talk. Perhaps we could have some tea?" Even in this crisis she did not blink an eye.

"I'm coming with you!" called Trudi, clinging to her side and Kirsten laid a protective hand upon her hair.

"Yes, I'd like that," she said. And they left, with Jurgen tagging along on behind.

Trudi cast a last glance over her shoulder. Per's sleigh was out of sight now, out of earshot. No more yoiking. The authorities wouldn't allow it.

"We've got so much to tell you," she said picking up one of Kirsten's bags. "We've been having such fun."

All Barbara's hopes of concealing her crimes were now well and truly dead and she boiled the kettle with a heavy heart.

But for Kirsten, the chaos and deception were only part of the problem. If she was truthful, the thing which upset her most of all was the feeling of happiness which filled the room. It had been a shock and it made her feel like a stranger.

She supposed she was jealous and that was why she had taken Trudi away. The presents she had brought for the children from Finland seemed trivial beside the gift of laughter they had all been sharing. She did not want them to enjoy such pleasures in her absence. She wanted *her* house back, spacious and serene. She would have it too, even if the laughter had to go. Surely that was reasonable - like demanding the return of an instrument which sounded sweeter when others played it. No one could blame her for that.

Her anger with Barbara was silent and terrible. It would take little less than a miracle to make her forgive. But miracles are not unknown in tales about magic and that evening, long after Corky and Miss Vincent had departed for home and Scarp had decamped to his truck, Fate struck a lucky blow.

Sven and Professor Saxmund arrived just before supper, bringing a new guest, a student waif with a rough-cropped head of dyed, black

190

hair, and a metal stud through her tongue. And this wonder was called Birgit.

"Our plane was late, darling," said Sven, snatching a kiss from his wife. "Professor Sax is staying tonight and - er -" (this in a lower voice), "he wondered if we could look after Birgit for a couple of days." His lips were at her ear now, whispering: "Keep her out of trouble, if we can! She's a little bit unstable."

Kirsten felt her cup was full.

"Anyone else?" she demanded loudly. "Uncle Tom Cobley, for instance?"

"Kirsten?" Sven sounded disappointed. They had agreed to bury all their differences and start afresh, and he had been so looking forward to their reunion. Seeing the fury in her eye, his hopes began to fade.

"When I came back" Kirsten smouldered, "the house was in an uproar. I found a drunken riot happening right here, with farm animals traipsing round the kitchen. Now you tell me we are to become a mental asylum too. Marvellous!"

"Kirsten, please, please. We said we would make a new beginning."

"Yes, well the new one is already worse than the old one."

"Look on the good side, darling. The children are well. I don't think I have ever seen them looking brighter or happier." That was an unfortunate stroke. "And Barbara has done a wonderful job with my father." Unluckier still.

Sven gave it up. The delight which had come with Trudi's ecstatic welcome, now began to drain away. Kirsten noted it with a pang, but her pride would not let her intervene. Since she had been mortified, it seemed only fair that others should suffer too.

She felt robbed of the happy homecoming she had planned: a cosy coming-together, with the children confiding their achievements to her and she, full of loving approval, sharing all that she had seen and done. What had become of the house she had left behind? What had become of her education programmes? Barbara had stolen and corrupted them with her ridiculous tomfoolery. Now, to cap it all, she was supposed to take under her wing a vegan with a nose ring - a young earth warrior - whom even Professor Saxmund classed as a liability.

191

Once again, Trudi heard her parents arguing and shed some tears on Sticky Bear. As for Barbara, engulfed in her disaster, she took refuge in silence, all the cheery, here-goes-what-the-hell jollity knocked out of her once more. Professor Saxmund failed to raise a smile. And Per had withdrawn to the Arctic. The day dragged painfully by, with each of them locked in chilly isolation.

Birgit alone seemed to feel really at home. Oblivious to everyone around her, she perched herself on the arm of Professor Saxmund's chair, and launched into a homily on the ills of the world, which so consumed her energies, she had no time to help with anything else. Birgit's strident ego simply flattened those around her by dint of continuous battery. She never tired or hesitated. She knew the answer to every question. She had been sent to save. And save she would...

One after another, the members of the Larsson household retired from her company feeling dizzy and bruised.

Yet there was something about her which could not be denied. She had the gift of uniting people and just when it seemed they would never see eye to eye, she, single-handedly, brought them back together. By the end of the evening, they were all finally agreed.

Life with Birgit was simply a nightmare!

Chapter 25

Birgit

Breakfast proved tricky.

Birgit was an activist; a feminist, anarchist and urban rebel. Her parents lived in a nice house in Wandsworth, but Birgit had cast them off as capitalist wasters for they did not understand about greening the planet, they ate meat and they had money invested in stocks and shares. Nobody knew what her real name was. At the age of nineteen she had chosen for herself the sacred spirit-name 'Wild-fly'. This, she said, was the name used by her personal angels. But, since Northern Gods were then in fashion and friends of hers had already called themselves 'Freya' and 'Meirikhi', she had also settled on 'Birgit' for practical, everyday use. This suited her fine - Celtic, with a Scandinavian twist.

Her conversation today consisted of commentaries upon everything from her hair-dye and exercise regime, to her taste in biscuits, her adventures in Borneo and her friends, of whom there were literally thousands, spread across the expanses of the internet. She had been arrested more times than she could remember, through her membership of a group known as the 'Woodsland Warriors'; passionate activists, who obstructed chainsaws in the rain-forests of the Amazon.

"We're moving in on Siberia, next," she announced, between rye crackers. Her job was to sell the T-shirts and CDs.

She was in the second year of her botany degree with Professor Saxmund. Her boy-friend, 'Wolf-Moss' Thomas, ran the website blog for a pop group which performed Tantric Rock on Tibetan instruments.

Trudi pushed her muesli round her bowl, wondering how this calamity could have befallen them, while Barbara, white-faced, ate nothing at all. Per sat silently crumbling up his bread. Jurgen kicked out under the table but Trudi felt too upset to kick him back or give him the grin he was looking for. Somebody had put out the light - and just when they were so close to doing something really important.

After breakfast, Professor Saxmund made his excuses. He had to attend to some things at the University, but he would be back in a couple of days. And if they could just keep 'Wild-fly' out of prison until then, he would remain their eternally grateful etcetera etcetera. He gave bear hugs all round and Trudi was enveloped in the folds of his sweet-smelling jacket and emerged crumpled and smiling. "Try to keep her busy," he said. "She's all right really, just young - a bit too enthusiastic."

But Birgit needed no help from others.

When she had finished regaling the world with her personal profile, she busied herself with improving the running of the house, reorganizing the recycling, and suggesting schemes to reduce the 'carbon footprint'.

"You should run your shower water straight out into the garden - water butts aren't really efficient - I know someone who could do that for you...

"You could fit a wind turbine on that roof there...

"You know, you shouldn't throw cardboard out at all - even for recycling – you're releasing deadly PCBs...

"You could make all these boxes into houses for hedgehogs and ladybirds..."

Sven fled back to his study. Per wrapped himself in a protective coma. Barbara went to do her packing, but Trudi followed her and implored her with real tears:

"Please don't go - please. We *need* you. *Grandfather* needs you. Don't go *now*!"

"Honey, what can I do? Your mother is so mad at me, I just can't stay."

"She'll change. She'll come round. She'll do her meditation and be fine."

"She's not in a mood to meditate, Trudi - I think she's more likely to murder someone!"

"Then you must stay and protect us!" Somehow a giggle slipped out.

For the second time that day, Trudi was swallowed up in a hug, but unlike Professor Saxmund, who felt hard and tweedy, Barbara was voluptuously soft, and smelt, as only Barbara could, in these reformist times, of hairspray and patchouli.

"Is that a deal?" said Trudi, mimicking an American drawl. She had already dried her face.

"Okay sweetheart, that's a deal. Though the Lord knows how we'll do it!"

Somehow they waded through the day. Kirsten, picking up the threads of her old life, found that almost all her instructions had been ignored or flouted. Jurgen's cello was collecting dust. The piano had not been opened for weeks. The history project consisted of a title page in fancy typescript - and nothing more.

"I can't believe you have wasted so much time," she lamented, upstairs in Trudi's room. "You've got your new class in just a couple of weeks - and you promised me... I blame myself. I should never have gone away." Trudi bit her lip. She couldn't begin to explain how much had happened and how much she had learnt in that time.

"I'm going to town to get some things. Are you coming with me?"

Trudi looked away and shook her head.

"Oh, like that, is it? Well, I'm going anyway. I can't stand another minute in this house." She stood for a moment in front of the mirror, collecting herself, then walked out, took four paces along the landing and opened Sven's study door:

"I'm taking the car. Going to Tilchester. Is there anything you want?"

Sven looked up. "Yes, plenty, but you won't find it there." His eyes were eloquent but his voice sounded flat: "Actually, I'm not sure if you will get there. The car was playing up yesterday. Starter motor."

"I'll get there," said Kirsten. "Back for tea."

Sven made one last attempt at reason. "You know, you shouldn't take things so hard. Really, darling. I agree they made a mess - but - well - we did leave them to it."

Kirsten, however, was in no mood to be placated. Still furious, she spread her fingers like a starfish and pressed them against the side of the bookcase. When she replied, she looked at them, not him.

"Do I have to endure lectures even from you? That girl down there is telling me how to save energy. *Me*! It is bad enough that the children have frittered their summer away and things have got into

195

such a muddle. But at least Barbara had the good grace to wait till I was gone before she vandalized my home. Birgit is doing it under my nose! She has stepped into my shoes and is strutting about as if she owned the place!"

Sven opened his mouth but Kirsten had not finished.

"Do you remember? *I* am the one who is vegetarian, who drinks herbal tea, who does yoga, who cares about the planet... ?" Her words sounded childish and petulant, but she no longer cared.

"Kirsten," Sven managed at last. "It's for two days. She doesn't really mean any harm. She's just young and - well, she's probably insecure. Don't you remember being young and laying down the law?"

"No, actually, I don't!"

"Let Barbara work her magic on her. She'll bring her round."

"Oh yes!" Kirsten's bitterness bubbled over. "That would be the magic that has bewitched the whole house, I suppose - or am I getting confused with the spells your father concocts in the kitchen sink! Barbara's 'magic' has filled our home with freaks and gangsters. Sven, we had a tramp living upstairs! Don't you understand? All the rules we live by, the rules which are there to protect our children, have been deliberately undermined and now, to add insult to injury, I have this Birgit scolding me because my fridge is full of fat. *I* didn't put it there! I didn't put that lamb's bottle in there either! Have they no idea of hygiene at all?"

The words continued to drop like acid, but Kirsten stopped staring at her hand, and looked up, hoping, perhaps, for a response. If so, she was disappointed. Sven had withdrawn into silence and the moment passed.

"I'll see you later," she said and turned away.

At the kitchen she flashed a smile, brittle as a mask, and Barbara nodded meekly back: "Anything I can do?"

What was the use?

Kirsten's lovely eyes rested on her for a moment. Here was her oldest, her dearest, her poor, recently-bereaved, and utterly contrite friend, yet, though she pitied her, she could not reach out to her.

"No, no, thanks. You've done enough, really." She swept out of the house on a wave of impatience.

Get away. She must get away quickly now. Find the soothing

anonymity of the town, where she could forget that she had been so mean...

But Sven, alas, was right. The car was going nowhere.

Kirsten tried the key in the ignition over and over again. She beat her fists on the steering wheel, but nothing worked. A dull clicking indicated that some vital, inner connection was broken. Useless, stupid car! Stupid world! And not only stupid, but unfair. Why give up the ghost just *now*? If she could only get to Tilchester, she would not mind breaking down. But to be stuck *here*...! She almost wept with frustration. And all the while, that unnerving child was staring at her from the landing window next door.

She must think of something to do, for she certainly could not go back into the house and admit defeat. Birgit would be sure to have a friend who was the best mechanic in the world... And then Birgit would be tutting, anyway, about wasting petrol on a whim of a journey. Barbara would probably think it served her right, after her recent rudeness. Even Trudi had deserted her... The accumulated anxieties and frustrations of the last few weeks burst upon her fragile heart and swallowed her up so completely that the voice at her ear gave her a violent start.

"Need a hand?" She almost screamed, seeing Scarp's battered face so close to her own.

"No - absolutely not!" she replied, wincing at her own abruptness and regretting that she had left the window down. "Thank you, all the same."

"I wouldn't have come back," Scarp apologized, but I promised to bring milk for the lamb - for Trudi. I've got it in my truck." A pause. "I could fix that for you if you wanted. It's my job."

Could there be anything in the world more humiliating than to accept help from this creature, with his gold earrings and his snake tattoo wriggling out of his vest? He grimaced, waiting for an answer, then shrugged. Would he never go away? He was virtually leaning on the car. Now he laid an arm across the roof, his arm-pit distressingly near her face. He was working up the courage to say more.

"It wasn't her fault, you know." At last he found his tongue. "Barbara. She's done everything she could for your kids - and the old man, too. She's just kind, that's all. She reaches out to people.

197

Even," he snorted, "even no-hopers like me. That's her only crime... And they've just *lived* for you coming back. They were planning a special cake and everything..." Kirsten stared ahead, impassive. "The lamb was *my* fault. I thought the kids would like it and, well, it was going to die. The owners didn't want it and I couldn't keep it. They've been brilliant, bringing it on. They're really bright kids."

"I know *that*," said Kirsten, biting back her tears. She had never felt so out of sorts. But there is no sticky bear for adults who want to cry, even though they feel rage and shame, just like children.

"Please *stop!*" She forced herself to look him in the eye. Did he have any idea how brave or foolhardy he had been? "Can you imagine what it is like to come home and find everything that is most precious to you turned upside down?"

Scarp scratched his head. "Funny you should ask that."

"Pardon?"

"No. No I haven't - not in the sense you mean. I mean, I don't have a home in the sense you mean. But I *can* fix your car - and I'd like to - to try and make amends."

Kirsten weighed her options. For a moment she pictured herself, proud and foolish, winding up the window and waving him away. Then going in - running the gauntlet of *them* indoors. Stewing in her room. Submitting to more advice from Birgit... Impossible! The alternative? Let go and put herself at the mercy of a stranger.

A weather-front of emotion crossed her face. At length, eyes closed, she admitted defeat and handed him the keys. She was tired, she decided. She would rather someone else took charge.

"Hop over!" he commanded, pulling open the door and Kirsten did as she was told. "Let's get the bonnet up. I'll fetch my tools."

She watched him bobbing about, checking over the connections, like a medic testing a pulse. That hurt? That? He was all tenderness, listening, probing, and then suddenly spurred to action - a man perfectly attuned to his task - a strangely moving sight. Here was a master-craftsman of sorts - and the notion touched a nerve, for it was just what she had thought when she first saw Sven, mending a puncture on a rainy mountain road. Inside her, the ghost of the young Kirsten, who had kicked off her shoes and paddled there beside him, flickered back to life.

Scarp struck the starter motor with a hammer.

"Try her now!" he shouted, rocking the car, and she slid into the driver's seat. The engine started effortlessly. Scarp beamed and showed a filthy thumb.

"I'm afraid I've been very unfair," said Kirsten when he reappeared.

"'S all right."

"No. Not all right."

"It's your house." He was wiping his hands on his vest.

"My house - my husband - my children - my friend. You know, you can have so many things you have nothing at all - like a child with too many toys."

"Yeah, I've never had that problem."

"Please come back and have some coffee. You have saved me from doing something very stupid." Kirsten got out of the car and planted a kiss on Scarp's astonished cheek.

Yes! She looked round, remembering that this was a public place. *I don't care who sees. For once, I just don't care!* She tossed her head at Simon Stringer and led the way indoors.

* * * * *

For Trudi, her parents' return had come as a serious blow. Her plans and schemes, all those matters, which had filled her mind so urgently for weeks, felt suddenly cut off, without prospect of renewal. Miss Vincent had retired and firmly closed her door. Per had put away his drum. Nobody knew if they would ever see Scarp or Corky again. And Barbara was a helpless onlooker. The question of the treasure and the Sump and the forest garden and the thugs - not to mention the shaman's magic - these would never now be resolved. Instead, the days would be eaten up with homework and before anyone knew it, the holidays would be over and she and Jurgen would be posted back to school... The whole thing came as a bitter disappointment.

To cap it all there was Birgit, with her black eye-liner and her sea-grass sandals, monopolizing everything: first the kitchen, then the computer, then the lamb. Now she had heard about the Sump and she knew exactly what to do with that. She would get 'Wolf Moss' to post details on his website blog, call on the Woodsland Warriors and stage a protest. They would hold a sit-in - get the Media involved. She knew plenty of anarchists who would stand up to the Water Company. She seemed unstoppable. And Trudi, an infant whom Birgit hardly noticed, could say nothing, because Birgit was 'special', was vulnerable, and Professor Saxmund had told them all to be nice to her. Trudi seethed with the injustice of it all. What had happened to the good magic Per had promised when her parents came back home?

She waited till she was alone with her grandfather and poured out her troubled heart.

Per listened, rubbing his brow with his hand.

"Trudi, Trudi, magic is not so easy. Magic is," he looked up, searching for the words, "like lightning. You cannot see which way it will go - where it will strike - until it actually comes. Can be dangerous, too. You know, the old Sami doctors used magic to heal the sick. Sometimes a healer would take all the illness out of a man - and then die himself. Magic cannot be rushed. You have to wait - wait for the right moment, like a skilful hunter. You remember your bow? When you hunt with a bow, it is not the animal you aim at, but truth. If you shoot true your arrow will fly home. Even if you cannot see where it goes."

"But it's already too late," cried Trudi. "All the things that mattered have been taken over or spoilt. Who is going to bury the treasure now, or water Corky's flowers, or mend Scarp's caravan, or call the birds...? The Sump was magical because it was 'Nowhere'. Nobody wanted it. It was free. Now there are so many people and they all want to have it and organize it - and there is nowhere left to be 'Nowhere' any more. Everybody knows about it. The whole *world* will know when Birgit brings her friends. And what was ours and special and secret will be just common nothing".

"Nowhere," said Per solemnly, taking hold of Trudi's hands, - and she noticed with surprise that his fingers were warm. "Nowhere is not out there - it is in here." He put her hands on his heart. "And no one can take it from you. This summer is not over and our work is still to do. You must be patient and brave till the time comes. Can you do that?"

Half terrified but exhilarated too, Trudi promised through her tears.

"Then let us see." He kissed her on the forehead. "Bright eyes! No tears now - the others are coming. Remember!"

When Kirsten and Scarp walked in, the kitchen seemed busy again and Birgit was still holding forth: how everyone should drink six pints of water and walk at least 9000 paces a day - how it would be better to give up wearing shoes and receive the influences of the earth's vibrations through your feet. The sight of Scarp gave her a new impetus. He looked like a Woodsland Warrior - one of *her* people - and she launched into an effusive welcome and disquisition on the merits of camping.

Scarp looked nonplussed, but Kirsten had retaken the initiative and seemed to know what to do. She gave Barbara a squeeze on the way to the kettle and announced in a loud voice:

"Caffeine anyone? And Brownies! Where are those wicked brownies? But I think we should have them with cream - don't you? Trudi, run and fetch daddy. Tell him we're having coffee now - and cake! He *must* come. And then you can help Scarp mix up the new milk for the lamb."

"Oh *I* can do that," said Birgit. "I worked at a vet's for my summer holidays last year."

Kirsten ignored her and added imperially: "*With Jurgen!*"

That was as good as declaring war and Birgit would not forget it. But Kirsten kept going. "Grandfather, how will you have your coffee, strong and black? And Barbara - cappuccino? You know we have a proper machine - or do you prefer to be a purist with your coffee pot?"

"Anyhow, honey. Just as it comes," said Barbara, holding her breath.

"And Scarp?"

"Black please - three sugars."

"Let's sit in the garden - it will be more relaxing and we can be with the lamb. Just water for you, Birgit?"

She had taken the wind right out of Birgit's sails. Really it was wonderful to see, and Birgit, who felt a headache suddenly coming on, passed a puzzled Sven on the stairs and spent the next half hour texting her friends in her room.

A snatch of chaos had crept back into their lives and with it, a little bit of merriment too. The new ewe's milk, more nourishing than the last, threw Cobweb into raptures. Scarp had bought a proper teat for the bottle and the lamb sucked so hard, the milk ran down his chin, while his eyes rolled and all four legs floundered. Even Kirsten laughed in delight. Wherever the children went, Cobweb now followed. When they ran, he ran, kicking sideways and skittering at shadows.

Beor heard them and lunged at the fence, but he gave only one or two strenuous barks and did not jump up. Instead he satisfied himself with gargling and prowling back and forth.

Trudi looked up in surprise.

"What's happened?"

"Perhaps they have tied him up," suggested Sven, but Per dismissed this, shaking his head.

Scarp crept up to the fence and put his eye to a knot-hole. Beor stood just a few feet away, his magnificent body straining to attention, huge paws firmly planted, and tail whisking back and forth.

"Nope!" he reported. "No tether, but he is wearing a big collar. Perhaps they've rigged up an electric boundary. You know, if he crosses the line, the collar gives him a shock. That would stop him jumping."

"Well, that will help," said Kirsten.

Per looked grave. "Bad thing to do," he muttered. "It will madden him more."

"Let's enjoy the peace while we can."

Kirsten made another round with the coffee. Gradually, conversation eased over the rifts and ruptures of the day. They talked of Jackson's harvest, of Helsinki - of crocodiles - the sun passed through the web of voices and the fretwork of summer leaves. Birgit reappeared and sat down on the grass, hugging her knees.

She looked resentfully at Kirsten, so effortlessly making an art of living. But then everybody looked at Kirsten - they could not help themselves. Sven could not take his eyes off her. Only that morning Birgit had felt quite affectionate towards her, adopting her as an amiable mother-figure. But how quickly that had changed. Kirsten had laughed at her and wounded her spirit and for Birgit, that meant daggers drawn. Kirsten seemed to relish the prospect.

"Scarp you *will* stay for supper, won't you? We've got sausages."

"You don't *eat* sausages!" objected Barbara.

Kirsten smiled. "I do today."

When Birgit crept off for a smoke, Kirsten followed her and settled herself nearby. Birgit saw her chance.

"Like one?" she challenged.

In a move which surprised her, Kirsten accepted the offer. She might as well burn all her boats and prove she was no better than the rest. She was tired of being superior; beyond reproach. Somewhere inside her, she felt the stirrings of a self long forgotten, a youthful rebel, who had kicked her way to maturity, and now provided a glimpse into Birgit's soul. In those far off days, the magic had been easy. A flash of wit and wickedness were all it took to dazzle friend or foe...

Birgit handed her the tin. She was making roll-ups, teasing out shreds of tobacco, but Kirsten, who had never smoked before, ducked that part.

"You do one for me," she said. "I never liked licking the paper."

Birgit shrugged and applied herself, handing over an article still wet with spit.

Kirsten looked at it and swallowed hard.

"Do you do this because you're angry?" she asked, squinting at the proffered match.

"I suppose so."

"What is the point of drinking all that water to stay alive and then killing yourself with this?"

Her antagonist shrugged again. "It's cool."

Kirsten inhaled and spat out the loose tobacco. She had an overwhelming desire to choke, but she must not lose face now. The blue smoke drifted away. How did one hold these things? Between the fingers, or between finger and thumb? Technique was all. Then there was the question of ash. Should you dispatch it with a flick, or tap it gently? Neither method seemed to work. This cigarette was too flimsy.

Birgit turned away to make another for herself.

"You're not really enjoying that, are you?" She might score a point, but Kirsten held on tight.

"It just doesn't seem very strong," she lied. "Must have been different in the old days."

Despite her ironmongery, Birgit had a pretty face: fine lips and wide, baby-doll eyes which gazed out innocently through their mascara. Whatever in the world had made her so fierce and defensive? Not just a passion to save the planet, surely. Kirsten recognized something familiar in her - an anxiety - a trying-too-hard which chimed with her own embattled state. Fear, was it? What were they both afraid of? Life was like a grand masked ball where everyone had to second-guess their neighbour.

Did Birgit sense it, too? For these few moments they shared an uneasy truce - outcasts together; then finished their smoke in silence before rejoining the others. They did not yet have an understanding, but there had been a shift. Kirsten now knew what she must do.

Once back at the house, she put on a fine performance: flirted generally, sharing a private joke with Barbara, patting Scarp on the shoulder, leaning over to whisper something in Per's ear. She was tender and affectionate to the children; bright with Birgit. Only Sven, it seemed, missed out. Pretending not to see him, she lavished the attentions intended for him, upon everybody else, while he watched open-mouthed. He had seen one Kirsten go out of the door and another come back in and he recognized this one - this coquette, who now turned her back so mischievously. *She* was the woman he had fallen in love with, all those years ago, before life made her hard. Whatever had brought her back?

Birgit renewed hostilities straightaway. She insisted on cooking her supper in separate pots. She was thinking of giving up veganism, she announced, and living only on produce from living plants. That way she could live a truly blameless life. She didn't know how people could bear to pollute their bodies, eating meat. Didn't they feel ashamed when they looked at little Cobweb? As for Scarp's caravan - all her friends would be able to help. She knew a master-carpenter …

Kirsten pricked up her ears. "But Sven here is a master-carpenter!" she exclaimed. "He made all these shelves and cupboards to his own design. *We* can help with the caravan. No need to trouble other people!"

"Scarp won't have it," said Barbara dryly. "People *have* offered. Miss Vincent even promised you some of her china."

Scarp grinned. "Can you see me drinking out of that?"

204

"Yeah! I can!" retorted Barbara. "With your little finger stuck right up in the air!"

"*I* can make curtains," Kirsten persisted.

"Scarp, you should accept this kindness," said Per. "Many hands, you know …"

"Then there's Corky," added Barbara. "He'd fix you up a wind pump."

Birgit saw her chance: "I've got a friend who runs a solar technology company."

Trudi and Jurgen drifted away.

At one point, Per caught hold of Scarp's arm and pulled him close.

"Did you get it?" he whispered.

Scarp looked around. "Not yet."

"Get what?" asked Birgit, butting in.

Both men stared.

"Get what," she continued unabashed. "I might be able to help."

"I doubt it," said Scarp. "We want a hide for a drum."

"Oh, no problem." Birgit stretched out her many-bangled arms. "Wolf Moss will know. They use sacred drums all the time in the band. In fact we know several shaman drummers. We're in a kind of drummers' forum. We meet at special festivals and pagan rites, you know - an organic brotherhood."

"And tell me," asked Kirsten, closing in. "How does a fruitarian manage to bang a drum with a hide?"

Birgit swiped back. "Polypropylene. All the best drums are plastic these days."

"I'll keep trying." Scarp squeezed Per's arm and moved away.

But Kirsten's blood was up. "I've got something," she said and disappeared upstairs.

"Why do you need to *make* a drum?" asked Birgit. "You can get them really cheap on the internet."

Per was smiling now. "For a shaman's rite, of course. Why else?"

An awkward silence fell and finally Birgit laughed: "Oh yes, of course!" They laughed politely, too.

"Jurgen's putting together a one-man-band," explained Barbara, trying to smooth things over.

"Oh, he *must* talk to Wolf Moss. Wolf can teach him so much!"

There was simply no stopping her and they all let it go.

When Kirsten returned, she was holding a buckskin waistcoat.

"Dear Sven brought this for me from Wyoming - one of his trips. But I've never actually worn it. It isn't properly cured - distinctly smelly. And it doesn't fit my vegetarian image." She winked. "But you can cut it up - do what you like, can't he Sven? *Can* you use it, Grandfather?"

Per took the garment in his hands and tested it for suppleness and strength.

"Ya! Ya, Kirsten, thank you. This is good! Very good!"

"You make as much mess as you like. Finish it!" she commanded.

Finally, Sven caught up with her on the stairs. "Kirsten?"

"Yes?"

"You - " he choked in disbelief. "You smell like a *bonfire!*"

"Oh, that!" She gave a knowing smile.

"I don't know what you're up to," he lectured sternly, taking hold of her wrists. "But, whatever you do, don't stop."

"It's not me," she replied. "Something in the air."

"Barbara's magic?"

"If you like."

"It's outrageous! You - smoking!"

"Shan't do it again." She wriggled. "It stinks."

"And *sausages!*"

She shrugged.

"I'll never understand you, but please, please don't change again. You are such fun like this - I might even ask you to marry me!" He tried to kiss her, but she broke free, laughing.

"Cure Birgit first!" she insisted.

What was it Per had said? Magic was like lightning. You couldn't tell which path it would take. As it happened, Kirsten did not have to do any more. Something else changed Birgit - and something no one could have predicted.

At eight o'clock Hubert Jackson appeared, towering, bronzed and tired from a long day in the sun. He had cut two fields, yet his hair shone sleek, his hands were clean. He was looking for Scarp, who hadn't answered his phone all day. He'd hit a stone with the combine, and needed help to fix it. Scarp, his mouth full of sausage, muttered an apology.

Hubert gave jovial greetings all round, cracked jokes, declined food, promised to return another time and clipped Scarp affectionately on the head.

After they left, the conversation flowed on, but Birgit stayed transfixed.

"What was *that*?" she said, at length.

"*That*," replied Barbara, pointing her fork and gazing with a lovelorn smile, "was Adonis."

"*Who*?"

"Oh, don't worry, - it's ancient Greek. To you and me, girl, let's just say - A HUNK!"

Chapter 26

Home, Sweet Home!

Trudi had pictured Scarp's caravan to herself many times during the last few days. Though she had never actually seen it, she knew what caravans were like and this one, she decided, was an old-fashioned tourer, pinky-cream and stained with algae where it stood beneath the trees. Inside it would be damp. The windows leaked and the lino was chipped. Scarp had crammed the inside with furniture from junk shops. They would have to bring all those things out before they could get the van back on its wheels and in her mind she saw Scarp's saucepans and tins of soup, his radio, his slippers, all neatly lined up on the grass.

Harvest had been interrupted until a new part for the threshing drum came through, so, the next day being fine and the men therefore free, it was generally decided that this would be a good time to salvage the wreck. There would, of course, be a picnic too. Another excuse for a party.

A message was duly sent to Corky, telling him to join them if he was able. Barbara and Kirsten prepared a lunch. Sven disappeared into the shed to sort out some tools, and Trudi and Jurgen hung about, hindering everybody. Birgit, once her nose was out of joint, had renounced any desire to be involved, but when she heard that Hubert was coming, she brightened up, put on her commando trousers and reported for duty. So much for all of them.

Relishing the prospect of some time alone, Per settled in his corner of the kitchen with a box of threads from Kirsten's workroom.

Today it seemed best to avoid the Sump and the rescue party squeezed inside Sven's car and drove to Jackson's farm. Scarp met them at the gate, leading the way on foot, and whacking the roadside hogweeds with a stick. "Mind the ruts! Pothole!" He was feeling confident today. Here was the farmyard with its huddle of buildings. And there, old Jackson himself, waving hello. They saw him stooping, shading his eyes with his hand - grey-haired, dungareed and touchingly dwarfed by his son.

208

The rough track carried on, past another cornfield, then took a turn to the left. Directly ahead lay the outline of the Sump and there, beneath some trees, the remains of the caravan.

With a surge of excitement, Trudi realized that she had imagined it all wrong, for this was no tinny holiday camper, but a proper gypsy vardo; a wooden bow-top with a turquoise tarpaulin, sprawling, like a dying horse - its ribs all sticking out.

"Oh, but it's beautiful! It's *beautiful!*" she squealed, struggling to get out of the car.

"Well, Mr. Scarp," Barbara put her hands on her hips. "Aren't you just full of surprises!"

"I've got a friend who restores all these…" began Birgit, but seeing Hubert striding towards them, she forgot her friend and the Larssons exchanged thankful smiles.

Scarp, gave them a conducted tour. He had mastered a momentary fit of embarrassment and now took pleasure in pointing things out. Perhaps four men, with long poles, could lever the undercarriage? With any luck, the whole structure could be raised without breaking up. Some of the hoops had snapped and were poking through tears in the canvas and the glass in the door had shattered - but otherwise things did not look too bad. Landing on the brambles that grew nearby had luckily softened the fall. Everything inside, however, was smashed - Hubert thought *that* seemed deliberate - and subsequent rain had done further damage. Scarp did not appear to have many possessions, though he had rescued some personal treasures - his flints, some old clay pipes, cast iron cooking pots and a set of harness bells. These now lay, stacked in a wooden crate. Everything else had been flung into the cab of his truck.

Even at this early hour, the field had begun to bake and high swallows sliced the air, hunting for flies. Below, the stubble lay parched, shimmering under the webs of thousands of gossamer spiders. Candy-pink convolvulus straggled in the headlands. This was dry country - a progressive farm - and summer flowers were scarce. A cloud of dust on the horizon announced Corky's arrival on his bike.

"Half a helper, at your sevice," he announced, shaking Sven's hand, then Hubert's and nodding all round. "Not much muscle, but plenty of enthusiasm!"

209

If Corky was fit enough to help, Birgit decided, so was she, and she took her place next to Hubert to prove her mettle with the men. Barbara and Kirsten, who had no intention of getting involved, exchanged knowing smiles.

"You kids stay away!" ordered Barbara.

Now that she was forgiven, she was beginning to sound like Barbara again. "Go exploring - or come and help us."

That meant catering. The children scampered off.

In the distance, they could hear the men debating: should they rope the chassis and all try heaving together? Or prop whatever they could and shove with their shoulders? Or try both ways? Or think of something else? In the event, Corky proved himself worth *two* whole men, his engineering mind knowing instinctively just how much pressure to apply and where to apply it and the team trustingly followed his directions, though it seemed a gamble to do so. At one point it looked as though the whole contraption would fall apart. The canvas top sagged horribly and all the joints strained and creaked, as gravity took its toll. Then the weight began to shift. The vardo picked up momentum and they had to stop pulling and push for all they were worth to stop it crashing down.

"Mind your hands!"

"Get away from that side now!"

"Easy does it!"

The shouts rang through the trees.

"If it comes down wrong, it will kill them, you know," said Barbara, calmly setting out sandwiches.

Kirsten had been assessing the damage to the canvas. Of course it would all have to come off to be mended. She thought, with a smile, of the fancy materials she used for her professional 'creations' - all that went by the name of 'design' in Helsinki. This, by comparison, would be a bodge of a job, economy patching and darning, though both were only sewing, after all. Today the darning seemed more companionable.

A final cheer went up.

"They've done it!" said Trudi. "Come on!" and they hurried back to the camp.

She was right. The caravan was up. It looked surprisingly high off the ground - still rather a wreck - but *up*, and, with its chimney pipe and jolly, red paint, presented a homely and inviting appearance.

Scarp leapt onto the front ledge and let himself in. The others waited respectfully while he rooted about inside but his face quickly reappeared at the door. "What a bloody disaster!" he grinned. "Thanks, all of you. You've been true mates. You must come back when I've sorted myself out a bit and I'll cook for you. I'll show you what a real feast is!"

"Coffee?" Barbara had a flask to hand, though no one was listening. They wanted to see inside the van.

"I spent half my childhood here," said Hubert wistfully. "I used to scramble through my homework and then Scarp would help me with my ferrets."

"*Ferrets?*" cried Birgit. "You kept *ferrets*? That has to be one of the *grossest* things anyone can do! Keeping ferrets should be banned by law."

Barbara smiled in delight. She had found herself a log to sit on and was rocking gently back and forth. Now this was real company - all sparky and complex and no one would ever iron out the wrinkles - not even Tod, whose ghost was standing over there, quietly inspecting the caravan door.

"Who did the scrollwork?" she asked on his behalf.

"*I* did," Scarp's face looked suitably smug. "My uncle taught me."

"Have you still got family on the road?"

"Nah. Only part of my family was gypsy and they lived in the council houses at Newbridge. My granny..." he buttoned his lips, deciding not to go on."

"But you've got a big family?"

"Yeah. Yeah. Don't see them much. My sister works in the garden centre at Tilchester."

What happened? wondered Barbara. *Did they get on in the world and leave the young hoodlum behind?* She could see why Marylin Jackson, grooming Hubert for girls from the gymkana, might have reservations about Scarp. *Were his own family the same? Getting on in the world could cause a lot of trouble.*

Scarp had fished out a wooden ladder, also painted red.

"Coming up, kids?"

Such days should last in the memory forever. After lunch, Trudi lazed on the ground, with her arms behind her head, letting the hum of conversation flow over her. Nothing mattered for the moment, but the immediate reality of this grass with its shiny beetles hurrying to and fro, and the distant prospect of sky and trees. Her former world, the world of lessons and projects, seemed impossibly far away. Shifting leaf-shadows here were the only measure of time. And this wasn't wasting time; it was *making* it. Hours, minutes, merged into a continuity - a magical state she felt she knew from long ago and her only fear was that she would lose the way here again.

They collected sticks and lit the stove - the 'queenie', as the gypsies called it - to see if it had cracked in the fall. This was a dainty piece of ironwork with an open grate and decorative legs. The hob would heat a kettle, or boil a stew and keep toes warm in winter. The flue went out through a metal plate in the roof and was capped with a conical top, which made it weatherproof.

"They spent most of their lives outside," Scarp was saying. "Women and children slept in the vans, the men camped underneath. A mate of mine built this one, years ago and then didn't have anywhere to put it, so I bought it. Hubert would have been about 6 years old when I came here."

The stove had miraculously survived, and a ribbon of smoke now curled up into the trees, adding a fragrant bite to the air. How could one explain the deliciousness of hearth-smoke? It smelt of kinship and safety and hope and comfort and had done so through all ages and all cultures. The smoke of war, that smelt of burning lives, but this was a peace-fire to bring free minds together.

"So, what about the pheasants?" asked Hubert, changing the subject.

"They're still about, some of them. I've picked up dead ones, but I've spotted others, in the hedgerows."

"It's obscene," said Birgit. "Raising birds to kill them."

Hubert looked hurt. He genuinely loved his pheasants, both in the wood and on his plate. Life was simple for him. He didn't have ethical complications.

Opinion split and the conversation blew hot and cold. Trudi wanted the pheasants to stay wild - she had always thought the pens were sinister. If freedom meant death, was that better than being safely confined? She remembered Miss Vincent's words and then

212

she thought of Beor, now chafed by his electric collar. Life was full of fences. Some you could see and some you could not, but they rarely made you feel any safer. In many ways they made things worse. Per did not like them. "Fences," he said once, shaking his head. "There were none in Samiland years ago. The Arctic was free. Now roads and fences are cutting it up. The old routes, the old ways, are broken. Borders! Passes! Explain that to a reindeer." Trudi knew already that fear came from inside. The times when she felt most free were also times when she was taking risks. And forbidden ground like the Sump was a good place to test your courage. For a moment she recalled her sketching-trip with Miss Vincent; the vision of the lichen tuft.

She tried to imagine life as Per had known it: a waste, a forest without limits, where wolves might come and snow, and tempest. Instinctively she felt for the bow he had made her. Since the night she outfaced the *kelet*, she had neither seen nor heard from them again. They had abandoned her. And she did not know whether it was the power of amulet, or her own sudden determination which had frightened them away. She wondered where they had gone to now. She almost felt sorry to have lost them. But of one thing she was certain - the hunter's bow made a difference. It drew a vital connection between life and death - figures in the sun and those in shadow. She couldn't quite work it out. Wild animals walked a precarious path. At any moment their lives could be snuffed out, but they did not seem to mind. They never wanted to be caught and saved. Perhaps gypsies were the same? She felt her own soul's craving to take wing and fly.

On the other side of life, there lay another world entirely – the world of Pumpkin, curled asleep beneath his tree... No, she could not work it out.

When she next took note, the conversation had moved on.

"Sowing and reaping," Corky said. "The problem with our modern way of living is that the giving and taking is out of balance. Today we take a great deal from the Earth: our food, our fuel, our water, our habitation... But we don't give much back that the world can use." He was warming to a well-loved subject, and his voice gathered pace. "In Nature everything belongs to someone. Even the things which disgust us - poop - corpses - fungus - It's all either

213

somebody's dinner, or somebody's home."

"Keep your eyes off my van!" said Scarp irreverently.

Corky smiled but carried on: "That way nothing stays still. The whole planet is forever reinventing itself. The molecule which is in a blade of grass, goes, in time, through the cow, the dung-fly, the swallow, the hawk and finally falls back to earth where it will make compost for more grass. We are the only ones who don't follow the rules. We bury our rubbish, or send it out to sea, where it can't return to its source. We take natural materials and convert them into indestructible things that clutter the planet. Our water escapes. Our soil blows away." He looked, for a moment, at the parched stubble field. "It could be so different. Killing one bird here or there is not such a sin. We are all destined to die and birds are made of very good meat! Taking the wood the birds live in - that's another matter. That kills them all. We just need to do better maths."

Sven closed his eyes. Self-appointed experts were generally bores, but Corky had the gift of self-deprecation, and he was enjoying this little lecture in a subject which was properly his own.

For once, even Birgit forgot to interrupt. She sat deep in thought, doing some mental calculations of her own.

"So I'm allowed to hunt, then?" said Hubert cocking an eyebrow.

"Man has always been a hunter," Corky hadn't finished. "If he doesn't hunt animals, he hunts other things. The problem is we are just too successful and don't know when to stop. Primitive people with primitive tools, take what they need and leave a bit for later. Industrial man wants and takes it all. Those of us who care, turn away from cruelty or greed, but we fool ourselves if we think we can live detached from the cut and thrust of Nature. A hunter has to know his prey, watch it, love it. That is why, in old tribal ceremonies, the dancers often dress in animal skins, to touch the spirits of the creatures which they kill. Knowing the spirit brings respect - a kind of thanksgiving for the gift of life. When our meat is pre-packaged in the supermarket, we cannot see the animal - feel the connection. The cheetah and the antelope know one another - preserve one another."

"Of course it doesn't quite work like that commercially," said Scarp.

"Commercially nothing works like that," said Corky. "The drive for profit destroys every principle of balance. Profit is theft in nature. That's why squirrels forget where they have hidden things - so that others can find them!"

"And that's why I'm an anarchist," said Birgit, calmly picking a leaf out of her sandal and admiring her toes. "I would abolish money altogether." She looked up innocently into the face of a stranger who had joined the group.

Marilyn Jackson stared back.

"Hubert, I was looking for you," she said, eyeing the company, and Birgit in particular, with disfavour. "Weatherby's have rung up. They've got the part for the combine. I don't know why I couldn't get hold of you. I tried to phone!"

Marilyn was fifty-five, with dyed, auburn hair and hard cheek-bones. She had a leathery appearance from much baking in the sun, but she had kept her figure. From behind, you might have guessed she was thirty. She wore a skimpy summer top and riding slacks and her shoulders were covered in freckles. Trudi marvelled at the quantity of gold jewellery she wore: necklaces, bracelets, rings, earrings... Kirsten took a different view. Flashy, she thought. Brass.

Hubert started guiltily. "Must have sat on my phone. I keep doing that." He stood up. "Well, duty calls. Come on, Scarp!"

Scarp, who had been lying like a lizard on the soil, dusted himself down and they set off across the field together. Hubert turned, as if he had something to say, then changed his mind.

"So he will inherit all this..." mused Birgit, clasping her knees, and following him with her eyes. "...*and* the Sump too, if his mother gets it." Who could tell? Perhaps she might be able to swallow a pheasant or two, after all.

"Why don't you call the birds back with your flute?" asked Trudi, returning to the original question. It seemed too soon for Scarp's brood to have to die. "You told Jurgen you could call turkeys with a yelper. Why don't you 'yelp' the pheasants? Then you could catch them and keep them safe."

But the picnic was breaking up.

"Trudi, we have to get back," called Kirsten.

Somebody damped down the fire and someone else collected the plates.

"Don't forget you have to feed your lamb."

Sven and Corky agreed to stay and measure up, but the rest of the party began to pile things into the car.

"*Can't* we do it?" asked Jurgen, pulling Corky's sleeve. "You did promise to show me."

Corky scratched his head. He had been foolish enough to preach about something he only half knew, forgetting that children with sharp ears, have memories to match. How did one actually make a yelper? He really wasn't sure. That would teach him to make rash promises in future. Now he had homework to do!

Chapter 27

The Wingbone Call

The wingbone call, was thus dreaming itself into existence. Now, when night fell and the waxing moon rose over the Sump, Trudi thought of the silly young pheasants, roosting in all the wrong places, and the foxes, creeping up on them, sniffing after dinner!

In a few days Scarp was free again. Work continued on the vardo and Sven made good progress, fixing up new shelves and replacing the glass in the door. They loosened the tarpaulin and brought it to the Larssons' house to be mended and Sven cut green ash laths to splice the broken hoops. And all this time, Trudi fretted and worried about the birds.

"Ask Corky again," she pleaded with Barbara. "There won't be *any* left alive if he doesn't bring his whistle soon."

Corky, for his part, knew that honour was at stake. Having set himself up as an expert, he now had to prove his worth. He spent a morning ploughing through references at the local library. By the following evening, he had fashioned a set of whistles and was ready to be put to the test.

Accordingly, at dusk, Scarp collected the children in his truck and drove them back to the farm. A red sun was setting behind the pines on Wat's Field and long shadows were settling for the night. Sven watched them go with a twinge of regret. He had had this same feeling the other day, seeing them clamber into Scarp's caravan, or swing along the field side, looking for kindling, returning in full war-cry with feathers in their hair, hands all stained with blackberries. Theirs was an exuberance he seemed to have lost. He had been away too long; left too much ground untilled. He had assumed, so confidently, that his children would always be there, waiting for him, turning to him for companionship. This summer things had changed. They had found a new independence. And they had found Scarp to fool about with. Tonight, he was busy - he had a report to write – he would let them go without him. But next time it would be different...

In his mind, he pictured a long-forgotten day - a different place - a

217

young boy waving good-bye to his father and the father, gazing blankly back, leaning against the door, as the car which tore their lives apart, spun out of sight. It wouldn't happen again. He wouldn't allow it!

Corky had begged a selection of poultry wings from a butcher at Newbridge market. Fair exchange being no robbery, he had paid in the usual way, with eggs and spinach and tomatoes. The pheasant bones seemed too tiny use. He would have to cheat with those. But chicken looked more hopeful and turkey and goose promised real results.

After hours of patient boiling, cleaning, gluing, and polishing, he produced a range of whistles which could be coaxed into sound by sucking and clucking. Twice he choked. Once he bit his tongue. But at last he felt sufficiently proficient to give a demonstration. He arrived with an excited sense of anticipation.

Scarp took them to the field-edge site where he had erected new pens.

"This is a better place altogether." He was talkative today. "More light - more room for the birds to scavenge when they're bigger. Mrs. Jackson's worried they'll damage the crops. But she worries about everything. I think they'll hang around the bushes here. In any case, there aren't enough of them to matter much this year and the corn's already in. I think it's *me* she doesn't want too close. Hubert's still hoping that they'll buy the Sump, and he can make it his covert with me as official game-keeper. I laughed in his face. Do I look like a game-keeper? I'm the poacher round here! He might as well have it, though. I can't imagine what other people want it for. It doesn't look right for building, not with all the trees there. And the treasure rumour is rubbish. We all know that."

"Would it even be *safe* to build?" asked Corky. "Suppose the land is contaminated? The Water Board might have dumped stuff in the past."

"You mean chemicals? Who knows? It's stood idle for decades."

"They won't care," said Trudi quietly. "They are only going to build a few houses at first. They're selling on to another company for the real development. Miss Vincent's got a letter."

Scarp whistled. "What about planning?"

"We overheard the developers talking once. They've got two

plans. Eco-Homesteads come first, with designer houses - then it's going to be a big estate. Comfort Living. I think our neighbour is doing a deal for them."

"Stringer!" Scarp spat in contempt. "Have we got proof?"

"Only the letter."

Scarp rubbed his neck. "Stringer! I might have known. That's why I was scared off the land. The skunk! Must have been 'friends' of his who wrecked my van."

Corky sat down and began to play his 'yelper'. He sucked in his cheeks and drew the air deep into his throat. At first he produced a sweet peeping sound, then a low clucking. Then he popped a cork like a loud cock-pheasant. He had been practising hard.

"Let me try! Let me!" urged Jurgen, but his efforts made everyone laugh.

Corky tried again.

"If they've done a deal, that's me pretty well finished here," muttered Scarp.

A young pheasant poult emerged from the hedgerow, pecking this way and that in the sun's last rays, following the trail of corn they had laid. As they sat, holding their breath, another followed and then another. Hubert turned up and squatted down beside them, his face beaming.

"Well I never - it works! You're a genius, Corky!"

The pheasants pattered nonchalantly into the pen, investigating their new quarters. All very acceptable: nice dry litter, fresh water, shelter from the rain. Every home comfort.

"Only trouble is I shan't be able to eat them now." Hubert said.

"You *what*!"

Hubert shrugged. "I think I might be turning vegetarian. For Birgit."

Scarp's eyes boggled and Trudi laughed out loud, but Corky cautioned silence. The birds were still coming.

Now a mature hen-bird flew in. A male was answering in a neighbouring field. They counted twenty-five in all. Not bad."

"Try the other whistles," said Jurgen when the birds were safely penned.

"You won't catch a turkey," smiled Corky, but he demonstrated the call in any case. "There were huge, wild flocks of them once in

America. Can you imagine the row they must have made at dawn?"

"Now the goose."

The goose whistle gave a haunting, plaintive cry that lingered on the air.

"Again," said Jurgen.

The call rang out across the field to the distant trees. At this magical hour anything seemed possible. The sun had set and a rosy light suffused the sky. White moths with feathery wings, began to stir amongst the grasses. The dew was settling. Trudi felt once more that she had entered an unnamed place. Out of this stillness, they heard a solitary reply. Corky stopped blowing and waited.

Slowly, winging over the treetops, came a lone bird, repeating the cry which Trudi had heard at night.

"That's a greylag," said Scarp. "I've seen it in the Sump before."

"There's your feast, then, Scarp! Michaelmas goose!" Hubert slapped his thigh, forgetting he had forsworn meat. "If only I had my gun..."

Trudi leapt to her feet and clapped her hands in a frenzy. The goose wheeled low as she tried to wave it away.

"Don't! Don't touch it!" she screamed, turning on the men. "If you hurt it..."

She faltered, aware that she sounded ridiculous. "...if you kill it, you will kill *me*!" She fell silent, embarrassed and angry that her eyes were full of tears.

"Hey, hey. Okay!" said Scarp. "He was only joking. Don't fret!"

But a chill had entered the air and they all felt uncomfortable.

Corky put his pipes away.

"I want to go home," said Trudi. "Please, can we go?"

Chapter 28

Tracks

Trudi had decided to tell her father everything - everything from the very beginning - about the Sump, and Grandfather Larsson's boyhood, about the *kelet*, and Miss Vincent and the Stringers. She wanted to visit the Sump with him, and show him just where everything had happened and why it all mattered. Here would be their old camp, here the log where Jurgen slipped and she had made her drawing; there, the lagoon, the Trollstones, the badger sett, not forgetting her own forest garden. She worried that it was drying out and dying of neglect. There were so many things on her mind.

Cobweb needed a new home. He was already beginning to nibble things in the garden and he was too boisterous to come indoors any more. Two shiny black horns were beginning to grow on his head and Scarp said he mustn't be a pet any longer. He was a ram, after all, and it would be too dangerous for him to get used to playing with people. He must go back into the country and learn to be a sheep.

The holidays were speeding to an end and she could not imagine how there would then be time for private adventures. Before the demands of school overwhelmed her, she wanted to share some of the discoveries she had made.

Everyone seemed to have forgotten about the Sump. The beech trees whispered on, as though they had all eternity before them still, but only Trudi had ears for what they were saying. The others were busy, preparing for Scarp's feast, relaxing, planning the future. For them, the wood was condemned already and there was no more to be said about it. As for Grandfather Larsson, he kept to the silent labyrinth of his thoughts.

The drum had become an all-consuming passion. Though sometimes tired and visibly frustrated by his work, Per laboured on, honing the birchwood frame and cutting and stretching his hide. Nobody complained any more about the mess. The family indulged, encouraged him. If Kirsten groaned inside, she hid it well, while Jurgen watched over his present with proprietary pride. Sven alone

221

seemed uneasy about it all. Perhaps he remembered something his mother said - something about drums and northern magic. He didn't explain but he held aloof, noting how the instrument, as though exerting an invisible influence, pressed first one person, then another into its service.

Kirsten had been right when she said that Sven was clever with wood. Day after day, as he worked on Scarp's van, shelves - cupboards - benches, materialized as if from nowhere. Scarp filched timber from Jackson's barn and Sven chopped and planed according to the improvised plan in his head. He liked the feel of pine. Working with your hands, he joked, was easy as pie, after brain-work! Tools were like friends. Comfortable and reliable. His own hands were tools he could trust; his mind, a good master.

But to come home and find his father struggling, with trembling fingers, to tie the simplest of knots, finally wrung his heart. Per had the knowledge, the skill, but old age had stolen his strength. One evening, unable to stand by any longer, Sven put aside his reservations and quietly began to help, steadying the old man's grip, holding this and passing that, until they found a rhythm working together. Entrainment, drummers called it – synchronizing, till two hearts beat as one. A flow of understanding passed between them, shyly at first, but then in open smiles. Agneta's warnings became a distant echo. Father and son found one another, after their long estrangement.

That night, Per announced that he was tired and took himself off to his room and Sven carried on working alone. So that was how Trudi found him when she returned from calling the birds. Now she sat at his side, watching *him* work and the pattern repeated itself.

Already this drum was passing messages from one generation to the next and from the world of unseen, unknown things, to the everyday here and now. The fabric was practically complete. Decoration would follow but Per would insist on doing that himself. He alone knew the symbols which his Sami forebears used and Miss Vincent had supplied him with beads and trinkets for the rim. Then, and only then, when all was complete, would he strike up and rouse the sleeping spirit within. Sami drums were beaten with a deer-bone hammer. He would order a joint for dinner!

Trudi wanted to talk right away, but Sven's head was too full of thoughts and he took her hands in his: "Tomorrow! Tomorrow, Trudi, tell me everything. We'll look at your Sump, I promise."

She nodded, knowing that the moment, by then, would have passed.

"*Be patient, Trudi*" she heard Per's voice, echoing like a stream in a ravine. "*You have so many battles to fight - and things will come right. You will see. You have a good heart. Do not be unhappy. Your time will come and then you will do much.*"

The words lingered on, long after.

* * * * *

When Trudi opened her eyes, she found herself gazing up into the vastness of a Norway spruce. A sombre light trickled through the canopy. The air hung thick with the scent of resin. Above her, branch after branch receded skywards - a squirrel's staircase. The top seemed to be in lost in heaven. She was lying on a bed of soft, dry needles and around her, the great roots of the tree formed solid buttresses.

She could feel those roots plunging down into the earth, into an unseen underworld that smelt of mystery and fear. How long she had been here she did not know. When she scrambled up, she saw the forest stretching away in every direction. Huge boulders lay tumbled amongst the tree roots, sunk under quilts of moss. Here and there, the tiny white flowers of wood sorrel nodded between the ferns. It was delightful to step on the soft, springy earth, to hear the rustle of a breeze in the tree-tops, the voice of a distant stream. Over there, she knew, the boulders lay drenched in spray, with shiny liverworts plastered to their sides. In this clearing, the few shafts of sunlight picked out the tips of a young tree - emerald fingers, jewel-bright against the distant gloom.

A magpie fluttered onto a branch ahead and dived into the forest.

"Follow me!" he called.

Trudi stepped out of the light and began to follow.

He hopped on and waited, hopped on and waited, until she could detect only the white parts of his plumage and her feet stumbled over invisible obstacles.

Suddenly, she sensed danger.

223

The ground gave way beneath her feet and she realized, too late, that the magpie had led her into a trap. She had foundered in one of the treacherous, forest swamps and her legs were sinking fast. She tried to pull herself along by her hands, but it was useless. All power, all feeling had deserted her.

Away in the distance she thought she heard a sound. Something so faint, so far away, perhaps only her skin could hear it. Then silence. A branch creaked. As her ears strained, the sound reached her again and now her pulse began to quicken. There could be no mistaking it - that was the howl of a wolf - and alternating with it, the beat of feet approaching through the dark. Helpless as she was, she recognized, with a terrified certainty, the creature now making its way towards her. Here he came, loping easily along, snapping the dead twigs in his path, breathing harder, closing in, swift, inexorable and deadly - Beor! She could almost smell his breath upon her cheek.

She tried to scream but her mouth was full of moss…

When, at last, she wrenched herself awake, the moon was shining in at her window; the house, lay quiet. It would be a long wait till sunrise. But a lone robin twittered, anticipating day. His voice, defied a world still sunk in sleep. Brave robin. She was not alone then. She would live. She lay back on her pillow, and reasoned with the tumult in her heart.

* * * * *

Next day, Barbara and Kirsten drove to Tilchester to look for fabrics. Whatever bedding Scarp had once possessed, had been drenched by the rain and then left to moulder in his truck and they planned to throw it all out and present him with something new and altogether more tasteful. This would be their joint 'house-warming' gift.

The outing also gave them a chance to indulge in a cosy lunch, and they talked of old times as they sat at their café table, mending the recent tatters in their friendship.

Meanwhile, Professor Saxmund called for Birgit. Friends of his had agreed to rent her a flat, so she would have somewhere to live for the coming term, and he could relax his role as guardian. He was full of his usual good humour. Would he come to Scarp's feast? Why, yes of course. Somewhere, amongst his collection of curios, was a Spanish gypsy cauldron. He would bring it with him. Six o'clock - Tuesday - Jackson's Farm? No problem. He'd be there. Birgit coyly announced that she would be coming with Hubert.

Per settled down to paint the figures on his drum. He, too, was in high spirits. He hummed as he dipped his brush in the alder dye. Blood red. Crimson. "Hep!" He nodded. His drum would be ready for its debut at the party. All he had to do now was carve the hammer.

Jurgen, with typical inconsistency decided to practise his cello.

Seeing everybody occupied, Trudi and Sven helped themselves to some cinnamon buns and slipped out of the house, past the crazed barkings of Beor and past Cobweb's offer to play - to the garden fence and the secret way into the Sump. Trudi looked nervously around but no one seemed to be watching. She scrambled through first and lifted the wire for Sven, but he must have grown fatter, or stiffer with age and he didn't quite fit. Losing patience, he ripped the fastenings from the concrete post. They were old and rusty and came away with ease. In a few moments he was through and brushing his hands on his knees. The atmosphere of the Sump closed quietly over him. This was the moment Trudi had been waiting for, but today she noticed things which bothered her.

Someone had recently been through and planted T-shaped pegs at intervals, trampling the vegetation. Trudi's plants, being small, had survived, though they looked somewhat dry. But the trees had been marked with red and white daubs of paint. A dot here, a line there. What did it all mean?

"I think these are instructions for loggers," said Sven. "You see the same thing in the forests where I work. Someone comes through first and decides which trees they are going to fell…"

"There's a mark on *our* tree," said Trudi, turning to the beech that grew four ways.

Sven frowned. "I thought they would keep the big ones," he murmured. "The trouble is, Trudi, that to an outsider this is just waste ground. A naturalist wouldn't say it was particularly special. The beeches are old, but the original woodland flora was buried under sludge when they dug out the lagoon. That's why there are all these nettles here. The storm of twenty years ago wrecked most of the decent specimens. Some of these are badly diseased. See the fungus there?"

"You can't know what's special," said Trudi passionately, "just by looking. You have to listen - feel it in your bones. Who knows what this place could be, given the chance? Given time?"

"Oh, yes," he conceded sadly. But time was the most expensive commodity of all. Time had already run out for people like Per. Even Sven, committed as he was to living life to the full, had let it slip through his fingers. They were all getting older. How else explain his inability to crawl under that fence! It was Earth's tragedy that Nature needed time, vast swathes of it, and man was always in a hurry.

They climbed up into their old camp and, squeezing into the hollow where the branches forked, unwrapped their buns.

"So," Sven smiled, brushing the crumbs out of his beard. "Begin at the beginning. I want to know everything." He looked so eager and hopeful, so determined to be happy today, Trudi knew she could not tell him everything. Nevertheless, she made a start. She told the story of the Wulfstan forgeries and the Museum. She explained about the Jacksons and the fall of the house of de Fraisey - and she painted pictures of Miss Vincent's study, of Corky's chalk-pit, and of Barbara and herself, all covered in flour. Telling stories was like following tracks. Sometimes they disappeared and you had to retrace your steps. Sometimes they ran into other tracks. Life was crossed by invisible threads, linking things together. Story-lines wove them into a pattern you could see.

Trudi came at last to the Sump itself - the prospect of the sale - the meeting she had overheard with Miss Vincent, the letters and the attack on Scarp.

Sven had prepared his response well in advance.

"Trudi, my love, these things are out of our hands and really we shouldn't interfere. The Sump doesn't belong to us. It won't even belong to the people who buy it. Not forever, anyway. No matter what happens, long after we're all gone, there will be something surviving here, I'm sure..." but the speech sounded fatuous and he found he couldn't finish it.

He had never muddled up the two halves of his life. At work he was a fearsome campaigner, outspoken, controversial, but when he

226

came home, he came to relax. In Bockhurst, he was known as a mild-mannered, family man who did not complain to the neighbours. Battles were for other places, not home. Home should be a haven. Why else let Kirsten always have her head? And that word of Trudi's, 'special'? What was 'special'? He couldn't honestly say that anything here, with the exception of the big trees, was of particular ecological value. He sighed. Trudi, with her child's eyes, saw things he wouldn't be able to defend in a paper.

"If only you had a rare lizard, or a salamander, or an endangered butterfly," he murmured, "then we'd have a fighting chance. But the pool is too shaded to have much life in it."

"There's *something* big in there," objected Trudi. "Jurgen nearly caught it."

"Darling, it might have been an old shoe. How do we know? This here, Trood, is just scrub. I know it's special to you, but it's prime development land."

Trudi's fierce, young face remained intractable.

"You're like the rest, who give up because something is difficult and let the worst people win! All along, people have just used this place for their own selfish purposes - but inside, it has a soul - I've seen it!" Disappointment made her desperate. "You could *do* something to save it. I was so sure you could."

Sven took a deep breath and stretched his legs. There was to be no easy solution, then. Trudi's alternatives left him no room to manoeuvre: take on the impossible or lose her trust again. It wasn't really a choice.

"Let's go," he said, nodding his head. "Let's go and see Miss Vincent."

* * * * *

Marjorie Vincent was sorting the contents of the great, black cabinet in her parlour when she spotted the Larssons coming over. The parlour shared the same dimensions as Kirsten's workroom next door, though it formed a mirror-image, for the houses in Beckley Road had been built in complimentary pairs. But this room seemed light years away from that bright, airy space. This, with its high marble mantel and funereal furniture actually smelt Victorian -

mothballs and camphor - all the staleness of a room never used. Miss Vincent scanned the street and paused for a moment, a teapot in one hand, a soup ladle in the other, like a monarch posing for a portrait. Then she set both down and applied herself properly to the art of spying.

Through the gap in the curtains she could make out figures in the street - Trudi, of course, and that must be her father - but there were other people too. Now they were stopping to talk at the gate. Ah, yes! The au-pair hussy from number fifty-five and the Stringer boy. What an odd couple *they* made. They must be off to the park, for he was clutching a football and she - Lord knows - she was in sunglasses and gold slippers, a top with a gypsy neck, unlaced, and a micro-skirt, (could one call it that?) snakeskin, hugging her shapely thighs. She was all smiles. Red lips wide, like a gash. If you did not know better you might actually think she was flirting. And the boy looked cocky too, smirking at her back, one finger tracing the stitching on his ball. Now they parted. The Larssons were coming on.

Like a housemaid, caught with her ear at the door, she hurried back to her table. Yes, she would put the teapot here. Royal Doulton on this side - Worcester, on that. She started as Sven knocked the door.

"Miss Vincent, I wonder if we can trouble you?"

Trouble. That was all there seemed to be these days.

"I'm sorting things - in here." Head down, she led the way. "Please excuse the muddle - there is no time…"

The dishes, with their gold-leaf and lustrous colours, gleamed on the table.

"They're lovely!" cried Trudi.

"They're very *old*, and never used. What is the point? I was going to give some to young Scarp."

Sven stifled a smile, finding the idea absurd.

"How kind," he spluttered.

"*Not* as stupid as you think," said the old lady, ruthlessly reading his thoughts. "The gypsies used to collect all this stuff - the prettier the better. Scarp will know that. I'm sure his grandmother would have had some." She wagged an emphatic finger. "What can I do for *you*?"

"Well, it's that letter, about the Eco-Homesteads deal. I've promised Trudi that if the developers *are* up to no good, I will try to do something about it. I don't suppose that will be enough to save the Sump, but if it only gives us time, well, it might help."

Miss Vincent scrutinized his face and laid her icy hand on his arm. She had a glitter in her eye.

"Precisely my thought!" she said with relish. "But watch your step with that lot. They are *mafiosi*! Bandits!"

"I've just been talking to the nanny."

"I watched you." There was no point pretending otherwise. "Something is up. That one doesn't normally speak."

"She was full of herself today," said Sven. "Quite friendly." Any darker motive seemed to have escaped him. "She told me they are moving. Imminently. Seems she's very happy about it."

Hearing this for the second time, Trudi still could not dare to hope it was true. Were the Stringers really leaving? All of them? And taking Beor with them? Imagine life without the ghastly menace of Beor... Would they really be free to play and talk in the garden and not worry who was listening or watching? Imagine the relief! Remembering their last meeting she had not dared to look Simon in the eye, but she sensed, just now in the street, that he was gloating and that could only mean one thing. Whatever the future promised, his business was still unfinished. It would be too early to celebrate his departure yet.

Miss Vincent seemed unsurprised. "Yes, well, I suppose Nigel Stringer would have to, wouldn't he? Move on." She led them through into the study and began to rummage in her bureau. "I put it here somewhere. Just hope the blue-tits haven't eaten it. Ah!" She plucked out the letter and continued thinking aloud. "You see, *here* his hands are tied. He has to declare an official 'interest' because the land adjoins his garden. That means he can't handle the case himself. And if he is trying to cheat the system - pull strings to get planning permission through - well, he will need to move away. Then he can look after things without raising suspicion. He must be pretty sure the sale is in the bag!"

"The closing date for offers is Friday. I checked."

"Then we have a couple of days."

"Miss Vincent, there are several parties, aren't there, who are

229

bidding?"

"Oh yes, the Museum, the Manor, the Jacksons, and there may well be more."

"And all have the intention of exploiting the Sump in one way or another?"

"I'm afraid it's the tale of Wulfstan all over again."

"I beg your pardon?"

"Trudi will know." She sank into her chair and motioned them to sit down where they could. "Greed." She nodded ruminatively. "And glory! It's the old Cherokee story of the two wolves."

Trudi glanced anxiously at her father. Perhaps he would not appreciate Miss Vincent's circumlocutions. But he was leaning forward, attentive, his elbows on his knees.

"A man and his grandson were talking about good and evil. And the grandfather explained that he had two wolves living inside him. These two wolves were locked in deadly combat. One was white; a noble animal, peaceable, compassionate and loving. The other was black. The black wolf was a terrible beast, full of savage hatred. Their contest raged day and night without a pause. Sometimes it looked as if the black wolf would conquer the white. Sometimes it was the other way around. Fortune swung this way and that, ripping up his heart as though it was a battlefield. The young boy listened and thought the matter over. At last he turned to his grandfather. "But which wolf wins?" he asked. The old man smiled before he spoke. "Whichever one I feed. Inside me are all the powers of goodness, kindness, honour, generosity. And inside me too, are depths of selfishness, greed and aggression. I have to choose which to nourish, my white wolf or my black. We all have to choose. And whichever we choose, will win.

"The Sump is an opportunity, just as Wulfstan's riddle contest was an opportunity. It can develop in a good or a bad way. You may judge for yourself which way most people are tempted to use it. All the bidders that we know of propose to exploit the land for their own vanity or greed. Whether they desire horse schools, or visitor centres or housing estates, I suppose makes little odds. Any which way, the wood is doomed."

"Miss Vincent," said Sven carefully. "If the treasures that your uncle made were handed over to the Museum, if you came clean

230

about the whole thing being a hoax - the Wolf Stone, the manuscripts, the missing pearls and all - would the archaeologists drop their interest in the Sump?

She thought a moment, guessing his drift. "Very probably. It's the brooch they want though. That *is* genuine, and that cannot be found."

"All the same, Trudi tells me these are exquisite things which deserve to be seen. Your uncle may have been led astray in what he did, but the skills he possessed were real, no? - and good enough to rival the Saxon goldsmiths. People would love to know his story, see his work. It would be so sad if both were lost to the world again. History would surely judge us if we kept these things selfishly to ourselves."

"You are something of a devil's advocate, Mr. Larsson! You have turned my own story against me. But I will consider what you say."

Sven nodded and smiled. So far so good.

"And we will go and see Alison Quick at the Manor." He rose to leave. "Our young lamb needs a new home. May I keep this letter for a while? I have some telephone calls to make, and shall need all the evidence I can muster."

Chapter 29

The Bluebird

Fraisey Manor had begun its existence as a simple hunting lodge. The great chamber, which had once warmed guests round its Medieval central hearth, gained a chimney in Tudor times and rapidly expanded into a labyrinth of passages and rooms whose crooked timbers still deceived unwary visitors into many a bang on the head and stumble of foot in the night. The floors sloped one way, the ceilings went another, and the windows had a secret logic all of their own, appearing in random places, sometimes at knee height, with panes as small as a hand, sometimes soaring into grandiose mullions, according to the builder's fancy.

Now converted into a hotel, the manor appeared in all the tourist guides. The gardens alone attracted visitors from far and wide and carefully embellished tales of the ghost under the mulberry tree, and the spectral dog in the library, kept public interest keen.

Alison Quick and her husband had bought the property for a song back in the seventies, when there was damp in the bedrooms and death watch in every wainscot. The roof leaked. The house creaked. One staircase was completely boarded up. Lovingly, they restored every lath and tile. They unearthed brick floors, polished the boards, set flowers on the window sills and opened their doors to the Americans.

Breakfast here might cost a mint, but it was a genuine banquet, served in style. Why confine yourself to three courses? Stewed fruit compote, homemade yoghurt, melon, eggs and bacon, freshly made toast and coffee were only some of the delights on offer. Food arrived on delft-blue dishes, at a table resplendent with silver and crisply-ironed linen. The local girls, who waited, wore demure grey dresses and white aprons. Here you absorbed History with a capital H, while enjoying every modern comfort.

Though Trudi had passed the wrought-iron gates innumerable times, she had never set foot inside them, so to be marching with her father, past the secluded rhododendrons, tulip trees and beds of

232

lavender and box, filled her with excitement. Now the trees gave place to lawns and the house itself came into view - a jumble of brick and plaster, oak beams, chimney-pots and a roof of Horsham stone. Additions had been tacked on willy-nilly. To the right, Jacobean gables rubbed shoulders with a stone façade, all windows and parlours, where the Georgians had taken tea. Over on the left, stood the workaday slab of a Victorian coach-house and a stable-block, surmounted by a weather-vane. The effect was haphazard but provided an honest, if quirky account of evolving fashions. The de Fraiseys had never quite known how to organize their wealth.

Trudi analysed none of this. She saw a fairy-tale mansion and her imagination instantly peopled it with the characters legend had supplied.

Mrs. Quick was deadheading roses in the drive. Though she employed several gardeners, this was a job she liked to keep for herself. She had once been beautiful and she had never forgotten it. Now, at nearly sixty, she was still blonde and slender, with a carefully tended face, but her arms and hands looked old. She might have been going to a party in her white dress and floppy hat. She received them courteously, but there was something indefinably hard beneath her smile; a shadow, which flitted from eyes to mouth - a ghost of ambition and ruthlessness? Trudi decided she did not like her much and fell to wondering how anyone could become rich enough to own all this grandeur.

The people at Fraisey Manor knew nothing about their renegade ram and the subsequent birth of the lambs and Alison listened to the tale with an air of polite detachment. She had started by keeping peacocks, she explained, but they had disgraced themselves, waking everyone with their screams in the early hours and attacking their own reflections in the visitors' cars. In the end, it proved too embarrassing, explaining to irate owners why their BMWs were scratched and bloodied. Bad for business too. That plan was hastily abandoned and the sheep were a later compromise. Hebrideans looked the part - stately and exotic, with their jet black fleeces and finely sculpted horns. Of course, it was the rams, which everyone liked to photograph. She did not know that sometimes they escaped.

She led them round to a paddock at the back.

"*We* put in the ha-ha," she said. "We so loved the one at

Glyndebourne. Have you ever been? Are you music-lovers?" She was so busy being gracious, she could not hear how patronising it sounded.

Confined by their ingenious ditch, the sheep needed no fence to keep them out of the garden and grazed picturesquely beyond the dahlias. The outlines of the Sump provided a suitable backdrop.

"Of course we're all in a state of dread about *that*," she pointed towards the wood.

"The developers?"

"We've put in our own bid. Well, we could do so much if we owned the land. Concerts - wedding parties – a little Glyndebourne of our own! - So many possibilities... All in the best taste, of course! But to think they could just flatten it! Well, you can imagine how that would affect us! We've tried protesting - signing petitions - we've written to the DoE. What more can one do?"

Sven murmured in sympathy and she collected her thoughts.

"Well - this lamb. Yes, I'm sure our groundsman here could feed it. He looks after our all the other sheep. It would be rather a treat for the visitors. They do like to feel they have had a full countryside experience. *I* don't see a problem. I suppose the poor creature belongs here, really." She turned to Trudi. "You'll miss him, though, won't you? You must come and see him now and then."

You could tell from her voice that she didn't mean it but she knew how to make a pleasant end. "Come into the house and I'll give you William's number. You can make the arrangements with him."

They wandered back, past flower urns and topiary pheasants and in through the open front door.

This led straight into the original hall, now sumptuous with rugs and whisky decanters. The age-old smell of soot mingled with the scent of flowers. And while Sven and Alison talked business, Trudi's eyes scanned the room, from end to end. There was a cavern of a fireplace, and a carved oak chest beneath the window, topped with a china bowl of pot-pourri. From there on, everything was Jacobean: lion-headed dining chairs around a solid refectory table and a sideboard, where clusters of photographs showed the Quicks when they were young, talking to royalty, receiving awards, relaxing in tennis whites... Then more flowers - a huge display - a stuffed fox and - no - it couldn't be... there in the corner, as if it had been there all its life, a clock, identical to the one from Tilchester Museum. Case, dial, pendulum - Trudi squinted across the dusky room - everything looked the same. There was even a bluebird, awaiting his cue to take to the wing. Off he would go and then be lost forever. Another bird was already waiting to follow... Curiosity made her bold and she tiptoed over to take a closer look. Now she felt certain. This was in every respect the clock she remembered. There were the posies of flowers, in crackly paint, the burnished hands and the motto, in copperplate, which Kirsten must have read aloud a dozen times:

"I have a secret which cannot be told,
More precious by far than silver or gold..."

Of *course*! It came to her in a flash. *Now* she understood why the inscription from the Sump had seemed familiar. She already knew it by heart. The treasure box and the clock said identical things. It was simply that one was in English, the other in Anglo-Saxon:

"...Neither lock nor chain can bind me
And those who chase me will not find me."

"You noticed our clock," said Alison Quick, moving across to join her. "The little bird flies, on the hour, from one side to the other. We simply love the piece. The answer to the riddle, of course, is 'Time'.

"It's from the Museum at Tilchester," said Trudi, rudely. How could this woman have it all to herself, when its proper home was there, where people could see it?

Sven shifted nervously, anticipating some unpleasantness, but Alison seemed unperturbed. "You're quite right," she acknowledged with some pride. "We did a 'deal' a few months ago. This clock really belongs here. It was auctioned in the sale following Lord de Fraisey's death and disappeared for many years. Then the Museum got hold of it. Now they are giving the Museum a face-lift. They want a cleaner, more modern look. Less clutter. More focus. They're redesigning the foyer."

"I know," said Trudi.

"Well, it happened that we had papers here, old deeds, and letters, which our solicitor released to us when we registered the property. The Museum was desperate to have them. They are building a profile of all the houses in the area - an online archive, or some such thing.

Unfortunately our oldest deeds were missing."

Trudi nodded as if to say '*I know that too!*' What a conceited child she was!

"Anyhow, they weren't too bothered and basically, we did a swap. We agreed to clean and house the clock (the poor thing hadn't been overhauled since a London clockmaker did it in 1914) and we let them take charge of the papers."

Sven broke in: "Which is how they came across Sir Vivian de Fraisey's notes about Saxon treasure."

"Precisely. My husband was quite upset when he found out. We wouldn't have let those go if we had known. But we didn't have time to trawl through everything and, in any case, we couldn't decipher the writing. However, the Museum might still prove useful to us. If their bid is successful over ours, they will generate a lot of interest and interest means customers. Everyone who wants to know about the de Fraiseys will need to come here."

"All's well that ends well," said Sven, sensing they had stayed too long. "Thank you so much for your time. We'll certainly speak to your man about the lamb." He took Trudi by the hand and they hurried out.

"That's *it!*" Trudi danced along beside him, pulling at his arm. "Don't you *see*? It's the same riddle on the clock and on Miss Vincent's box."

"And so?"

"There must be a link."

Sven smiled indulgently.

She thought for a moment, puzzling over the words: "*I have a secret that cannot be told ...*" Then light dawned and she stopped in her tracks. "I've *got* it. *That's* the secret," she said. "The brooch is inside the clock!"

"Darling, I don't think..."

"It's the treasure which sits under your nose - at home all the time!"

"Now you've lost me. If the clock was restored, then they would have found anything hidden inside it, years ago."

"Ask Miss Vincent," said Trudi. "She'll know!"

* * * * *

Miss Vincent listened to their tale with interest.

"It would be quite typical of Edward's maverick humour," she reflected. "He had decided to conceal the brooch at the Manor, right? Well, what better place to choose than the grandfather clock? The clock was part and parcel of the house. No one could imagine the family ever parting with it. So, say he uses my uncle again... He pretends he is sending the clock to London to be restored, but instead he rents a place nearby - somewhere where Uncle Roger can work unseen - and has the original piece delivered there. It is a small task for Roger to devise a hidden compartment. He places the brooch inside. He also forges any necessary paperwork, say, labels, invoices etc. from a bogus restorer. He presto! The clock comes back with a little secret no one knows. There would have been time to do it, *just*, before Edward left."

"But we can only put this theory to the Quicks, if we come clean about the rest of the story. Do we have your permission, Miss Vincent?"

The old lady shrugged. "It's out now anyway, isn't it? Uncle Roger, realizing the game was up, must have used the riddle as a clue to *his* own secret. Certainly the rhyme existed on the clock long before Edward began his Machiavellian schemes. My uncle simply took the deception one step further. He translated the words into Wulfstan's language, and inscribed them on his private treasure-box. That would have been a simple and satisfying task for him. In one neat stroke he performed his last great sleight of hand and created a forgery so obvious, it would, in time, unravel Edward's crimes - as indeed it has. However," she wrung her hands, theatrical to the last, "I don't believe that the answer to the riddle is 'Time'. You will have to think on that again."

Chapter 30

Messages

The revelation of Edward's plot put Alison Quick into a frenzy of excitement. The Museum called up an expert and the press arrived, as if by magic. Each party saw a chance to promote their cause and hoped that events would unfold to their advantage. This news would make the national headlines and provide material for interviews and articles and television programmes for years to come.

Miss Vincent pulled down her blinds and resigned herself to a season of annoyance. She relinquished all the documents and artefacts in her possession, on condition that she be left alone. She had no telephone, but reporters found her door implacably barred against them. She had said her piece and, as far as she was concerned, the subject was now closed. Even Trudi had to accept that. Nevertheless, her final words had been a tease: "It was lucky for my uncle that Edward de Fraisey died, otherwise he would have got sucked further in. Who knows what depths he might ultimately have sunk to? I think the demise of the gardener set him thinking and he worked out the riddle of the bluebird for himself. From that day on, he made amends for his errors and lived a blameless life."

Marilyn Jackson read about it all in the local '*Echo*'.

"Listen to this, will you!" she shrieked above the noise of her husband's television. "They've found that Saxon brooch. It's all in here: '*...a tip-off led to the discovery in an old grandfather clock. Hidden behind a fake restorer's label, a false floor in the case, revealed the antiquity. Wulfstan's brooch lies at the heart of one of the most ingenious crimes of the century. The clock is now where it belongs, at Fraisey Manor, but specialists from the Museum at Tilchester, have sent the jewel to London, to have its authenticity confirmed.*' Walter! Walter, are you listening?"

Old Jackson nodded, but his eyes remained glued to his film.

"Walter, that brooch belongs to you." shouted Marilyn. "Oh, for heaven's sake!" She pounced on the remote control and turned the picture off. "*Listen* to me, for once."

Walter knew it was useless to remonstrate. He should not have married a tyrannous wife, but it was too late to say so now.

"That brooch by rights belongs to you," she went on. "It was in *your* family - the de Fraisey's."

"Oh, Marilyn..."

"No, I'm right. Assert yourself, for once! That's an heirloom that should be yours - be *ours*. It would be the saving of this place. Just think - we could pay off the loans - have a new kitchen. We could probably buy back Fraisey Manor, for ourselves!" She was soaring now, carried away by her own fervour.

"That's all past and done with," said Jackson. "Let's just make do with the present."

"Oh, the *present*, yes," Marilyn came down again, hard. "Your precious present is that we can't pay our bills - and that your son..."

"Yours too," muttered Jackson.

"...has taken up with an eco-warrior with a nose-ring. Suddenly, he won't eat meat and he's more interested in building that wretched caravan of Scarp's, than getting on with the harvest. He's off, tonight, to a Swedish summer party - and the seven-acre field's still waiting to be cut."

"It's too *wet* to cut after yesterday's rain," objected the long-suffering Walter. "Otherwise I'd be out there myself."

"Never mind that. You should talk to him! Set him an example. Where's your spirit, your pride? You should be up at that Museum demanding your rights. And if you won't," she raked her gold-ringed fingers through her hair, "I tell you I will. I won't see this family go down, after all the work I've put in!"

Jackson made no reply. If he kept his head low, she might lose interest and go away. But not yet.

"Do you know that Tamsin Smythe-Philipson rang Hubert three times yesterday? She's a lovely girl - *lovely*. And her father is president of the golf club. Hubert hasn't had the decency even to call her back."

Jackson stealthily retrieved the handset and returned to his film. Heaven help Hubert. But he was a strong boy. He would stick up for himself, no doubt.

Dapper, in his country-casual cotton, Hubert was too busy preparing for the party, to heed any tirades from his mother.

239

The other guests were getting ready too.

Per attached the last bead to the frame of his drum and held it up to the light, turning it this way and that, inspecting it with a critical eye. It looked a fine, handsome piece now, with its bold, red characters. The symbols all had special meanings. There in the centre, sat the sun, with figures from Sami life encircling it: reindeer and beaver; a conical tent, a tree; a man on skis and his little boat and sledge... Uncle Roger's beads, now strung on laces jingled along with other protective charms: tiny flints from Scarp, and a crocodile tooth. Wrapped in silver thread, the thongs which held them glinted in the sun. There was a good grip for the left hand at the back, a strap to attach to the drummer's belt and a hammer, now engraved with mystic signs.

"Jurgen, come and see," called Per when he had finished. "You must treat this always with greatest respect. It is not a toy. It is something - can be very powerful - something for singing and dancing - creates happiness - teaches wisdom. Listen to voice of the drum. Get to know it."

Jurgen wanted to bash it, but Per placed it gently in his hands and turning him round, wedged him between his knees.

"Hold the hammer and I will guide your hand."

"How do I do it?"

"Listen to your heart," said Per. "That is your best guide. This drum will link your heartbeat to the silent rhythms of the world - will give them both a voice."

Softly at first, he began to tap a pulse and the drum-spirit answered back. Per relaxed his grip and let Jurgen continue alone. The boy had a good ear. He picked up the rhythm and explored the instrument's surface, testing each of Per's pictograms in turn. Those towards the centre sounded deeper, those at the edge, sharper. The drum had many voices.

"What do the figures mean?" he asked.

"These are symbols from the far north of my country." Per pointed them out "This is the wind god, Bieggolmai, this is a hunter, and here are his animals and this here is for good luck."

"And this?" Jurgen picked up a triangular counter made of metal.

Per dismissed it with his hand. "That is for something else. It is part of the ancient purpose of the drum - for seeing into the future.

Sami people call it a 'frog' because it jumps on the skin when the drummer strikes it. So - in the old days, the villagers can tell if it is a good day for hunting or not. We don't need it today. We have the weather forecast. You see? Hup! That old life has gone for good."

"But show me," insisted Jurgen. "What do we do? I'd like to see into the future."

Per snatched back the piece of tin and his eyes flashed with a warning fire. "This, I told you, is not a toy! Jurgen, you had better believe me!" He was so terrible when he was angry, Jurgen quailed before him. After a while he mastered his breath and said in a calmer voice. "This is a hard gift for me to give you, because you are so young and I do not have time to teach you properly. I have to trust that you will listen, so that my knowledge can come to others through you." His anger had changed into sorrow, a sorrow which alarmed Jurgen even more.

"Will you try?"

"Yes, grandfather." It seemed a pity to forgo the fun of messing about - Jurgen really *was* too young to understand - but he nodded anyway. He didn't want Per to be unhappy. And he did feel honoured in a way. For once, someone was treating him with respect - had seen the lion somehow inside the boy.

The old man smiled and his eyes softened. "Go and enjoy the party. And when it is over bring the drum to me." He patted Jurgen's hand. "Remember, the spirit in there is like your own heart. It will watch over you."

* * * * *

Hard as she tried to suppress it, Trudi could not help feeling jealous about the drum. It was so unfair of Per to say that only boys did drumming. She knew she was every bit as good as a boy!

In her new summer top and trousers, she frowned at her plaits in the mirror. She wouldn't have plaits any more. She would be like Birgit and shave her head! Birgit had done it once for the polar bears - but Trudi would do it out of spite. She was missing Cobweb. And then, there was school next week. Her sunburnt reflection scowled back. The adults had taken over all her projects, leaving her only hideous History to do.

Nevertheless, the Stringers were leaving. Others had confirmed what Amber told them. And the misery of feeling hated by them would finally be over. That, at least, was worth a smile. When she told the news to Per, he nodded gravely and didn't seem pleased at all. But then you never could tell what her grandfather was thinking. Sometimes he just liked to be contrary. Sometimes he seemed to be listening to voices no one could hear, just as she had once listened to the *kelet*. She wondered about this. Did he know the *kelet* himself? Did they talk to him?

There was still so much she did not understand. His insistence on being patient, for instance. How could one be patient when life itself would not wait? The Museum, and the beech trees would be gone if one waited too long. The holidays had already run their course, and if she did not grab the moment, and live it for all it was worth, she too would lose her chance and be old, like Miss Vincent and then she would have whiskers and warts and never be able to look in a mirror again!

She put out her tongue at the reflection-girl in blue, wrinkled her nose and wagged her head in the best playground tradition. Then she giggled and slipped off to find Barbara, who was making Tuesday buns.

Chapter 31

Scarp's Feast

Tell me, have you never tasted Tuesday buns? Oh reader, you do not know what you have missed.

Picture to yourself a dumpling of sweet dough, light as a puffball, and baked to a delicious, butterscotch brown. This vision arrives from the oven in its own cloud of cardamom-scented steam. The top is cut off and the centre filled with almond paste and lightly-beaten cream. Then the top goes back on as a hat. The confection is dusted with a snow-shower of sugar, and set down to paddle in a pool of fragrant milk. It is sops made in heaven. Breakfast at tea-time.

Barbara, never happier than when busy, in her baker's apron, was setting the buns to rise. Kirsten, meanwhile, was preparing some savouries and cutting up slivers of salmon, on a separate board. Scarp had volunteered to cook all the food, gypsy-style, but they couldn't resist bringing something along with them. And Kirsten was so artistic. Her dishes always looked the prettiest at a party.

"Here we are, still stuck in the sink," she mused, clasping her knife mid-air like a baton. "I've spent my life trying to be a liberated woman and, you know, in the end I'm not sure what liberated is."

"No worries." Barbara, spread her plump fingers as if dismissing the subject.

"That's just it," said Kirsten, ignoring her. "The more I struggle to break away, the more worries I seem to have. Am I doing this right? Am I achieving my potential? Am I keeping up with everyone else? I've so wanted Trudi to do better than me, I think I've just made her worried too!"

"No, Trudi's cool," said Barbara.

"You think so? It's so hard to tell."

"We're all forever looking over our shoulders, wondering how we are doing."

"Tomorrow I'll be back at my drawing board. I love my work so much, I can't live without the buzz of it. Don't you miss the bookshop?"

"Yeah - sure I miss the bookshop. And, don't worry, I'm going back - soon as we get this party over - and then you can have your house to yourself again."

"I didn't mean that."

"No, but *I* did. I *ought* to go back."

"So, what would make us free?"

"From worries?"

"Yes."

"Having something bigger to worry about! You can't see things when you're on top of them. If disaster struck now, we'd look back on this as a golden time."

"But it *is* a golden time. I know that. It's why I don't want you to leave. We shall lose what Sven calls 'Barbara's Magic'. You make the silly little things seem important."

Barbara puffed herself up in mock indignation and gave her dough a protective pat: "You call this *silly*?"

Kirsten smiled, thinking of her frugal lunches: half a cracker and fennel tea. How many times had Sven searched through her cupboards for a biscuit, in vain?

"Perhaps you are right. But there's normally no time."

"Ah," Barbara nodded. "That's why the children are wiser than us. They have no sense of time and they sure never say no to a bun!"

She grinned as Trudi came and hovered hopefully at the table.

"Trudi, you can put these in the fridge and stick some parsley in-between." Kirsten handed over the salmon, adding a cautionary: "I've counted, so don't eat them now."

"Oh hell!" said Barbara. "There you go. Let's *all* have some and then no one will have to cheat!"

* * * * *

The rest of the day was spent sorting tablecloths and packing plates and cutlery, for this was to be a proper feast with candles and wine glasses and those paper lanterns, which had at last turned up in the shed. Sven and Jurgen went on ahead to light the fire. Hubert provided the furniture: old stable doors, balanced on trestles, for tables. There would be fresh straw-bales for seats.

Scarp, resplendent in baggy, pirate trousers and waistcoat, had borrowed Hubert's cap, which he wore irreverently back to front.

"I say, Hube," he mocked, as he stirred up the fire. "Dashed fine headgear you've got here for keeping off the flies, what?" He was excited, ebullient, possibly even a little drunk, despite the early hour.

Hubert, deciding that the Swedes were not to have it all their own way, had contributed a keg of English cider, and, since the harvest was *almost* home, set up a corn dolly at the head of the table. Scarp, naturally enough, had offered to test the cider, just to make sure it would 'do'.

"Look out. The band's arriving!"

A cloud of dust bowled along the farm track, bringing Corky on his bike. When the dust settled, they could see him, dismounting, armoured like a beetle. His sidecar bulged with provisions. He was babbling behind his visor, and it was not until he had peeled off his leathers and divested himself of his helmet, that they could understand a word. He was itemizing the things that he had brought. This was the wine; this, fizzy for the children; *that* was the big drum and that under there, a trombone. More percussion *there* - some lettuces and plums from the nursery - oh dill – and..." he pointed to a large plastic pail with a lid.

"Blimey - weighs a ton!" said Scarp, lifting it out.

"That's crayfish. Don't put your hand in - they have a powerful nip. I promised Per I would find him some. Not natives, I'm afraid. These are the villainous American cousins which have taken over our local streams and driven the natives out. I have a licence to catch them and the river authorities are glad for me to take as many as I can. They're bigger too - so more meat for us!"

"You want to cook 'em here?"

"My contribution," said Corky.

Only Hubert looked unhappy.

"Wassup Hube?" said Scarp.

"Well, I don't know what Birgit's going to say. I was going to be a good vegetarian and refuse all flesh, but now you've gone and brought crayfish, what can I do? I can't say no to crayfish. No man could!"

"If she loves you, she'll forgive you." Corky assured him.

"I've already upset my mother..."

"Well *that's* not hard to do." Scarp offered scant comfort. "You'll have to do penance. Celery and golf for a week!"

Sven clapped Corky gently on the back, his eyes shining with pleasure. "This will be a *real* feast. Thank you!"

"'Spose nobody wants my hot dogs, now," whined Scarp.

"Oh yes. Most definitely," Corky was insistent. "I've only come for hot dogs. Where do you want the music?"

Kirsten and Barbara arrived with the children, in a car stuffed to bursting and Trudi ran back and forth, arms loaded, while Kirsten oversaw the laying of the table. Barbara held a council of war with Scarp over the cooking pots.

"You know these critters are supposed to cool for hours and hours before you eat them?"

"Well, cook 'em now. I'm sure they'll be okay."

"Where's father?" said Sven, suddenly. "Why isn't he here?"

"We can't do it without Grandpa," seconded Scarp.

"Darling, he won't come," Kirsten replied. "He was quite adamant. He sent his love but he doesn't feel up to it. We've left him lashings of food."

"That's not the point," objected Sven. "He *must* come. We can't celebrate without him."

He strode to the car and drove off without looking back. A hush settled momentarily on the party before they resumed their tasks.

Corky touched Barbara's arm and pulled her to one side.

"Is everything alright?" He looked suddenly anxious in the fading light.

"The old man? I don't know. He just dug in his heels." Barbara shook her head. "Something is bothering him but he won't talk. Ever since he finished that drum, he's been a worried man."

"Perhaps he wore himself out…"

"Oh, sure." She had put on her Italian shoes: green, pointy suede with a black tassel on the tongue, and she scraped a dust-pattern with her toe. Didn't know why she had dressed up, really. As a rule, she liked to be comfortable - blend with the wallpaper. Corky was rigged out too in his buskers coat and red neck-tie, but he had a preoccupied air.

"Are *you* okay?" she asked at length.

"I'm being turned out," he said.

"Turned out?"

246

"I received a letter from the Planning Department this morning. You know all my post goes to a P.O. Box in Newbridge. Someone has shopped me to the authorities and I've got thirty days to demolish my shack."

Barbara stared in disbelief. "*Who*? Who would do such a thing? Who could know or care?"

"I've upset somebody..."

"Wait," said Barbara. "You did an interview, right, with '*The Echo*', about finding the Vincent fakes? Your picture was in the paper. Someone is unhappy about the publicity around the Sump..."

"Surely, not the old lady..."

"Never! She'd die rather than speak to an official. And there's no malice in her."

"The Museum? But they are quite happy with the story. It's still a scoop for them."

"The Planning Department, did you say? Well, anyone who visited Newbridge Market would know who you were. And it wouldn't be hard to find out where you came from. They only had to ask. Any of the stallholders could have told them..."

"Well, the damage is done now." Corky gave a defeated shrug.

"Stringer!" said Barbara finally, narrowing her eyes. "Who did for Scarp, here? Who was behind the letter threatening Miss Vincent?" She broke into a grin and squeezed Corky's arm. "Don't give up hope. We've got Stringer in our sights. I think his days are numbered."

* * * * *

When Sven returned, he was still alone. Per would not yield to persuasion. He was well, he insisted, and wished them all a good feast, but he was tired - too tired to venture out. They had to leave it at that.

By now the scent of sausages filled the air. As daylight faded, the Swedish, moon-faced lanterns gathered strength. Candle-beams glinted on Kirsten's silver and crystal and made flower shadows dance on the tablecloth.

Another car drew up and out hopped Professor Saxmund, in white tie and tails. He cut a noble figure, his leonine head (mane and beard

247

neatly brushed) looking striking in the lamplight. He opened the passenger door with a flourish and a roar of welcome greeted Miss Vincent. She too had come in fancy dress: an antique flowered frock, a stole and pearls.

The third passenger posed something of a puzzle. Petite, blonde and self-conscious, she emerged in a pair of spangled pumps.

"Lordy, will you look at that!" whistled Barbara. "It *can't* be!"

But it *was*. The mystery guest turned out to be Birgit, who had had herself done up! Saving the surprise for Hubert, she had declined his offer of a lift and travelled with the old folk instead. She still wore her nose-bead, but, this aside, her looks had changed beyond recognition. Her hair, dazzling, dye-bottle blonde, now tumbled (thanks to some ingenious extensions,) in bubbly tresses to her shoulders. And the feel of them was so novel, she could not resist patting and stroking and fiddling with them, while Hubert gazed on in wonder. She wore a peacock blue sarong, with false finger-nails to match.

"Well I call that a shame." whispered Barbara, regretfully. "I did so *like* her all in black!"

Kirsten nodded, watching the lovers meet. "What happened to Wolf Moss?" she asked.

Professor Saxmund knew the answer to that: "Disgraced himself, I'm afraid. It seems he played at a *'Change the World'* festival and heard a sermon on the spiritual power of money. From that moment on he was lost to the cause. Pledged himself to a new career, selling insurance and left the Woodsland Warriors..."

Out came more presents: the tea service from Miss Vincent; a vegan cookbook from Birgit; the cauldron from Professor Sax. Scarp downed another glass of cider and grinned over his cooking pots.

When they had taken their seats, Professor Saxmund rose to give a toast.

"No, no, no!" cried Sven, remembering Swedish etiquette. "The host must give the first toast. Where is Scarp?"

"Get off!" said Scarp. "If *he* wants to give a toast, let him!"

Saxmund raised his glass: "To friendship and loyalty!" They repeated the pledge.

Then Barbara stood up: "Cakes and Ale!"

"Cakes and Ale!" they responded, just as if they were in church.

Trudi watched the large-winged bats come out of the Sump. Big as blackbirds, they seemed to hang in the air, then suddenly, miraculously, speed to a distant point and hover there. The harvest moon, fat as a cheese, rose over the dusky stubble. Moths beat their wings against the lanterns. The smell of the earth mingled with campfire smoke, the tang of old nettles and dry leaves. How she loved it all. Away from the firelight and laughter, the Sump lay dark, hugging its secrets. From out of the shadows, a came a soft, insistent pulse. Jurgen had unpacked his drum, which meant the music would soon begin.

Corky's crayfish marked the climax of the feast. They arrived on a platter, a delicious, rosy pink, with their little tails stuck up in the air, and a ticklish job it was, winkling the flesh out of their shells, but even Birgit, who had also hit the cider, grabbed herself a cocktail stick and set to with a will.

"Save some fish for Per." That was Corky, fitting his trombone together.

Scarp now staggered to his feet. "I *have* got a toast," he said, casting a lordly glance the length of the table. "It's to old Grandpa. Long health to him!"

"To Per!"

"Skål!"

Corky launched into a ragtime stomp, with glissandos on the trombone and fancy percussion that made him jerk like a puppet. Torn between admiration and envy, Jurgen put down his drum. Should he have taken up the trombone instead? *"Don't try to be clever."* He could hear Per's voice in his ear. *"You will find only emptiness that way."* He shrugged.

They were getting up to dance: Sven and Kirsten, Birgit and Hubert...

"Come on, gorgeous!" Scarp caught Barbara round the waist and jigged away like a madman. Who would have believed that he had it in him? The cider had stolen his shyness and out came the toe-tapping, thigh-slapping rhythm-swagger of his Romany ancestors.

Professor Saxmund made Trudi a formal bow. "Miss Vincent is sitting out. Would you do me the honour?" And off they went, as incongruous a couple as you could ever hope to find on a summer's night, under the stars. After the dancing, came trifle, and the famous

Tuesday buns, and then stories round the fire: tales of the everglades from Sven, and of the jungles of New Guinea, from the Professor, and of fashion and culture in Helsinki. Birgit had kicked off her shoes soon after arrival and slipped reassuringly back into character, topping every story as it came.

"You know, everyone should have a spirit name. We all have a familiar, like the old wise women of long ago."

"Witches, you mean," said Scarp.

"Yes, of course, witches. Anyone can be a shaman or a shape-shifter and contact the guardian spirits, for advice. I'm rather good at it. That's how I knew I was a 'Wildfly'. But your guardian-spirit might be anything: a butterfly, a rainbow, a dewdrop... a fairy mushroom..."

Scarp made an ill-concealed guffaw and received a cuff from Barbara. But Wildfly winged on, unperturbed, and even Trudi felt too lazy and satisfied to object.

"Hubert here is a stag," chirruped Birgit. "I can *see* - I have the gift. I can read auras, too."

"And Kirsten?"

"Kirsten is a swan, and Sven is a giant redwood."

"What am I then," asked Barbara. "An elephant seal?"

"No, no!" Birgit had no sense of the ridiculous. "You're a little baby, fluffy owl."

Scarp stuck two fingers down his throat. "...and I'm a rattlesnake and Professor Saxmund over there is a sly old crocodile, creeping up on unsuspecting natives... Gub!" he gulped, "Swallowing up their secrets in the jaws of his laptop." He snapped the imaginary lid shut between his hands.

"No," Jurgen stepped in. "Professor Saxmund is a magpie. You can see, look. Black and white."

"I sincerely hope not!" objected Miss Vincent. "A most detestable bird. I've seen them, working their way round the bushes in my garden, stealing the eggs and fledglings of all the songbirds. I cannot abide the sight of them."

"Poor things can't help their nature," said Barbara. "And they *are* beautiful."

"They are the birds of death," the old lady pronounced with her customary vehemence. "I wish Professor Saxmund to be something

250

else."

"It's true." He wrapped his hand thoughtfully round his beard and held it there. "Magpies have always been considered omens of misfortune. In the Old Norse religion they were birds of Odin, like the raven and the crow – wise, but dangerous..."

"You have to greet them if you see them," said Corky, throwing in his two-pennyworth. "Doff your cap. Then you will be all right. After all, they are not all black. White for goodness too."

"And there's a rhyme for counting them:
> *"One for sorrow; two for joy;*
> *Three for a girl; Four for a boy;*
> *Five for silver; Six for gold;*
> *Seven for a secret never..."*

But before Birgit could finish, Barbara cut in with something else.

Trudi felt convulsed by a sudden shiver. The talk had broken her dream and she saw again the bird which had enticed her into the forest.

"There's a better story," Barbara was saying, "about magpies. You know how jaunty and know-it-all they are, always chattering, never listening?" She cast an indulgent glance at Birgit. "Well, on the day the birds are taught to build their nests, the magpie is away on other business and misses class. When she gets back, she has no idea what to do. So the other birds take pity on her and decide to teach her what they know.

"The heron takes a big stick and wedges it in the top of a tree. 'You start like this,' says the heron, but the magpie can't sit still long enough to listen. 'I get the idea!' she squawks and flaps away to visit the crow. With the crows it's just the same and while they are trying to help her she chips in: "I know all that already." And off she goes to hear what the wood pigeon has to say. The wood pigeons have hardly begun when she starts strutting and wagging her tail. "Anyone can do that." And she hasn't even seen the little birds - your birds, Miss Vincent. Though they know how to make a whole variety of exquisite nests, they can see they are wasting their time. At last, the magpie comes home to her own jumbled heap of twigs. Now she has to cobble something together, but since she hasn't paid attention, she can't really recall the designs of any of the nests she has seen. All she has in her head is random bits and snatches. So, she does what

251

she can. She takes the sticks of the heron and the moss of the blackbird and the mud of the house-martin and she makes herself a nest which is quite unlike any other. And that is why, my dears, to this day, the nest the magpie makes has such a curious construction."

"And why, perhaps," added Corky "magpies are said to be thieves. For it is not just ideas they borrow. Tinsel, silver paper, anything that shines... If they can get it, they'll pinch it for decoration. That's the way to impress, if you're a magpie!"

"Just like storytellers!" laughed Barbara, thinking how all the best tales were made up of shreds of others.

She looked at Scarp, who now lolled, half asleep against a tree, and the children, dozing like puppies on the straw. Time to pack up - scrape the plates - blow out the lanterns. Tomorrow, the business of the world would reclaim them all and this lull would seem no more than a summer dream.

Chapter 32

Beor

By the time the revellers returned, Per had already gone to bed. His supper lay untouched. Trudi felt a moment's anxiety. Was he actually all right? Suppose he was ill or sliding back into apathy? But the dark was warm tonight and she fell asleep with Corky's rhythms dancing in her ears, and the memory of firelit faces, smiling.

Her awakening next morning, came as something of a shock. It was early - no later than seven. The weather had changed overnight and a rough, dry wind now harried the leaves in the garden. But above the sea-swell of the trees, she could make out another sound. There was no mistaking it now. That was the whine of chain saws. There were several of them. And they were busy in the Sump.

She leapt out of bed and threw her window wide. Without a doubt, the felling had begun. But how could it be? How could they touch the trees before the land was sold?

All through breakfast the whining continued, aggravated by the roar of other machines. Brush cutters? Strimmers, were they? There must have been a sizeable gang at work. Per sat stony-faced, drumming his fingers on the table, refusing any food. And Trudi pushed her muesli bowl away. Barbara's coaxings had a hollow ring:

"Eat up, honey. Your father's going to phone them and sort it all out. Don't you worry. Everything will be just fine."

What rubbish, Trudi thought. Of course it wasn't fine. Anyone could see that! If only Birgit was here with the Woodsland Warriors, they could form a human shield and fend the developers off. But Birgit was away, and, in any case, she had rather over-stated her influence with those doughty activists. The Warriors were busy frying other fish.

Sven marched to his study at nine o'clock to telephone the Water Company.

"You want to speak to Mr. Malting?" sniffled a young secretary with a cold. "I'm afraid he's not in the office today. Would you like to leave a message?"

"I'd like to enquire about the land for sale at Bockhurst."

"I'm sorry. There's no one free to speak to you right now. Perhaps you could contact the agent."

"Can you give me the number?"

"Newbridge. 01387 944733. You want Mr. Westwick."

"Thank you."

The office in Newbridge was equally unhelpful.

"Mr. Westwick? I'm afraid he's in a meeting."

"It's about the land sale at Bockhurst."

"Do you have a professional interest?"

Sven swallowed hard and lied, affecting a cold himself to disguise his accent. "Yes."

"Well, the bidding closed yesterday."

"The sale is on Friday, surely."

"All the main bids were in, so they brought the day forward. They've had trouble with threats from protestors. I'm not really supposed to say - it's confidential. They haven't notified all the parties yet."

"Well, can you tell me who was successful?"

"I'm afraid not. We have to protect our clients' confidentiality. Shall I say who called?"

Sven hesitated, but he had now ploughed in so far, he thought he might as well go on. "Yes - Stringer - Nigel Stringer."

"Oh, Mr. Stringer," stammered the receptionist. "I'm sorry, I didn't recognize your voice. That's a nasty cold you have. Yes, we managed to bring everything forward. I thought Mr. Westwick spoke to you yesterday. I know he was trying to contact you. The money from Eco-Homesteads all came through by electronic transfer - no problem at all. Mr. Beamish was notified straightaway. I'm surprised he hasn't been in touch. Mervyn Towner, the contractor, said his boys were ready to make a start. I think they were going in today."

"Thank you. That's excellent news." Sven hung up.

Well, Miss Vincent was right when she called them crooks and swindlers. They had stitched up a deal between them, in advance - cash on the nail - no time for appeals. They must have had contracts ready and waiting. And now what was he going to say to Trudi?

She must forget the Sump and all her games and adventures there. It would be a shame to lose the trees, but if one thing was certain, it this: there would be no point in contesting matters now. Stringer and his friends would have covered their backs very carefully and would employ the best lawyers to defend them. They had already proved themselves ruthless with opposition. Suddenly the Museum, the Manor, even Marilyn Jackson appeared preferable neighbours. Miss Vincent's letter looked like flimsy evidence now. And he had no grounds for a professional objection. In any case it was all too late. He certainly had no intention of letting anyone he loved cross Stringer's path.

Yet, one last, desperate idea occurred to him, and before he broke the news to Trudi, he sought out his father, who was sitting blankly in his room.

"They've got it," he announced. "By whatever devious and criminal means - the developers have bought it already."

Per nodded as if he already knew and Sven pushed on. "I'm worried about Trudi. She takes things so much to heart."

"I have told her to be calm," the old man replied.

"But you know her better than that. You know she won't be calm."

Per looked away. And Sven dropped on his knees to meet him eye to eye.

"Father, can't *you* help?"

The appeal sounded odd, coming from him. Was he, the scientific rationalist, really asking for some kind of alternative intervention? Magic? No matter if he lost face, he needed to believe in some resort to justice.

Per opened his hands to show that they were empty. But Sven was not deceived. The old man knew something. He was sure of it. He thought of Proteus, sea god of the Greeks.

In ancient legend, Proteus had the gift of divination but he would not tell what he knew without a fight. Those who wanted his counsel had to catch and pin him fast, while the crusty old merman did all that he could to escape. It was nothing for him to raise a storm, or change himself into a monster - a series of monsters, even. You had to cling on tight till he had finished all his tricks. Only when he was thoroughly weary, would he resume his natural form and yield his secrets up.

"What can *I* do, a useless invalid?" said Per, closing his eyes.

255

"You *know* things," Sven persevered. "You *see* things. My mother told me. I remember. She said you had the power to make things happen…" He took hold of his father's hands but the old man shook him off.

"No. All that is past. It lost me your mother's love. Lost me everything that was dearest to me. Such knowledge could not bring you back when I most needed you. I will not use it now. I will not lose Trudi as well."

"She will believe we let her down."

"No. She will learn that failure makes the spirit stronger."

"Can *nothing* change your mind?"

Per looked away over Sven's head, unable to hide the conflict which raged within him and his voice, when he next spoke, sounded deeper than ever: "If you want magic, it has to happen on the inside. What Trudi has done already here - *that* is magic. I hope it will be enough."

Sven could hold onto him no longer. Sadly, he let him go.

Throughout the day the sound of the chainsaws continued. You could hear the thump as the distant trunks crashed down. This was clear-felling. The contractors must have been working in haste before anyone could protest or intervene. But the trees of the camp swayed on. Their imminent end meant nothing to them. What did they know of execution?

Barbara tried to contact Scarp and Hubert - neither were answering their phones. Miss Vincent had taken to her bed and would not come to the door.

To make matters worse, Simon Stringer carried his football into the garden and spent an hour kicking it straight at the fence. When he wasn't kicking, he was peering through the gaps which had begun to appear, revelling in adding to the general annoyance. They could hear Beor beside him, panting joyfully up and down, astonished find he had a friend to play with.

At last, Kirsten could bear it no longer and took Trudi and Jurgen to Tilchester to buy their school uniforms.

"These things just happen," she said, tucking them into the car. "Think of poor old Corky losing his home. It's not fair - of course it's not fair - but you simply have to keep going. Work hard. Then you can do more good in the world."

256

Trudi had no interest at all in her uniform. What hogwash adults talked - even Per, who had forbidden her to set foot beyond the garden. None of them had any real courage to stand up for what was right.

Children see justice in an unequivocal way and for Trudi there were no legal complications or moral ambiguities to consider. The Sump belonged to the trees and the badgers and the ancient flint-makers. It belonged to Scarp and Miss Vincent. Even to the *kelet*, whom she feared. What would become of *them*, she wondered? Where would they hide their hairy, spider legs and white, moon faces if the Trollstones were taken away? Maybe they had lived there for hundreds of years. Maybe they would die? She even felt a stab of pity for them and wished they could come out and make a stand. Surely *they* could frighten Stringer's men away.

At four o'clock, the chainsaws ceased. The sound, like a nagging pain, had drowned all other sensations and now softer voices could be heard. The wind was just sighing in the tree tops. Trudi, who had been quiet since the return from town, pulled Jurgen aside as soon as tea was over:

"Come on! I'm going in to see what they have done."

Jurgen hung back. "You can't," he objected. "It's too dangerous. They might catch you. Anything could happen."

"Are you too scared to come, then?" Trudi sneered. But she could taunt him all she liked, Jurgen wasn't playing dares today.

"Yes," he whispered. "Grandfather said…"

No matter. Her blood was up. "Well, *I'm* going anyway. Will you at least keep lookout for me?"

He nodded unwillingly and followed her to the fence.

"Trudi, be careful." His small hand caught her sleeve.

"Oh, *baby*!" she hissed and put out her tongue. She did not need to be careful. She had a Sami hunting bow to protect her. She would be like the old hunters, when they set out on their skis. This was *her* ground. She squeezed through the gap Sven had made a few days before and disappeared into the wood.

"Be *quick*!" Jurgen pleaded, looking anxiously up and down "You're going to get us into trouble." But there was nobody about. Sven was busy working. The women were talking in the kitchen. And Grandfather Larsson had done nothing all day but prowl round

257

his room like a lion in a cage. None of them would be able to see what was happening down here; the shrubs grew far too thick. Only that boy next door could tell on them, peeking from his upstairs window, and when he caught Jurgen looking back, he turned away.

"Hurry up, Trudi. Hurry!"

Jurgen patrolled the wire, willing her to return. But his impatience only seemed to slow things down. The minutes limped and dragged themselves along as though they were half asleep. They would not be measured by a clock. They belonged to a different kind of time, a time which had no truck with a pendulum. Per knew all about it. He had talked of it when he was building his drum. He said that a good drummer could *create* time, just like that, as if it could be unwound, like a ball of string. But Jurgen's fear had frozen everything up. He could no longer hear Trudi moving beyond the trees. His ears strained foward, listening anxiously...

Then a new sound behind him made him start.

The minutes woke up and immediately started to run...

Someone next door had loosened a catch and Beor bounded out. He was barking, as always, but he must have escaped from his collar for he hurled himself at the fence with his old ferocity. Jurgen heard the spittle catch in his throat. Growling, he drew back and leapt again and with a splintering wrench, the panelling gave way. Now there was nothing to stop him - he was through.

Jurgen shrank back with a horrified: "Oh my God!" but Beor took no interest in the boy. He merely knocked him down as he passed and slipped, like an evil shadow, into the Sump.

What could a puny eight-year-old do now? How could he even call for help, when his voice had shrivelled up inside him and wouldn't come out? Dazed and shaken, Jurgen stumbled along the path, but before he had gone many paces something else ran into him. In his bewildered state, he could not even tell what this creature was - a pelt grey and white, long, sleek and soft, with silent paws. It darted after Beor and was gone. Jurgen mustered all his strength and charged towards the house.

"Beor's out!" he yelled at the kitchen door. "Beor's out and he's going to kill Trudi!"

In the green hush of the Sump, Trudi tiptoed along the old

familiar path, past Jurgen's log and the nettle trail, into the willow-herbs. The silence was palpable. The wind had dropped and a still, white sky showed above the trees. No birds sang. The insects had suspended their summer hum and in that unnatural quiet you could have heard the snap of a twig.

There. There was a sound just like a twig snapping. The silence settled and then it came again. It took Trudi a moment to register the fact and in that instant, her heart began to quicken. Someone was out there, somewhere in the wood, but, lost in the tall willow-herbs, she could see nothing either way. She pushed on, steadily increasing her pace. If only she could reach the Trollstones, she might hide behind them and wait till whoever it was went by. But this person or thing was moving at speed and gaining on her fast.

Suddenly, her mind was flooded with fear. She felt herself back in the forest of her dream, or lost in the charcoal chase which had scrambled across her drawing paper, weeks before. The message of both was essentially the same. If this was a hunt and the hunter was behind her, then some unknown foe had marked *her* as its prey. Her lungs gasped now for air. Her legs turned into lead. She broke out of the undergrowth by the lagoon and glanced in horror at the water. Dear God, not there! Wherever she must meet her doom, please let it not be there. Not in those filthy depths!

Ahead of her, the trees had been felled and the open sky presided over a clearance of some size. Only the far beeches remained. Perhaps she could climb into one of them? The very thought was impossible. Already she could hear the drumming of Beor's feet and his wheezing, coming up behind. As she staggered on, tripping over branch and bramble, he sprang out of the willow herbs and launched himself at her back. The weight of his great body threw her to the ground and the heat and stink of his breath was suddenly upon her.

Instinctively, she curled herself into a ball. She knew she had been hurt but a voice inside kept saying if only she could keep him away from her face, she might live a few seconds longer. She wrapped her hands round her neck and buried her head between her elbows and Beor stood for a moment, triumphant, one heavy paw upon her side, before he opened his jaws.

How many times he bit her she could not tell. Her fingers remained resolutely locked together. Consciousness of anything beyond the will to hold on had drained away, like her own life-blood. For those few seconds she felt nothing, heard nothing but a fiendish, gutteral roar. And then a calm.

Having raised the alarm, Jurgen turned on his heels and, without waiting for the others, raced back to the Sump. He had lost his fear now and the running was easy. He was the 'rocket' of the football team. He had quite forgotten his sprain.

At the Sump, the trampled stems, told him which way to go, and he plunged on, listening for Trudi's screams. The wood lay quiet on every side. Silence in the willow herbs. Silence by the lagoon... Then he heard a cry - a voice like thunder itself:

"Beor!"

There, in the clearing, he saw the dark shape of the dog worrying at something on the ground, and beside him - huge - with arms outstretched, the figure of a man.

As Jurgen watched, this figure struck the dog upon the haunch and Beor wheeled round snarling, closing his fangs upon his assailant's hand. His victim did not flinch. He was forcing his fist deep into the creature's maw, trying to choke the life-breath out of it, while his other hand reached for something at his belt. Now he had hold of it; lifted it high above his head. Jurgen glimpsed a flash of steel. Bright silver. A hunter's knife. Within the span of a moment his mind grew clear. Man and knife, of course, were known to him. And that shape, lying still... he knew now, what that was. The blade hung, quivering like a hawk, then plummeted down, straight into Beor's heart.

In the silence which followed, slayer and slain looked hard at one another. Beor's eyes, clouding fast, met the cold, blue gaze of a northern wolf.

"Forgive me," said Per, placing his hand on Beor's head. "Be at peace now."

With one movement, he rolled the dog's body aside, and, casting his knife away, knelt over Trudi, gathering her into his arms. The last thing she saw, before the dark closed in, was his beloved face, all wet with tears.

Sven burst into the clearing, with Kirsten at his heels.

"Trudi!" He cried out, rushing wildly forward, and Per lifted her

260

body and held her out to him. "Gently, gently - she will live - I promise."

He cut a terrible figure himself, hands, arms, clothing drenched in blood, but he had assumed an authority that brooked no questioning. "Take her, my son. Fetch help." Sven paused a moment, trying to speak with his eyes, then turned and made for the house.

"Grandpa, you are hurt!" said Kirsten, reaching out her arms.

"No, no. Go with him! He will need you at the fence." Dishevelled and shaken, she looked quite pitiful, all her composure gone. She cast a look of horror at Beor's body, turned and fled.

"Jurgen. Quick!" With his remaining strength, Per seized on a broken stem of stripling ash. "Hold this." Jurgen did as he was told and watched as the old man recovered his knife and lopped the leaves away. A few deft strokes soon sliced and sharpened the ends.

"Now this way - hold it level!" Steadying himself with the elbow of his injured arm, he made rapid incisions in the bark.

Jurgen tried but could not make them out. These scratches did not look like English words - not Swedish, or Anglo Saxon either. But all the same, the signs were familiar. Belatedly, he realized, they were runes – the rune-figures Per had cut for him before. He wished he had paid proper attention at the time. What did they mean? What was it Grandfather said? He could not ask him now. Per, for his part, did not blink or falter. He knew exactly what to write and he spoke as he cut the letters: "This is a *game* we were playing. You remember? Yes? You will tell them?" But this game had a deadly urgency. He dropped his knife into its scabbard and, smearing the script with his bloodied hands, read it again and nodded.

"Good." He thrust the rune-stick into the earth where Trudi had fallen. "Good boy. Brave boy." His eyes shone at Jurgen. "You have done well. Now you can help Grandfather home. He is tired."

By the time they returned, the emergency services had arrived. All along the road were vehicles with flashing lights - ambulances, police cars. And strangers had taken possession of the house - kindly men and women in uniform, their radios crackling, calmly taking notes and offering comfort, as Trudi was taken away. When Sven and Kirsten left for the hospital, they turned to Jurgen and Per:

"This was the boy who raised the alarm..."

"This man needs help too. Lost a lot of blood…"

They were quiet and efficient, smiling reassurance and Jurgen clung to Barbara's side, feeling suddenly overwhelmed.

"We've tried the house next door. There's no reply," reported one young sergeant.

"The boy is there," said Jurgen. "I saw him."

They had strapped Grandfather Larsson into a tiny folding chair and wrapped a blanket over his knees. Somebody attended to his hand. Someone else attached a drip. To Jurgen, he seemed to have shrunk in size. He looked a mere dummy of himself. But Per had no intention of giving in. As they carried him to the ambulance he sought out Jurgen's face and wrinkled a smile. One long finger tapped his nose. The questions would all come later and he would need an ally then.

"Honey, don't fret. It'll all come out just fine! You'll see," fibbed Barbara dropping to her knees.

Jurgen hugged her back and pressed his face into her shoulder. He did not believe her, but he clung to the words, just the same.

Chapter 33

The Path to the Ancestors

When Trudi came round, her bedside was crowded with friendly faces.

"Darling, it's all right. We're here. You're safe." She tried to move, winced and fell back. "Just rest, just rest," said Kirsten, smoothing her forehead.

She looked about as though searching for something she could not find, then gave up and drifted back to sleep.

Later, when her sedatives had worn off, she recognized Per's face amongst the others. Now she smiled.

Her injuries were not too terrible. Apart from a nasty bite on her shoulder, she had protected herself pretty well and the most serious wounds were to her arms and hands. She had scraped one leg as she fell. The doctors marvelled that she had survived the attack at all. She would be kept in for observation, until she had recovered from shock and loss of blood. However, she could expect a long and difficult convalescence. Dog bites went deep, causing trauma to body and mind. They would give her medication for the pain.

Under different circumstances, she would have loved the attention, but she was too confused and weak just now to take it in. She found it hard remember what had happened. She knew that she had gone into the Sump and heard something there which frightened her. There was a shock - a terrific blow on her back and after that, nothing the but Per's eyes, burning into hers. Others had to explain to her that Beor was dead - that she had become a newspaper sensation - that Nigel Stringer had been taken for questioning, pending further investigations.

Beor was dead.

That incredible fact came back to her over and over again. She would try to touch whoever was at her side, just to hear the words again.

"Is it really true?"

"Grandfather killed him."

263

And the question which everybody asked, but no one could answer was *How*?

How could he *happen* to be there? Just then? Per's story baffled them all, but they could not for sure refute it. He had been worried, he said, and gone, like Trudi, into the wood, alone. He had not known his grand-daughter was there. When he heard the dog, the old hunter in him had rushed to the rescue.

At which point they still asked: "How?"

"I'm not so feeble," he replied indignantly. "An old man, yes, but I am not finished yet."

"You are a hero," said Kirsten, laying her head affectionately on his shoulder. "Where would we be without you, dear Grandfather?"

He smiled and nodded and a little more ice melted in his soul. Indeed, he seemed a different man entirely. The passivity and remoteness of the previous weeks had gone, and he now showed a determined spirit. He would not stay in hospital. Though he permitted them to stitch and bandage him, he declined all pills and medicines. He roared at his doctors. He would walk to Bockhurst, if necessary! Trudi heard of the rumpus with satisfaction. And finally, Sven and Kirsten took him home.

At the house, the police had finished for the night. Dodging the reporters, the Larssons hurried indoors, where Barbara had hot coffee ready and where they found Scarp, fuming for revenge.

"No, no," said Per, calm once more. "Revenge is done. I did it! Now it is time for healing." All the same he declined his supper and, looking drawn and weary, withdrew for the night.

Jurgen sat on the sofa, listening to the grown-ups and thinking how odd the house felt without Trudi. Of course, she had been away before, but nothing important had happened then, and usually, when she was away, he was away as well. Now, he felt he needed her. The events of the last few hours swirled around in his head and for the first time he could remember, he did not have her there to tell him what to think. The police had searched and photographed the wood and taken Beor's body away in a bag. They were coming back tomorrow to ask more questions. They had interviewed the neighbours, including Miss Vincent, and spent some time inspecting the Stringers' house. All work in the Sump would be suspended until the enquiry was over. There had been a lady from the RSPCA. They

264

did not seem to believe Grandfather Larsson.

Tired as he was, even when he lay in his bed, Jurgen could not stop this mental merry-go-round. He did not know what he should say to the authorities. He did not even really know what he knew. He had begun his story with Beor's escape and his brush with the second wolf, but the police did not seem to understand him. They would not believe there was a wild wolf in Sussex, and later, when he heard his grandfather's account and learnt that he had made no mention of it, he began to wonder if he had made the creature up. He remembered Per tapping his nose like a conspirator. Did Per really not see the wolf? Was it a ghost? Or did the old man know more than he would admit? He had counselled secrecy over the rune-sticks and Jurgen did not want to contradict him and land him in trouble.

Gradually, the sounds of the house died away. The last light went out. Even the voices in his parent's room fell silent. Everyone had gone to sleep and in time he, too, drifted off.

He was woken a few hours later by his own heart, which was beating louder than usual, drumming, as though entrained to a distant rhythm. He lay still, listening for a while - then opened his eyes. He *could* hear something, far away: a pulse, beating, way out in the dark - slow - steady - like a summons - a spirit, calling. Tiptoeing to the window, he gazed out into the night. His room lay next to Trudi's, at the back of the house and, like hers, looked out over the Sump. Though the moon had not yet risen, a soft glow suffused the sky. And as he watched, other lights flickered above the trees. Could there be someone out there? Someone carrying a torch? Or lighting a fire?

Grandfather would know. Jurgen stole downstairs in his pyjamas, and pushed open the conservatory door, but from the threshold he could see Per's bed was empty. The French windows stood ajar. Perhaps Grandpa could not sleep either. Perhaps he was in the garden... Not sure whether he was waking or sleeping, he stepped outside, drawn by the distant sound. Fear and curiosity fell away. The summons came from deep inside the Sump, where the strange lights played. What he could hear, he realized, *was* the voice of a drum, insistent, full-toned, like the drum Per made.

Barefoot, he ventured down the garden, feeling his way with his hands. The fence at the bottom had been pulled away and it was easy to pass beneath the white tape which the police had left. On he went, like a somnambulist. Ahead of him, a green finger of light flared up and rippled across the sky, beckoning beyond the dark shapes of the trees. Then it was gone. Was somebody working there? Manning a searchlight - letting off fireworks?

The measure pounded on.

He reached the willow herbs and passed them. He must be careful not to slip here, for he knew the water was nearby. And instinct told him he was getting close to the source.

Gradually the rhythm quickened and the display intensified. Once more the sky was flooded with emerald light. A giant will o' the wisp, a luminous fringe, unfurled and wavered overhead. Yes, not much further to go...

At last, he came to the clearing where, only hours before, he had seen the terrible sight of Beor's death. That was where Trudi fell, and there... he stopped, with mouth agape. He had arrived. Here, beneath a flare, new-tinged with rose, was a figure dancing - man, was it? or demon? - whirling, like a dervish in a trance. Eyes blazing, hair flying, he beat a Sami drum. As he turned, the skirts of his coat swung wide, revealing a long tunic with a beaded belt. His coat was old; the inverted pelt of some wild beast. On his head he wore a cap. From beard to naked feet, he seemed possessed by the invisible spirits his dance invoked.

It was Per, the magician. Per the shaman. So Trudi had been right about him, all along!

For Jurgen, crouching in the shadows, the spectacle held the primitive wonder of a pagan rite. Cries, like the voices of animals, broke from the old man's lips and his eyes rolled as the aurora flickered overhead. In some inexplicable way, the heavens were answering him. Now an arc of light bent down like a celestial causeway. The drum hammered faster and the whirling spun into a frenzy which almost threw the dancer off his feet. Now the arc faded, giving place to a crown of light.

Jurgen felt that if he stretched out a hand, he could touch the light, so close did it seem, so beautiful, so unlike anything he had ever known in his brief life. But fear of breaking the spell prevented him. His limbs congealed. His breathing ceased. Perhaps the rapture and the agony would never stop, and he would be locked forever, with his grandfather, in a maelstrom outside time...

Convulsed by a final spasm, Per collapsed on the ground. The lights gradually faded, then expired. When Jurgen crept from his hiding-place he found the clearing empty. The moon was up. He stumbled here and there in the shadows, calling, but there was no reply. And no sign of what had passed, save a snatch of trimming, lodged in a tangle of ivy.

Daylight found him in his own bed, safe and sound, but his feet were sore and he clutched a blue bead in his hand.

Chapter 34

Ghosts

Hospital visiting was not allowed till after lunch, so the morning was given over to practical concerns. Per accepted some breakfast in bed and, to Barbara's surprise, made short work of a boiled egg with soldiers, a bowl of wheatie-puffs and a positive mountain of toast. He had abandoned his sling and seemed to be making good use of his hand, though he complained that he was feeling his age, stiff and rather tired.

"I'm not surprised," said Barbara. "It's not every day you kill a hell-hound!"

Per grinned, then grew pensive. "Jurgen..."

"He's in *there*," she jerked a thumb towards the lounge, "talking to that nice young policeman. But he's fine. Sven's with him."

The old man bit his lip. Then shrugged. Nothing he could do about it now.

"Any chance..." he queried, "of a bun of some kind?"

Barbara squeezed his good hand and picked up the empty tray. "A bun, huh? Is that *all*? You sure you wouldn't like a steak as well? There's a bucket of crayfish out there, all swimming about, just waiting for you, you know!"

Per gave this some thought and tugged at his beard. Then he closed his eyes:

"I will have *those* for lunch!"

There were two police officers: a pretty, dark w.p.c. and the sergeant who had attended the house the day before - a mountain of a man who tried to gain Jurgen's confidence by sharing football stories.

"So, when you got to the clearing, was the dog already attacking your sister?"

"I couldn't see really," said Jurgen. "Beor was in the way."

"And your grandfather?"

"He came up behind and hit Beor."

268

"You mean, Sammy? Which is when the dog turned on him?"

Jurgen nodded.

"And what about this then? We found this at the scene." He brought out a plastic bag with the rune-stick in it. But Jurgen had been primed. He knew just what to say.

"It's a game we used to play," he replied without hesitation.

"A game?"

"Grandfather made it for us." Jurgen's oh-so-innocent eyes turned to the policewoman. She was nice. She wore her hair in a bun. "It was a magic game. Swedish. We're Swedish, see. Trudi must have had the stick. She was probably making a spell when Beor grabbed her."

"It's got blood on it."

"There was blood everywhere." This was certainly true.

But the sergeant had not finished yet. "What about this writing, then?"

Sven stared in disbelief. Did his children really play with such things? But Jurgen had his answers ready.

"It's magic writing."

"Who taught you that?"

"Why, Grandfather, of course. He's Swedish, too."

The sergeant nodded. "Well, that's very helpful. Very helpful indeed. Thank you. You've been a very brave lad. Well done." He cleared his throat in a theatrical way, caught Sven's eye and nodded towards the door. As they stepped outside he confided: "There is a children's counsellor available, if you think your boy will benefit… He's been through a lot."

Sven nodded politely. "We'll let you know. He's got a dozen counsellors here in the house already, but thank-you. You are very kind."

"Fine," Sergeant Kirby wrinkled up his nose. "I just need to revisit the site with you, then, and get your story - oh, and interview your father - and we're all done for the moment. We can leave you in peace."

"What about my neighbour?"

"It seems that the dog was an ideal family pet. A bit territorial - that's normal with that breed - but obedient, well-cared-for. I think the dog wardens came out once before at your request and they

269

concluded that there was nothing wrong with him. Their report has him down as a lovely animal, devoted to his master. The fence was getting old, but we've got no proof of actual negligence. This has just been one of those tragic accidents. I'm told any animal can turn, if provoked or exposed to sudden stress. Your daughter was lucky that your father was there. It seems almost too good to be true."

"So," said Sven, ignoring this last innuendo. "No charge?"

"There's really no case to answer. I understand that the family are moving away. That is probably for the best. Of course, they are very shocked. Especially that poor little lad. I think the dog was his best friend. Pity he couldn't have known your children better. They could have played together and this might never have happened."

Sven gritted his teeth.

"I'm coming with you," announced Professor Saxmund, laying a fatherly hand on Sven's shoulder. "I want to see this Sump anyway. I've heard so much about it. That's all right, isn't it, officer? I'm Mr. Larsson's boss - Head of the Department - his minder, if you like!"

He had arrived at the house sometime earlier, bringing bunches of flowers and gifts from Hubert and Birgit. His presence, as always, brought reassurance. Sven could not lose his temper while Professor Sax was looking on.

Today the reporting pack had set off on another case and visitors were free to come and go. Corky turned up with a pumpkin and a box of eggs. Scarp could not stay, but poked his head in at Per's door and made a 'keep-it-up' sign with his thumb. Miss Vincent left a pile of books. All morning long, the telephone rang and cards and messages from friends poured in. And Barbara found herself, for the first time, dreaming of home.

To sit in her little window-seat above the shop and watch the people pass in the street below; to sit with a book, on a rainy Sunday, hearing the water gurgle in the gutters, and the splash of feet in the pavement puddles; to sit on a spring evening, with the window open and the chestnut buds just breaking over the rooftops... Yes. She wanted to be home. *Her* kettle, *her* mugs - and the old tom cat that came for milk, from the alley behind the shop... She hadn't realized how much she missed them or the freedom of running her life just as she pleased. Certainly, the place was ramshackle and too expensive for her to manage on her own. But perhaps she could take in a lodger; someone quiet, who might do occasional stints in the shop? At any rate, it was a prospect to consider with pleasure. To have *time* to read again...

Sergeant Kirby led Sven and the Professor back to the Sump, talking all the while in his breezy manner. "So, you took down the fence sometime earlier, you say, sir?" He stopped at the boundary.

"I came with my daughter a day or so ago. I'm afraid I was too large to squeeze through the little hole that was there before."

"Little hole?"

"Yes, the little... where they - where the children used to scramble through." He sighed, knowing that it sounded bad.

The Sergeant merely smiled. "Kids eh? Little monsters, aren't they?" Perhaps he remembered escapades of his own. Perhaps he disapproved. He liked to think of himself as inscrutable. Often, when he did not know what to make of a situation he would deploy this trick to good effect. "Go in there often, did they?" He so wanted to prove himself smart and perceptive.

"We didn't encourage it, at least not unaccompanied," said Sven hastily. "But this summer, they formed a fascination with the place - and, well, we can't chain them up!"

"Quite. Well, let's go through."

It all felt deeply uncomfortable. Sven prickled, feeling himself under suspicion. He resented this policeman's patronising manner. What could such a man know about the private world he was trampling through?

"Technically," said Sergeant Kirby, "this business should be a case for the dog wardens, since it happened on private property." He was getting into his stride now, marching ahead, intoning observations to the air, so that only partial phrases drifted back: "...but as the injuries were so serious... police matter... and the dog itself was dead..."

Professor Saxmund was glad they couldn't hear him. Least said, soonest mended, he reckoned.

Now the three of them stepped clear of the willow-herbs and the policeman's monologue ceased. The day had been overcast since dawn. The black depths of the lagoon, now exposed to open sky, had turned a muddy green. Here, where the chain-saws had done their work, the ground was littered with woodland debris. Here, Beor had met his end. But just beyond this point, an unexpected sight arrested them.

There, by the Trollstones, stood the surviving trees. Four or five giants, they were, their boughs, in places, touching one another, their branching trunks, muscular as Norman pillars, stained with dark patterns, where the rain had run; their grey bark wrinkling at the joints, like living skin. How beautiful they were! They had spread their leaves to catch every vestige of light, creating caverns of cool shade below, where little grew. Their reticulated roots covered the ground.

But something here was odd. A trick of the light? Beyond the police tape and official warning signs, lay a pallid efflorescence, so thick in places, you would think that snow had fallen.

"What the...?"

They stared in astonishment.

A carpet of flowers had sprung up overnight. Their blushing stems carried no leaves and their waxy spikes, winged, like spectral moths, spread in a deathly mantle as far as the eye could see. Their existence was unheard of in these parts. Their profusion beggared belief.

"You know what they are?" said Professor Saxmund, dropping to his knees and cupping a specimen in his hands. Sven nodded in silence. Textbooks. Yes - he had seen pictures.

"Ghost orchids!" Saxmund almost choked. "Ghost orchids. Thousands of them! The rarest, strangest plant in all the country... *here!*"

Sven made some rapid calculations. Perhaps the upheavals of the last few days had prompted their appearance, though these freaks of nature needed little light. Some called them saprophytic for they seemed to grow on nothing but leaf litter and the fungal threads which proliferated in it. They hardly belonged to the living world of the sun. They had no green parts at all. And though science would continue to speculate about them, they were so elusive it was almost impossible to study them. Albinos, which buried themselves alive for years at a time. A man might count himself blessed to see one in a lifetime, but to see thousands was nothing short of a miracle!

"This changes everything." Professor Saxmund pronounced, abruptly asserting himself. "It takes priority, you understand. The land must not be disturbed in any way. I shall be reporting this to the highest authorities. And I am afraid it will mean no more machines in here. No more workmen. No more policemen, even. The whole area will come under protection of the Countryside Preservation Act and compensation will have to be paid to the owners. This has, overnight, become a site of national, no global importance and it must be sealed off from outside world. Orchid-hunters would come in their thousands to steal these plants. They will need to be guarded night and day."

Suddenly, roles were reversed. The case of Trudi and Beor slipped into second place and the officer, who had so confidently led them in, backed out in confusion, hardly knowing where to put his feet.

From that moment on, the Sump would be officially out of bounds.

Kirby's case was beginning to crumble. Though he suspected a cover-up somewhere, he could not find the proof. Key witnesses could not or would not speak. Per had mysteriously forgotten all English and rambled vaguely in his native tongue. Trudi, evasive, remembered next to nothing. Every attempt to get to the root of the matter met with similar frustration.

"I still say there's something funny going on," he complained to his superior at the station. "Looks like a ritual killing to me. I read a Swedish thriller about a werewolf, once..." But his theories fell on unsympathetic ears. Funding was short and a matter like this needed wrapping up swiftly.

"What are you suggesting?" mocked the Inspector. "That the little girl lured the dog into the wood and then attacked him with a stick? Didn't you ever play with sticks when you were a lad?"

"I'm just saying it has the hallmarks of something fishy... The old man knows more than he's admitting. There were other sticks with rune-markings near the fence and a colander, just lying there."

"Come on Kirby! Every child knows about runes. They've all seen '*Lord of the Rings*'! Where have you been all this time?"

He had to give it up.

Sitting in her hospital bed, Trudi heard how Professor Saxmund had taken the Sump under his special protection. Today she was her old self again, bright, imperious and miraculously untroubled by her injuries. People who have survived a scrape with death inspire a certain respect, so Trudi and her grandfather were spared many awkward questions. In private moments they exchanged enigmatic looks and smiles.

"Your daughter is extraordinary," confided the consultant, taking Sven aside. "The fever has gone. Indeed, she has made such a remarkable recovery there hardly seems any reason to keep her here. She might just as well convalesce in comfort at home and continue her treatment as an out-patient. I've never seen anything like it. No post-traumatic stress. No trouble sleeping. She seems to have very little pain. Dog bites normally cause deep and lasting damage. Somehow Trudi has been spared."

Sven nodded. "A mystery," he said.

"And I only believe it now because I have seen it with my own eyes." As if to stress the point he took off his glasses and polished them on his shirt. "If I could do magic like this every day, I tell you, I'd be a happy surgeon."

Sven shook his hand with feeling, but his own doubts lingered on. Like Sergeant Kirby, he had been sifting through the evidence and found that things did not add up. Suppose Per just happened to wander into the Sump... and Trudi and Jurgen really did play a rune game with carved sticks... and the developers did unwittingly ruin their own plans by causing the orchids to bloom... well, all these things might conceivably be true. But why should Per have taken his hunting knife? And why should the rune stick be daubed with blood from all three victims? Not merely spattered, Sergeant Kirby said, but *daubed*. And by what improbable coincidence did the orchids decide to flower just *then*? Scarp had spent years roaming the wood and never seen hint of them before. If there was some conspiracy - enchantment - downright magic at work - why then there was no need for probability. But those who knew the truth, Per and the children, had closed ranks and, like Miss Vincent before them, decided to bury what they knew.

"Oh hell, Sven," said Barbara, shaking his arm. "You have to stop brooding! What does it matter? They're alive and well, and Beor has gone. Nothing else matters two hoots! Maybe Per did decide to put on his shaman's coat and come to the rescue after all. Maybe he does change himself into animals when he pleases. You and I will never know. We're just ordinary mortals, like strangers on a magic island. The kids might be in on the secret, but they're not telling. They can hear things we don't. And that's how it *should* be. Someone has to be the straight guy. Decent, proper, normal people, they're needed too and that's you, my dear, and me. Those children are much too old for us."

Sven gave a beleaguered smile, so she went on:

"You know what Sergeant Kirby will do? He'll go home tonight and sit on his computer till he finds a spell that matches the runes on that stick. It's probably a healing spell. You find them in the Old Norse Sagas. And at the end of it all, he'll be no wiser than he was before. The story will flow on, like a river, carving new courses."

"You see everything as though it was a book!"

"But of course," she declared, folding her arms as if she had trumped at cards. "Know where that word comes from? '*Book*'?"

Sven shook his head.

"The Saxons! Good old Wulfstan and his friends. 'Beoc' is Anglo-Saxon for book, but also for beech tree. There's a theory that the first books were carved on tablets, made from wood, just like those old rune-sticks! The Saxons were pretty keen on runes too. Runes are riddles." She paused and then forged on. "Bockhurst - your village - would have been Beochurst, said with that gorgeous lilting tone you Swedes still have, you lucky devils. It means Beechwood. See how old the Sump just might be now? And how close young Edward might have been when he pictured Wulfstan dying there? Who's to tell if that lagoon isn't the very swamp where Eadric met his fate? Of course, we'll never know. The real treasures, in the end, were the orchids - Trudi's 'ghosts' which she was always so sure were hiding out over there. But there's something else. 'Bockhurst' also means Bookwood - a place full of stories - a real enchanted haven from our mad whirlwind of a world."

"You should be the lecturer!" laughed Sven.

"Not me, sir. I'm just the cook. Which reminds me, I invited Corky to stay for supper. I'm making pumpkin pie. I hope that's okay."

"Everything is okay, Barbara."

"I mean, with Kirsten."

"Kirsten loves pumpkin pie."

Barbara had been thinking of Scarp, and feeling angry with herself for thinking of him. Since the night of the feast he had seemed a distracted soul, preoccupied with thoughts he could not share.

"Penny for them," she asked once.

"Oh," he grinned with his broken teeth. "Must be getting soft. I blame you lot! I keep thinking about my family. I really ought to go and see them."

"I should think so!" she scolded cheerfully.

"Yeah. Maybe I'll go. Look up some old mates as well."

Of course he would have old mates; other worlds. A line of the 'Gypsy Rover' came into her head. Easy come, easy go. What did that riddle say? "*Neither lock nor chain can bind me…*"

"Your granny still alive?" she asked. He had so often made mention of her.

"Nah. She's gone. Gone completely. When she died, my uncles cleared the house and got rid of everything. You know that's the gypsy way. In the old days they used to burn the vans with all the possessions in them. No keepsakes."

Barbara nodded. "Let go."

"Well, maybe I let go a bit too much. My granny was the only person who ever really understood me and I took it hard when I lost her. Walked out on everything. But they're not really bad people, my folks, just… not like me. I've always been a bit wild."

"You'll stay in touch, won't you?"

"You bet."

"I'm making pumpkin pie for tonight, when Trudi comes home…"

Scarp pulled a face. "You're doing *what*? Who's going to have to eat that?"

"Don't say that to an American, you ass! Pumpkin pie is heaven on a plate!"

"Do I get some, then?"

"*If* you behave yourself."

"Put out a plate for me. I'll give it a go!"

276

Chapter 35

Pumpkin Pie

Barbara needed to put her thoughts in order. The time had come to pack and sort out her affairs. Term would begin next week. Heavens! Just think of all the books that would be wanted by those bright, young school-kids - all the Shakespeare texts, soon to be defaced in roundhand biro, scrumpled up and thrown into lockers with bags of crisps and soggy swimming things. Perhaps one in a thousand would be loved. The thought sent a shiver of excitement through her. Selling books was rather like releasing tadpoles. You never knew if any would survive for long, but there was always the hope that one or two would make it through. Somewhere, out in the great world pond, would be a shelf, a pocket, a pair of hands to hold them... and a bookworm, with luck, to devour them.

As her knife plunged into the belly of her pumpkin, she paused to savour the moment. The flesh was orange, like a Colorado sunset, the mass of seeds inside so perfectly aligned - the whole thing a miracle of practical design. The incredible bounty of nature struck her with new force. So many seeds! Some for the mice to eat, some for the birds, some to rot, some to be cooked, maybe only one to grow out of all these hundreds. A pumpkin was just like a bookshop, after all!

Corky said that seeds were spies, smuggling information around the world. Insignificant, commonplace, often too small to see, they carried encrypted messages, ambassador thoughts, blowing on the wind, buried in the soil, hitching a lift on the rump of a cow, just waiting for their chance to keep life moving. They were the most successful infiltrators ever. By that reckoning, Autumn, seed-time, was the real beginning of the year; the source of all that was to follow. What would Corky make of the ghost orchids, Barbara wondered? Maybe he wouldn't even be surprised. He believed the lowliest clod of soil was a miniature cosmos, simply brimming with surprises.

Dear Corky! However would he manage without his shack to live in? And he was talking of bringing that boy of his to England... Wherever could he put him up? She finished dicing the pumpkin and piled it into the pan, winked at Tod, who was watching from the door and added an extra pinch of nutmeg, just for him.

Kirsten came in, looking agitated.

"They're here!" she announced. "They're bringing Trudi in now. Are you sure she'll be all right here, on this sofa?"

"She'll be perfect. She can keep an eye on everything from there."

"Oh, Barbara. What are we going to do without you?"

"You're going to go back to work."

"Has it really been only six weeks? It seems an eternity."

"Well, we've been busy."

A pause.

"Per wants to go home." Kirsten patted the cushions and stared at her hand, as she often did when she was upset.

"That's good," said Barbara.

"Is it?"

"It means he feels well. And he thinks you can manage here."

Kirsten shook her head without looking up. "I don't know anything, any more."

On an impulse, Barbara came across and gave her a squeeze. "Then you're just about like me!"

"What will *you* do?"

"Soldier on."

"What about the others? What about poor Corky?"

"Oh!" The sentence just came out. "He's coming to live with me. He can have my top floor and share the kitchen. Well, the place is too big for me alone. It will be easy for him to get to the market - only a few minutes to the quarry on his bike - and then he can help with the stocktaking!"

"Has he agreed?" Kirsten livened up.

"He doesn't know yet. I haven't asked him."

"Oh Bee, that's marvellous! Wait, they're coming in..."

Voices in the hall were audible now: "Jurgen, hold that door! Now then, can you manage?"

"I'm fine. I'm fine!"

"Jurgen, hold the door!"

"Trudi, welcome home!"

278

"Quick, get the flowers!"

"Darling, are you okay?"

Barbara stepped back as they piled into the kitchen. She glanced across to wink at Tod but he had disappeared. She couldn't see him anywhere. How strange! She could have sworn he was there a moment ago. He had been with her all this time... ever since the accident. She felt a sting of disappointment. How could he abandon her like that? Of all the mean, rotten things... it was too bad to sneak off the moment things were starting to go right! "Well," she warned the empty air. "I shall just have to eat your slice of pie for you!" She winked at nothing. Love goes on, the same.

* * * * *

"So tell us! Tell us!" she said later that evening, when the pie was all gone and they had settled down to gossip. "What has happened about the brooch, first of all?"

Hubert put his head in his hands and groaned. "Well, it's genuine all right, but my *mother...*" (here Birgit poked him with her elbow), "and the Manor and the Museum are having a tug-of-war over it! I think they will go to court. She will be the ruin of us all."

Miss Vincent nodded in satisfaction. "I did warn you. Bad gold never did any good."

"We're thinking of going out of farming when Hubert takes over, and setting up a sanctuary for birds," said Birgit.

"A sanctuary?" spluttered Scarp.

"Well, maybe we'll keep one or two for the pot." Hubert reddened.

"I suppose if your mother wins the brooch, she can rent it out. Then everyone can be happy. She'll have her horsey parties, the Manor will have a story for the Americans, and the Museum will have its exhibition," said Professor Sax.

"They don't see it like that."

"Nah. Didn't think they would," muttered Scarp.

"However, the Quicks would like Trudi to come and visit Cobweb and have her picture taken."

Trudi smiled in a sickly sort of way. She had eaten too much pie and felt strangely detached. Looking round at the familiar faces, she wondered what alchemy held them all together. There had been so many mischances and false starts. How come they had all arrived here, safe and sound? Everyone kept asking the same thing. And Jurgen, whose dream should have given him some insight into the matter, professed to be as baffled as the rest. After a tantalizing description of the Northern Lights, he insisted that he had seen them in his sleep and Per dismissed his account as pure delirium. Which left speculation just where it was before...

The old man seemed cheerful tonight, drinking toasts with Scarp, paying court to Miss Vincent, singing songs in his rumbling, bass voice. And her father, her dear father and mother, look at them! They sat, quite lost in the midst of it all, like survivors from a wreck, who had washed up somehow among the coffee cups and whose eyes, met across the room, still shining with briny tears.

"Tomorrow morning," announced Professor Saxmund, "if Trudi is well enough, we will go, one last time, to see the orchids. Jurgen, Corky, Scarp, you must come, too - well, *all* of you who have had a hand in this. After that, I'm afraid, the Sump will have to be closed - really closed - except to the one or two experts who will observe and manage things. The place is far too precious and important, now, to have people trampling about and disturbing things, any more."

Scarp made a face.

"They've been trampling about in there for hundreds of years! And what about the badgers?"

"The badgers are a problem."

"You leave them badgers alone, do you hear - or you'll have me to reckon with - and *her*, with her wire cutters!"

"And me!"

"And us!"

Professor Saxmund took off his official hat.

"I suppose you're right. But we can't let the public in. The whole affair is out of my hands now, in any case. The land is under a protection order. I'm afraid Eco-Homesteads made a very bad investment. They'll only receive basic compensation."

"And what about Nigel Stringer?"

"Well, for the moment, he is safe. He got his money early, as we know, through Amber, and, though it's not the fortune he was hoping for, he's actually done rather well for himself."

"Unless someone gets revenge on him," said Scarp.

"Now why would anybody want to do that?" mused Barbara.

"Well, not Eco-Homesteads. They would simply ruin themselves."

"Nor his colleagues in the council - ditto."

"Nor the crooked agents. They'll all keep quiet. They've got too much to lose. They're probably already cooking up another scheme somewhere else."

But Barbara was dreaming on. "No, no, it's too late to catch up with any of them that way. They will have covered their tracks too well. But there are others, who don't have much to lose. His wife, Felicity, for instance. And someone who was, maybe, hoping for more? His mistress, Amber. I think Stringer's fate will be extremely satisfactory. He will be torn apart by two jealous women, like those prisoners of Genghis Khan who were tied between two horses. Somebody fires off a gun and lets them run and - hey ho!" She smiled. "That will do him nicely."

Chapter 36

Last Secrets

Despite the jollity of the occasion, the pumpkin party left a bitter taste behind. Trudi felt somehow betrayed. They had tried so hard to fend off the threats which besieged the Sump, and now, when they had succeeded, nay, had *triumphed* over their adversaries, they were to have victory snatched away. The place was to be sealed up. True, the birds could come and go and Pumpkin could sleep on in peace and the wild strawberries might send their runners wherever they pleased, but Trudi and her friends would be barred entry forever. The door which had opened on that secret world, was to close and vanish, locking part of her heart inside.

Professor Saxmund's final trip proved a dismal affair, for the orchid blooms were already fading and their petals looked brown and dry. A fetid smell hung on the air. Autumn had come. There would be fungi soon, but since no one would see them, what was the point? Two men were taking photographs and soil samples with a detached efficiency which Trudi resented.

Miss Vincent sat down on a stump.

"Well, you got your miracle." She looked bereft and Trudi, too sore to give her a hug, rested her chin on the old lady's shoulder.

Of course, Grandfather Larsson was right. Magic was like lightning and you couldn't tell which way it would go. Just now, it seemed, there were many miracles, each astonishing in its way. Everyone knew about the orchids - the ghosts of the wood - which had finally come out of hiding. But there were other surprises, too: developments still emerging, apparently from nowhere. Take this bizarre little friendship, here. Could anything be more curious?

"You are a good girl!" said Miss Vincent, dabbing her nose and adding, after a pause: "I had a sweetheart here, you know."

The photograph of the young airman! Trudi *knew* it!

"It was long ago. During the War. He was a pilot in the RAF. He ran out of fuel on a return trip from Germany and crash-landed his plane over there, on Jackson's field. My uncle saw him come down and, of course, we dashed across. In those days, when the lagoon was still in use, the land around it was mown like a meadow and the only trees were the beeches, which they kept, for camouflage. A pumping station could have been a target then, you see - for enemy aircraft. There were no security fences. All sorts of things grew over there. Seeds escaped from the sewage beds. I'm afraid my uncle used to pick himself tomatoes. Think of it! Several people round here did! We've been trespassers all our lives!"

"But the pilot..." prompted Trudi.

"He was lucky. Just a broken leg. He was sent to convalesce near Newbridge. I suppose the war provided many such romances: love at first sight; no time to waste..." Trudi pictured the pair, for a moment, through Marjorie Vincent's eyes. She could see them quite clearly in a blur of golden light, exchanging addresses, snatching a stroll by the river. Kisses under lilac - stars and distant sirens and brave goodbyes. His face she knew from the photograph. Marjorie she imagined with nut brown curls, slim ankles, sensible shoes.

"What happened to him?"

"Not so lucky next time. When he recovered, he returned to his squadron. He was shot down over the Channel. A comrade saw him go." Trudi gazed at the old-leather face and pebble-grey eyes beside her. What transformations time and tears could make. But the old lady would have none of it. "Bah! No good moping. It was a thousand years ago." She pushed Trudi and her sympathy away.

"You must cut the new fence! You mustn't give up!"

"No, no. Enough is enough. Nothing stays the same for long. One day, when you are old like me, other folk will be telling other stories here. That's quite right and proper."

Trudi, unconvinced, smarted at the words. Was she the only one left who cared? She looked for a last time at the Trollstones, the water and the camp, with a dejection, plain to all.

Professor Saxmund took pity on her. "I'll try to get you a pass now and then," he cajoled. "But you've done something wonderful here. You should feel very proud."

She didn't feel proud. She felt cheated. It wasn't a good note to end on.

* * * * *

Two days later, Per was packing.

"Do you have to go?" asked Trudi.

"Ja." He gave a determined nod. His hand, now free of dressings, showed the marks Beor had made. All were healing well.

Trudi watched in silence, sucking her lip.

"Are you homesick?"

"Ja," the intonation changed and the nod became a sideways waggle, which meant No-Yes. He folded a shirt and laid it in his bag. "Winter is coming. There is much to do in my house. I need to get in wood for the fire, lay up some food. The snow will arrive soon enough."

"Are you going back to the forest?"

He paused and his eyes settled on her, sparkling with life.

"I'm going back!"

"I wish *I* could come."

"Ney, ney Trudi. You live here. Your work is here. You have many people to look after."

"But you have your forest. I haven't got a forest any more." A wave of self-pity brought a lump to her throat. Per nodded again as she went on: "Everyone else is fine. Barbara is going back to the bookshop with Corky. Hubert and Birgit are getting married. Cobweb is happy at the Manor. Professor Sax has got his work. Jurgen's playing his cello again. But I haven't got *anything*. All the magic is over. We won and now we've lost it all."

Per picked up his belt with the little blue beads and handed it to her.

"Listen!" he said solemnly. "The magic is *never* over. This was given to me by an old man in Lapland. It is something rare. The Christians took these, years ago, and destroyed them, or put them into museums. This one survived. It is not a toy. You must look after it very carefully. It is a shaman's belt."

Trudi started, hearing him say the word.

"Yes," he continued. "Look after it. The wisdom of the ancient Sami is a memory now. But Sami hearts do not forget. The ancestors are inside us all - and you - they have given you the gift to see and hear more than usual. For you, the magic will never end, I promise. You feel sad to lose something you hardly knew you had - but remember the Hodja. The treasure is *always* at your feet. Hep! I will

284

tell you one more story about my country."

He turned and sat on his bed and Trudi plumped herself down at his feet, waiting for the words...

"It is winter in Finland, long ago. Deep snow. The trees crack and bend under the weight of so much snow. The little wooden houses in our village are huddled under drifts that reach almost to the eaves, but the smoke curls up out of our chimney pots, the coffee boils on the hearth. The pigs and chickens are safe. We children have good clothes and ruddy cheeks. And when we want to go out, we have our little skis. We can go faster than the pigs! All week long we have been hearing thunder in the forest. The Russians are coming. Everybody says it, but we have never seen Russians. When their planes fly overhead, we dive for cover, but they are flying to the big cities - don't bother with us, for we live in the middle of nowhere! We hardly even have roads in this corner of Finland, just frozen marsh and forest. We stretch out our arms and fly like the Russian planes, in our games, and life goes on. Strangeness becomes our way of life.

"The war started a few weeks ago. Nobody knows why. My father is away, helping at the front. He is a doctor. He volunteered to go, but our whole army has been just scratched together. Here the units are made up of irregulars - village men, with hardly any training. My father knows many of them by name. They have no battle plan. They have had no time to make one. But everyone does what they can - even boys and old men, on their wooden skis. They are tough and not afraid of the cold. And they are passionate about their homeland. Soldiers turn up from nowhere, needing coffee - needing a bed for a night. Then they disappear into the snow. The forest and the wide, white land simply swallow them up.

"But today, it is different. I am seven years old. Today is my birthday. The thunder sounds nearer. A neighbour rushes in to say that the next village is on fire - tanks are coming - then, suddenly, the shooting starts all round us. My mother drags us into the barn and hides us behind some barrels. Everywhere, the deafening sounds of explosions - shouts - shrieks - women - pigs screaming. We are three little brothers, holding hands, too frightened even to cry. And when the shooting stops, we find the world has ended."

He shifted tense, as if to stress the point. "Next day, a neighbour found us, stumbling through the ruins, and took us to join the refugees on the road. Horses, carts, women and babies. Hundreds of us, fleeing together, And now the planes flew low overhead, spitting out their bullets as they passed. We walked, not knowing what would become of us, wrapped in white sheets, like little sacks of flour, hoping the pilots would not find us; hoping the kindly snow would hide us. We left without looking back.

"At the nearest town we were labelled, and bundled onto a train. The train took us to Sweden. They meant it for the best. They thought they were saving us. Perhaps they were... Everything else I learned years later. My father was shot, trying to rescue a friend. And my mother, thinking we were dead, made her way back to her people in the north. As for my brothers, I do not know what happened to them. They were sent to different families. Maybe, like me, they gave themselves Swedish names and stayed. Maybe they went back. We never saw one another again.

"Long after all this happened, I learned the bigger story: how our makeshift army, with just a handful of guns and only the snow for an ally, held out against the powerful Russian forces. The Russians offered to settle for peace. Our men returned to their villages full of hope. They thought they had won the war. But when the peace treaty was signed in 1940, my country, Karelia, was given away. And when I returned to Finland, people still spoke about it in disbelief. How could we win and still lose everything? They could see their woods, their old homesteads across the border, but the land was no longer theirs.

"On that cold winter day, it was as if the snow entered my heart.

"In every place, I was an outsider, always expecting the worst. When your grandmother left me - when I came to England - I felt lost all over again. The world changes so fast now, Trudi, sometimes whole nations feel like exiles. And to a refugee, everywhere looks like someone else's home, so it is harder still to be outside.

"Yet, though I thought I had lost my land, it had not lost me. Wherever I found a pattern of ice, or a rising sun, the old magic would overwhelm me as if the wilderness had been inside me all the time, free as ever.

"That is how you found the path to my old heart. And in this house, I learnt something new: that home is only and always *here* -

286

wherever there is a coffee-pot, a hand to shake, a story to tell - human love.

"What is my nation? I cannot tell. But I am going back with a warm heart to begin to live again."

"But what about the magic?" asked Trudi. "Won't you need the belt?"

"I did not do the magic," replied Per emphatically. "*You* did!"

"I shall miss you."

"You will come and see me. Christmas!"

Chapter 37

Touch Down

In a few days, Trudi was to start her new school. Having missed her summer courses, she felt suddenly unprepared. She had almost forgotten how to be Trudi Larsson, top girl. Per had introduced her to a self who wasn't even sure she wanted to go to school; a self who craved other satisfactions.

That morning the Stringers had moved out. And this time it was Trudi who stood watching from the landing. Grim-faced, they piled into their waiting car. But the euphoria Trudi expected to feel had already spent itself, and she almost pitied them. How would they manage without the Larssons to hate next door? Simon's white face glared resentment. "Not finished yet," it said. But now she could see the fear behind his fury. He was trapped, just like the white squirrel. As long as he was afraid, he would always be in prison.

The adults were discussing 'things' in the kitchen. She knew, because they had closed the door, which meant it was all the more important for her to hear what they were saying. Barbara, too, was leaving and the time had come for final arrangements.

"I'm sure she'll be just fine when all the fuss dies down." That was Barbara's voice.

"You'll come and visit often? Promise!"

"Promise." A pause. "I wonder..." Barbara hesitated and then plunged on. "...I wonder if you ought to buy her a puppy, so she gets to know there are *nice* dogs out there in the world?"

In the silence which followed, Trudi pictured, quite accurately, her mother's look of horror.

"It's - you know - it's just an idea..." Barbara realized straightaway that the idea was 'no-go' in this house.

But Scarp stepped in: "It's okay. You don't need to. *I'm* getting one."

"You?"

"Why not? I reckon I ought to have a companion. Might be a bit of security for the caravan. The kids can play with it and take it for walks. A mate of mine has a bitch with pups. Nice mongrels!"

"Scarp, you're a star!"

"No - I'm a mug!"

"Good mug," said Per laughing.

The door opened and Scarp came out, with Barbara hard on his heels. Trudi retreated to the top of the stairs.

"Scarp, are you really getting a puppy?" Barbara whispered.

He gave her a look. "Well, I am *now*, aren't I? You and your brilliant ideas!"

"You're crazy!"

"Yeah - like you!" As an afterthought he added: "Best keep it secret for a bit. I'll have to find a puppy first."

"No probs. Oh, Bless you!"

More people piled into the hall and the volume went up.

Scarp again: "You coming then, or what?"

"Trudi! Jurgen!" Kirsten called. "Auntie Barbara's leaving! Come and give her a hug good-bye!"

"K, phone me - e.mail - *promise*!"

"Promise!"

Scarp held the bags. He was running her back in his truck.

Trudi sidled down, looking sleepy.

"Oh, honey, look at you!"

"Thank you, for everything," she said, but she wasn't being polite. She really meant it.

"I can't even give you a proper hug, with all those bandages! You be good, and come and have cake with me soon! Jurgen. Where's Jurgen? I want to hear that Bach cello thingy. Note perfect, mind!"

"Ring me!"

"See you Saturday!"

"Goodbye guys!"

"Goodbye!"

Laden with gifts, Barbara, staggered out onto the pavement and gave a disconcerted look at the cab. "How'm I gonna get up there?"

"Gawd 'elp us! Here. Gimme that. Grab that. Now!" Scarp dealt her a shove from behind, and with a wink, slammed the door.

"Cheers nipper!" He swaggered round to the driver's side and gave Jurgen a private salute.

"Bye, Captain!" Jurgen raced the truck down the street. Then the next street. And the next. He was a good runner. He had a long walk back when Scarp finally hit the accelerator and shot ahead.

* * * * *

Two days later, the Larssons stood awkwardly at the airport, saying the usual platitudes that precede farewells.

"Got your ticket? Passport?"

"Telephone when you get to Stockholm. You'll take a taxi all the way, won't you?"

"Ja, ja." Per kept looking uneasily to left and right and Trudi felt miserable for him. He looked so out of place in his reindeer skin.

"Have you checked his luggage?" asked Kirsten in a nervous aside.

"It's fine," Sven nodded.

"What about the - the - thing?"

"The knife? He gave it to Scarp, when the police returned it. Stop worrying."

"Oh my God! 'Stop worrying', you say. Now I'll worry about Scarp!"

"He's not going to use it. He put it with his flints in his private collection. Stop worrying!"

Kirsten traced the floor-tiles with her toe.

"When will you ask him about the jacket? He'll stink the whole plane out in the coat he's wearing."

"At the last minute - Kirsten, please!"

Trudi wished she was anywhere but here, with the clock counting their last minutes away. She tried to catch Per's eye, but he had withdrawn into himself. He was reserving all his energy for the ordeal ahead. She slipped her hand through his arm instead, so afraid that she was losing him forever. Without his special things, how would he survive? Without his magic, how would he even be himself? He had given everything away - his bag seemed empty. He gave a reassuring squeeze:

"Christmas Trudi! Come and meet some real trolls!"

"That's it," said Sven as the information board changed. "Your flight's up. Gate 17. Stockholm. You must check in now."

"Ja - Okay."

290

"Father," Sven seized his moment. "Kirsten wanted to give you this - a winter coat. She has been working on it all week long." He opened a carrier bag and pulled out a modish jacket, with faux-fur collar, pockets and, close-fitting cuffs. Kirsten had stitched designs across the yoke, red, like the figures on the drum. There was a belt. Her eyes pleaded silently.

Per hesitated.

"No!" cried a voice inside Trudi, but Per decided otherwise.

"Why not? Tak! Tak! You, Sven - my son - take this one. Keep it!" His eyes were suddenly full of tears. "I don't need it any more. You should have it." He shrugged off his shaman's garb and put on the other, which dwarfed him. "Like Sami coat," he said, patting the sleeves. "Very good!"

"There's a hat too!"

Now he was going, his face broke into smiles. A kiss for Kirsten. Bear hugs for the children. To Sven he put out his right hand, but neither could simply part on a handshake and, having waited for this moment all their lives, they clasped one another in a long, un-Swedish embrace.

"Christmas!" gulped Sven.

"Christmas!"

"We'll write!"

"Remember, Trudi!" Per caught her eye and gave her an unforgettable look.

"Take care!"

"Remember!"

He was gone, shuffling amongst the other passengers; swallowed up in the crowd. Kirsten smiled and touched Sven on the cheek. "We *did* it! We got him into something respectable, at last. Thank heavens - we can now dump this old thing!" But Sven was having none of it.

"Oh no!" He insisted "This 'old thing' now belongs to me. Whoever touches it, does so at their peril!"

They trooped back to the car a little downcast, a little lost in thought. Trudi found it too distressing to see Per stripped of his possessions. Remember. Remember what? He had slipped away from them like the shamans of old, who would not stay in jail. Professor Saxmund had told her all about it. The authorities would lock them up, pocket the key and then find them calmly smoking on the steps outside. Masters of old magic, with their inexhaustible fund of disguises, they would trot past as a hare, or a goose and no one would realize till they had gone. Now Per had gone and a passer-by would never guess that there was anything extraordinary about him. He was just an eccentric old man, a little out of step with the world. And it would be more difficult than ever to remember him as the enchanter she had known, secret, fearless and true. She was so afraid that she would forget what he had taught her.

Of course, he had known everything, all along, though he wouldn't let on. He even knew the key to the bluebird riddle, when no one else could solve it. She herself was still struggling to find the answer. The harder she tried, the less she could grasp what it was. For it wasn't 'time'. Nor was it 'love', nor 'magic'… What in the world could you *have* but not explain? What lived in the doing and died in the telling? Something Corky found when he put his hands in the soil? Something Barbara added to her bread?

As the car joined the motorway and gathered speed, a greylag goose appeared from nowhere and flew level with them for a while. Trudi wound down her window to get a better view. "Look!" she wanted to cry. "Look! It's Grandfather!" But before she could open her mouth, the bird wheeled up and away. Now nothing could stop her spirits rising. She had had a sign. Here was a summer migrant, heading home.

Remember? Yes, yes! Of course she could remember! And she had the answer to the riddle too: this feeling which flooded her being; she knew just what it was. The day was too fine for feeling sad. In Sweden, the first birches would be turning yellow and her goose would be winging over them by the light of tomorrow's moon.

She gave Jurgen a playful dig in the ribs and, as he poked her back she wriggled into her corner and let her thoughts soar free.

"Hey, hey. No fighting!" called Kirsten. But Trudi didn't care. In a sudden burst of joy, she wanted to provoke the world. She was alive. *Everything* was alive! Unable to reach the world, she kicked the driver's seat in front and Sven half-turned.

"You all right, trouble?"

"Yes!" she beamed. "All right!"

Epilogue

Curtain

When Trudi had to rest, she would sit on the sofa with her History Project, listening to the comings and goings of the house. She had renamed the piece - this time, in a scribble of biro - "*Bockhurst - the History of a Wood*," though the story in her head was not the one she would submit to school.

"I can't think what to say," she confessed to Barbara. "It's just a jumble of other people's tales."

"Dear girl, that's exactly the point," said Barbara. "What else *is* history? You can't make bread without wheat, you know."

Trudi's story was a medley of woven thoughts - all that her young life had experienced of the world this summer. The Sump still lay at the bottom of the garden with its white moths in the evening, the croak of a heron at night. Corky had brought new plants, to establish a patch of wildwood this side of the fence, so perhaps the forest creatures would venture there, too. The story that Trudi had chosen, likewise, spread and grew...

When, half-dozing, half-dreaming, she put down her pen, she would picture to herself a clearing, like a stage; the old-fashioned, open-air sort that suited a summer play. And here, she would summon her cast for a farewell curtain call.

She can see them now, even though her eyes are closed...

First comes Per, sweeping in, with his shaman's belt and drum. The skirts of his coat swing wide. Per the magician, doffing his cap and bowing low while his eyes rake the gallery with a glitter of icy blue. His cap goes back on his head and he departs.

Second, herself, as heroine, leading Beor. The beast makes a pantomime snarl as she kneels by his side, her pale hair gleaming on his shoulder. His red tongue lolls and he too rolls his eyes. He is milking the applause!

Now three figures, running, hand in hand: Barbara, with Corky and Scarp on either side. For some reason, she is dressed in a Shakespearean ruff and gown. The men step back as she curtsies and

293

then come forward, grinning, like a brigand and a mountebank.

The stage clears and on dashes Jurgen, taps his nose, plays a little tune on his flute and races off again.

A pause for Professor Saxmund and Miss Vincent, who perform a stately quadrille.

And no sooner have they gone than Sven and Kirsten steal from the wings, look around to make sure they are alone and embrace, to wild hurrahs.

Hubert and Birgit seem late and are dressed for a shoot. Trudi checks them off - so far so good. Her pale face rests on her pillow.

Now the lesser members of the cast:

The villainous Stringer household, all arguing and glaring at one another, with a retinue of corrupt and devious accomplices. Boos and hisses. Then the Museum experts, the Quicks and the hapless Jacksons, waving writs.

Lastly, ghosts, who flit, half-seen between the trees: Neolithic hunters and the Saxons, Wulfstan and Eadric; Sir Vivian and Edward de Fraisey, and dear old Uncle Roger; the young airman and the beautiful Agneta and maybe even a kelet or two. Is that everyone? Not quite.

When they are sure that Trudi is asleep, a flock of little birds announce the presence of two black lambs, which stand for a moment centre stage, then kick up their heels and scamper away... leaving just the magpie, to do what magpies do best – that is, picking up bits and pieces for another tale!

FINIS

www.ingramcontent.com/pod-product-compliance
Lightning Source LLC
Chambersburg PA
CBHW062127170626
46813CB00002B/599